Zardi Cross

SYSTEM: THE LIMIT

D1526771

Zardi Cross

SYSTEM: THE LIMIT

I.

2005

1.

At about 5:20 in the morning, Ian was already halfway to DC. It was a chilly morning. The sun was at least an hour from rising, which put him at ease. These moments before dawn gave him the chance to immerse himself in that peculiar state of... synergy with his inner world.

He was truly concerned about many things. Many things that weren't present in his day-to-day life, but inhabited his consciousness in the hours before 6 a.m.

He was barely twenty-one years old, yet he already felt like he was running late. Even though he completely fit in with the conventional standard for his age, he kept feeling like he had insufficient time to find his own place.

He was 80 miles from home.

He hoped to find his parents as he was used to at 7:15 in the morning – in the kitchen, surrounded by the aroma of freshly ground coffee.

Elizabeth Dunne was a child psychologist. She was very young when she found herself passionate and truly curious to understand the behavior of others. Later, she found a path to the answers and her innate tenderness led her toward the youngest patients. Most of them, because of her classic beauty, golden blonde hair, or maybe the warmth of her smile, seemed to open up to her right away. So had her husband, Jeff, a long time ago. Long before he became Jeffrey Dunne – one of the most respected lawyers in DC.

His career had progressed with stability and sustainability, in line with his work ethic. After he graduated from Princeton, he was recruited by one of the largest law firms in the US. The same firm he'd dreamt of joining once he decided on a career in law. He was barely twenty-three at the time, but his characteristic determination and decisiveness already formulated the basis of his personality.

He spent eleven years at that firm. Years in which he succeeded at much more than just a senior position and an office with a view. Jeffrey Dunne had become the name of truth. Everyone who had the advantage of his uncompromising defense was almost automatically absolved in the eyes of the jury, court, and the media.

Somewhere in his mid-thirties, he decided to take an independent professional path. Central to his decision was not so much his desire to establish himself apart from the firm, but rather his concern that young law graduates and interns joined the corporate world with principles and beliefs that were *too* flexible, and the lines between acceptable and unacceptable were blurred.

He aimed to found an institution where young people would find meaning in preserving their initial drive for justice and truth. A place where they wouldn't need to prioritize money over conscience. So he did just that – Dunne's Central opened its doors on October 21, 1985.

He hoped to be doing it for his son, too. From a very early age, Ian had clear positions and an attitude toward the world that Jeffrey, with a warm feeling of nostalgia, recognized as his own.

In the twenty years that followed, Dunne's grew into Jeffrey's initial dream. He took pride in the thousands of cases taken and won, and he was deeply convinced that each ended with a just verdict. In all this time, The Pillar, as the media dubbed him after one of the most publicized trials of his career, continued being as steadfast in his selection of causes and clients. Money did not debase the meaning of his work. And so, Jeffrey Dunne's law firm was established as a desired career for young and educated people who were ready to fight for the truth.

Not long after the first rays of sunlight, Ian traveled back to his childhood. He was driving down 20th Street, his peripheral vision appreciatively taking in the rows of beautiful plane trees that lined the sidewalks, all of which he knew so well. He marked every tree he passed with a blink – he'd been doing that since he was a kid. He tried to remember when and how he came up with that game, but his mind went back to the road – he was approaching Calvert Street. He smiled. It was 7:10 a.m., and his self-satisfaction was exuberant. He liked to confirm his ability to manage time.

He'd made it. His dad was probably impatiently waiting for the last drops of espresso to trickle down into his favorite cup, while sharing the news from the *Daily* with his mom.

"Jeff, are we expecting anyone?" Elizabeth was coming down the stairs when she heard a car engine outside. Its outline was becoming more visible through the shaded windows of the front door.

"Wait..." she squinted her eyes. "That looks just like..."

The car's horn revealed Ian's arrival. Now that there were no doubts as to who the unexpected guest was, Beth rushed outside.

Jeff got excited as well. He took a sip from his coffee and smiled at the view displayed in the kitchen window.

He'd always been proud of his own ability to make his wife laugh out loud. But every time Ian did it, it was different. His son had a special relationship with his mother. He watched them from inside and suddenly realized how much his son had grown. Luckily, the passing years didn't bother Jeffrey much. Except for some silver locks of hair, there was barely anything that betrayed his age – from his proud posture and the spark in his brown and green eyes to his fighting spirit and contagious energy.

That morning, the driveway in front of his house became the sight of a beautiful future memory.

"I'm coming for you, old man!" the boy yelled from outside after putting his mom back down on the ground. As if he had sensed the wave of sentiment taking over his dad.

"Go Lions!" he emphatically screamed right from the door.

It was Ian's customary greeting since he had become

the quarterback for the Columbia Lions. His college buddies put more hope in his sporting career than they did in their own undertakings. He showed the same potential with his academic achievements. He picked economics and political science as his majors and excelled despite the rigorous curriculum.

For the people around him, he was a leader – on the field, in class, and on the pages of the university's paper, which he edited. But more than anything else – it was his sincerity. His appearance added a final touch to his charismatic personality. His six-foot stature accentuated his athletic physique, as his amber-hued gaze did to his dark-brown hair.

"The score matters more than the touchdown!" Jeff jokingly asserted. "I'm so happy to see you, son! How long do we have before duty calls?"

They both moved to the round table in the dining room, just like they had done every morning before the boy left for New York. Lately, Jeffrey remembered these moments with a tender pain in his heart.

"The big game against Berkeley isn't until next month," Ian started to calculate. "I've written all the articles for the paper two months ahead. I need to prepare for my microeconomics exam. Which would mean that I can be at your disposal until... say... tomorrow morning." Then, he sighed and added, "I'm sorry, Dad. You said it yourself – 'It's the score that matters!'"

"I see that you've mastered the art of prioritization," remarked Jeff.

Although not quite consciously, the pride he felt at the sense of responsibility his son was displaying trumped the regret that they wouldn't have enough time.

"I hope you still remember the rules of the house. Dinner is at seven," he specified with mock severity before putting his shoes on.

"I wouldn't dare deviate, boss!"

Jeff patted him on the shoulder and checked his watch.

8

"Are you ready, Beth?" he shouted toward the kitchen. "It's eight, we need to go!"

Their conversation gave Beth the chance to leave the dining room the way she liked to find it when she got back home at night.

"Well, keep up then!" She quipped. She grabbed her beige coat from the hanger and quickly slipped by Jeff so as to be in front of him.

Sometimes, their interactions were reminiscent of the way they had provoked and challenged each other when they were children. Because indeed, Elizabeth and Jeffrey had known each other since they were kids. Their friendship began somewhere in the distant year of 1956, at a children's chess club, where dedicated upper-class mothers left their children when they felt the need for a bit of social interaction. They earnestly believed they were sacrificing the time spent together in order to invest in the future of their children. Chess would help them assimilate very important lessons – patience and strategic thinking. Even though they didn't realize it at the time, under the guise of innocent teasing, Elizabeth and Jeffrey had actually embraced these principles as the foundation of the relationship they later built. Without, of course, ever outgrowing the impulse to challenge each other.

Jeff's eyes followed Elizabeth as she walked to her car, then he turned around.

"One day, son, you'll realize that losing to the right person is a priceless privilege," he said with a wink before stepping outside.

Ian thought again about something of which he would often remind himself. Aside from the high standard of living his parents had provided, the worldview they'd helped him form, as well as all the other advantages that the financial and social status of the Dunne name gave him, he clearly realized what the most valuable part of his parents' legacy was. Few of the young people around him had grown up in a real family environment. Their family, though, enjoyed something more than harmony. The three of them were a team.

"He took got that urge to surprise from you," remarked Elizabeth when Jeff got in the car.

They headed downtown. Her office wasn't far; it took about 20 minutes to get there. And these moments were her favorite time. They both appreciated good music and surrendered to it, even if just for a short while.

Today, they chose jazz.

"*Out yonder where the blue begins. The moon will guide us...*"[1] Jeff sang along with his beloved Ella Fitzgerald. "I sure hope so. Means more surprises for my favorite girl. But I was thinking... When Ian puts his mind to something, he doesn't let off even for a split second. Nothing can lead him astray from the goals he sets for himself... Do you know where I'm going with this?"

"Not just a surprise, huh?" Beth guessed.

"You know how focused he normally is. With exams, before an important game, all these side projects, and he drives all this way?" reasoned Jeff. "And just to stay for a day!"

"You're right, it's unusual," admitted Beth, before waving her hand. "Whatever it is, I'm glad he's here. Even if it's one day. Tonight, I suppose, we'll find out the reason for the pleasant surprise," she concluded, while her husband continued to sing along:

"*With love beside us. To fill the night with a song. We'll hear the sound of violins.*"

"I only ask that it really is violins this time, because last time, it was drums. When he told us he robbed the school library!" Beth reminded him before stepping out of the elegant Volkswagen sedan.

"Still, they had no right to punish him so severely." She turned around. "The children from that home had a much bigger need and a much smaller chance to get access to all the books he piled on them."

"Don't ask the lawyer to skirt the rules, dear." Jeff put his hands up and then drove off.

At exactly 9:00, Ed Thompson hurried to open the door of

---

[1] *From Ella Fitzgerald's song "Stairway to the Stars."*

Jeff's car, just like he did every morning.

"Jesus, Edward! I don't even know where you jump out from!" Jeff teased and handed him the keys. "I hope you aren't as fast behind the wheel."

Ed parked the car on level E2 in the underground garage of the ten-story glass building that bore Dunne's name. Jeff liked it there because it was close to the elevator.

He was already swiftly walking across the luxurious lobby when the loud clacking of high heels on the shiny granite floor made him turn. Mary Rogers, the firm's senior assistant, had jumped up from behind the reception and was galloping his way, clearly worried.

"Mr. Dunne, hold on! Mr. Dunne!"

"Mary! What's the rush?" stopped her Jeff. "What's wrong?"

"I couldn't stop them, Mr. Dunne..." she replied as she tried to catch her breath. "They're in your office... Senator Preston and another man. They showed up without warning, without an appointment."

"Take it easy, Mary. When did they get here?"

"I told them you're booked for the day..." she continued with the explanations, without acknowledging the question. "But they just burst in and declared they'd wait all day if they had to. I'm sorry, I..."

"It's alright, I'll manage," Jeff reassured her and sent her back to reception.

He was familiar with this style, but he was not expecting this particular visit.

2.

Oliver Preston was a California senator in the fifth year of his term. During this time, he somehow managed to maintain a relatively respectable reputation. Even before he took office, his attorney, Martin Smith, made sure to wrap the future senator in a veil that wasn't too thick, but not exactly transparent either. Over the years, Preston had not allowed himself to abuse his power and connections too much, at least not when compared to other representatives of these circles.

Jeff, however, was not fooled. This was certainly not abstention, but rather a delay for the times when the lights would be shining on the next lucky senator. Jeff knew the senator well, after all, despite his efforts to avoid him. Regardless of his attitude toward the senator, Jeff deeply respected his father, Roger Preston. He had been one of the great lawyers of the 20th century, a man of exceptional intellect, and morals as well. Morals that, unfortunately, he'd been unable to pass on to his spoiled son. Preston Senior had been simultaneously a father and mentor to Jeff. He was the one who had helped and guided his early law career. They remained very close friends until Roger's last hour struck about fifteen years ago. Roger's last request to Jeff had been to "to not be too hard on Oliver." In order to keep his promise, the young lawyer had to stay far away from Junior – his arrogance and snootiness could easily make Jeff lose his temper.

The display of the elevator counted every floor by lighting the button in red. During the short ride, Jeff went through the possible reasons for the unexpected visit. He tried to remember the last time he'd seen the senator. It was a few months earlier, when Preston organized a charity auction. The event took place at his Hamptons residence, and the guests were representatives of the elite – politicians, lawyers, artists, actors, reporters. Each one of them had to pick one of the senator's prized possessions – antiques, art, books, even cars, and pay excessive sums for the special objects. The proceeds were to be donated to underdeveloped African countries.

Jeff took a deep breath right before the 10th floor button lit up. He straightened his graying hair as he always did when he needed to collect himself and headed down the long corridor. His office was at the bottom of it. Each side of the corridor had four doors, where Jeff's most trusted

12

associates worked. They weren't separated by walls, but had glass panels instead.

Dunne wanted the atmosphere in his firm to convey transparency and allow an open view, as well as contact between the members of his team. He wanted to predispose them to reflect this feeling in their manner and method when it came to work.

Jeff greeted each one of them with an unobtrusive nod. He was about eight meters from his office's glass door, behind which he could make out Preston's figure. Or rather, his back. In any case, even without actually seeing the senator's sly blue eyes, Jeff couldn't confuse him for anyone else – the raven-black hair, carefully swept back with a heavy application of gel, had become his characteristic – and often ridiculed – feature.

Across from him, facing the corridor, there was another man. As expected, it was Martin. It seemed like these two were an inseparable tandem in the last few years.

Jeff noticed how much Martin had changed since their last meeting five years ago. Thirty-five years old at the time, had Smith exuded vivacity, and his bearing betrayed his strive to reach high peaks in his career. Whether coincidentally or not, the two of them looked quite alike – the hair color and the eyes, the calculating expressions on their faces, only that Smith was a mini-version of his eminent companion – several years younger, a number of pounds lighter, some inches shorter, as well as a few degrees less abrasive. But today, he looked somewhat different. He had the expression of a man who's seen enough and had allowed cynicism to permanently lodge itself in place of any principles. Aside from that, there wasn't even a trace left of that former, somewhat aggressive, vivacity. His eyes predominantly showed apathy.

Jeff walked into the office and continued forward.

"Etiquette was never anything but a formality to you, was it, Preston?" he said, concealing his irritation behind a smile, as he shook the visitor's hand.

He maintained the grip slightly longer than was customary for a business interaction. Long enough to convey reproach. Preston pulled his hand away. He understood Jeff's message very well but chose to ignore it.

"I'm always eager to see you, Dunne," he replied and pointed to his companion. "You know Martin, I believe."

Smith stood up from the granite surface he was leaning on and stepped forward. Before that, he made sure to display his displeasure that someone would find it necessary to introduce him to a colleague, even if it was The Pillar himself. He winced, and his sideways glance was visible enough to be noticed by all, but also measured in a way that didn't cross the line of good manners. Dunne, irritated by the childish faces, headed over to his chair on the inner side of the long table, walking past Martin. He coughed at the exact moment they were close enough to each other to show he expected at least some sort of superficial manners.

After everyone in the room seemed to tacitly agree to forgo unnecessary and insincere niceties, Jeff could begin the conversation in earnest.

"So, gentlemen, what can I do for you?"

Preston had once again slumped back into one of the chairs, perhaps too comfortably. It seemed like his upper body was sprawled on the table. His elbow had the significant task of holding the weight of his content-laden head. His nonchalance was obviously premeditated and overdone. The fingers of his right hand were busy spinning a heavy fountain pen. The luxury line of the Caress fountain pens was famous for its exclusivity – there were exactly 36 in the entire world. This made the accessory one of the most sought-after status symbols in upper society. Alas, the pen was the only solid element in Preston's presence at the moment.

In the meantime, the senator was trying, with a string of verbal and non-verbal methods, to lighten the seriousness of the case that he had come to discuss.

"Did you hear about the Libra case, my friend?"

14

Libra was the charity organization through which the large sum collected at Preston's auction was sent to those who needed it. During the decade it operated, it handled over 350 million dollars. For several weeks, however, there had been rumors of a festering scandal regarding the transparency of the funds' distribution.

Jeff had a firm principle – to avoid acknowledging words thrown into the air without any factual substance.

"A favorite subject, huh?" Jeff said sarcastically, and then, with mock severity: "'Embezzlement of funds from charity organizations'.... Repeated statements and empty chatter," he concluded.

At last, Preston firmed up a bit and turned his chair to face Jeff, so as to emphasize that this was the essence of the conversation.

"Unfortunately, you'll have to delve into the case. Thomas Mason will personally introduce you. " he announced, then added: "Remember? You met him at the auction."

Jeff's face remained expressionless.

"I offered Martin's services to Mason, but he refused," continued Preston. "he said that he wants attorney Jeffrey Dunne. No one else."

The senator stood up and started pacing around the table. He spoke slowly, as if leaving pauses for what was unspoken, without failing to glance at Jeff now and then. He wanted to make sure he was being fully understood.

"I don't know what the reason for his attachment is. But it seems one-sided, judging by the look in your eyes... Whatever the truth behind this mystery is, I want to be very, very clear about one thing."

The culmination of the interaction brought them face to face with each other. Preston stood at one end of the table in a pose as domineering as he himself was. His fingertips clenched the edge of the table and made his hands look like the tentacles of an octopus ready to seize everything around it.

"That man is guilty!" he stated categorically. "And must be convicted!" he made sure to emphasize.

Jeff was in no rush to answer to what he was beginning to recognize as an ultimatum. He leaned against the desk and posed a question to himself: why would the senator and his lawyer want to get involved in something that seemingly didn't concern them? He was getting the feeling that in the last few minutes, he'd been forcefully dragged into a case with an ending that was clear to all but him.

"What exactly are you telling me, Oliver?" he pressed the senator. "I don't remember agreeing to defend that man. And if I remember correctly, lawyers still have the right to choose whom they defend. Am I right, Martin?" he asked, turning to the other intruder.

Smith lowered his head, then stared out somewhere beyond the office's big window. He looked like he was mentally shuffling all the versions of what he could say. He was a lawyer, after all; he was supposed to pick his words more carefully than anyone.

"The rules... don't always apply, Mr. Dunne," Smith began. "Yes, you do have a choice, but not all laws are subject to the Constitution."

"Let's not be dramatic, Jeff!" interjected Preston, before softening his tone. "Don't make things more complicated than they actually are. It's all clear! Mason will call you, you'll hear him out and take over his defense," he explained diplomatically. "When the trial begins, it will turn out that no matter how hard you try, you can't dispute the facts. That's it! Nothing else is required of you."

"Nothing else is required of me? And who might it be that requires it, Oliver?"

They both remained silent but kept looking into each other's eyes.

"Listen," sighed Preston and looked around, as if trying to find the right words. "There's no politically correct way to say it, but... yes. You must accept, and yes, you must lose the case."

Jeff could feel his self-control slipping away little by little. In all his years as a lawyer, no one had dared threaten him.

"Gentlemen, thank you for the visit!" he snapped, placed his palms on the table loudly, and stood up. "It was a pleasure to be in your company, but, unfortunately, I have a pressing engagement," he said.

Preston slowly headed for the door and opened it.

"Martin?" he said with a gesture that implied he should be left alone with Dunne.

Smith understood the hint. He also understood that in the climax of their conversation, there was no place for a single word from him. He left quietly, and the senator shut the door behind him.

"Dunne, I never thought I'd say it. But... in the name of my father and your friendship, please do it!" he declared before walking out.

He kept his stare on Jeffrey for five or six long seconds. A warning that the lawyer understood. He also remained motionless for a few heartbeats, while a particular phrase intrusively crossed his mind. Is there a defense for the guilty?

The memory of the first and only time he met Thomas Mason surfaced. It was at Preston's auction. Piece by piece, his memory, intuition, and experience pieced events together. Libra was the intermediary foundation, Mason its executive director, and Preston – a depositor of seven-digit sums.

Shortly after they were introduced, Mason found Jeff in the crowd again. "Is there a defense for the guilty?" the director had asked right before Preston invited him onstage to accept recognition for his noble deeds.

At the time, Jeff understood the comment as a form of self-deprecating humor, even if said with disproportionate seriousness.

3.

It was almost noon when Elizabeth finished her first session of the day.

"See you soon, dear!" she said as she led the fair-haired girl to the door, adding, "Don't forget to tell mom to call me when she can."

The kid had walked only a few steps down the corridor before a smiling red-haired lady, who was waiting behind the reception, took her by the hand to lead her out. She always did this. For Jessica Frost, who had been Beth's assistant ever since she started the practice, it was a pleasure to be around children. In her late 40s, she had accepted the fact that she would never have any of her own. That made her feel great joy for being a part, however small, of the help that the children received in Beth's office.

"Jess, can you please make an appointment for Erica for next Friday?" Elizabeth asked her when she got back to her chair behind the reception.

"So soon? How's she doing?"

"It will be difficult. The stress she experienced is devastating for a seven-year-old's psyche. But you know, that girl is a fighter!" smiled Elizabeth. "I've never applied the methods I use in her therapy to such young patients."

Elizabeth smiled when she heard her cellphone chime from the office. It was someone close; her personal number was rarely given to people outside the family.

"I need advice from my best friend," she heard her husband say. She looked at her watch.

"I've heard lunch may do the trick!"

"I could try that, I suppose..." Jeff answered, somehow sounding closer than he should have been.

She turned around, only to find him leaning comfortably against the doorframe. So comfortably, in fact, that it seemed like he'd been there for hours.

"Fortune favors the bold," she smiled. "I have about an hour... Pasta?"

"You got it."

One of their favorite restaurants was a five-minute walk from Beth's office. They liked to go by Ragu on weekdays, even if it didn't happen as often lately. They had three blocks to soak in the rays of the November sun.

"*Ciao*, Enzo!" Jeff spoke Italian with a very convincing enthusiasm, but he had actually memorized only the most important phrases. Half of them were names of different dishes. "I'll expect a quick tagliatelle porcini and penne all'arrabbiata!" he melodically placed the order with the waiter straight from the door. The open vowels in his words emphasized his passion.

"You better do your best, Enzo!" Beth quipped. "The man's about to ask me for a favor!"

The Dunnes were a charismatic couple. They always subtly drew everyone around them into their witty and humorous vibe.

They headed over to the third table by the window, where they always sat. Jeff pulled his wife's chair slightly, then walked around the table and sat across from her.

"How's your day going, doc?"

"Let's postpone my story till tonight, shall we?" suggested Beth. She could see her husband was distressed, despite his effort to conceal it. "What's going on?"

If someone could point out a solution, it was Beth. She knew him as well as he knew himself. Besides, their way of thinking and reasoning was remarkably in tune. That made her his most prized confidante – she had the ability to assess the situation from the side, as if through his eyes, to make the decisions he himself would if he could be impartial.

"Oliver Preston came to see me this morning."

"The senator? He must've certainly surprised you."

"Definitely. And not just me! You should have seen Mary's expression. He and his lawyer burst into the lobby and headed straight for the elevator. When she finally caught up with them to say my day was fully booked, Preston hissed back that they'd wait all day if they had to."

"Overly dramatic, even for him." Beth furrowed her brows.

"So what was so urgent?"

The server interrupted them to place a bottle of water and a small antipasto platter on the table. A compliment that they would have enjoyed, if it weren't for the conversation they were having.

Jeff leaned over the table to make sure no one else heard them. "Did you pay any attention to those accusations around Libra circulating in the media?"

"As far as I gather, they're being investigated for embezzlement of charity funds, but... what does that have to do with Preston?"

"I asked myself the same question" agreed Jeff. "Do you remember the charity auction in the Hamptons?"

Elizabeth's expression changed several times, reflecting her thoughts. Subconsciously, she made an instinctive step in the right direction – the link between Preston and the foundation. That gave rise to the doubts and questions.

"Preston and Libra, of course! But... no, no!" She started to debate out loud. "It doesn't make sense. Why would the senator risk publicizing the campaign, if he had something of the sort in mind?" Elizabeth wondered aloud.

She leaned back on the chair and stopped talking when she saw the server approach. "It looks wonderful, thank you!" she said gratefully.

"It's an honor!" earnestly replied the young man with his hand on his heart. "*Salute!*"

A few minutes went by, but they hadn't touched their food. Elizabeth started anxiously stirring the pasta in front of her. Finally, she rolled some around her fork, but then put it back down – her emotions were in turmoil. Her throat only had space for the words that were welling up.

"I can't believe Preston allowed that! How did he expect to get away with it? Especially considering he drew the media's attention to the initiative? And now what, he wants you to defend him? Like you owe it to him?" she kept adding, and her tone escalated with every question.

"That's precisely the problem," muttered Jeff after he took

a sip of water and looked out the window. "He didn't come to me asking for himself. He came to tell me that Libra's executive director insisted that I defend him. That he wouldn't accept any other lawyer."

Jeff could see that his wife was still puzzled.

"It turns out that the investigation led to Thomas Mason, at least for now," he explained. "Preston claims that he offered his own lawyer, Martin Smith, but..."

"I'm sorry," Elizabeth interrupted him sharply. "You mean to say that Oliver didn't do it? Do you know Mason?"

"Not quite. I've only seen him one time, at the auction."

They both stayed silent for a bit. The worry Jeff saw in Beth's eyes made him wonder whether to share Mason's words with her... that question he asked at the charity cocktail. Finally, he admitted, "You know, he asked me something at the time. Right before Preston's speech," he began, "which you missed, because one of the other ladies, I think you said it was Melissa Gordon, got a merlot stain on your dress?" He searched her eyes for an indication that he had reconstructed the memory. "So during the speech you were somewhere else, furiously trying to save the Escada's life."

"Oh god, that was a disaster!" The memory amused Beth.

She saw Miss Gordon's genuine horror and her lips trembling with panic all over again. At that moment, it was only the committed scrubbing of the yellow chiffon that allowed her to suppress the uncontrollable laughter bubbling inside.

Jeff laughed, too. Not so much at the story about the lady's misadventure, but rather at his wife's effort to keep her manners – the way she recalled a memory that made her laugh uncontrollably, right when her mouth was full of her favorite pasta. It was a substantial challenge even for his elegant lady. What was most charming was that she kept intending to cover her mouth with her hand, as etiquette prescribed, but prevented by the urge to laugh, her hand never managed to find her face.

After they calmed down, Jeff brought up the subject again.

"Is there a defense for the guilty? " Jeff he quoted, and then clarified: "Mason's question..."

Elizabeth leaned back again and folded her arms. "That's all? 'Is there a defense for the guilty'?" she repeated quietly.

"That's all," confirmed Jeff. "I don't know why he insists on having me defend him. He'll explain it himself, I suppose. He should be getting in touch any time now."

After a short pause, with both of them immersed in thought, Jeff looked around for the server to ask for the check. Beth's next session was in twenty minutes.

"Dear, there's something else I need to tell you," he admitted soon after they walked outside. "Preston doesn't want me to actually defend Mason. He wants me to lose."

Elizabeth froze one step behind her husband. "What's that supposed to mean?" she asked rhetorically.

Jeff stepped back and moved her away from the bike lane. "The last thing he said to me before leaving my office was that in the name of his father and my friendship with him, he was begging me to do it."

"You do realize how that sounds, don't you?" she asked insistently.

"Let's go, dear, we're running late." Jeff tried to distract her. "It's almost 1:30."

Beth held him against her body, without moving from her place. "I think they're threatening you, Jeff!" she insisted, with a clear accusation in the face of his calmness.

"Let's not jump to conclusions. You know Oliver, he's probably overreacting."

"You mean to talk to Mason? Wouldn't it be better to stay away from the whole thing?" Beth reasoned.

"I'm hesitating. On one hand, I have no desire to get in the mud. You know I don't like dirty games." Jeff waved his hand. "To be honest, Preston's warning doesn't worry me all that much."

Without realizing it, they'd reached Beth's office.

"You know, I think you should hear what Mason has to say," she advised him. "My instinct tells me to keep you away from this, but whatever decision you make, you need to know all the points of view."

Jeff agreed. "I'll see you tonight, dear. Thank you for your support," he said softly and kissed her on the cheek.

4.

Ian was almost done preparing dinner when he heard his parents from the yard. He meant to surprise them with the culinary skills he had learned in his years on campus.

"I can't believe it!" exclaimed Elizabeth right at the door, then turned to the driveway and shouted: "Jeff, someone beat you to it!"

She left her coat and headed to the semi-open kitchen, from where her son was peeping as if from a large TV screen.

"You didn't expect that, huh?" Ian praised himself.

"I hope you did a good job, young man!" She teased him. "Your dad intended to go crazy in the kitchen tonight!"

Jeff joined them and set the bags of groceries he was obviously not going to need tonight down on the counter.

"Greetings, boss!" Ian glanced at his father, wrapped a towel around his hand, pulled the hot pan out of the oven and placed it on the countertop. "Please, please!" he said, waving his hand with false modesty, trying to cool down Beth and Jeff's loud enthusiasm at the appearance of the golden roasted turkey. Then he carefully led them to take their places around the dining table. He followed them with a bottle of young Jeunesse, their favorite merlot, and three crystal glasses. Then, he proceeded to pour – his favorite part.

The Dunnes appreciated quality wine. The summer after Ian's freshman year, they had spent three weeks in a small village in Provence, learning the arts of the sommelier. He remembered every single rule about serving and degustation.

120 milliliters and not a drop more! More liquid in the glass is a display of ignorance and poor manners!, his mentor never failed to remark.

"To justice, truth, and loved ones! And now – the moment of truth!" He rubbed his hands before starting to carefully slice the meat.

"Stop trying to be funny and get to the point!" Jeff rushed him .

They dedicated about two minutes to silent appreciation of the result of Ian's three-hour culinary marathon. From time to time, their eyes met, even though they were all trying to avoid eye contact, as no one was ready to make a positive observation. Positive, in this case, meant realistic, but also encouragingly presented.

"Damn, it sure is bland!" the chef himself spoke first. "I knew I should have added more salt!"

"You've done a wonderful job, son. Let us all play a part here!" Jeff winked as he reached for the saltshaker.

Ian took a sip of wine. He let it caress his palate for a few seconds, using them to choose the right words.

"Mom, dad... My visit probably surprised you."

"Well..." Elizabeth started, before Jeff interrupted her to speak for both of them.

"Let's say that considering your busy schedule, we're expecting an important announcement."

"I do have one, actually... I'm going to do it."

"Do what, buddy?" nudged Beth.

"Go to Nigeria."

Drumroll. Elizabeth and Jeffrey sat very still. It was as if they had mentally taken hold of each other's hand, and now that they heard the silent explosion, they were left wondering whether it was better or worse than their expectations.

"You remember, right," continued Ian. "English lessons for disadvantaged children. I told you about it."

There was still no clear reaction from the other side. Beth started to retrieve the memory of what their son had told them a year earlier, some charity program for the education of children under 14. She ran her fingers over the hair flowing down her neck, as she always did when worried or nervous.

"Don't get me wrong, dear." She cleared her throat. "What you carry in your heart is my biggest pride! I know you're impatient to help, but..."

Jeffrey took his wife's hand under the table, insisting that she entrust him to lead the conversation.

"So when are you planning to leave?" he asked calmly.

"After the fall term."

"Three terms before you graduate?"

"I know what you're getting at, dad. The thing is, I can barely fit in my own skin! I have an awesome family, a high standard of living, I go to a prestigious university."

"Yes, so tough..." Jeff couldn't contain his sarcasm. Its aim was not to offend, but to remind him to appreciate and take advantage of his chances.

Ian understood him correctly.

"I mean to say that... I'm terrified of getting used to all that! And just forgetting the things that are happening out there! I feel ready to do something for these people, to sacrifice something of my own."

"Son." Jeff brought him back down to earth. "I understand how just watching is burning you from the inside..."

Elizabeth didn't show it, but her husband's gradual approach was starting to annoy her. Still, she didn't doubt his judgment for a second.

"You know that I would never try to manipulate you. We've always been straight with each other. So just hear me out... Our entire lives, your mom and I have put everything on the line to ensure opportunities for you. Step by step, with every undertaking, you tackle these opportunities. The education you're receiving at the moment will give you good prospects, because you're smart and resourceful. Even if you don't graduate, I'm sure that you'll find a way to ensure a good life for yourself."

He appeared to support him in the end. His words surprised Ian almost as much as they did his mother. He was alert, ready to defend his decision, but to his own surprise, he found himself in agreement with everything his father said.

"But..." Jeff emphasized the word that was going to turn the direction of his statement. "When you want to change the lives of others, when you want to save the world, you have to have trump cards in your hand, my friend. Brains and money – the main instruments of change. You'll need a lot more of both to make it happen. If you leave now, you'll spend time with these kids, you'll give them some attention, you'll teach them something... but you won't change their fate. On the other hand, if you give yourself time and continue to make an effort, one day you'll get there and you'll know that you can truly change something, really be a real factor – build a school, a hospital, housing... The people in Africa need a lot more than attention and time. You have no right to sacrifice the end result for a moment of weakness, and impatience is exactly that."

"You have a long way ahead of you," Elizabeth interjected. "so many chances to make the world better. Now is the time to make yourself better, to gather everything that you'll give later."

He leaned back, his left ankle casually positioned on his right knees like the numeral four, and stared at the glass that he held above his lap. However, there was a conflict brewing in him. He could see the logic in their words. They were right again, only this time he really did not want to be dissuaded. But their arguments were undeniable.

"Yeah, maybe..." he barely muttered, before Jeff interrupted him.

"Tell you what," Jeff interrupted him. "Let's organize a rematch for tonight one year from now. And yes, you're making the turkey again!"

Ian couldn't contain his laughter, and he didn't want to. He agreed.

"Let's do it, really!" insisted Jeff. "Then you'll repeat what you told us, we'll tell you again how much we love you and believe in the help you'll give these kids, and we can all think about how to make it happen!"

"Only if it's Thanksgiving. I'm not making turkey for every gathering!"

The hours until midnight flew by. Ian retired to his room, tired from the long day.

Elizabeth and Jeff stayed behind to clean up a bit – they had always done that together, ever since he was a kid. They used these moments to discuss things they wanted to keep away from his mind. Naturally, tonight the subject was Ian.

***

At 7:20 the next morning, Ian came running down the stairs. Elizabeth had not seen such a morning rush in years. While still on the staircase, he focused on the coffee cup in his mother's hand. She was reviewing her schedule by the countertop.

"Make yourself another one – I'm late!" He excused himself without stopping, as he grabbed her favorite yellow cup.

He drank a quick sip and headed for the shoe cabinet in the anteroom. He put the cup on top and pointed to one of the three picture frames on it.

"The year 2000, Rome. It was an awesome vacation. Right, boss?" he shouted to Jeff, who was just coming down the stairs and rushing to the espresso machine.

Ian noticed that one of the important elements of his father's daily routine, the *Daily News*, was missing. He was by the door anyway, so he checked if the newspaper man had covered his route on time. *The man never misses!*, he thought as he lifted the paper from the mat.

He headed to the kitchen to hand it to his father. Right then, Jeff's phone chimed and he answered immediately.

"Jeffrey Dunne."

"Mr. Dunne, hello, it's Thomas Mason," the man on the other end introduced himself hesitantly. "We met at Oliver Preston's charity gala."

"Yes, I remember. How can I help you?"

"I would like a personal consultation with you, Mr. Dunne. When can we meet?"

"Look, I don't think it'll be possible this week, I'm pretty busy..."

"Please, this meeting is of the utmost importance to me. Please consider it, I'll fit myself to your schedule."

"I'll see what I can do and get back to you. Have a good day, Mr. Mason."

In his peripheral vision, Jeff could see his son following the conversation with astonishment.

"Mason? Thomas Mason?" Ian asked, barely containing his excitement.

Elizabeth was quietly pouring some more coffee into a thermal cup. She wondered whether they should share any information with Ian on the case that was developing around Jeff. She cast a quick glance at her husband, then decided to redirect the pressure of the expected reply from his shoulders.

"Have you heard of him?" she asked calmly.

The boy's eyes expressed shock and darted back and forth between them.

"Have I heard of him? Are you kidding? The man is a hero to me! Do you know what he does? Do you know what he does every day?" His questions grew louder.

"Son, it's a good thing to judge a man by his deeds, but sometimes what we see isn't the whole story," replied Jeff.

"What I see is enough for me! Did you know that last year, Libra sent 760 volunteer teachers to Chad, who all pledged to spend three years there? Do you know how many lives that changed? Even the program I was going to apply for is run by Libra. Dad, these people are amazing! By helping Mason, you'll help thousands of others!"

In spite of his son's exaltation, Jeff still tried to clarify his own position in regard to Mason and his honesty.

"Alright, young man, hold your horses," Beth tried to cool him down. "Decisions are yet to be made."

Ian sneaked behind his dad and, like a devoted coach cheering up his player before the most important match of his career, shook him by the shoulders. After a final manly tap, he went over to his mother.

"Why do you always have to be in a hurry, son?" she took his face in her palms.

"Because I'm always late!" joked Ian and kissed her.

In truth, he was never late. And he was rarely more than five minutes early. He grabbed his leather jacket from the hanger and shouted, "Maybe I'll come again at the end of next week. I think I'll get a chance. And dad, do the right thing!" he said patronizingly.

"We'll be waiting, dear!" waved Beth.

Jeff smiled as his eyes followed Ian out. His mind, however, was occupied with the Libra case. He did not want to enter into preliminary deliberations before knowing the facts. But he didn't have any, which forced him to do what was necessary – to meet with Mason.

The roar of Ian's Mustang had quieted down. Jeff remembered how long his son had dreamt of that car. For four years, the walls in his room were literally covered by posters of the classic vehicle. He got it when he turned eighteen. By then, he already knew that dreams travel a long way. And in his dreams, Ian had imagined the car just like that – a model 69 coupe, arctic metallic, with a 4.7 8-cylinder V engine. It was a model respected by aficionados, and the boy just worshiped it. The leather upholstery may have been a bit cracked, but still maintained fairly well.

"We've always known that there are no coincidences," Elizabeth said to her husband.

"I'm going to hear him out," announced Jeff. "Even though the picture seems clear."

"Do hear him out," Beth agreed. "Don't rush to conclusions."

* * *

Ian could not stop thinking about the call. It might have looked strange to an outside observer, but it was a big deal to him. He was exceptionally proud of the fact that the founder of Libra was being advised by none other than his dad. Whatever Mason had done, whatever he was afraid of, he had clearly understood the meaning that truth and justice had for the Pillar. All the things that he himself really admired in his father.

He was 300 miles from New York. He didn't rush; he was a calm driver. He enjoyed the feeling of driving far more than speed itself. The vibrations moving between him and the Tank, as he called his 330horsepower gasoline pal, seemed to merge them into one.

5.

Jeffrey's workday began as usual; the Friday mood of nonchalance had not taken over his firm. The last workday of the week was designated for group discussion and internal consulting on current cases. At 9 am, the entire team gathered in the large conference room on the ninth floor. His team was a benchmark of professional synergy, and also equality between the sexes, as half of the sixteen attorneys were women. After sharing their morning coffee together with some exchange of opinions in regard to more publicized cases, Jeff once again heard the name of his dilemma.

The divorce attorney Tim Dawson, one of the first lawyers to join the firm, was looking through the latest news in *Affairs* – the favorite publication of lawyers and a nightmare for politicians and businesspeople. The former used it to collect some preliminary information on their future clients, while the latter, the potential defendants, ritually opened it every Friday, just as people had searched for friends and relatives in the obituary section since the last century. Nowadays, however, the sorrowful news came in the column "The Red Line," and when people were still very much alive. The column had begun eight years before, with the premise that any reporter with facts and proof regarding criminal acts by high-ranking officials could find a platform there. It could be said that its audience had become impressive, and many people got excited about the articles in *Affairs*.

Tim started reading out loud:

"'The sum funneled by Libra's charity fund to Thomas Mason's offshore account in Panama is 12 million dollars.' My God!" Tim took his glasses off, and nodded, clearly impressed. "That girl caused him a lot of trouble... I hope she doesn't suffer for it. Other reporters would think twice before publishing something like that."

"What was her name? Layla something..." Susan Hill said over his shoulder, as she waited for her coffee by the machine in one corner. "It seems like she has a killer instinct, even though that's just her second investigation. And it's not like the previous one was large-scale. Remember that story from last summer about a public contract for military uniforms?"

"Was she the one to sniff out the connection between the Military Fit CEO and the mayor?" Jeff asked and then spent a few seconds trying to remember more details about the case. "Cronyism in these circles is probably not a surprise for anyone, but if you think about it, a lot of effort must've gone into that investigation. Just imagine..." he continued and stepped closer to Dawson. "May I?" He took the paper from his hands and turned the front page with the headline "You're Lying, Libra!" toward the others around the table. He pointed his finger to the reporter's picture and asked, "How old do you think this girl is? I doubt she's older than my son... Can you imagine what it took to obtain this information? She's staking a serious claim for presence among investigative journalists."

The others agreed and shuffled in their chairs, showing their readiness for the meeting to proceed to specifics. Susan, who specialized in copyright law, called attention to her latest case. She needed to consult her colleagues on several aspects that were in their areas of competence.

Jeffrey followed the conversation until a thought distracted him – he realized that he was constantly thinking about Thomas Mason, or rather, his own attitude toward the man. This case, even before he was familiar with it, was shaping up to be one of the knottiest in his career.

First of all, the demand so brazenly presented to him by the senator had left Jeff with a negative impression of the people involved. Later, it seemed like Ian's extreme praise had convinced him to consider some sort of exonerating explanation. And now, hearing parts of the article about Layla Pierce's investigation, this consideration nearly evaporated. The Pillar felt himself becoming impatient to know facts.

After the end of the meeting, he headed for the elevator to go to his office. He sat on the chair behind the massive oak desk and reached for the intercom button. He kept his eyes on a picture of Ian – his son was reading a speech at his high school graduation. *I hope I won't have to disappoint you, son*, he thought before putting the golden-plated frame back on the desk.

"Mary, would you please look at my schedule for the late afternoon? I think my last one is Edison at 4 p.m."

"Of course, Mr. Dunne, one sec."

He could hear her shuffle the calendar's pages. They had become accustomed to the new way of working after she asked to combine two positions. She wanted to remain his assistant, but also welcome colleagues, clients, and students that came to the office for instruction or internships.

For years, Mary worked from a room next to his office and they discussed his schedule in person. He preferred it like that, but when she had asked for additional responsibilities in order to afford her daughter's private school, Jeffrey could not come up with a more adequate proposal.

"Right... good memory!" she remarked. "Your last appointment is at 4:00, but not with Edison, it's with James Parkins, the dean of Santa Maria college, regarding the media law seminar. Your meeting with Edison is at 2:30 tomorrow."

"You spoil me. Thanks Mary."

Jeff took his cellphone and dialed Mason.

"Mr. Dunne? I'm glad to hear from you," the voice in the

speaker greeted him with appreciation.

"Mr. Mason, I'll have some time in the late afternoon. Would 5:30 p.m. work?"

"I can make it. Your office?"

"I'd rather we met in private. Do you know the Woodley Park area? There's a large parking lot 21st Street."

"I know it."

"Let's talk there, outside. My car is a dark-blue Volkswagen sedan."

"Understood. See you soon!"

It was deeply uncharacteristic, but Jeffrey went through the next consultations absentmindedly, in a professionally controlled shuffle between different cases and Mason. At 16:45, he anxiously reached out to shake Mr. Perkins's hand.

"Not to worry, Mr. Perkins. The 6th floor hall has 180 seats. If for some reason that isn't enough, we'll go down to the 5th floor, where we have 300 seats. The more students who are interested, the more successful our mission is. That's the important thing!"

"Of course, Mr. Dunne! What you're doing for them is priceless. Santa Maria college is indebted to you!"

Jeff left the dean and headed to the underground garage. As always, his car was in E2. He drove up to Connecticut Avenue and headed to Woodley Park. Before he knew it, he had reached the parking lot. While he waited at the light to make a U-turn, he looked around the meeting spot. He could not see anyone in the driveways or between cars. He slowly entered the parking lot and headed for the far side of the fence.

He found a suitable spot between a plain Ranger and a Corolla. As he parked in reverse, he noticed a cab pulling over by the bus stop. A tall man of about 50 stepped out of it. He quickly scanned the perimeter as he reached over to get his coat from the back seat.

It was 5:29 p.m., and Jeffrey appreciated punctuality. He took his cellphone from the passenger seat and dialed.

"I see you. Look to the left," he instructed and flashed

his headlights.

Mason saw him immediately and headed over.

"I'm glad you agreed to meet. And so soon," he said as he got in Jeff's car.

"To be honest, I had serious doubts," admitted Jeff as they shook hands. "Let's just say that the people you're involved with didn't approach me in the best way."

"They came to see you?" Mason shook his head and smirked, showing this didn't surprise him. "Preston is trying to parry every independent move I could make. He didn't like my refusal to go to court with Smith's 'defense.'"

"Look, let's start from the beginning. You'll have to introduce me to the case from your point of view, because it's the only one I haven't heard. And something tells me it's of key importance."

Mason paused for a bit; he felt the weight of the words he was about to speak.

"I met Oliver Preston six years ago. He came to my office. He said he wanted to 'personally meet the man who does all these good deeds.'"

"Six years ago?" repeated Jeff.

"Yes, at the time he was still his father's son, rather than his own person. Because of that, my attitude toward the father was a leading factor in my judgment of Oliver. I knew Roger..."

"He was an honorable man. A great professional," Jeff interrupted and Mason nodded in agreement.

"My opinion of Oliver was formed by association and guesswork – a young man from a respected family, affluent, and with the desire to invest money in good causes... that's how I saw him. In fact, in the beginning of our relationship, he was pretty much that. Soon after we met, he asked to donate 150,000 dollars to one of my campaigns. I admit that at the time, I believed this first impression of him..." Mason sighed with disappointment.

"Am I to understand that changed later?"

"About a year later, he was sworn in as a senator. I

hadn't heard from him for a while, and I didn't follow his politics. I had my own problems..." He paused again for a moment and drew a deep breath. "One day, about a year later, he called me and asked to meet. He was excited and told me about the giant sums he wanted to bring to my charity programs. And the protection he would ensure for me and the foundation."

Thomas avoided looking at Jeffrey too often, as he didn't want to interrupt the continuity of his story. Now, however, he tried to make eye contact with the lawyer so as to gauge his reaction to the last sentence. But Dunne was exceptionally practiced at controlling his emotions and expression. Mason continued chronologically.

"Back then, I didn't quite understand what he meant by 'protection.' I was doing good things, I helped people, why would I need protection?"

"I'm assuming that it came up soon enough?"

"For a long time we didn't discuss the subject, and I didn't ask, either. I somehow missed that detail, even though I should have been more focused. Some months later, the senator came again and declared that after working on mission Libra for a long time, he'd finally managed to secure funds – 25 million dollars."

This time, the Pillar couldn't quite hide his surprise. Thomas continued.

"Yes... he definitely managed. 25 million, I said to myself... The things we could do in Africa with that money! But even if I didn't realize it before, I unconsciously connected the sum with what he said about protection. Preston's approach was very shrewd," Mason remarked with frustration.

"In what sense?"

"He distracted me, he put me in a position where I had to defend the foundation's right to receive the funds. To account for the different causes and programs, whether they make sense, the transparency of the monetary distribution. He seemed to really care about how and what the money would help!" he justified himself.

"So when did you realize there was something else?" asked Jeff.

"I realized it when he asked me how my daughter was doing." Thomas paused again. It was obvious he was suppressing a strong emotion. "I have a daughter. She's twelve."

Jeff didn't quite get the turn, but he felt he shouldn't interrupt.

"She was eight when they diagnosed her with leukemia," Mason continued, in spite of the lump that was stuck in his throat. He could feel that Jeffrey was sympathetic and appreciated his decision not to interrupt. They both knew this would only make the conversation harder.

"In all those years, we went through every possible therapy and method. The result was always the same – she'd be stable for a while, then she'd develop a resistance to the therapy, and sometimes even deteriorate. Vivian was withering away in front of our eyes. Sometimes I think that these awful procedures are more cruel than the disease itself."

"I'm truly sorry that you've had to go through this pain," said Jeff. "But I fail to see what these circumstances have to do with Preston."

The lawyer's question returned the focus to Mason's mind.

"That's what I asked myself when he wanted to know about Vivian. Because I'd never mentioned her to him, let alone the nightmare we were going through! I was so surprised that I didn't even consider how he knew about her. I answered that we were doing everything we could. Then he asked me if I'd heard of Hope."

"Hope?" Jeff tried to retrieve information from his memory, or at least a connection.

"Barely anyone had back then. After a while, it became a favorite of conspiracy theorists."

"Hope! Now I remember!" Jeff recalled bits and pieces of the theory that had reached him through different channels. Unfortunately, all unreliable. "You're talking about the rumors that the US government is hiding the results of an exclusive secret therapeutic program for..."

"For curing incurable diseases. It's true! They've provided the most qualified medical specialists, methods and medicaments for the upper echelons of society. Access is severely restricted, and the success rate – a proven 100%. Preston assured me of that. You can understand what it meant for me to hear that," Mason tried to justify himself.

"Right, but I don't understand what Hope has to do with the charity money?"

"You have the power of deduction, Mr. Dunne. You can see the connection, even if you don't yet understand it. At the time when Preston was telling me about the therapy, I still didn't suspect it. I didn't even allow for such a connection."

"Connection? Where's the link here?" insisted Jeff.

"You've already put A and B together. You know there's a link between Hope and the 25 million. All you have to do is find B – the mutual benefit," Mason guided him.

Jeffrey didn't like to play detective. His profession taught him to work with facts, not assumptions. But in all these years, he dealt with the people before he got to the facts. He had established that respecting people's emotions was of paramount significance, because emotions were at the bottom of every action. In this sense, he felt that Mason aimed to provide him with a path to discover his guilt.

"Therapy for your daughter," Jeff grasped.

"Oliver offered to provide Vivian with access," confirmed Mason. "Access to our last chance."

"What did he ask for?"

Thomas kept his eyes down on the rubber mat beneath his shoes. Although he knew the reason for accepting the senator's offer, he was still conscious of having committed a crime.

"A huge part of the donations," he mumbled, after which they both retired to their own thoughts.

His admission did not come as a surprise to Jeffrey. He knew Preston well, and it was entirely in unison with his persona. For him, however, the dilemma was becoming ever more palpable. With every sentence Mason said, he realized that the case was complicated... even more complicated than he'd expected. But what really stirred his emotions was the difference in his previous position. Not even an hour ago he had been almost categorically against getting involved. But now, he felt himself becoming sympathetic.

At that moment, as if to give them more time to think, the owner of the beat-up truck appeared. The exhaust of the blue beast from 1989 popped two or three times before it drove off.

"What do you expect from me?" asked Jeffrey, while simultaneously searching his mind for potential answers.

"*Expect* is not the right word, Mr. Dunne. I want to fight for justice in spite of the deal I made. I believe I still deserve that. My daughter deserves that," he emphasized. "And if there's someone in whose sense of justice I believe, it's you."

"What went wrong? I doubt you took the deal without discussing the conditions and consequences of such actions?"

"Our arrangement was clear, or at least that's how it sounded. I needed to regularly make sure that certain sums from the hundreds of millions that Preston raised for Libra were diverted to his pocket. To do that, I had to risk my name and reputation by sending the money to my own offshore accounts. As I mentioned earlier, I'd received multiple assurances about the protection I had. And all of this in exchange for my daughter's treatment."

"And did it happen, did she get treatment?"

"Well, ostensibly, she's still getting it... but the procedures are becoming less and less frequent. I'm assuming they do it to keep me under control."

"Let's return to the protection for a moment. What did it consist of?"

"Happily for them, they haven't needed to apply it. But now, after the article in "The Red Line," the threat to all of us is serious. The prosecution is building a case. A case *against me*, clearly."

"You sound like you believe you'll be hoodwinked?" Jeff tried to direct the conversation.

He very clearly remembered what the senator and Smith had told him in his office a few days ago. They were completely intent, even eager, to see the trial end with a guilty verdict for Mason. In the mind of the Pillar, the elements given by both sides of the scheme started to find their places in the puzzle. It was becoming increasingly obvious that Preston would benefit the most if Mason were accused and tried. For Vivian's sake, he would be forced to go behind bars and confess to being the lone perpetrator. And to guarantee his silence, the results of her treatment would, naturally, be perpetually open-ended. And the senator would retire from his post clean – and considerably richer.

"I wouldn't have been as suspicious if I hadn't been literally ordered to go to court under Martin's 'protection.' What's more, Oliver knows quite well what my opinion of that reptile is. He shouldn't have assumed that I would put my trust in him. But he didn't just offer Martin's help. It was almost an ultimatum."

Jeffrey allowed himself a few seconds before deciding whether to warn Thomas that he was on the right path with his suspicions. The rules of confidentiality prevented him from saying it directly, but he sent a signal he believed was received.

"I can see that you also have the power of deduction," said Jeff and saw understanding in the other man's eyes.

They remained silent for a moment before Mason continued.

"Look, I understand what I've done, and also what I've risked. It would be naive to imagine that there was ever a set of circumstances under which I could come out clean. Still, I hope it was worth it. I want to know that I've done everything in my power for Vivian's future, that her place is in the elite checklist, that she won't be erased when I go to jail, like I expect. She needs to complete that treatment!" he said with desperation. "That's why I need your help. And as far as punishment for Preston, regardless of my own guilt, the man deserves it! His only motive was never anything but greed!"

"And you believe that I can deliver this punishment?"

"No, Mr. Dunne, but I do believe that you'd do everything in your power for that to happen. Thanks to your name and reputation, people will know the truth regardless of my sentence. I don't want my family to be stained by this. In its essence, Libra aimed for nothing more than to help. I won't forgive myself if I don't fight until the end to at least reveal why I sullied my own name. I owe it to all the people around me."

At this point, the pauses between them said nearly as much as their words, as if they understood each other better through the unsaid. Once again, Thomas felt the lawyer's unspoken thoughts and decided it was time to leave and give him the necessary space to find his way in the case.

"Mr. Dunne, I sincerely thank you for your time and attitude. I'm aware of your moral principles and I knew that the chance for you to hear me out was small, so I'm indebted to you. Your support would really mean a lot to me and my family, if you accept to fight with us." Mason gripped Jeffrey's hand tightly. "It was an honor!"

Jeffrey maintained eye contact and held on to his hand, underscoring the significance of his words.

"Mr. Mason, you are aware that my participation in this case would inevitably reflect not only on my work and name, but my family as well. I want to emphasize that I understand you... what you did. Probably anyone would have done the same in your position. But I can't be part of the case until I've given enough consideration to the potential consequences for both of us. I'll get in touch and let you know about my decision."

"I'll be waiting," nodded Thomas before stepping out of the car. He wanted to give the lawyer privacy and quiet as soon as possible. He realized how necessary they were in moments like these.

6.

February was in its early days. The sun was shining high above Manhattan, provoking the students from Columbia university into thinking about the upcoming spring rather than the spring semester.

Ian was heading to Low Library to meet Chester and Megan, his best college friends. Although he was a favorite of everyone, he allowed very few to get close. Not very typical for someone with his qualities. Despite his charisma, he didn't provoke rivalry and competitive sparks in his peers. Ian was the uncontested leader, and the sympathies that he enjoyed left no place for jealousy. The Invisible Man, as they called him on campus because of his lightning speed on the pitch, was one of those individuals that people just knew were destined to achieve great things.

Chester saw his friend creeping up behind Megan and he understood the signs he was giving him. Ian meant to startle Megan. The impulsive reactions of the curly-haired, olive-skinned girl were inordinately energetic in such situations, which contrasted with her usually modest nature. This really amused Ian and the people around him.

Just like every Tuesday, they were attending the debate course they took together and loved so much. Ian looked around the hall like every student did after going to yet another class for the day. It was emptier than usual; he counted only 23 faces. He had seen all of them before but knew less than half of them personally. The students were used to the feeling of regarding people they had never spoken to before as acquaintances or even buddies, only because they bumped into each other at least twice a day. On the one hand, it was pleasant because it gave them a sense of community. On the other, it could become rather confusing. After the first month in college, they adopted a key communication technique – they just nodded or smiled each time they met someone's eyes. If they still didn't know each other personally, it was almost inevitable that a course, a project, or a seminar would introduce them. It was something like an introduction in advance.

For this reason, Ian applied the technique to his future acquaintances and walked toward the far end of the auditorium. Set up as an amphitheater, it allowed everyone to watch him as he walked to his preferred seat. As a matter of fact, he considered this hall to be utterly unsuitable and uncomfortable for the purposes of the course. After all, debates were conducted there, and people stood up to defend their positions on a given subject. Only here, when speaking one had to spin in all directions to make eye contact or give a direct reply to one of the other students scattered all over. Ian considered a round table set-up a much more adequate choice.

Megan and Chester came in about ten minutes after him, right before Professor Blair. The 73-year-old professor was a former reporter who still wrote the occasional piece for political publications. Politics was the main focus of his professional career, even though his erudition allowed for more. For a man who had devoted so much of his time and attention to such a rational pursuit, he was remarkably open minded. Although his large square glasses, his thinning hair, and his suit one size larger than needed contributed to his stern academic appearance, his knowledge spanned multiple and varied fields. In a fascinating mix of interests, it combined sports, AI, classic literature, and the esoteric. This was precisely why Blair was so well respected by students. Just like the course he had created five years earlier.

"Hi, Professor Blair!"

"Hello, Professor."

One over the other, the greetings came from every corner of the auditorium as Chester and Megan took their seats next to Ian.

"You've come to debate instead of basking in that alluring sun outside? What's wrong with you?"

"And miss out on the verbal wrestling?" Aaron Rain chimed in from the left side. There was laughter. It was typical for Aaron to lighten up the atmosphere with one of his wisecracks.

"Ian, what's the topic for today?" Megan asked in a whisper against the exchange of jokes in the background.

"I don't know, I missed class because of the game."

"Don't you remember, Meg?" Chester nudged her. "Professor Blair warned us that this time he'd surprise us..." He fell silent while he attempted to remember something. "Yeah, right, with a verbal ophthalmological analysis."

"What?" Megan and Ian just gaped, unable to comprehend, before turning to the professor for an explanation.

"Dear colleagues," he began. "I know that normally, we prefer designated subjects. Situations that require concrete actions and measures."

Everyone had quieted down, expecting to hear the connection between the last lesson and every uttered word.

"But I have planned something more abstract for today," he explained and ran a conspiratorial look through the students like a laser. "I'd be curious to hear your ideas about the future."

"Right!"

"Now I get it!"

The exclamations came from the students who managed to spot the connection between the theme and the ophthalmological analysis. They gradually started to get excited about the diagnoses they were about to receive – would they emerge as shortsighted, unable to think in perspective, or people who chase the future so desperately that their present was engulfed in fog.

"So..." Blair prepared to insert a pin into an imaginary time axis. "The year 2036."

A silence ensued, and he needed to be more specific.

"Let's start from somewhere, then. Today, February 7, 2006, I ask you: what would we see if we somehow, through paths unknown, all end up exactly here in thirty years, on February 7, 2036?"

In this course, the students were used to reacting in

seconds to a given subject. Normally, the first comments started coming no longer than 20 seconds after the question was posed. This time, however, they were all quiet. Only professor's steps could be heard as he paced back and forth without looking at the students very often.

"Professor, the question wasn't put correctly."

Blair's rhythmical steps suddenly stopped. He turned around and smiled for a split second.

"There he is! I thought you'd fallen asleep, Dunne. It took you way too long to counter me!"

One could take the professor's remark seriously, but only if they didn't see his smile. Blair liked Ian. A lot. He respected his readiness to look at every angle before allowing himself to voice an opinion. Unlike the great majority of his peers, he had a very high internal standard for the significance of his own opinion – as if it had to meet his internal expectations first. He even had requirements for the way through which he was to form his position. His beliefs and philosophy were adopted after meticulous analysis and were refracted through his own prism.

The sympathy was mutual. Ian didn't take provocations from just anyone, but he regarded the professor as an authority figure.

"I'm sure that you'll find my words reasonable. The subject is excellent, but I believe that something in the question itself contradicts the idea, and the objectivity, of an ophthalmological analysis," he chuckled, but he was left alone in his amusement, since the others had yet to understand his statement.

They would have probably understood if they could repeat it in their minds.

He continued his thought.

"There's a paradox in the idea of imagining a realistic scenario, possible in thirty years, in combination with the unrealistic and impossible element that all of us are here again together. Allowing for a paradox in the premise of the hypothesis wouldn't allow us to reconstruct a realistic picture of the future."

"I swear Dunne, sometimes you're a bit much!"

Even before the heavy sigh that preceded the comment, the students were already rolling with laughter. They were accustomed to the teasing banter between Ian and the professor and always found it refreshing. Besides, Blair kept the boy in a position closer to that of his colleagues through sarcasm, though benevolently and in the name of a friendly tone. He believed that it could help dissipate any irritation on their side, even though Ian – without even knowing – smashed any hints of envy. It was impossible for those surrounding him to keep that attitude up for long; it usually evaporated as soon as they got to know him.

"Alright, then. Would you be so kind as to explain to us what kind of imaginary scenario would facilitate the visualization of life in 2036?" the professor encouraged him.

Ian put down the pen which he occasionally tapped on the desk in order to accentuate particular moments of the conversation and slowly stood up. For a moment, he looked at the bright view out the window. He kept quiet for one more second, then shifted his weight forward to his palms, like he was trying to focus a thousand thoughts in a tight column of a few sentences.

"Please forgive my remark, Professor Blair, I allowed myself the liberty in the name of an optimal treatment of the subject... which is very personal to me. I often think about this future world, and unfortunately, what I see horrifies me."

"So what's wrong with flying cars, Dunne? Are you afraid of heights?" Aaron Rain remarked from somewhere on the left. This time, the comedian's ego took a blow – only a couple of people reacted.

"Oh come on Aaron, I've said barely a few words and your brain is already incapable of handling the pressure," Ian interjected.

"Love and peace, bro," humbly replied the comedian with a manner intentionally reminiscent of his favorite Bob

Marley.

After a short pause, Ian continued.

"If I could jump to the year 2036 and observe from here... I fear that everyday routines, jobs, interpersonal relations, and just life itself will be digitized to a degree to which people will ignore real contact. You ask what I imagine I'll see right around here?" He lifted his palms and expressively looked around. "I don't see anyone."

"So you think that in 2036, education will be a thing of the past?" asked Blair, taking care to grasp Ian's theory before passing judgment.

"I think that live communication will be a thing of the past. Education, just like every other aspect of modern civilization, will be adapted to the modern environment."

"And how would that work out, Dunne? You mean that institutions that have existed for centuries will be disregarded in the future? Right when it is assumed that humanity will seek ever newer knowledge, skills, scientific discovery?"

Naomi York cut in over his shoulder. She was an ambitious and well-read girl, but too narrow minded, Ian thought. "You seem to question not just the moral aspect of society, but its ambition to evolve as well?"

"Very good, Ms. York," the professor remarked before turning to Ian. "Mr. Dunne, Naomi pointed out some very valid concerns regarding your thesis. Let's focus on education for the moment. It's clear that, given the historical development of the education system, knowledge has been placed at the absolute center of modern society. Think about it, would it be possible to find realization in our day without education? Is there a place in the system for those who don't make an effort to contribute to its advancement?"

Ian carefully thought about his position before presenting it, since he knew it could provoke sharp reactions.

"Please allow me to quote you, professor. You say, 'education is at the center of society,' and 'one must contribute to the advancement of the system.'" Before he continued, he shot a glance at Naomi. "So let's look at education and the system as two separate elements, and I can clarify my concerns. Let's begin with the first. May I ask you to share your majors?"

Naturally, Naomi was the first to jump up.

"Business management."

"Alright, Aaron? Stand-up comedy, was it?"

"Ha-ha! Linguistics, you smart ass!"

"Economics and statistics," someone said from the right.

"Computer science," Megan raised her hand and said, looking at Chester as if handing him the relay.

"I'm good, you can continue..." Everyone laughed at his shy answer.

"Drama and theater studies, this is from the shy gentleman next to me," Ian pointed out dramatically before turning both his thumbs to his chest. "And here we have economics and political science."

"Very well, Mr. Dunne, it was refreshing to get introduced again," the professor teased. "Would you enlighten us on the purpose of this exercise?"

"Patience, Professor Blair, I propose that we will all clarify it together. What do we have here? Business management, economics, statistics, let's leave linguistics and drama aside..."

Ian looked around and noticed some of the students were starting to get bored with this approach of stating the obvious.

"Please, don't get bored yet! I'd like to direct your attention to the purpose of these sciences. Why do we choose them? Personally, I picked economics and political science because I wanted to understand how to work with this world's main driving forces – money and politics. Naomi, you probably want to learn how to build the foundations of an enterprise and turn it into a successful, thriving business, and a product that would benefit society. As for statistics, it makes use of analysis and categorization of data that benefits the system and is necessary for its sustainable development. The system," he repeated. "Now we get to it."

Blair realized that Ian was methodically leading the students on a particular path, and he couldn't wait to find out its final destination.

"What's the system, Ian? What does it mean to you?" he asked.

"Before I tell you what it means to me, I'd like to acknowledge the opinion of my colleagues. Let them answer first. Naomi, I'm assuming you'd like to start?"

"Thank you, Ian! To me, the system is a benevolent mechanism that helps the development of society. The interconnectedness between different spheres is constructed in a way that channels its functions and points them in a direction beneficial for our future."

It was almost as if the national anthem was playing as a background to her words. It was obvious that Naomi was raised in a conservative American environment.

"I can see your logic, Naomi, I really do." Ian nodded and the others did, too. "The point of the system is the common good, right? Do you all agree? And our majors were created entirely in support of this mechanism? So the system can continue existing just as we happily evolve within it?"

He observed the reactions around him. Unfortunately, he saw – even among his friends – nothing but agreement. Only professor Blair's facial expression betrayed the fact that the words "within it" had called his attention. The pauses in his rhythmical pacing, which normally didn't stop throughout the entire debate, showed when something aroused his interest.

"Because no one would want to be outside of it, right? What would our lives be like outside of the system?" Everyone remained silent, so Ian continued. "Is there anyone among us who can build something? Build a house from bricks and wood? Or cut wood for heating? Or hunt... Anyone?" he looked around again.

"Are we Neanderthals or something? What's with the primitive attitude? How could you chase an animal to eat it?" Bethany Gray, an animal rights activist and vegetarian, said with disgust.

"Of course you couldn't. And why would you, when you can pick any part of the corpse of all kinds of known and exotic animals, which are carefully chopped to pieces on a daily basis? We see them on every other shop window on the street. Well, maybe not exactly you..." He tried to soften her predatory stare with a joke. Unsuccessfully. "But someone else, for instance, would gladly take advantage of this plenty. Let me ask you this, Beth, as someone for whom plant-based foods are so important. Have you ever grown any?" he provoked her. "I'm not talking about a house plant, I mean carrots, for example. Can you claim that you could independently survive outside the system? After all, you don't need so much, right? A roof over your head and vegetables."

Suddenly, the irritation that the mention of killing animals brought to Beth's face dissipated as a consequence of the thoughts that flashed in her mind. Finally, she collected them and began patronizingly.

"Ian, it's the 21st century. Maybe I've never grown carrots or potatoes, but I put enough effort in my education to be sure that I'll manage somehow, regardless of what life brings. Information is all around us, I don't need to know everything, especially such basic stuff. For god's sake, I'm studying statistics at one of the oldest US universities! If I must, I'll figure out how to plant a potato!"

Although she was allowed to explain her position un-obstructed, Miss Gray seemed like she wasn't too happy with her exposé. She felt that despite her effort, her claims did not have the weight to dispute Ian's arguments. That was obvious to the others as well. They had already started to grasp his idea and waited to hear its conclusion.

"What horrifies me is the fact that, starting with our first steps in society, we are encouraged to adapt to this machine. To find a way to be highly prized and necessary in it. Until one day we realize that we reach career peaks that have meaning only within the frame of that same system. At the same time, we're incapable of surviving for even a day outside of the modern world! Imagine, for example, a natural disaster that destroys all the comforts and amenities of present-day life. Would we manage? Would we be able to build, to plant, to grow...?" Ian spoke passionately, and it seemed like it was only to the professor. He wanted to make sure that someone would understand the importance of his anguish. "What's the use of politics outside of the system? Of statistics? Economics? What's the actual point of the monetary system?"

"Oh, dude! You're going too far, bro!" Aaron Rain found another chance to speak out. "My brain is starting to hurt..."

"Think about it, man, we're so deeply buried in this matrix, that normal and natural things seem unthinkable to us! Does anyone really need money? These pieces of paper, that today define us more than any knowledge or ability..."

Ian realized that he was dwelling too deep into a subject that he had no time to properly expand. So he judged it was time to return to the beginning of the debate.

"So, back to your question, Professor Blair. It's 2036 and I don't see anyone around. No one needs personal contact, real debates..." he smiled with nostalgia, as if he were already living in this bleak future. "People will study their pointless professions and develop those skills entirely digitally. And what would follow from that? As a result of complete digitalization, we would gradually lose the knowledge of how to interact with nature, we'll seek, and find, a way to subdue it completely. We'll probably raise... no, we'll construct animals and plants in an artificial environment, with ones and zeros. Until finally, this system that we guard so zealously, that we were placed in with such foresight, cripples us completely," he summarized, trying to keep his emotions in check. He then sat down to show he was finished.

The other students remained quiet. Most of them had

seen reason in Ian's words, but they seemed to hastily strike this conceptual challenge from their minds as a redundant worry that could distract them from their personal plan for success. They did not need to brood on such dark scenarios. Even if true, they would materialize so many years from now. Years during which these people, still young, would be able to give to the system – and, of course, also take from it.

Professor Blair looked at the watch on his left wrist.

"Well, time's run away from us, and we need to start wrapping up. Ian, I understand your concerns and I can see why you're worried. But could I give you some advice?"

"Yes, professor."

"This actually applies to all of you. It could be the case – that we're the product of a selfish matrix that only aims to turn us into its own product, one it can greedily consume before our expiration date. But the true essence of man – the intellect that separates us from animals, our ability to reason – no one can take that away from you. Not even the system. And don't forget that the difference between the thinker and the doer is considerable. You know the saying – 'Be the change you want to see.' Let's not just perceive it as yet another cliche. I want each one of you to know that you can be the agent of change, instead of just waiting for it."

He looked at the faces in front of him and waved his hand.

"Alright, scram! The weather outside is beautiful and you have my full permission to spend it according to your youth – freely and fully. Think, dream, and plan, but don't forget that you have your whole lives ahead of you. Be young for a while longer," he winked at Ian and returned to his desk to collect his notebook and the marker he had not used on the board today.

Ian nodded, but deep down he already knew that these thoughts would not give him peace. He was walking silently to the exit behind Megan and Chester when the professor called him.

"Ian, could you please stay for a minute? I want to

discuss something about your essay, it won't take long."

"Yes, of course. Wait for me outside, will you," he shouted after his friends, who were a few steps ahead.

The professor stretched to the side to reach the podium. He leaned back and folded his arms on his chest, while he debated how to give some advice to the young man without sounding patronizing. What he wanted to say had nothing to do with Ian's essay. It was about his entire worldview.

"Ian, I'd like to share something I've been observing for a while. Actually, ever since you started attending my course. I've noticed the rage you feel when we discuss global social developments. We touch on it during different discussions, to different degrees, but that rage always comes through."

Ian had a tight grip on his backpack's strap and stared at the ground while the professor expressed his concern. This wasn't because of any feeling of uneasiness. He understood Blair's worry, but he had no intention of changing his views.

"Professor, I'm aware of how I come across. Maybe it's quite unacceptable, considering I myself am part of the system. But it needs to change!"

"Hear me out, son," interrupted Blair. "I know how difficult it is when you first begin to see. But you have so many opportunities ahead of you! Opportunities for which other young people would give anything. I'm not saying you need to be blind or indifferent. I'm only saying that you shouldn't turn your back on your potential in the name of a cause without any real prospects."

Impatience bubbled up inside Ian. He didn't expect such words from his favorite professor.

"So this is the situation and it'll remain the same? There's no point in trying to change anything at all, we're only expected to enjoy our opportunities – if we have them, that is. What about the ones who don't? What do they do, professor?"

"One day you'll realize that power is a privilege for the very few, far fewer than you ever imagined. Only here we aren't talking about power, we're talking about absolute control, Ian. You don't deserve to waste your future on a struggle with a predetermined result. Sooner or later, you'll have to realize it. I was just hoping it would be sooner."

Ian had more to say on the subject. And although the professor was the right person, now was not the time or place. The subject required respect and attention, which neither of them could provide at the moment. Ian shuffled these thoughts in his mind, but his expression had already betrayed them clearly enough for the professor to recognize. Blair put his hand on Ian's shoulder.

"I don't want you to say anything. Just think about it, alright?" he suggested with concern.

They silently headed for the door, where Blair had to slow his pace. The huge keychain that weighed down his pocket justified his inability to lock any door in less than three minutes.

"See you soon, professor Blair," said Ian as he walked away.

He needed to quickly reach the steps by the front entrance, where he assumed his friends would be waiting. This was a universal meeting spot for the students. At any point during the day, one could see the symbolic Alma Mater statue surrounded by young people.

Their arrangement was to spend the free hour before Megan's next class together. Since Ian and Chester's next classes were at five o'clock and 6:40, they meant to take advantage of that time and go by the High T store on 67th and Broadway. They had promised each other to go check out the brand's latest products. That was mostly for Chester's benefit – he followed technological innovations almost fanatically.

7.

Ian looked for his friends on top of the stairway. He saw Megan first, sitting right by the statue. Her bright yellow shirt stood out among the throng of students, even more than Chester's ginger hair waving in the air.

"2:20 p.m.," stated Megan, after looking at her phone's display. "It may be better for you to head to the store, so I can look over the stuff for my next class. Plus, I can see that Chester can barely contain the excitement."

"You got that right! The new SlimBook, man!" he said excitedly. "They say the issue with the shiny screen has been..."

"I got it, I got it already!" Ian laughed. "Spare me the ode, at least until we get there, okay?"

Half an hour later, the boys saw the famous brand logo on the facade of the huge tech store. Surrounded by solid brutalist buildings in the brown to gray range, the store gripped one's attention – it looked like an ethereal hologram, completely in unison with the brand's image.

Chester headed straight for the first store consultant he laid eyes on, with the excitement of a kid at the door of an amusement park.

"Hi. Where are they?" he said without looking at him but scanning the store instead.

The environment was very similar to a student workshop. For the comfort of the customers, long tables were set up where they could immerse themselves in the new product. The place was full of high-tech enthusiasts who thirstily absorbed the blue light that radiated from the displays, while occasionally casting a glance at the toy in the hands of their neighbor.

And while Chester could barely wait to join them, the consultant didn't seem to share everyone's enthusiasm. He had probably already experienced it and made use of the resistance he had developed to be more focused on his tasks.

"Please, go ahead," the consultant said and apathetically pointed to one of the tables with three empty chairs. "What would you like to see? Probably the latest SlimBook or the new BeatPro?"

"The SlimBook please. Let's start with the basics." Chester turned to his friend, pulled his sleeves up and flexed his neck back and forth, as if preparing for a very serious wrestling match. "Let's see what our guys have done!"

"You seem to have prepared for a very expert examination," Ian remarked with surprise. "Are you inspecting anything in particular?"

"If you listened to me more carefully, bro, you'd be in way, way deeper... Thank you," he said to the consultant who brought the elegant laptop. Then, Chester dove into the lesson that he had already been impatient to give on the way over. "Earlier I told you, or at least tried to tell you, that the previous models had a few issues. The visibility of the display, for example. It was too shiny and it turned out that it messed with the resolution and the contrast. Well, maybe not the contrast itself, but everything around reflected on the display and the picture wasn't always as clean as you'd want it to be."

"Sounds nearly intolerable," Ian remarked sarcastically and looked around, as if he needed to absorb more of the fervor around to fortify his sarcasm.

He himself wasn't such a big fan of the brand and modern technology. He was a lot more interested in the process of programming than in the thousands of gizmos that inundated the market month after month. He found the great majority of them, and especially their permanent upgrading, to be an unnecessary stimulus for overconsumption.

"Oh man! Ian, come see!" Chester pulled him away from his thoughts. His tone suggested that it was about something different from the original aim of their visit. He turned around and stood next to his friend. "Check this out!"

Chester pointed to the laptop's screen. The website was *Political Life*. The boy pointed to one of the articles. Its positioning implied that it was in the focus of events.

"Open it, come on!" said Ian, after he had already grabbed the mouse and was moving the cursor to a headline that read:

Where Is Libra's Money?

The subheading that aimed to keep the attention of readers followed:

"Lawyer Jeffrey Dunne with scandalous revelations about the case! Is Thomas Mason guilty?" The article loaded and the two boys stared at the screen. Ian began by reading out loud, but after a few sentences he stopped vocalizing.

The content was too emotional for him to allow even the sound of his own voice to distract him. Despite the pride the article gave him, he seemed to have just realized that the case was a lot more convoluted than he had assumed. A while ago he had asked his father about it, but Jeffrey only told him that he had met Mason, and he was now in possession of enough documents and proof that Mason had handed him personally. And although they were indeed a family, the lawyer respected client confidentiality and didn't reveal anything else to his son.

For this reason, by the time he had finished the article, Ian had mixed feelings. According to it, the Pillar was going to provide evidence to the court. The revelation about the involvement of a third individual with a very high public profile was upcoming but was to remain secret for the time being. The evidence didn't exonerate Mason, because the funneling of funds from Libra to his personal offshore account was a fact. The reduced sentence was seemingly going to be the result of the circumstances and motives behind the crime, but mostly because of the third person implicated. It was alleged that he was at the bottom of the entire affair. There were no specifics regarding the next hearing and when the trial would be held.

The boys looked up from the screen. Chester exhaled loudly and turned to his friend.

"Wow, man! So your dad really is a big deal! Thomas Mason, huh?" And after a short pause, he added, "And what happened again? Yet another saint falls from grace."

"Come on, dude, didn't you understand anything from the article we just read?" Ian was genuinely irritated. He still believed in Mason, but more importantly – he still believed in his father. If he stood by Mason, someone else was the guilty party. Without a doubt! But he saw no reason to discuss that. "Let's not talk about it, okay?"

"Sure, bro, forget about it. Let's go back to the SlimBook,

then. Nice, that's nice. You see that? The brightness is..."

Chester's voice slipped further and further away, until at some point Ian realized that he had shut him out. He couldn't stop thinking about the article.

Who was the individual with a very high public profile?

He had no experience with similar cases, but he could think logically. The pressure for the individual who stood behind the scapegoat would probably be challengingly high. He needed to speak to his dad as soon as possible.

Not long after, Chester finished with his expert examination, and they headed back to campus. His acting class was in 25 minutes, while Ian was free for another hour and a half. He had to talk to his dad; he thought about it all the way back. Soon after, Chester was running up the stairs of the Miller theater, where his class started in four minutes, while Ian headed down 116th street toward Riverside Park.

He liked these moments of solitude by the Hudson River. It was one of the few places where he could really retire with his thoughts. He sat on the most isolated bench and went back to the article again, as well as to his last conversation with his father. He tried to remember every word, pause, the intonation, in search of hidden clues he might have missed. Clues that would help him evaluate the seriousness of the case. Finally, he decided to stop wasting time and he took his cellphone out of his pocket. It was 5:20 p.m., and he assumed Jeffrey would have time for a chat.

He heard the receiver beep twice before his father's voice answered.

"Ian! How are you, son?"

"You sound surprised. Not that rare for us to talk!"

"True, I was just expecting a different call. These days have been busy," mumbled Jeff.

"I can imagine. I saw an article today, in *Political Life*, and I know that you're not allowed to share details of the case, but... Dad, do I need to worry?"

They were both quiet for a bit. Each one of them was trying to choose the words with which to continue. Ian did it first.

"It feels like you're about to find yourself in the crossfire."

Jeffrey felt the anxiety in his son's words and knew that he needed to reassure him. There was no need for him to spend his nights concerned and worried. This case needed to stay far away from him.

"Just a professional liability, buddy," he said in an attempt to lower the tension. "Look, that thing you read wasn't supposed to be published, I don't know who managed to get their hands on that info. In any case, you don't need to worry about anything. Regardless of their power, the guilty are powerless if there's no one they can bribe to hide their crimes," he asserted confidently. "Once they come out in the open, facts give everyone what they deserve."

"I was just unprepared. When I asked you last month, you weren't even sure you were going to defend him, and suddenly I read this, and... As much as I respect Mason, I'd rather know that you're safe."

"You know that I think through things carefully, son. And yes, I really did hesitate whether to defend him. Shortly after we met and he told me everything that had happened, he sent me all the proof and documents in his possession. A risk that can't be taken lightly, by the way. I looked everything over and I decided that this man has the right to be heard... and that other people have no right to go unpunished."

Ian took a deep breath in an effort to calm his growing anxiety. "I'm thinking of coming to see you next week, if it's alright?"

"If it's alright? Of course you'll come! Your mom will be so happy!" He kept silent for a moment, then added, "And I promise you that we'll have a serious talk about the case. And don't get me wrong, I'm not going to go into details. But in any case, it's only right for you to know certain things."

"Alright, agreed, then. I'll see you very soon."

"See you soon, son!"

Ian hung up and counted the days that separated him from seeing his parents. It was barely Tuesday. But it wasn't just any Tuesday. Actually, the days until Friday were highly important to him. He had distributed his tasks so as to avoid piling up too many, but that didn't completely reduce the pressure.

His thoughts raced forward to his return to DC. He couldn't stop thinking about the promised conversation.

***

The next two days went by in a way customary for this time of year.

The students bustled around, but also had a premonition of the relief from the term's approaching end.

Ian's last Friday class finished at 4:20 p.m. It was his statistics course, where he had to present a project. Before going home, he decided to drop by one of the computer labs to start preparing one of the assignments due next week. He had plenty of time until evening, and he still felt like working.

He entered one of the campus buildings, walked through the lobby, and took the first corridor on the right. He had just reached the lab when he decided that he would need another cup of coffee after all, so he walked by the door and headed for the cafeteria.

"A cup of coffee, please," he said to the nice lady behind the counter. Alice had worked on campus for over six years and many students called her by name, but Ian hadn't talked to her that much.

"Cream, sugar?" she asked.

"Black, thank you."

"A dollar fifty, young man."

Ian busily dug in his pocket in search of change.

"Oh, Lord..." Alice unexpectedly exclaimed. "What a tragedy!"

"It's really not such a big deal. I keep putting it in the same place, but..." He finally fished two quarters out and handed them to her.

"What?" she gaped at him with confusion. "No, I mean the news," she explained with unease and pointed to the TV behind her. As soon as Ian looked up at the screen, he saw a burning car. Apparently, the footage wasn't live, because Alice seemed to have already known about the incident.

"What happened? Could you please turn it up?" He always followed similar tragedies with particular empathy.

Right then, he saw five letters, which, among all the other letters and colors on the screen, stabbed him through the heart. He grabbed the remote and turned the volume up, his pulse racing almost as quickly as the cold chills that ran up and down his spine.

Attorney Jeffrey Dunne dies in an incident

Ian was clasping the counter with both hands, as he gradually started hearing the voice of the reporter, until now muted by the shrill noise in his ears.

"... shortly after he presented new revelations in regard to the Thomas Mason case, Mr. Dunne's car burst into flames on Connecticut Avenue. According to unconfirmed eyewitness reports, Jeffrey Dunne was in the company of a woman, presumably his wife. The police are investigating the case, but there has been no official statement..."

Ian's limbs froze, and the forms in front of his eyes were consumed by darkness.

"Young man! Hey, young man!"

Alice's voice echoed in ascending degrees. Muffled and distant at first, but increasingly clear. He opened his eyes and realized he was on the floor. He had fainted. It took him a few more seconds to fully regain his focus and vision. The woman was leaning over him and gripping his shoulders tightly. He tried to stand up.

"Wait, where are you going?" She held onto him.

Only a couple of minutes ago she was making him a cup of coffee, but now she was suddenly the conduit of the sharpest pain he had ever felt in his life. She seemed to subconsciously feel that.

"Please, leave me alone," he barely uttered as he pushed her aside to open the way toward the exit.

He went outside, but still didn't know where to go. A tense pain spread on his temples and forehead, probably as a consequence of fainting. He put both his hands on his head and looked around. He felt helpless. He still didn't fully grasp what had happened and didn't have the courage to contemplate what was to come. He didn't even know where to go in these otherwise overly-familiar surroundings.

He hadn't used his car in a while, and it required an effort to recall where he had left it last week. He, Megan, and Chester had decided to take Tank on a trip to the botanical gardens. He remembered that on the way back they had left the car in one of the underground garages on Broadway and 114th street.

Six minutes later, he saw the attendant, Carl, sitting in his booth. It was a stroke of luck that he was at work.

"How are you doing, my boy?" he greeted Ian.

"Carl..." Ian started speaking some distance before reaching the booth. "I need to leave immediately, but my receipt is at the dorm. I don't have any time, please! I need to..." he quieted down at the horrifying realization that he had no idea what he needed to do or where he needed to go.

"Alright, alright, take it easy," interrupted Carl, clearly aware that the boy had a serious problem. "What's your car's license plate?"

"385 AAA"

"Head down to level one, L6."

The attendant's eyes followed the young man to the stairway at the end of the ground level. Their relationship had never crossed the line of a hello and small talk, but even at this level of acquaintance, he could feel that something serious had happened to the student. A few minutes later, the Mustang roared from somewhere beyond the garage's barrier.

8.

It was close to 10:00 p.m. when Ian saw the DC city sign. He could barely remember how he got here. He had yet to speak to the police, but that explained the eight missed calls while he was in class, and before he had found out. He didn't call back; he wasn't ready.

The only thing he knew was that his father's assistant,

Mary, was the only person he could turn to at this moment, and she would be waiting by his house in half an hour. Hers was the only call he took.

His phone rang again.

"Mary?" he answered quickly. "I'll be there in twenty minutes."

"Listen, I'll be waiting in front of St. Thomas. I went by your street and I don't think it a good idea for you to be there. At least not now. The churchyard will be more peaceful." She tried to sound composed, but her tone carried anxiety.

"I'd really rather go home, I can take it," insisted Ian.

"Yes, but your house is surrounded. The police have been there for two hours, I watched them. Please trust me and come to the church. I'll be there in ten minutes."

The church of St. Thomas was a favorite of Jeff and Beth's. Although they were not so religious, they liked to go and listen to the service from time to time. After he turned eleven, Ian had rarely accompanied them. For reasons unknown, from a certain moment on he preferred to stay away from religion.

He saw Mary sitting on the church's stairs. The reflections of the street lights flickered on her black, frizzy curls. He parked on the corner right across from the church. The car's engine was still running when she stood up and walked over.

"I'm so sorry, Ian!" She couldn't finish her condolences and burst into tears. She gave him a tight hug. The way only a mother could hug. The way he would never be hugged again.

Ian also gave up on suppressing his grief.

"Come, let's go sit." She took him by the arm and they walked back to the church. She remained silent in an effort to find enough composure to continue talking. Whatever she said next was going to turn her into an accomplice of his cruel fate.

"God. How did this happen?" Ian interrupted her

thoughts. "Where... where are they now? And the funeral?" He sobbed.

He realized that with all the shock, he had neglected to think about all the responsibilities that awaited him.

"The... Their bodies were burned," she sighed and looked to the side so as to swallow the lump in her throat. "They're in the morgue, there's an ongoing investigation."

"Fuck!" Ian shook his head as if to deny what he just heard. The initial shock, which had considerately sheltered him in the position of an observer gradually gave way to the brutal reality.

"Listen, Ian, you need to keep it together. Your father meant a lot to me! I won't let all his work go to waste!"

"What?" The sudden change in the direction of the conversation surprised Ian. Mary's words even provoked some irritation in him. "What do you expect me to do? I'm sorry that this affects your life, but honestly, I don't really have the strength to deal with that right now!"

"I don't mean me, son! I'm talking about you!" She cut him down to size. "I won't allow you to ramble all alone and turn your back on everything that Jeff did for you. I'll help you get back on your feet and take over the firm. Our team is brilliant and I can assure you that every single person in that building will toil for you just like they did for your father!"

Ian listened to her as he stared at the concrete underneath his soles. He knew that her readiness to help was genuine. But one thought circulated in his mind with increasing obsessiveness.

"And how did that help him? Where is my father now?"

"Ian, this case was different."

"If there's anything that you have the obligation to do, it is to tell me what happened. Who killed my parents, Mary?"

His icy tone dismayed her. She realized that she really truly owed it to him, that explanation she didn't have. "Your father never shared details about cases and clients, Ian. But it wasn't hard to see that the last case put him under a lot of pressure. After that, I learned from the media who exactly the case was connected with. I think everything started in November, with senator Preston's unexpected visit."

"Preston?" Ian repeated with bewilderment. "What does Preston have to do with it? We're talking about Thomas Mason and the embezzlement of charity funds from Libra."

"Exactly. Your father found proof that Preston was behind everything. Information leaked that Mason was forced to divert the funds. But that's all I know."

"Mason is the one I need to speak to. You have to help me find him!" Ian pressed.

"On the news they said he's under house arrest."

"Where?"

"His villa in Annapolis, Maryland. I think they mentioned Sherwood Forest."

"On the Severn?"

"Yes, I think so. I'll find a way to get the address. Give me until noon tomorrow."

"Thank you Mary," Ian nodded and stood up. "Go home to your daughter, she's probably worried."

"Wait, where will you go? Why don't you stay with us? At least for the night?"

"Thank you, but it's enough that you had to come so late."

"That's the least I could do for you. I'll call you in the morning, okay?"

Ian nodded and climbed inside the car, but soon realized once again that he didn't know where to go. Only now he did he recognize how rude he had been to Mary, out on the streets alone, and at this hour of the night!

Idiot! You didn't even think of giving her a ride home.

At once, he turned the Mustang's engine on and drove down the street. She was still within sight, he could see the dry figure and recognizable military gait of the 45-year-old woman about 300 meters ahead.

"Mary, let me give you a ride home..." he said through the open passenger window.

"There's no need, really." She came closer and leaned over the window. "We both need to be alone with our thoughts. We're in one of the safest neighborhoods in town."

Although Ian didn't even want to admit it to himself, he agreed with her. Every other word he would have needed to articulate would have cost him immense pain.

"Are you sure?"

"Trust me. There's a cab stand down the street." She tapped the roof of his car twice. "Go, and take care. Talk to you tomorrow."

Ian continued forward and took the first right. It seemed that he had subconsciously decided where to go. He was heading to Cleveland Avenue, and then home. He was really close, after all.

He could already see the yellow tape that surrounded the house, even though he pulled over at a 200-hundred-meter distance to observe. It seemed that most police officers had left, except for the patrol car that was parked a little further away. Thank God no one was loitering around. Ian had no desire to cooperate right at this moment. He was angry even at the "law enforcement." What kind of "enforcement" was that anyway? For years there had been blatant and insolent violations, but the hands of the authorities were always somehow tied for justice. He was certain that the tragedy with his family could have been prevented. Even if the one who ordered it was a senator from California. Or rather – in spite of the fact that the one who ordered it was a senator from California.

He left the car there and walked to the house. He needed to be as inconspicuous as possible, so he went in through the backyard. He looked at the houses – a row of four on each side of the street separated him from his. That meant that he needed to count on the eight families being busy with something other than watching the events in the Dunne house.

Ian slowly walked on the left sidewalk, looking at both sides. He went around the streetlamps situated a few meters from each other. He hoped that the strong light they emitted would make the space where he was moving more favorable to concealment.

Fortunately, the majority of Woodley park residents were people with serious professions and status. The kind whose biological clock had learned to obey a strict regimen – wake at dawn, go to sleep before midnight.

The windows of most houses were dark.

There was one where they were lit, even if only on the second floor. It was the Lawrence house, the closest neighbors. Ian had known these decent people for eleven years, ever since his parents moved here. It couldn't really be said that he worried about them, but he still did his best to walk the distance through their yard as quietly as possible.

Less than a minute later he grabbed the "POLICE LINE DO NOT CROSS" tape and pushed it over his head. The entire property was wrapped in it. As he snuck through the backyard, he wondered why the police would seal the house when his parents were killed in a blast that destroyed their car.

Fucking far from here!

They probably wanted to find clues about the killer, like notes or other proof that Jeffrey could have kept at his house. He started to regret not coming earlier. The police questioning would have been long and harrowing, but on the other hand, they could have given him more information about what happened.

He would still be reasoning further in that direction of possibilities if the grief hadn't struck him again. It knocked him down as soon as he opened the door. Everything in his home was the way he expected to see it when he returned there. That's how his mom was – every piece of furniture, every object had its carefully designated place. Even if for whatever reason something was moved, Ian couldn't remember a single case in his entire life where Elizabeth didn't turn around before leaving to make sure everything was back where it belonged. That's how it had been on that morning, too. She had left the house in an impeccable state. For the last time.

Ian was very aware that the pain of the memories would distract him from his goal of finding his parents' killers. As a matter of fact, the opposite was even more true – that goal was his only chance of deflecting the pain and moving forward. These thoughts accompanied his walk from the front door to the stairway at the end of the room.

If his father ever brought home any documentation to do with the case, it was probably here. The investigators had probably made the same assumption. They were most likely to have just taped the house today and left the search for tomorrow. And if they had already searched, they definitely made an effort not to leave traces. It was even too much – everything looked untouched.

Ian had one foot on the last step and the other on the second floor of the house. He looked around as if he were an impartial observer, and he walked along the rooms from left to right. His room was at the bottom and to the left. Then there was a bathroom that he used, then a larger one for his parents. Finally, his eyes lined up with the rest of his body and Jeff and Beth's bedroom was in front of them.

With a pang of grief, he walked in and headed for the mahogany desk at the other end. He opened every drawer – the two small ones on the left, the big one underneath, the four on the right – but he didn't find anything. Only a few case folders that had nothing to do with Mason.

He shut the last drawer – another that didn't provide the needed information. He turned around. He put his palms on the desk and rested some of his weight on them. Physical exhaustion started to take over. But not nearly as much as the emotional. He looked around. The fatigue blurred the lines between memory and reality. He slowly continued forward and laid his back on the large bed. Just for a bit, just enough to put his thoughts together.

∗∗∗

He opened his eyes after what felt like just a few moments. The birds that were chirping in the backyard woke him. He looked at the alarm clock on the nightstand – it was 6:38 am.

He wanted to lie to himself. To believe that it had all just been one of those horribly realistic nightmares. He forced himself to remain under that illusion, but he couldn't keep it up for long. He stood up and walked to the window without caring if someone could see him. The beautiful view of the snow glimmering under the first rays of the sun didn't chase his headache away.

Maybe he needed some oxygen. He opened the window and breathed in the February air. Chilly, but not freezing, as one might expect at this time of year. In the deafening silence, an unexpected bang startled him. It wasn't too loud, but it turned his stomach. A big pinecone had fallen from the tall pine tree onto the tin awning that covered the basement cellar door.

He remembered when they moved in the house. He was ten or eleven years old. Right around that period, he developed an interest in explosives. Undoubtedly the fault of Cartoon Network. Naturally, he had no access to anything but small fireworks, which were supplied by his best friend's 14-year-old brother. They weren't exactly gunpowder bombs, but some of them popped seven times, which was enough of an adventure for the mischievous kids.

After the third complaint by Ian's teacher, Jeffrey started to suspect the existence of a secret stockpile in the house, and he found it under that same basement door not long after. The Stash, as Ian and the other little "bombers" from his class called it, held an impressive quantity of fireworks, clearly assembled through a joint effort.

Jeffrey Dunne wasn't the type of parent that scolded and punished. But as one could imagine, he was brutally persuasive, and proof was his strongest weapon. It took him a few hours to put together a scarecrow adorable enough to provoke empathy in the children. Two or three fun firecracker tosses later, Straw Sam was left without one of its arms, and the boys never looked at fireworks or anything of the sort again.

After a few moments of unavoidable nostalgia, Ian turned his eyes back to the basement. He stared with a frown. He realized something almost insultingly obvious – where else could his father put something that shouldn't be found?

Ian knew that his neighbors were probably up by now, but too busy with their morning routine to be peeking into the Dunne's backyard. Ian turned around, stepped onto the metal staircase, and closed the door. Nothing had changed since the last time he was here. Their basement, with its six-meter walls and red brickwork, didn't exactly conform with general expectations. It was actually pretty cozy, if one ignored the cold.

One of the walls was dedicated to cinema. Four massive black frames held posters of film classics – *Some Like It Hot*, *The Godfather*, *Once Upon a Time in the West*, *Casablanca*.

The opposite wall was almost entirely covered by racks arranged in three vertical and three horizontal rows. That was plenty of space for their household. Ian and Jeff weren't the type that collected screwdrivers and hammers, nor Elizabeth the kind that piled up dinner sets and vases in the basement. Naturally, some of the usual objects could be seen around – a lawnmower, two bicycles, three tennis rackets, as well as photo albums, a wine collection, and a few paintings for which she never found the right spot in the house.

And document folders – lots of them, carefully arranged in large white banker's boxes. One of them had to have Thomas Mason's name on it.

Ian headed for the middle rack that was designated for documentation. He started from the bottom. He pulled out a box and took three folders. He looked at what was written on them – A.D., L.R., I.I. – clearly, initials. Which meant that he needed to find the one labeled T.M. One feature drew his attention. There were no details whatsoever on the boxes. It would make sense, and definitely make it more accessible, to have an indication of at least the year. But maybe that was the idea – it wasn't meant to be accessible. That made sense, too.

At 9:40, the phone rang. It was the second call for the day in spite of the early hour. At about 8:30, an unknown number called, probably the police. He never found out, because he didn't answer.

"Mary, hi."

"How are you handling it?" she asked with concern.

"I'm at home."

"At home? And the police?"

"They were gone when I got there last night. If they were ever inside."

"That means they'll probably do it today. Probably any time now. Do you mean to stay there?"

"I wanted to take some things before leaving for Maryland."

"Sherwood Forest, Beech Road, shorefront by the Severn," Mary recited. "That's all I could get my hands on. It'd be best to just ask there, I'm sure someone'll show you."

"Do you think I should wait for the police first?"

Mary remained silent for a moment before replying.

"They'll find you one way or the other. I'm surprised they haven't called you yet. Go now, so you get a head start. It's fairly certain that whatever you find out on your own will be different than what they tell you"

"Alright, I'll leave right away."

"Call me when you're done, okay?"

"Of course!"

Ian closed yet another folder and returned it to its box. He wasn't able to find Mason's file, but he knew that he didn't have much time before the police were back to investigate.

As he walked through the front door, he remembered that his car was parked some distance up the street. He was way too late. Calvert Street was already pretty crowded, and he had to walk unnoticed for 200 meters. He put up his hoodie and his sunglasses before heading over. At least there were few pedestrians on the street. He could only hope that none of the drivers or passengers recognized him.

Seven minutes later, he made it to the Mustang. He opened the glove compartment to get the map out. Annapolis was close, but strangely enough, he had never been there. He remembered hearing that it was beautiful and quiet, with several quaint bays where affluent people liked to buy vacation houses. Obviously, Mason was one of them.

He opened the map and found that Sherwood Forest was only about 50 kilometers east of DC. He needed to get on the 50 freeway, then take the secondary highway and get on the shorefront, where the house was located.

9.

He was getting close to Sherwood Forest. He had been on the road for about half an hour, but he felt like he'd been there for days. Maybe because he kept replaying in his head the conversation that he was about to have. Within the narrative of this conversation, he had sporadic thoughts about everything else that could happen from now on. Then he came back to reality and the road that led to Mason. To the answers he was seeking.

He was just off the ramp to the highway when the worn-out melody of his cellphone chimed. Once again, it was an unknown number, probably the same one from earlier. He didn't want to answer, but he also knew that he couldn't hide forever.

"Hello?"

"Mr. Dunne?" a man said with a flat tone. It was definitely the police.

"This is detective Tim Jones, homicide..."

"How can I help you?" Ian interrupted. Of course, he knew exactly why they were calling.

"I'm calling you in regard to the murder of Jeffrey and Elizabeth Dunne, your parents..."

Ian didn't answer. The detective had conducted dozens of such conversations and could feel the grief through the speaker just by the changes in breathing.

"First of all, I would like to express my sincere condolences. What happened to them was terrible. But Mr. Dunne, I need to ask you to come down to the station. Your cooperation will help us establish what happened and why."

Ian made another pause that was longer than the previous one. He really had no idea what the right words for this conversation were.

"Listen, Detective Jones, I'll need some time to establish the circumstances... At least a few days. My parents have been killed, my home sealed off, I don't even know where to go..." His voice rose, forcing the detective to react.

"I'll tell you what," Jones suggested. "Take today and tomorrow to collect yourself. You can go home; I'll warn my colleagues not to bother you. We'll keep the police tape up to prevent pesky reporters and neighbors from disturbing you. Alright?" His tone was firm, but also had compassion, which calmed Ian down. "Then on Monday you can come to the station. The criminal investigation division on Indiana Avenue. Let's make it 11 a.m."

"Thank you, I appreciate it."

"Mr. Dunne, I must warn you that after our conversation, we'll need to go to the morgue. The bodies of your parents are being examined, but you need to identify them. I'm very sorry." Before he said the last words, Jones felt like Ian was trying to swallow his tears. It seemed like he managed, because they didn't register in the intonation of his answer.

"I understand. I'll be there on Monday, Detective."

He could see the water in front – the Severn. He needed to focus on the road, and that helped him keep it together. He was about to talk to Mason. He needed to arm himself with the necessary concentration and composure to reach the truth.

He saw a small sign for Sherwood. There was no doubt he was on the right path. He was certain once he realized that the beautiful river, especially bright blue on this winter day, would fall on his right.

He rolled the window down to allow the crisp wind to refresh him. He liked to drive in winter. With the heater on and the window down. Small and medium houses, villas, mansions, and large residences lined the road one after the other. He kept driving without stopping, but sooner or later he was going to have to ask about Mason.

After another four or five blocks he reached a beautiful, yet not very large house. Its yard, like that of the other houses, was covered by a blanket of snow, but unlike the other houses, it wasn't empty – a sinewy man of about 75 was energetically stabbing the snow with a shovel and tossing it at least a meter and a half away. He didn't look like the owner. It was more likely that some wealthy lady trusted his services so she could park her expensive car somewhere without getting stuck. Ian judged that he was unlikely to meet a more suitable individual to give him directions. Usually, people like that knew everyone in a ten-kilometer radius and liked to talk rather than to ask questions.

He pulled over, shut off the engine, and climbed out. It wasn't all that cold. Even though he hadn't strayed from his thick down jacket for the last three winters, he still wore sneakers. After all, how often did he have to step in the snow like right now?

After about ten sluggish steps and after getting his jeans wet up to the knees, he reached the man with the shovel, who had stopped working when he saw a stranger approaching.

"What do you need?" asked the old man.

Ian hesitated about whether to beat around the bush or go straight for it.

"I'm trying to find Thomas Mason's house."

"Gotcha," the man interrupted unexpectedly, as if he had known already. Ian found that strange indeed, but he had no time to think about it. "Keep going until Brewer road," the man continued, "and count three houses on the left. "Mason's is the fourth one. You're close."

"Thank you, man!"

Ian couldn't understand why the man looked at him with a mixture of disappointment and pity.

"Bad business," he sighed and started digging again.

He managed to disconcert Ian with two of the four sentences he had said.

What was that about – *bad business*? Maybe he knew about the accusations against Mason?

It didn't actually matter. The important thing was that Ian knew where he was going.

Soon he saw a wooden pier. This was probably Brewer point. He looked to the left, one, two... One more and then his destination. He could see it. House number three, which separated them, could easily be missed against the background of Mason's mansion. It was definitely not some giant, ostentatious palace. It was in the Dutch Colonial style, with a graphite-gray slate cladding, as if chiseled out of a mountain.

He walked to the beautiful wrought iron fence. He was about to ring the bell when he noticed that the gate wasn't locked.

He headed down the pathway paved with white pebbles and flanked by piles of snow on both sides, no doubt garden spaces in another season. From here, he could see a lot more details – three stories, lots of French windows. There were six of them on the bottom floor, separated by a massive front door, four on the second floor, and one round one on the third. One might wonder what happened to privacy with all these windows. But even at this distance, only a few meters from the door, he couldn't see anything inside, even though the heavy beige curtains were pulled to the side. Evidently, the window glass was very special.

He set foot on the doormat – the last step before the truth. For a moment, he almost slipped into self-sabotage mode. He didn't know where to start, he didn't know what to say to Mason. Until a few days ago he had admired the man. But today, he was the reason for the death of his parents. He realized that only now. Then he once again remembered that the truth was his purpose. His chance to return to life. He took a deep breath, exhaled slowly, and calmly and rang the bell.

Fifteen seconds went by in silence. It started to seem like he had anxiously prepared for something that was not going to happen. He looked around; he didn't want to pressure the hosts, but he couldn't help it. He pressed the button two more times, one after the other, breaking the silence with the melodious ring.

After another twenty seconds he heard the sound of a key turning and tensed up. His stomach contracted, but he somehow immediately managed to get a hold of himself. The door opened.

"How can I help you?"

It wasn't Mason, but a woman of about 45. Beautiful, but visibly exhausted and... desperate.

"Hello. I'm here to see Mr. Mason," Ian answered after he shook off his surprise.

"You too?" she sounded distressed, but also annoyed; it seemed she had had enough.

"I must speak to him, ma'am. Please call him, it's important."

"Forget it!" she said abruptly and tightly gripped the door with her right hand, getting ready to slam it in the face of this insolent intruder. Ian, however, didn't shy away from preventing her.

"Wait, please! It's important to him, too! Please call him!"

"I can't call him, son," she finally admitted, while obviously making a big effort to contain her tears. "He isn't here!"

Ian felt like he was really going to lose it this time.

"What do you mean, he isn't here?"

"I mean he's dead! He *killed himself* two days ago!" she said, making finger quotes with both hands, which only served to increase Ian's insistence. "And I swear, if someone else shows up at my door within the next year, I'll shoot on sight!" These were her last words before she slammed the door.

"Wait!" he tried to stop her, but to no avail. "What do you mean? Was he killed?"

There was no answer.

Ian didn't just fail to get information – he left the house even more confused than when he'd arrived. All the way to DC, he struggled to calm the bubbling anger caused by the feeling that he kept slamming his head against the same wall, over and over again.

$$***$$

By the time he got on the 50, he had already gone through all the versions of what could have happened to Mason. The woman, obviously his wife, clearly thought that he had been killed. But how could he be killed in a house protected by the police? The premises also had security cameras, which meant that all of Mason's visitors had been recorded.

Ian himself was certainly among them. That didn't worry him, though. Actually, after yesterday, hardly anything worried him.

The flat asphalt seemed to speed his thoughts up as they kept swirling around Mason. How could they kill him and still make it look like suicide? His wife's attitude betrayed her extreme frustration and disagreement with the official version of her husband's death.

Maybe he could have gone to see her again in a few days, introduced himself, and tried to talk to her. But for now, he was going to search for information by himself. Starting at home.

He was already drawing a mental plan of how exactly to go about searching for the documents. It was Saturday, a little after 2:00 p.m. He had the rest of the day, as well as Sunday and a few hours on Monday morning at his disposal. This meant that he needed to find information and proof at all costs, and to decide what stance to adopt with the police.

As he was driving back, he felt his stomach churn. He tried to remember when he'd last eaten. Maybe Friday morning was the last time he put food in his mouth, or about thirty hours ago, when he didn't yet suspect that his life was about to be turned upside down forever.

Connecticut Avenue was coming up, which had a lot of restaurants. He had no idea what he felt like eating; he just wanted to grab something quickly and take it home without having to detour.

Rose's Burgers

He saw the flashing sign from a distance. Or rather, he saw the parking spot in front, which simplified his choice. To stop right in front of the establishment was not a comfort that could be enjoyed often, especially on busier streets.

Soon he had parked in front of the restaurant. He was about to go into what was likely to be the pinkest burger joint in the US. Pepto-Bismol pink. And a doorway decorated with pink and purple hortensias, guaranteed to be plastic. Ian thought about the absurd combination between burgers and flowers... Burgers, those greasy, caloric, culinary "masterpieces," the favorite of fellows with long greasy hair, leather pants, and dirty boots.

Apparently, this Rose person had decided to lead the fight for the right of women to eat dirty. Maybe it had worked.

Ian hesitated before stepping into this temple of absurdity. Maybe it was a bit too strange even for his open mindedness. Then he decided that he had no time to waste. If nothing else, this pink world looked cleaner than many other joints. It was enough for him to continue.

As soon as he stepped in, a fair-haired girl with a broad grin greeted him with open arms. "Welcome to Rose's! It's a pleasure to present our pink burgers!" she recited, somehow sounding genuine at the same time.

What a miracle! The burgers are pink! thought Ian, before the attendant's high-pitched voice assaulted him again. Strangely, this girl, who didn't seem much older than him, seemed to be the only employee in the restaurant. Ian really hoped that the cook was someone else. If there was no cook and this pink, pigtailed creature disappeared in a minute, he was probably about to have the honor of being served by Rose herself – the culprit behind this insanity.

She didn't let him finish his thought. "What can I get you, sir?"

"Well... maybe you should tell me?"

"Am I to understand that you aren't familiar with our

menu?" excitedly answered presumably Rose herself. "Wonderful! We love to surprise new customers!"

God, no more surprises, please! thought Ian, before allowing himself to be surprised.

"May I look at the menu?"

"Of course, sir." She handed him a laminated menu with few choices. "We have two kinds with beef, two kinds with chicken, and three dessert options. We source our meat from local Annapolis farms," she added with visible pride.

Ian had definitely had enough of Annapolis for a day.

"I'll try the beef one, thank you. To go, please!" he hurried to end the prolonged interaction.

"Which one did you choose, the classic, or the spicy with chorizo?"

"Classic." Ian reduced the number of words with each sentence.

"Very well, sir. Eleven dollars, please."

That was a pretty steep price for a classic beef burger. But then again, how traditional could Rose's traditional burger be?

A faint panic started to take over Ian. He couldn't predict what was coming, especially considering where he was, and in general he was absolutely no fan of surprises when it came to his food.

"Please have a seat." She pointed him to a small dining room to the right of the counter. "Your order will be ready in ten minutes."

The room had four white semicircular booths with a round table in the middle of each one. It wasn't spacious, but that didn't matter to Ian. He was going to take whatever came out of Rose's hands and take it home, far from Barbie's dreamhouse.

He walked past the first booth. He hated to take the easy way. Obviously. He sat in the next one with his back to the door and his face to the wall. Thank God, it was white and bare. Connecticut Avenue calmed him – the world continued to be normal on the other side of the window.

After twelve long minutes, Rose's ringing voice tore

through the silence. She was coming from somewhere behind him.

"Here we are!" she declared and was next to him before she'd finished, which meant that either the kitchen was very close or she was exceptionally speedy.

Only now did Ian notice the absence of music. An interesting choice. As if nothing was allowed to distract customers from the sizzling sounds of the kitchen. Evidently, Rose wanted true devotion to her creations.

The large mauve box with printed white flowers that dropped on his table was the pinnacle of irony, almost a mockery of the dramatic events that were happening in his life. Regardless, the girl's excitement disarmed him.

"I really hope you like it!" she said with a genuine expression, and her palms moved in a way that delicately encouraged Ian to open the box.

She probably expected to see surprise, admiration, or any reason to give meaning to her existence. But it looked like she hit a snag with this customer. Probably most of her customers would have by now given her plenty of opportunities to tell them more about the food and the inspiration behind it. He had limited her chance to present beyond the origin of the meat. And he preferred to keep it that way.

"I'm sorry, but I need to leave right away," he disappointed her.

"But aren't you..."

"Really, I'm sure it's great," he interrupted, even though he didn't want to offend her. He just didn't have the strength for it and wanted to go home as soon as possible. "Thank you, bye!" he mumbled as he snuck between the girl and the backrest of the booth.

Relieved, he climbed into his car and drove off.

* * *

Before long, he was able to see the yellow tape that surrounded his house. He wondered if he should remove it and enter the driveway, or just park by the curb. Maybe the latter was better. He didn't want awkward conversations with neighbors, or to receive condolences, and much less to talk to reporters. He chose to be as invisible as possible. He left the car a block away, even if he had the assurances of Detective Jones that he could go home safely. Then he walked around the house to go in through the back door.

It was a little after 4 p.m. and the soft sunlight shed light on the first floor as if life had stopped and nothing had happened.

He walked across the living room and left his keys and the mystery box on the kitchen counter. He looked around. The silence was priceless at the moment. He also became aware of the benefits of not having a large, united family.

Many times during his childhood, he had dreamed of holidays spent in the company of grandmas, grandpas, aunts, uncles, cousins... Like in an Italian movie. Over the years, however, he learned that Jeffrey basically grew up as an orphan. His mother died from complications during childbirth. His father was a good man who treated him well, but he never overcame his grief after the death of his wife. Finally, the alcohol in which he sought solace also took his life eight years later. Until his seventeenth year, Jeffrey had been raised by his maternal grandmother – the widow of a wealthy businessman, who had provided an upper middle-class environment that gave Jeffrey an opportunity which he fully comprehended and embraced.

Elizabeth had the luck of having been raised in a close-knit and loving family. What fate took from her was time with them. Her appearance surprised her parents ten years after that of her sister, also born when her parents were older. Their mother had been thirty-five when she gave birth to Rosaline, and their father, fifty. He did, however, get the chance to see his daughters grow up, dying when he was in his eighties. His wife survived him by two years, which is exactly what she needed to get the chance to meet her grandchild Ian. Although barely, he remembered her. Or rather, the feeling of her.

Beth's sister, and Ian's aunt, was a bit of a strange bird. She always had been, according to his mother.

She was somewhat estranged, not so much in her youth, but rather after their father's death. As if she had lost her roots. She lived her life in motion, she stayed in different countries for about six months to a year. She had casual, short relationships, and no children or an actual career.

Ian had only seen her twice. Once at his grandma's funeral, which he barely remembered. Their other meeting was a total coincidence. About ten years ago, Ian and his parents spent the Easter holidays in Europe. They bumped into Rosaline in Munich, on the famous Maximilian Strasse. She was accompanied by a gentleman of about seventy. Their interaction lasted barely five minutes, during which Rosaline didn't feel the need to introduce her sister. Elizabeth had to do it herself.

"I'm Linnie's sister, this is my family."

The gentleman seemed to be curious to get to know them, even making an attempt to invite them to dinner, but Rosaline impeded it.

For better or worse, she was now the only family Ian had. It was probably the former – he recalled once again that he really didn't need visitors, pity, or condolences. The only thing he needed was time. Time to comprehend the situation and assess his own options – whether to fight or to resign himself. To seek justice or to try to put his life back together. There were countless arguments for both options.

Ian heard his stomach churn again. He went into the kitchen to get a few napkins and carried the pink box into the living room. He didn't want to sit at the dining room table by himself – it would have brought back too many happy memories. His self-preservation instinct, it seemed, was working at full swing.

He made himself comfortable in front of the TV and put on a movie channel. He flipped through a couple, though it wasn't like it mattered, he just needed some background noise.

He opened the box. Everything inside looked fine, and the only thing that reminded him of Rose, except for the pink buns, was the red cabbage. The burger was a good size, the patty looked juicy and had a normal color, and he could see cheese, probably cheddar. In the end, nothing seemed unpalatable.

He leaned forward and took a bite. It was good... really good, actually. She had done well, this Rose.

After about fifteen minutes, when his stomach finally settled down, Ian stretched out on the couch. He felt super exhausted. His eyelids were heavy, and he felt like he was sinking. It wasn't exactly sleep, more like brief episodes of deep slumber. The third of these came forty minutes later. He woke from it with the immediate impulse to at once renew the search for the Mason case documents. That red light in his mind didn't go off for even a second.

He stood up abruptly, probably more abruptly than advisable. He went around the couch and headed for the second floor. While he was half-asleep, he had decided to go through his parent's bedroom once more. Something told him that what he was searching for wasn't in the basement.

He went into the bedroom, and the first thing that caught his attention was the crumpled sheet on the bed. He never made it in the morning. His mother would not have approved. The thought of that disapproval compelled him to return the room to its impeccable state. Exactly like Elizabeth would have wanted. He went to the bed, straightened up the bottom end, then tapped a few times on the right-side pillow – his father's side, and where he had fallen asleep the night before. He was pulling the duvet up to the corners when his hand hit something. The alarm clock on Jeffrey's side fell on its back, and since it was pretty massive, it left a scratch on the mahogany nightstand. It was one of those vintage clocks that rang hard and long without stopping until a button was pressed. Ian put it back in its place and noticed something on the floor, between the nightstand and the bed. If the circumstances were different, he would have assumed that the thin white folder had fallen there and was forgotten. But in this case, he believed that it was either intentionally put there, or it was the last thing his father read before going to seep.

Could that be it?

He rushed to lift it off the floor, expectant of the answers he was hoping to find. With irritation, he established that there was no name on the front. There were no initials, either. He opened the folder only to discover a number of empty compartments. Finally, there was one that apparently contained something – it looked like a handwritten letter. His impatience showed in his movements.

After a couple of seconds that seemed like an eternity to him, he finally held the piece of paper in his hands. He had yet to read a single word, but he was already convinced that the letter was the first clue in uncovering the murder of his parents.

He took a breath and started reading.

Dear Mr. Dunne,

Over the years, I have observed your work carefully enough to trust your judgment of good and evil, truth and deceit. I have reason to believe that you should allow me the chance to present my point of view on a series of events that will soon become a public scandal, one in which I will be the main point of interest. Even though I prefer the confidentiality of a private conversation, I insist on presenting a written outline of certain facts that, for one reason or another, I may be unable to share with you at our meeting later today.

First, I knew senator Preston before he was elected. He clearly used that time to build up an image that I would trust and take into consideration later, when I needed to decide whether to be part of his scheme.

Second, although I had no cause to doubt him before he made his offer, I would have refused to participate in any case. Probably aware of that, he was privy to information that I never personally shared with him. He knew details of the acute medical condition that my daughter Vivian suffers. He offered me access to exclusive medical treatment, available to an extremely restricted number of patients. You can understand that from this point onward, I was ready to accept anything.

Third, I never took a single penny from the appropriated millions.

Fourth, I have corroborating documents, including video material, which I can hand over to you in case you decide to take on my defense.

I knew that I was taking an enormous risk by agreeing to transfer funds from the official foundation accounts to my personal ones, even if offshore. I knew that there was a high probability of being incriminated. Our agreement stipulated that I would take all the blame, in exchange for my daughter's treatment. They assured me that in the event of exposure, I would be provided with the best defense available.

Presently, the situation is as follows – after Vivian's third treatment session, the facility in question stopped calling, making appointments, or providing any information whatsoever regarding the remaining six sessions of the first round of treatment. I fear that this is occurring as a result of the untimely revelations concerning the scheme, and the therapy will never be continued. I am assuming that their wish is to get me to court as soon as possible, where I will be convicted, which will in turn secure a formal perpetrator and dissipate the scandal.

I am being compelled to accept the "services" of Martin Smith, who is Preston's attorney. They will place the blame on me and ensure that Preston's name remains undisclosed.

This was the nature of our agreement, but I was only ready to accept it once my daughter's treatment was completed. Since they are certain to have surmised that I may take the actions I am presently taking – namely, to reveal everything and present the proof in my possession – I am afraid that time is of the essence.

They will no doubt attempt to dispose of me. They will not suffer the risk of leaving me alive. For this precise reason, I want to be certain that I have done everything in my power to reveal the truth. And you, Mr. Dunne, are the only person I can trust. I just know it.

I realize that your involvement in this case exposes you and your loved ones to the same risks that I myself face. I trust that you will be able to assess the situation, and I will understand regardless of whether you decide to stand with me or to step aside.

I sincerely hope they will receive retribution.

Yours truly,

Thomas Mason

Ian left the letter by his side of the bed. He was as stunned as if he had just read his parents' death sentence. Even more painful was the thought that when Jeffrey read the letter, probably in this exact same spot, he still had a choice. He had *made* his choice.

A profound sorrow ripped through Ian aggressively, reminding him that he had no chance of escaping this, no matter how much he reasoned or what goals he set to distract himself. Reality advanced and was closer to him with every second. Only a day separated him from his meeting with Detective Jones. He didn't know what to expect from this meeting, or rather – interrogation. He was certainly outside of the perimeter of those suspected, and the interrogation was probably not going to be tense. Ian was going to be one of their few sources of objective information.

At this juncture, he needed to play his cards smartly and determine what to do with the letter in his hands. If he took it to the police station, he risked allowing other interested parties access to the only real evidence in his possession. Suddenly, his mind tossed something at him that he had nearly missed earlier. Mason mentioned the existence of proof, including video footage, that he meant to present to Jeffrey. If the letter was here, the proof was probably here, too.

Maybe some of it had been in the folder that Ian held at the moment. Only it was missing now.

Exhaustion was affecting him again. In the short time since he'd learned the horrifying news of his parents' murder some twenty-four hours ago, he had gone through all types of emotional states. He had already established that when he was exhausted, anger prevailed over his other emotions. Anger toward his father. Not because he believed Jeff did the wrong thing. On the contrary, precisely because he had *chosen* to do the right thing. Regardless of the price he knew would be paid. *He knew*. He had known when they had their last phone conversation, he knew when they discussed getting together very soon... He knew every morning when he drove Elizabeth to her office. Every night, when they went back home. Until the last. Ian thought about his mother. Did she know as well? Did Jeffrey take the risk with her consent, or had his pursuit of justice doomed his wife?

Although he realized that pain was easier to overcome with accusations and rage, he also recognized that he couldn't smear his father's name after his death. Even if it was to protect himself from the pain.

Besides, once he thought it through, he judged that there was no way his father had put the family at risk. He would never do it. If he had really taken the risk consciously and deliberately, it must have only been because he was certain it would affect himself and no one else. Or he had truly believed in law and justice and was sure of a fair outcome.

Ian looked at the clock on the nightstand. It was close to 10 p.m. Normally he wouldn't go to bed so early, but he was really drained. He didn't even know how he would crawl over to his room at the end of the corridor. He somehow found the energy after fifteen tedious minutes devoted to hygiene, and though he felt like he was in a state of noctambulation, he finally made it to his bed.

10.

The phone was ringing again. The third call pulled Ian out of his interrupted sleep. He kept waking up during the night – twice from nightmares, once from parching thirst, and three times, including this one, from unanswered calls.

Who would be calling so insistently on Sunday, especially given the circumstances, and on top of that – so early in the morning? Judging by how sleep deprived he felt, it was early. Probably 7 or 8 am. He opened his eyes and for a few brief moments he felt calm, just like he always felt in this room. Everything in it remained untouched since his high school days. He looked at the posters on the wall, three of them of his favorite cars – Ford Mustang, Dodge Challenger, MG-TF. There was a Depeche Mode one, too

– he was a fan. He reached over to the desk to get his phone. He didn't foresee the possibility of being woken by it, otherwise he would have left in the living room. Or in the master bedroom. In any case, at least now he knew what time it was. He stood up slowly and carefully, so as to not give his splitting headache a reason to get worse. He could hear a rumble between his ears. He looked at his phone. It wasn't 7 or 8 am, it was 11:38 am. He didn't remember ever waking up so late. Never. Even after high school or college parties, he was always up by 10:00 a.m.

Someone really had called three times, it wasn't just his drowsiness. Two missed calls from Megan and one from Chester. On the one hand, he still didn't feel like talking to anyone. On the other hand, he couldn't afford to alienate them. He was sure they had already found out – they knew his parents, they certainly had access to the news and were definitely worried about him. He needed to get in touch with them. But that could wait, at least until he had a coffee. He also needed to think about the meeting with Detective Jones, which was in less than 24 hours.

He took a quick shower and put on one of his old sweaters and a pair of thick socks. Good thing that most of his clothes were still in this house. He usually brought all his clothes over from college, and got a fresh change to take back. This time, he hadn't brought anything.

He grabbed the phone and the folder with Mason's letter and headed downstairs. He couldn't start without a cup of strong espresso. Or maybe even two.

He opened the window in the kitchen. The same window his father had watched him from when he came for his last visit. As a matter of fact, the exact time he'd found out that his idol Thomas Mason was seeking his father's services.

The day was chilly, probably no more than forty degrees. Nevertheless, it was sunny. Ian turned the coffee machine on so it could warm up. No one had turned it on for a few days. Everything around felt orphaned, just like him. Every object, every appliance and piece of furniture brought a memory back. Today, however, his state of mind was a bit different from the day before. It felt like more time had passed than had gone by in reality. It was probably the rapidly developing circumstances, and the new facts he was learning, that made his recovery more bearable. Naturally, the sadness was crippling, but his focus wasn't on it. Rather, it was on the pursuit of justice, even if he didn't yet quite know how he would seek it. Or whether it would be a struggle or just a search for the reason behind their murder.

The light on the coffee machine stopped blinking. Finally.

As a devotee of high-quality espresso, Jeff had bought the machine on one of their wedding anniversary trips to Verona about six years ago. He and Beth had gone alone – Ian was in the period when he refused to travel. He was only interested in his group of friends and his girlfriend. And cars, of course. Usually, his three passions went hand in hand, and events intensified around the fact that he was getting an opportunity to be home alone.

The machine had a built-in grinder, which guaranteed freshly ground and exceptionally aromatic coffee, and also allowed Jeffrey to experiment with different types and varieties. He returned from every trip with at least five or six bags of different coffee beans.

Ian made himself a short espresso with an Ethiopian arabica. That's what is said on the package; he didn't know how to differentiate them himself. He just liked strong coffee. He put the phone and the folder on the table next to the windows that looked out to the yard and the street and sat beside it.

After the three sips that the size of the cup allowed him, he was ready to speak to Megan. Chester was a close friend, too, but communication with Megan was a little more personal. At the moment, probably as a result of his state of mind, he felt a bit closer to her. After a few seconds he heard her voice in the speaker.

"Ian! I'm so sorry! We heard about it..."

Megan sounded upset and unsure, with all the possible nuances of an awkwardness that was otherwise very uncharacteristic of her.

"Thanks, Meg."

"Where are you? Chester and I, we didn't know where to look for you."

"I'm home, in DC."

"Can we help you with anything?" She paused. "I know you, I know you prefer to be alone, but in this case..."

"There's no need, really," Ian interrupted her. "I know you're there for me, but I'll manage, okay? This is better for me. I'll see you soon, don't worry about me."

There was another pause. A pause in which a separate, brief, and earnest telepathic conversation took place. The things they knew about each other would become speech. After a few seconds, Megan actually voiced a part of it.

"Do you *really* mean that? Will we ever see you again, Ian?"

"I don't know," he stopped again, then added. "Of course we'll see each other again. But I don't know when or where."

"You're not going to graduate?" She didn't quite manage to say it without sounding patronizing.

"Maybe, I don't know. I need time. And I have a lot of things to take care of around here..."

"You can always count on me. I know the same goes for Chester. Even though he's useless, I don't see how he could help you."

Her last sarcastic remark made Ian laugh heartily.

"Thank you Meg, really."

"I'm not done yet! We'll leave you alone so you can recover, just like you ask. But I'll keep a close eye on you. In three months I will find you, Dunne. No matter where you are!" then added with a smile that could be felt even over the phone. "Not that I don't trust you..."

"Am I to understand that you don't require my permission?"

"Absolutely not! Just promise that if you need anything, anything at all, you'll call me. Alright?"

"I wouldn't turn to anyone else. Thank you for everything. Hey," he remarked, "can you please talk to Chester for me, please? He called, but..."

Megan didn't even let him finish. "You can count on me! Take care!"

The conversation ended, leaving more open questions in Ian's mind. What was he going to do, really? Was he going to detach himself from the circumstances and graduate? He didn't want to dwell on it at this stage, not before he got to the bottom of what had happened to his parents. Besides, Columbia University was one of the most prestigious on the planet and it had correspondingly high tuition. But it was also true that his family had always enjoyed upper-middle class status. The main family income came from Jeffrey's work, and he wasn't here anymore.

They had two properties – the house he was in right now, and a vacation home in Maine. In addition, the building where Jeffrey's firm worked was also an investment of his. He and his associates used the ground floor and a few of the top floors. The other seven floors were rented out in order to cover the mortgage. There were quite a few years left on it. And this meant that Ian was already in debt, even with the expected settlement from his parents' life insurance.

He let out the air that these questions had locked in his chest. *One by one!* he whispered to himself, which – as much as it was possible – cheered him up a bit. He had to resort to giving himself voice commands to put some order in the congested traffic of thoughts in his head. It needed to be regulated – his thoughts were racing from lane to lane on a multilane freeway. There were also endless possibilities for new thoughts to merge into the existing traffic.

Shortly after 1 p.m., he felt a slight hunger.

His biological clock was getting back to normal. Ian had no intention of sparing time for a ritual meal; he wanted something easy to both prepare and eat. He opened the fridge and found a yogurt that was fortunately still not expired and two overripe bananas.

As soon as he started eating, he felt as if he were getting hungrier.

Suddenly the phone, which had become an aggressive irritant, signaled yet another attempt by someone to reach him. This time, it was Mary. He had to answer, although he hated talking while eating. At least he was nearly done.

"Mary, hello," he said with a half-full mouth.

"Hi Ian, is this a good time?"

"No worries."

"How are you?"

"Well.... I'm alright. I think... Maybe I'm starting to pull it together."

He thought about the letter he found last night. Should he tell her? After all, his father had trusted her for years, she was more of a family friend than just an employee. In any case, she interrupted his dilemma, delaying the need for a decision.

"Listen, I just dropped Maya off at her piano lesson. I'm actually very close to your place. Should I drop by?"

Ian paused, which encouraged her to continue.

"I have to pick her up again in an hour anyway."

"Alright, I'll be here," he agreed with palpable reluctance. But when he thought about it, he realized that talking to Mary will probably help.

"See you in a bit."

In less than 15 minutes, he was greeting her. It was easier for him to have her as a visitor with a limited amount of time available. Mary had about 45 minutes, which perfectly suited his schedule and his currently low tolerance threshold.

"I brought fresh croissants," she said with a somewhat apologetic smile before even walking in, and waved a paper bag in her hand. "They're still warm."

"Oh, thanks, I just ate, but..." he needed to find a way to sound polite. "At least I won't need to worry about dinner!"

"Would you like some?" he remembered to ask, but

she shook her head.

"I already had one with Maya. We do it every Sunday. Something of a tradition."

"Sounds great."

"But I won't turn some coffee down, if it's okay."

It was obvious that she asked with a great deal of discomfort. Her aim was to distract him for a few minutes and get him accustomed to her presence in his house. She was keenly aware that Ian's emotional state was, and would remain, quite delicate. Probably for a long time.

"Sure, right away."

Mary remained standing between the dining room and the kitchen for a bit, then sat at the dinner table to wait for her coffee and the host. She didn't want to overwhelm him.

He seemed more at ease after she stepped away. He had already decided to tell her about the letter.

"Did the police call you?" he stalled.

"Yeah, on Friday. Right before I called you. You were already on your way here."

"What did they ask you?" Ian structured his questions as if to support his decision to trust her. "Did they actually call you to the station, or just ask questions over the phone?"

"Both. First they called me and informed me of what happened..."

"I wonder why they called you first?" remarked Ian with a clearly puzzled expression. He matched the coffee cup with a saucer and headed for the table.

"They didn't call me personally. They called the firm. They were fairly certain that it was attorney Jeffrey Dunne, and they just called his office number – the one I answer."

"Right, that makes sense."

"Then two policemen came to the lobby. One was a detective."

"Detective Jones?"

"Yes, the same. They asked me to accompany them to the station to answer a few questions that may help them with the case. Did they call you?"

"He did. I have to go tomorrow morning. They want to speak to me and I..." he paused to swallow. "I have to identify the bodies. Or whatever's left of them."

Mary was obviously a sensitive and very compassionate person, because Ian's words entirely changed her expression.

"Oh, Ian! I'm so sorry for everything!" she uttered, nearly in tears.

"Look, let's not go back to that!" he interrupted her sharply. "Not like that. I can't escape the fact that they've been killed. But I intend to focus all my efforts on finding out why and who is guilty for what happened."

She just nodded silently, while he repeated so as to emphasize what he was saying, "So let's not be consumed by grief, because we have lots and lots of work."

"What exactly do you mean, Ian?" she asked skeptically.

"First tell me about the questions they asked you at the station."

She shifted in her chair, in all likelihood trying to recall the conversation.

"They... wanted to know who he had been working for lately. If he'd taken on any other personal clients aside from Mason in the last few months."

"Did you know that Mason is dead"

"What?" Mary gaped. "They didn't say anything to me!"

"It happened a few days ago, Thursday, I think."

"How did you find out? Who did you talk to in Annapolis?"

"I found his house. A woman opened the door, probably his wife. She said he'd killed himself two days earlier, but she also clearly showed that she didn't believe that to be the cause of his death."

"And why do you think so?" Mary kept wondering.

"Her behavior spoke for itself. She told me indirectly that suicide is just the police's official story."

"The thing is, anything else would mean that someone broke into his house and killed Mason while he was under house arrest. Doesn't really make sense to me!"

"Well, not just to you. Anyway," Ian vented. "I'm more

inclined to trust his wife's judgment than that of the police. I found something... last night."

Mary didn't answer, but her eyes showed that all her attention was focused on anticipating the answer. Ian continued.

"A letter. Handwritten and signed by Mason."

"A letter?" she slowly repeated and leaned down to see better.

He nodded and clarified. "He seems to have written it before his first meeting with my father. He wanted insurance in case he was for some reason unable to tell him everything personally."

Mary stood motionless, all ears.

"He seems to have managed, after all. According to the letter, he also handed over other proof, including video footage."

"Did you find it?" Mary almost interrupted him.

"Only this," Ian reached for the folder on the other side of the table.

"Here." He slid it over to her. "I want you to read it."

After going through a few empty folders, she found the letter. She pressed her fingers to both sides and opened it. In the meantime, she didn't break eye contact with Ian, as if she needed to prepare for whatever she was about to find out. She took a deep breath and started reading.

Ian sat on the chair next to her, reconstructing in his mind the text that Mary was now holding. After six long minutes she looked at him again. She said nothing. She put the letter down and placed her fist under her chin as she exhaled. Only a second later she opened her hand and put four fingers on her lips. She was obviously thinking about what to say.

"I knew there was something..." She was the first to break the long silence. "But I never knew any details regarding the case. I drew conclusions only from what I saw with my own eyes and the news."

"So my father never told you anything?"

"Your father took confidentiality extremely seriously."

She sighed again and added, "He never said anything."

This time it was Ian who remained motionless and waited for her to finish. Her tone suggested she wasn't done.

"But I knew that something wasn't right after Preston's first visit. I told you about it, they just showed up one day and went straight into his office. Without warning, without an appointment. That was the first red light for me. No one barges in just like that. Even your father's closest friends respected his schedule and called to warn him."

"That's all that worries you?"

"Well, call it intuition," she said defensively. "Your father's behavior confirmed my suspicions. "The two crooks left first..." she made another pause and Ian sensed she was slightly embarrassed. He encouraged her to continue.

"And?"

"He came down to the lobby a full hour later. But my computer is linked to the security cameras, the ones in the corridor by his office."

"The one with glass walls?" Ian specified.

"Exactly. I know how it sounds, to sit there and watch your boss on camera... Anyway!" she waved her hand abruptly. "He sat on his chair, turned his back to the door, and sat like that for forty minutes."

Ian's expression was hard to decipher. As if he was both disappointed and impressed. He didn't expect such a preamble to the horrific event. Maybe Mary was not conveying it convincingly enough. What he heard didn't fit his concept of something that had such serious consequences, the way Mary had interpreted it at the time. And at the end of the day, it turned out to be precisely that.

"Trust me, Ian, it was obvious that something wasn't right!" she hurried to explain, as if she had picked up on the meaning of his expression. "He. Sat. Motionless! For *forty* minutes!" she put emphasis on each word and stared at him wide-eyed, expecting to be understood. "Then he just went out."

"Without saying anything?"

"Only that he'll be gone for a bit."

The sound of a phone ringing interrupted the conversation. The melody was different.

"Damn! What time is it?" she cursed before answering. "Are you done, dear?"

Ian looked at his phone's display – it was 2:34 p.m. Mary was running late.

"I'll be right there. Ten minutes, okay?" she promised and hung up. She turned to Ian. "I need to pick her up and go home. Can I call you tonight?"

Ian confirmed and walked her to the door.

Mason's missing evidence gave him no peace. He spent the rest of Sunday looking.

He started from the basement, again. This time he went through every single folder and box, but to no avail.

Then he went up to the master bedroom. He went through the desk, drawer by drawer, the nightstands, the armoire... Nothing.

He had the absurd idea of searching his own bedroom, just in case. He hit a snag again. Apparently, Jeffrey had only taken the letter home. The other evidence was elsewhere. Maybe in his office.

11.

It had been dark outside for a least half an hour before Mary called Ian as they had agreed. Before he answered he looked at the time – 7:05 p.m. He had barely noticed the afternoon slipping by.

"Mary, right on time," he said, getting straight to the point.

"We couldn't finish our conversation earlier..."

"I need to go into my father's office," he interrupted.

"Now?" she asked, surprised. For a second she went through the options in her head, but Ian rushed her.

"When else? Tomorrow, I have to go see the detective. I want to be sure that I've found everything there is to find before the police do."

"I understand, but they were there already, remember? The day of the attack..."

He had forgotten. And Mary had mentioned it when they spoke earlier.

"And? Did they find anything?"

"I don't actually know. One of them, the detective, went upstairs, and the other stayed with me in the lobby."

She paused for a moment, trying to remember more details.

"He didn't really take long. Jones, I mean," she added. "Maybe fifteen minutes, no more."

"Fifteen minutes..." he repeated. "Going up to the tenth floor and back takes about six minutes."

"He barely spent any time there..." Mary finished his thought.

"Nine minutes, of which he spent some time finding his way."

Ian became hopeful that there might be a chance to find something that the detective didn't. It seemed strange that Jones hadn't devoted more time to the victim's office, but he didn't want to contemplate that now. He would go back to it later tonight. He was likely to stay awake.

"Can you get me in now? I don't know where my father keeps the spare keys."

"I have spares," she answered with apparent hesitation. "But I'm not sure how we'll work it out."

"Why? I'm the owner's son. I've inherited not just the office, but the entire building. Why would there be a problem?"

"In principle, there isn't, of course. But it may be sealed for the investigation, maybe the police are there right now."

"I don't have time to delay, Mary. I'll be at your place in thirty minutes to get the keys."

"Alright, I'll be here."

"And you decide whether to come with me."

Ian hung up and headed for his room almost at a trot.

He grabbed his jacket and the car keys. Five minutes later he was already heading to Gallaudet University. Mary lived nearby. He knew that, because about a year and a half ago his father had asked him to give her a ride home.

At 7:47 p.m. he parked in front of a tall gray apartment building on Florida Avenue. He was punctual. So was Mary – she was already waiting for him. She was standing under the entrance's awning to keep out of the wet snow that had just started falling. She kept looking around and saw him as soon as he pulled over. She opened a large black umbrella and stepped forward.

"So, what did you decide?" he asked her impatiently, while she was struggling to close the umbrella and climb inside his car.

"Are you kidding?" she snapped. "Did you imagine that I'd let you go alone?"

Ian didn't reply or express his attitude. But he really did prefer her to come along. If nothing else, she was probably the only person around him that had an idea of what was going on. On top of that, she was guaranteed to react more adequately if something went wrong.

The possibility that the police could be in the building bothered Ian. He had done nothing wrong and there was no reason to be nervous. The things he was hoping to find, however, made him so. Mason's missing evidence could expose what was probably one of the senator's many schemes. If the proof wasn't in Jeffrey's office, then the detective was likely to have found it and collected it. And this could lead to two different outcomes.

One was for the detective to turn out to be an honest and truthful man who would use the evidence to seek justice for Preston. Unfortunately, this was the less likely option, even if more logical. Ian didn't quite trust the judiciary. He assumed that once again the result would be something more like Jones discovered the evidence and realized that he could gain more by hiding it than exposing it. So he just went to the senator and asked for the considerable a hush payment.

He had been quiet for a while when he saw the building that bore his father's name. The building that was now under Ian's care and was his personal duty. At least he didn't have to change the name.

Mary had apparently been focused on something herself, because she had not said a word on the way over.

"Let's see..." she muttered first, assessing the situation on the opposite side.

"It looks normal," remarked Ian. "I don't see patrol cars or detectives."

"It's just Norman, the security guard." She nodded toward the man who was pacing back and forth in the lobby, occasionally glancing out to the boulevard. "Let's go inside," she said, spurring him on, and opened the door.

"Hold on." Ian stopped her. "How well do you know this Norman?"

"Don't worry, he's a nice guy. I've come on Sundays to pick something up many times. We know each other well enough. Just don't get jittery!" Her intonation didn't exactly sound like advice, and it wasn't a question, either.

"Got it. But I need to park somewhere, I can't just stop on the boulevard."

"Try the first street on the right..." she pointed to a street about ten meters ahead. "I'll go inside and chat Norman up."

"I'll be right there," Ian replied. As he kept going, she confidently walked toward the entrance and started talking to Norman, who had already seen her. He reached for the key chain that hung from his belt.

"Hi Norman! We've come to get some things from Jeff's office."

"I heard about the incident," said Norman with regret. "Who would have thought..."

"His son, Ian, is with me," Mary got straight to the point. "He wants to take some pictures from upstairs. We won't be long."

"Of course, he can stay as long as he wants. I'm in no rush. That was him, right?" he pointed outside.

"Mm-hmm," she nodded as she followed his eyes. Ian showed right on time to distract the security guard. That was the moment when she needed to walk behind the reception, get on the computer, and manually turn off the camera in Jeff's office.

"Hello Ian," Norman opened the door for him. "I'm really sorry for your loss."

"Thank you," he answered distantly, although he felt sincerity in the guard's words. "Mary, are we going upstairs?" he asked as he walked up to her.

"Just give me a sec, I need to check something."

"Damn it!" Norman interrupted.

Startled, Mary looked up and opened the palms of both hands in an unconscious expression of surprise.

"The police called earlier," he remembered. "A detective."

"Jones?"

"I think so. He said not to let anyone through..." he admitted apologetically as he scratched the back side of his head.

Mary and Ian exchanged glances for a second. Somehow, she managed to keep it together and flatly stated.

"Well, you don't think he meant the son of the owner, right?"

Norman thought for a second, scratched his head several times, then waved his hand.

"You're probably right. They didn't think to mention that," he reasoned.

"Yes," she interrupted before deploying another argument. "Probably because he doesn't live in DC and they know that. They probably expected him to get back, but they didn't think he'd be here looking for pictures so soon."

"That's true," Norman agreed. "They'll probably understand."

"To make it easier on you, I'll stay here," Mary added.

"Only Ian will go up. You'll manage, right?" She turned to Ian.

"Yes, sure," he replied as he started walking backwards to the elevator. "I've been here plenty of times."

He stepped inside the stainless-steel cabin, thinking about the cameras. The detective was sure to review the footage from the weekend. What was more, he had warned Norman to keep outsiders away. The guard was probably going to excuse himself with precisely that – outsiders. Mr. Dunne's son and his most trusted assistant didn't exactly fit that category.

He pressed the tenth-floor button and decided to stop wasting time thinking about cameras and restraints. He needed to find something truly significant, and he had very little time. After he made a few preparatory visualizations of his father's office to ready him for the upcoming search, the elevator's doors opened out to the long corridor on the last floor.

Ian took a deep breath and stepped forward. He had forgotten how open the space looked with all these glass walls. He noticed a camera hanging on the outside of one of them and pointing at the elevator. He walked by it but not without noticing the tiny red light that blinked by the lens. He was now certain that his presence on the tenth floor had been documented. As he walked to the bottom of the corridor he noticed another camera – it was hanging from the window of the office next to his father's. He shivered for a moment. He had assumed there would be more cameras, but not directly pointing to the space he was to search.

Without changing the tempo and the span of his steps, he exhaled a long-held breath from his chest. He looked at the camera. It was unavoidable.

Always, whenever he wanted to avoid something, to not see something, he managed to look exactly there. Like peeking through the fingers of someone who has covered your eyes with their hands to lead you to a surprise.

At this point though, Ian noticed the most optimistic

course of events he could allow for. He looked the gadget over several times, just to make sure. It wasn't a mistake – the red light on the camera was off. This meant that if he was lucky enough to find the evidence, no one else would have access to it. No one would suspect it was him. Yes, he was on camera in the lobby, and Norman was going to confirm that Jeffrey Dunne's son had been in the building. But Mary's official version was good. Naive, but believable – the grieving orphan had come to collect sentimental reminders from his father's office.

Only now did Ian understand what she had been doing with the computer downstairs. *My computer is linked to the security cameras*, she had said earlier today, when she admitted she had observed his father for forty minutes after Preston's visit. Probably through the very same camera that she turned off while talking to Norman.

Ian took the office keys out. He looked inside while he put the key in the lock. It seemed much like the last time he had visited about half a year ago.

He went in and headed straight for the desk, walking by the long conference table. There were no scattered documents, boxes, or any other signs of a search. That struck him as odd – what had Detective Jones done up here? Or was it that the police academy was now teaching its pupils manners, too?

He sat in his father's chair behind the desk and decided to start with the drawers, which were a total of six and all on the left side. The right side had a tall rectangular compartment where the computer was. He hastily opened the first drawer. He didn't want to linger – he was supposedly here to pick up a few pictures, after all. The first attempt was unsuccessful. Just office stationery – scissors, paper clips, a stapler, pens. The middle drawer made him get his hopes up in vain. The thin folder in it didn't contain any of the things he was looking for. It had already been five minutes since he stepped inside the office and eight minutes since he'd gone inside the elevator. He had decided beforehand that it wasn't a good idea to take more than twenty minutes altogether. In other words, he had about nine minutes left before he needed to head back.

The top drawer took exactly three seconds – it was empty.

His best chance of finding something was the two-door filing cabinet against the wall by the desk. It had four vertical compartments only used for documents and folders. Ian assumed that they may take longer to review.

He opened it and counted ten binders. He felt hopeful when he pulled the first one from the upper left compartment. It contained three thin folders. While he was getting the first ones, he judged that he needed to check all of them, even if it took a few more minutes. He decided to pull them all out and then figure which one to dig in. Then he thought about it again – instead of that, it was better to go by compartments.

The first three folders contained nothing of interest. It wasn't related to Mason. The other binders were empty. In the back of his mind, Ian circulated the thought of Detective Jones rummaging around two days earlier. He reminded himself that he had no time to waste and focused on the next compartment. There were two minutes left of the time he had allotted himself.

He looked over the contents of the four binders in the second compartment without pulling them out. They were all empty. There was only one folder, a woman's case from 2003. As a precaution, he leafed through a couple of pages to make sure that the documents corresponded to the heading.

By the time he reached for the only binder in the third compartment, he was already a minute late. Lack of success dogged him through this compartment as well as the last one. Four minutes after his self-imposed time limit had passed, Ian had gone through everything that could contain some proof of the senator's involvement. He had more or less managed with the time, but not with the task itself. He was almost at the door when he returned to the desk to grab the only picture he could find, the one from his high school graduation. It would have been pretty suspicious if he had left it. He stared at it with a measure of regret. He felt like living that day again. Actually, any day before Friday. Back when his closest people were still alive.

He locked the door and headed for the elevator. He could

now go back to thinking about Detective Jones. Were the binders as empty before his visit, or did they become so as a result? The more he thought about it, the more desperate he felt. He only now realized that by not finding anything in Jeff's office, his only chance of obtaining objective information was probably gone. Anything that he may hear from now on – from his upcoming visit to the police station, the media, or any place else, could very well be adjusted to the senator's narrative. And was very likely to be.

The elevator doors opened on the ground floor. Ian met Mary's eyes and it took her a fraction of a second to understand that the mission was unsuccessful.

"There weren't any other pictures?" she asked and called Norman's attention to herself.

"That was it," Ian replied unemotionally. "Shall we go?"

He had almost reached the exit by the time he said it. Before he walked out, he turned around and thanked the guard.

"Have a good night, Norm," Mary said before she followed Ian out.

"Nothing!" he started before she had even asked anything. "Not just on Preston and Mason. Nothing about anyone!"

They crossed the boulevard in silence and headed for the street where the car was parked.

"How could there be no information at all?" he wondered, demoralized.

"What do you mean by none at all?" she timidly asked, trying to avoid pouring fuel on the fire.

"A few folders on old cases. Either my father didn't have any cases lately, or Jones took everything he could get his hands on."

Mary didn't know what to say. She shared Ian's puzzlement, but only now realized that she had no idea of Jeffrey's actual work, or where he kept the case documentation.

"It really is strange," she muttered after a few blocks.

They reached her home quickly. It was a Sunday night in February, and there were scarcely any cars or pedestrians out. Ian turned the car engine off at the same spot he had picked Mary up about an hour earlier. She spoke first, breaking the silence in which they had traveled.

"Do you think that Jones found something?"

He lifted his palms from the steering wheel and shook his head.

"I don't know what to think anymore!" his intonation and gestures indicated that his nerves were becoming more strained by the second. "Do you think that the contents of the cabinet was everything he was working on?"

Mary looked outside and for a split second her face showed a barely noticeable smirk, a telltale unconscious expression of self-accusation.

"You know, I just realized that after so many years as an assistant to Jeffrey Dunne, I know next to nothing about his work. One should wonder what exactly I was assisting him with?"

Ian felt her embarrassment. His desire to calm her eclipsed his frustration, however briefly.

"He was a lawyer, Mary!" he emphasized. "Did you expect that your job description included knowing details about his cases? Or where he kept confidential information?"

Ian was good at constructing arguments and using them. In reality, though, he had hoped for the exact opposite of his argument.

They parted without unnecessary words. He headed back to Woodley Park. Only now did he notice that the wet snow was falling in large, beautiful flakes. They fell on the windshield like cotton, without disturbing visibility – the wipers were humbly doing their job.

∗∗∗

After twenty-five long minutes, he was home again, confused and exhausted again. He tossed his jacket on one of the dining chairs by the table. Given that the hanger was by the front door, the random tossing was a subconscious raising of a white flag. Sinking ever deeper into this mess, only the hope that he would obtain information kept him afloat. Something that could help him seek justice. He had yet to find it. The house and his father's office were the only places he was aware of where he could find the documents or objects he *knew* existed. Somewhere, maybe in someone's greedy hands.

Hunger once again reminded Ian that his biological functions didn't recede with hope. He had just become terrified at the idea of wasting time and energy to prepare food when he remembered Mary's croissants. He thought about it – her support was invaluable to him.

He opened the brown bag on the counter, The four croissants still looked and smelled good. They only needed to be savory, and dinner was going to be saved.

He picked them up, once again faced the dilemma of whether to eat on the table, or – as his mother called it – on the "bachelor's table" by the TV. He had tried to eat on the couch many times over the years, just like all his friends did. According to Elizabeth, however, only "aging bachelors" ate in front of the TV. She said it with a wink, but she truly believed it to some extent.

Ian was far from that definition, but as of now he definitely felt better there than by himself at the big round table. He felt like watching tennis or boxing; he needed to better fit the profile, after all.

One of the sports channels was showing a repeat of a European football game. Ian didn't pretend to know much of anything about one of the founding versions of his favorite sport. For the moment though, the match between the unknown second, third, or even fifth-division teams was a perfect background to his dinner. They could even cheer him up.

He finished eating a little after 10 p.m. His newly rearranged biological clock made his eyelids interrupt the dynamic of the game that he wasn't following anyway.

While he walked to the kitchen to wash his dish, he

thought about the following day and what was to come. Detective Jones didn't sound like he intended to conduct an aggressive interrogation, or to apply refined psychological attacks. Or maybe Ian wasn't the focus at all? As a matter of fact, it shouldn't be him. If things followed a fair course, that was. Jones owed him an explanation of what had happened and how, who the culprit was... In other words, whether homicide and law enforcement in general were performing their duties correctly. And whether they held the evidence he suspected existed but couldn't find in the place where it was supposed to be. The same place Jones had searched before him.

He counted the last step to his bedroom as he prepared for an early rise. He meant to set his alarm for 7 am. His appointment with Jones was at 11 am, which meant that Ian needed to leave by 10.15 am. He needed the three-hour head start that waking early would give him.

12.

As usual, the alarm woke him on the first attempt. He opened his eyes to a strange state of mind – one of those confusing times when you wonder how long you've been awake. As if he had been conscious long before the alarm, the sound of which finally gave him permission to get up without remorse for stealing his own sleep. That happened to Ian frequently. In most cases, the false feeling of being well-rested evaporated within a few hours, leaving him under the pressure of real exhaustion. He could only hope that the scenario would play out differently today, at least while he was at the station.

As he waited for the espresso machine to heat up, Ian walked over to the long TV stand in the living room and pulled his laptop out from the middle compartment. It would have made more sense to keep it in his room, but he preferred to use it in the living room. On the whole, he wasn't in the habit of secluding himself, unlike most of his peers.

He put the laptop on the coffee table and headed towards the kitchen – the espresso machine had announced its readiness to perform its morning duty.

That's when his cellphone rang with an untimely interruption. This wasn't one of the sounds that Ian had much tolerance for in the morning, especially before coffee. He looked around a few times before realizing where the sound was coming from. He followed it to the couch. Had he left his phone there last night, or did he just toss it there when he was picking up the laptop from the stand? It was an unknown number. For a moment he hesitated as to whether he should answer, but then he figured it was probably a call he didn't want to miss.

"Mr. Dunne, hello. Detective Jones here," the voice introduced itself. "Just a reminder about our 11 am meeting."

"Yes, I'll be there. Where did you say it was?"

"The investigative division on Indiana Avenue. It isn't too far from you."

"Right, I think I remember it. Do I need to bring anything?" Ian regretted his question as he was voicing it. The detective paused, before replying.

"Do you have anything to show us, or...?"

"Just asking," he answered quickly. "Just habit. In my mind, visits to administrative institutions have to do with documents, that's all."

"Alright, I'll be waiting," the detective said after a considerable pause. "Please be on time."

Ian tossed the phone on the table and stared outside. Jones's question left him with an unpleasant feeling. He hadn't posed it with an aggressive or hostile tone, but the detective sounded different. It was hard to define a feeling like that. As if Jones wasn't pleased to hear these words, which he may have expected, but still hoped not to hear.

Ian decided not to dwell on it. He concluded that he was being unnecessarily suspicious, and under such circumstances there was a real danger of such thoughts twisting into paranoia.

After he confirmed the exact address, he flipped the channels between a few morning shows – he had plenty of time before he needed to head to Indiana Avenue. He needed about twenty minutes to get there.

He could leave at 10:30, but he opted to be on the safe side and left fifteen minutes earlier. Traffic at this time was normally pretty light. But after all, this was still DC and you wouldn't want to count on assumptions regarding traffic conditions at noon on a Monday. Ian considered the extra minutes an important element of planning his route.

This morning wasn't sunny like the previous ones. Gray, gloomy, and windy – full-on February.

He drove down Connecticut Avenue. The open spaces calmed him down even during rush hour, when cars crawled bumper to bumper.

He could reach the Indiana Avenue division via two routes – 17th Street and then Constitution Avenue or continue on Massachusetts Avenue and 4th Street. He considered it and chose the latter. He didn't feel like driving by the White House. In the last few days, he had amassed enough bitterness and disgust toward everything that had to do with statehood in all its forms and symbols. As he looked at the street signs with names of boulevards, he remembered Miss Gordon, his fourth-grade teacher. All his memories of her were radiant and warm, like the sun rays that illuminated the classroom each afternoon. Well, he had certainly gone to class in the winter too, but he knew how his mind liked to embellish past reality. That same teacher used to tell him that in DC there's a boulevard that bears the name of every single US state. Ian wondered why that information had impressed him so much.

He parked in front of the station twenty-five minutes before the appointed hour. The landscaped areas, which looked so pleasant in the spring and summer, now appeared deserted and muddy. Even this not-so-pleasant view seemed better to him than going into the station earlier and being surrounded by uniforms and gray walls.

He was going to have to wait for a while, so he didn't turn the engine off. He had heard that it wasn't a good idea to let the engine run idly, but in this case, he chose the comfort of heating.

His parking spot opened a good view to at least five sidewalks. He observed the passersby rush about, as gloomy as the weather. There weren't too many of them, but enough for Ian to notice that very few had anything alive in their expression. Truly, there were very few.

Right across from him, on the other side of the street, was the metropolitan police station. Somewhere in there, Detective Jones was waiting for him.

He checked his watch – it was 10:55. He climbed out of the car and headed for the entrance. He went through the metal detector without setting it off. In any case, one of the three uniformed policemen that stood on both sides came up to him to check.

"Where to?" he asked calmly.

"I have an appointment with Detective Jones."

"Ask at the registration desk," the man pointed inside the corridor while barely looking at the visitor.

Ian nodded and followed his instructions. The corridor wasn't especially long, and the gentleman had not considered it necessary to explain where exactly the registration desk was, but it was nowhere to be seen. He made it to the end and looked around.

"What are you looking for?" a deep, raspy female voice asked.

"I have an appointment with Detective Jones at 11," he stated to the lady, whose husky voice fit her physical appearance. She was middle aged, stern and gaunt, and obviously a smoker.

"Please wait here," she said with a visibly bored expression.

Apparently, the poker face and the depressing lack of emotion was a mandatory element for staff members. Ian was now almost certain what the conversation with the de-

110

tective would be like.

After two long minutes, the lady spoke again.

"Room number six, he's expecting you."

Ian looked around. Not that he had not had the chance to look around. But this time it was slightly theatrical, with open palms. After all, there weren't any numbered rooms around.

"And where is room number six?"

"The elevator down the hall," the woman pointed ahead. "Second floor."

The elevator doors opened, and Ian saw the first smiling faces he had seen in this building. Maybe even the first smiling faces he had seen all day. Except for the morning TV show hosts. Both men in the elevator were about sixty, gray, one of them with a mustache. They seemed to be in a good mood until the moment they saw him. At that point, they followed professional protocol and instantly frowned. It was becoming abundantly clear that the tough expression was a job requirement around here.

Ian pressed the second-floor button. Interestingly, all these absurdly stony faces cheered him up and distracted him from the tense expectation.

He exited the elevator and looked around again. A tall man in a brown suit walked toward him.

"Ian Dunne?" he asked and extended his hand. "Detective Jones, hello."

"Hello."

"This way, please"

The other two men walked in the direction the detective had come from. Ian inadvertently measured him up. Jones was a large, well-built man, unlike most of the specimens in the building. He was still in his active years and was probably no more than fifty. Like everyone else around, he also had a stern look, but his seemed to be more organic and genuine. Like the lady at the register – with a natural frown. Only Detective Jones didn't scowl but was rather serious. His hair was light brown, as were his eyes. They were expecting, but also mute. He certainly knew how to betray nothing with his expression.

"Please!"

He opened a heavy dark-brown door with a number six made of metal with worn-out plating. Underneath there was a sign printed on paper and tucked inside a rectangular transparent frame:

Detective Tim Jones – Homicide

Ian looked around the room as he followed Jones to the big desk at the other end of it. At least as much as the four steps that led to it allowed him. The office wasn't very spacious. A three-seat sofa, a lightly dusty mirror, and a sad ficus completed the furnishing. The atmosphere was reminiscent of the 1970s.

"Let's sit here." Jones sat behind his desk and invited his guest to sit on the revolving chair in front of it. He got started. "Once again, I'd like to express my condolences."

Ian didn't answer and just nodded.

"I can understand that presently things are extremely difficult for you."

Ian was stoically silent. This probably would have unnerved anybody else, at least a bit. But the detective remained unperturbed.

"I asked you here for several reasons," he continued calmly. "First, I would like to say that your father was a highly respected figure in our circles. And beyond, of course. As you know, maybe from the media or personally from him, his last case turned into a public scandal."

"My father didn't discuss details of his work with us, with me and my mother."

"And what do you know about this particular case?" asked Jones, trying to avoid pressure.

"As I said, he didn't share any details." Ian paused. Suddenly, he felt his nerves were strained, and he didn't want to betray that. He couldn't quite contain himself and said, "So why don't you explain to me what my father's last case was?"

Jones's face twitched ever so slightly, and he shifted in his chair. Compared with his attitude so far, it seemed that something had ruffled him. He just kept looking at Ian without replying.

"I'm sorry, I assumed that you called me for that... To give me some information regarding the death of my parents."

"Listen, son," he moved his head to the side apologetically. "It's only been a few days since the incident."

"The murder," Ian softly corrected him.

"Yes... We found an explosive device in the car, but we don't have a suspect yet."

"You don't have a suspect?" repeated Ian. His words voiced the affirmation he just received. So much for the hope that the police would do their duty! He wasn't surprised, but it still disappointed him. Then he added, "Well, you must have some suspicions? I read some articles that claimed Thomas Mason wasn't quite as guilty as it seemed?"

"Not quite as guilty as it seemed? What's that supposed to mean?" asked Jones coldly. "The facts are there. Mason received a large sum in Libra's charity account. He funneled a large sum from there to his own account. It took a while to follow because it was offshore. But things are crystal clear."

Ian was becoming increasingly irritated. On the one hand, there was the disappointment that the detective fueled with each word. On the other, he was furious because they both knew exactly what was being covered up. He decided to push a little further, but also decided against asking the obvious question about who the benefactor was. It would have sounded threatening. So he went in another justifiable direction.

"I understand," he said with apparent calm. "But, Detective Jones, the media has widely circulated reports that my father presented shocking new facts to the court, which put a question mark on Mason's guilt?" he remarked as he observed the detective carefully.

The detective's irritation showed in his face and gestures. He was quietly expecting the provocative question that Ian was getting ready to ask.

"So you don't have access to this information? To the facts that obviously forced someone to defend themselves?"

Jones didn't say anything.

"Don't get me wrong, I don't mean to play detective," Ian added. "But the way I see it, there's every reason for you to have at least one suspect. Is there a more logical answer than this: that the person the lawyer accused perpetrated the crime?"

"And who do you believe this person to be?" replied Jones, as if knowing that even if Ian knew the answer, he wouldn't risk saying it out loud. And he was right.

"You know that I have no access to that information. I'm just a regular citizen. But I didn't imagine that the jurisdiction of the investigative division was the same as mine."

"It isn't, son..."

But what I do with it is none of your business.

The last part remained unspoken by Jones, but his posture relayed the message. Or at least the feeling that this thought gave him. Of power and confidence. He was leaning his right hand on the chair's arm, while his left tightly gripped the other arm.

"We need time. We need to follow the necessary protocols. On top of that, Mason's suicide only complicates things."

Ian could barely contain the anger this cliched excuse provoked in him. This guy either took him for a fool or was very obviously ridiculing him. But he also realized that the conversation wouldn't end well for him if it continued in the same vein. It was futile, too. At this point, there were no doubts. The detective clearly knew plenty about the case, the murderer, and the victims. Ian's expectation had proven to be correct – Preston had ensured his own peace of mind. Any provocation from this point onward would be pointless. The only thing that could change in his situation was for it to become worse.

"I guess that's true," he answered hastily. He took a deep

breath, with which he quenched the impulse to rebuke the detective and steered the conversation toward its end. "Well, if there's nothing further to discuss, shall we head to the morgue? I'm sure you have plenty of other work today."

Jones paused for a few seconds without taking his eyes from Ian. This time, however, the expression on his face didn't seem as unbending. He appeared to be uncertain about something he was yet to voice. Ian looked at him with an unchallenging calm. The situation didn't need any additional tension.

"Look, like I said the other day, the bodies burned," explained Jones.

Ian winced, as if the picture in his mind filed his eyes with salty tears that he didn't want to set free. He still didn't move.

"Their identity is unquestionable," the detective stated. "So unless you want to make sure for your own sake, we don't need to do it."

Jones leaned back again, probably relieved after his last statement.

"It's up to you, son."

At several points during his conversation with Jones, Ian had been left speechless in an attempt to contain his rage toward this injustice and the brazenness and corruption of the "authorities." This time, he just didn't know what to say. He was torn by uncertainty – would looking at their disfigured remains afford them the respect they deserved, or instead sully their memory and all the happy experiences they had created as a family?

Deep down, he already knew the answer. It wouldn't be Jeffrey and Elizabeth he would be seeing. It would be a reflection of everything they had fought against their entire lives – greed, shadiness, corruption,

"In this case, Detective Jones, I wish you a good day." Ian stood up and pushed his chair back against the desk.

The detective tried to stand up.

"Please, there's no need." Ian raised his hand to stop him.

He could think of at least ten ways of assuring the detective that they didn't need the pretense any longer. He decided against it and headed for the exit.

"I'll let you know as soon as we have more information," Jones called out after him.

Ian left the room without dignifying the last display of hypocrisy with an answer. He left the building without even looking at the other officers there. But he assumed that now, with his expressionless face, he blended in fine.

At least the weather had cleared up outside. The sunrays were attempting to break through the gray clouds that hung over the city. He got into his car and headed back to Woodley Park. He wasn't frustrated or enraged at this point. The ugly realities of the last few days stubbornly tried to extinguish all emotion in him. It had even flattened out his grief, even though its roots were burrowing ever deeper. He had heard people say they were empty on the inside. Now he understood what they meant. He couldn't have described it better!

If all of this were happening to a friend of his, he would have advised them to be strong. To not waste their life in disappointment. To chase their bravest ambitions. To become an agent of change.

Presently, all of this seemed like total nonsense to him. The world didn't want change. It didn't want agents. It was fine as it was. Whoever doesn't like it can get off!

***

Ian parked in the driveway, fully experiencing the sensation of not knowing what direction to take. He didn't feel like going inside, and he definitely didn't feel like going back to New York and Columbia, to waste time in preparation for the meaningless career of a meaningless cog in the meaningless system of today's world.

He needed something else, something *real*. That thought sobered him up. For the first time in years he was absolutely certain of what he wanted to do. He had charted this possible course many times, but always followed by an "either/or." Either education, or experience, or a career... There was no "or" this time.

The idea to go to Africa had been blossoming inside him for so long. To give himself to a cause that saved lives was the only thing he could have faith in. Now this faith gave him purpose. Nothing held him back in the Land of Opportunity.

He realized that dwelling on the murder of his parents wouldn't give him peace or a way forward. But he could use this break with his past to fully devote himself to helping people in real need. Far from everything he had come to hate.

He went inside the house with the burning thought of how to execute the plan developing in his mind. He needed to take care of quite a few important things before leaving. Most of them were in the financial realm. He had to evaluate the perspectives that stood before him and assess the possible outcomes of his departure. This would determine how he would protect his assets – the savings his parents left, the two houses, and his father's building, which was still mortgaged to the bank.

Ian spent the next few hours nearly motionless on his back, on the couch in the living room, staring at the ceiling. He was impatient to begin his mission, and the questions that came up around every probability were starting to annoy him. The more he thought about it, the more he was certain of one thing – this house wasn't his home any longer and its place was in the dear memory of his parents. The proceeds from its sale were going to help Ian build a future, instead of staying buried in a past that he didn't want to go back to. Woodley Park was one of the upscale DC neighborhoods, and it was rare for properties to stay listed for more than a week.

With the observations that Ian had on volunteering, as well as the property market – which had always interested him – he could assume that it would be possible to live on the money for at least 20 years. He decided on half, because he was keen on investing as much as possible in Africa.

There were so many places in need of development, serious investment, and true dedication to the betterment of life there. Every penny was of paramount importance. He intended to begin in Malawi and Somalia, and he believed that within a decade he would find a way to not just support himself, but also help those who couldn't fight for themselves.

The fate of Dunne's Central was more complicated. To resolve that, Ian decided to consult Rich Mills – the man that his father had entrusted with the accounting and management of family funds. He was Jeffrey's college friend and consequently a family friend. His task was to ensure the proper payment of taxes and loans. Like pretty much every US household, they also had credit obligations. But thankfully, it was only for their vacation house in Maine.

Ian believed that the highest probability was for the bank to foreclose on the mortgaged property because it had been built with a considerable loan. If there were any other favorable possibilities, he could certainly count on Rich's expertise.

When it came to the firm's obligations and payments, however, he needed to consult Mary. He didn't personally know anyone from the firm's accounting department. There wasn't much of a point in thinking about it, even if he wanted to be prepared. But the fate of the firm and its associates was going to be the hardest responsibility he was going to face.

He hadn't forgotten about his mother's practice either. The scale was a lot smaller, but the significance was the same. Elizabeth adored her profession and gave all her attention to the children she worked with. It was his duty to make sure that there was no chaos at the place where she had given her all.

He waited until the end of the workday to call Mary. To wait until 5:10 was a challenge to his impatience. He spent that time planning the next steps before his departure.

He had long followed the missions and endowment programs of the Libra foundation. Maybe it was slightly ironic for him to join the exact same foundation that had become a death sentence for his parents. Ian, however, didn't see it that way. First, he was sure that Mason had been a victim of Preston much like his parents had been. Second, ever since he started following Libra's activities, he had noticed that the organization undertook projects that helped the future of communities

– educating children, building schools, kindergartens, hospitals, farms... And third, he believed this step would have healing properties. As if he were interrupting the vicious cycle by planting something good which would exist for the benefit of others.

That thought reminded him of Mason's daughter, Vivian. Another serious concern he had before leaving was to check on what was happening to her. Although indirectly, their paths had crossed, and he felt genuine responsibility.

Mary answered after the third ring.

"I've been waiting for your call all day!" she started without mincing words. "How did it go with Jones?"

"As expected. He was lying, I'm sure of it! They supposedly don't know anything, these things take time... I doubt anything will change."

"Preston's tentacles are long..." she sighed after a short pause.

"Anyway, listen, Mary, I want to get out of here."

"Are you going back to New York?

"I'm done with Columbia. I want to be done with everything here in DC, too," he declared.

Mary remained silent. As a mother, she believed the boy was about to throw his life away. To some extent she even felt an obligation before Jeffrey to try and stop the young man. On the other hand, though, after everything he had been through, she felt she had no right to interfere. She could only support him.

"How can I be of help?"

"I need funds to be able to leave. I need to somehow support myself until I get back on my feet. I have no interest in anything I can't take with me."

"So you want to sell the house?"

"I want to sell everything I can," he said firmly, even though he could sense Mary's growing concern. "And regarding the firm... we need to decide what would be best for the business. And for you, of course."

"I was hoping that you would take over," she said timidly. "You can do it. We can do it together!"

"There's no way, Mary," he uttered. "My place isn't here. But I don't want everything you've worked for all these years to go to waste. We need to decide who will take over from now on."

"Are you home? I can come by; this is a serious conversation."

Ian agreed, hung up, and started looking for Richard Mill's phone number.

He meant to devote the next few weeks, maybe months, to closing the book on this town, his and that of his parents.

And then, to say farewell to Mary, Chester, and Megan. It wouldn't be right to just vanish like that. Only then he could leave the continent and his old life.

The day he landed in Africa was going to be the day when he would become someone else. Without belonging anywhere. Without a home, a phone, friends, plans. The only place he would be able to go back to would be the secret room in his mind where he was about to lock up his past.

II.

2024

1.

I was fifteen minutes early, but my guys were already sitting in their places. I had failed with many things in my life. But I was certain of one thing...

I had a good team!

The buzzing of the cooling systems of the thirty computer processors, which we all became irrevocably used to in the last seven years, prevented them from hearing my arrival.

There was no way they could actually see me from there. First of all, I was standing at the entrance of the base, about three meters and ten steps above ground level. I was eight meters from Matt, but he happened to be severely shortsighted: his vision was 20/400. Maybe Austin was going to notice me first – his station was three meters from Matt's. Which meant that eleven meters separated me from the first pair of seeing eyes.

Besides, the contrast between the bright monitors and the dim light – my people preferred to work this way – was too strong. So strong that once you removed your eyes from the display, it took about seven seconds to start distinguishing details from the blobs before your eyes. We would have probably had bigger problems if I had compromised with the quality of our air filtration system. Down here, two levels below ground, it would have been completely unsuitable for breathing.

"How long do you mean to spy from up there, boss? Come this way, I want you to see something!"

In the end, it was the only woman on our base who spotted me. She always beat me to it. Considering that Fiona worked at the end opposite the entrance, I couldn't quite see her. Actually, I couldn't see her at all. And although we all had our tasks, each of them of enormous significance, one could claim that hers was the most important. She was the coordinator – from plane tickets to combing through archives, satellite surveillance, and disabling security cameras.

I stepped down, trying to not think about how absurd I must've looked perched up there. Anyway, knowing what we were fighting for here and what we were about to do for the world, I had the right to be proud. Not of myself, but all of us working toward this goal.

And we weren't few.

In the last years we achieved the unthinkable. We managed to recruit people from the underworld who were unknown even to the authorities. We united people and clans who had been enemies for decades. They did coincide in one thing – the belief that I was right. That change is imperative. That the system must be smashed.

And we were getting there, slowly and methodically, although we still had so much to do.

"You're up early, boo bear!" I couldn't walk by Matt without teasing him a bit. If you opened the dictionary to "IT specialist," there would be a picture of Matt there. Heavy-duty, curly-haired, with giant bifocals in front of his eyes. I met him in the third year of my five-year stay in Malawi. Matt was the first to believe in my idea.

We started working together in 2011, even before we started our first operational base in Belltown, Seattle, under the guise of eleven floors of offices and a two-level underground garage.

Shortly before that, I had received a solid sum from the sale of my father's properties. At first, the firm was taken over by his most experienced associate, but this only continued for a few years. Not long after, most of their lawyers decided to strike out on their own. We decided to offer the building to the company that was renting half of it. It was a tech enterprise, and it was growing quickly. They bought it from me and took on the mortgage.

On one of my returns to DC, in the process of making the deal, I met an employee of theirs. The best, as I was to find out later. Aside from the fact that he was about thirty back then, everything else was as it remained today, fifteen years later.

And it could be said that now, in his mid-forties, he looked better. We often joked that the clean air and lack of harmful sun rays compensated for the damage from his other unhealthy habits – fast food and sedentary lifestyle. Naturally, he made the excuse that his job description required his presence downstairs more than 12 hours a day. My job description, on the other hand, required the exact opposite – endless flights, regular sleep deprivation, and last but not least – constant mortal danger.

But, as they say, to each their own.

So, in 2009, I met the young Matt and got to know him well enough to like him. Aside from finding him open and honest, I also noticed how similar our thinking was in terms of society's problems and the world as a whole.

Well, I was also disarmed by his charming sense of humor.

At that time, I had an idea for a website with access restricted only to the investors that I was working with in Africa. I wanted them to be able to see in real time the results we were achieving with their money. Thanks to Matt, the platform was soon up and running... but the two of us had gone much further than that. We already knew what we could do together. And how exactly we could make it happen. Despite the dangers and sacrifices, despite the lifetime commitment.

Two years later, we were both ready to start. After all, it takes some time to erase yourself from every register. Not that you can disappear without a trace, but with enough precise planning and patience, you can hide fairly well.

In the meantime, Matt had the difficult task of finding more people for our team. From the standpoint of quantity, he hadn't done too well. In three years, he recruited *one* person. But he was flawless. Austin Miller had for years been Matt's only pain in the ass and his most serious competitor. It was nothing personal; they both wanted to see their companies succeed, but the real battle had been between the two of them. Between the two minds behind the logos that would later become tech giants. Matt and Austin played a cat and mouse game in their pursuit of the most innovative solutions, programs, and upgrades that could give their company the edge.

When Matt introduced us, Austin was an introverted person – tall, gaunt, shy, perpetually avoiding eye contact.

As I was to find out later, the latter represented a giant leap of progress in his communication with people. Matt once shared that before Austin left the company where he spent eight years, he was known as extremely antisocial and highly unwilling to even approach other human beings. He only cared about ones and zeros.

Matt, however, recognized that there was an obvious equal sign between them, and their work methods made it apparent that they thought alike. This encouraged him to speak to Austin about the purpose of their knowledge. And more specifically, the social aspects it could have – something that Austin hadn't considered.

I don't know by what means, but somehow the Bear managed to get on his good side. He didn't just recruit him for the mission, but he also unleashed him to the point of making him unrecognizable. The Austin we knew now even smiled a few times a day. And however awkward he may be, he was an extremely solid human being above all else. In his own way, he was the soul of the team.

In some unfathomable – yet glorious – way, our fourth pillar appeared – Fiona Rider. It was 2012, and Matt, Austin, and I were still adjusting to each other, when I saw Slim (we called him that for obvious reasons) furious for the first and last time. It turned out that he had been developing his own tech project, which was beyond my understanding. His newly built app had been ruined irrevocably. It had been hacked by a *slimy weasel*, as Austin put it.

I've learned one thing in all the time spent with this breed of people – only a hacker can find another hacker. We managed to find the weasel. Or rather – Matt and Austin did. But without me it would have taken them at least two days longer.

Tucson, Arizona. More or less in the middle between our

former and present quarters.

Back then, GPS navigation was mostly worthless, and apps were at an early stage of development. In a word – finding anything was a lot harder. After we circled around town for two hours, with a joint effort and some help from at least two or three tipsy Tucsonans, we established that the address was on the outskirts, in the direction of Phoenix.

At about 2 a.m. we finally laid eyes on the intruder's den. An old wreck of an RV. A weed-infested lawn and barely any signs of life. Except for the pale light that flickered behind one of the windows.

The capture occurred as one would imagine after hearing the description of the place. We three stood at the wooden porch in front of the door, dirty and sweaty from the road and the summer heat, which had already drained our energy. Soon, a small and frail creature opened the door. My own assumption was that the alleged monster that ruined Austin's project was yet another brat whose hobby was to just make a mess. But of the more gifted kind – the kind that took the mess to the next level.

He opened the door, and even before he could finish exclaiming, "What the fu...," he was promptly grabbed by the collar of the camouflage shirt that covered his basketball shorts nearly down to his knees. Austin freed his left hand and rapidly slapped the visor of his baseball hat, which landed two meters away. Suddenly though, our friend stepped back, shocked. Austin had seen something we only noticed a few seconds later – "he" was a girl. And so, the scrawny youth suddenly became somewhat likable – at least now the porcelain skin and the soft dimples that completed the mockery in "his" eyes made sense. As Matt and I looked her up and down with surprise and curiosity, she was very obviously having fun with the embarrassment that took over Slim's face and didn't spare him a jab at his predictability.

They spent nearly forty minutes with insults, yelling, and curses. Matt and I didn't participate much, and soon the three of us departed the ring.

Before we reached downtown, I stopped the car. The thought circling in my head couldn't stay in the dark anymore. It turned out that we were of the same opinion again. As annoying as the brat was, one couldn't deny her skills. If she had managed to break through Austin's defense, she had plenty.

We went back and lined up on her porch in the same configuration. After she again received us with the now familiar expletives, we went in and told her part of what we were intending to do. We knew that with the capabilities she had demonstrated, she would understand if she wanted to. After all, she had already reached into Austin's cyber-expanse.

It took Fiona a few years to stop using *every* opportunity to prove herself in *every* mission. She still was the youngest and scrawniest among us. At 35 she was nearly a baby to us, yet she literally controlled our lives, especially mine. Not a single turn was made outside of the path and sequence approved by her. And in the last few years, the paths have been many.

The organization we built gradually developed into a global network with offices on every continent.

The goal? To change the direction in which the world moves. The cage in which the system confines us, blind and dependent.

Investors and *instruments* – that's how we categorized our members. Both groups came with their capabilities, functions, and sometimes their shortcomings.

Instruments – the founders and backbone of the new society. On the one hand – the operatives behind the execution of missions, mostly IT, AI and military specialists. On the other – also experts in technology, medicine, ecology, energy and sustainability...

Investors were the source of power and money we needed to bring about change. They were the ones who could turn our mission from a utopia to an opportunity, which governments certainly wouldn't want us to have.

We quickly realized that the only world that possessed capabilities on a par with those of the state was the **criminal world**.

The only means to combat the state was the underworld.

Over the years, we became ever more convinced of the subjectivity of the definition of crime syndicate. What was more, many of them could contribute to the establishment of new rules and a better perspective for society. It just was a question of a little tuning.

We now had about 280 groups in more than fifty countries, with five to eight groups in each country. The average number of members of a small group varied between 150 and 400 people and was considerably larger for more powerful groups with truly deep roots. Like that old, almost mythical Japanese organization. When they joined us two years ago, we added close to 30,000 members to our ranks. This was, and still is, our most successful hunt.

I had two responsibilities. The main one was to recruit members for the organization and convince them of the significance of our mission, and the function of their money and influence. The second one, of course, was to survive.

Among Fiona's responsibilities, aside from everything else to do with my traveling – documents, routes, safehouses – was that I made it to my targets in one piece. In most cases, my meetings were prearranged through the appropriate channels. Usually, we had people embedded around our targets and we organized meetings with their assistance. But still, they tried to take me out more than once.

Two of the three attempts to get to me before the meeting happened in the Balkans, and the other was in Mexico. The end result, though, was worth it. Only one of the three potential investors refused to join us. And the one with the most rabid dogs later became one of my strongest allies. He recruited organization leaders from three neighboring countries. In turn, they recruited more.

Our instruments grew in number each month, and so did their spheres of development and activity. Naturally, we selected our political scientists and international relations experts with special care. In order to isolate the type of politics we suffered from and someday – maybe even money in its familiar form, we had to develop an effective and benign government model that would become the fundament of the new world we wanted to build.

We believed that in time and because of international interrelations, the structure and the functions of that new system would be perfected. But its beginning had to be now, and we were going to present it in a little more than two years.

The moment had come to sever the vicious cycle of global government. The way in which we were getting fleeced, generally under the pretext that we were being helped. Credit debt that robbed us, medical treatments that made you sick, media that misinformed, laws that killed.

The puppet masters seemed to change, but somehow the play always remained the same. And quite often, the alleged culprit for all these problems was the mafia – the informal economy or the so-called criminals. Were these two worlds all that different?

Well, I'm right out there in both. For my forty years, I can claim one thing with certainty – there were as many scoundrels *below* and there were *above*. The former at least purged themselves systematically. They had rules and laws, many of them older than the US constitution. I was not a sociopath who decided to join the side of the bad and marginalized. I didn't idealize the mafia and the underworld.

Maybe I realized very early on that we lived in a system akin to slavery. But I never learned to be a slave. I learned to be the change.

✳✳✳

They say that power can only be taken with blood.
Change requires casualties.

There were moments when my belief in the plan was torn by doubt. Could we bring it to its conclusion, or rather – its beginning? Had we chosen the right way?

In fact, at first we believed that a coup seemed like the only certain way. The definitive way. And given the scale of our organization, it was achievable. Our "terrorists" were capable of wiping out at least 60% of world leaders within two days. The execution wouldn't have been an issue. Or in any case, no bigger than the hundreds we had overcome over the years.

That logic started to crack as a result of the consequences we feared. We realized that society was not ready for the shock of one day waking up without its most influential public and political figures. For some, it would have been a feast, and for others, horror and panic. Similar circumstances brought out primal and animal instincts in people. And this would have prevented us from achieving the result we were after. People would have been too appalled by the brutal suppression of the old system to be able to look forward to the new one.

We would have been more likely to be remembered by history as the "monstrous revolt of the conspirators," quickly quashed by the next lot of corrupt puppet masters, than to prevail for a new future of humanity. People preferred to remain in their comfort zone, to bitch and complain, but continue along the same trodden path.

We needed a more gradual approach. More subtle.

And we found it. We changed direction in 2019, at the dawn of the COVID pandemic. The developing health, demographic, and economic crises forced leaders to speak. They were expected to provide daily updates and decisions on how to solve all the difficulties. The great powers needed to sit at the same table more often than they were used to. Words like *unification, reciprocity,* and *unified policy* were spun like mantras in the media. A total **charade**, of course.

And right there, in the thick shadow of mass psychosis, we saw our opportunity. It was something that we had been aware of, but never thought of using this way. Global power and 90% of world GDP were concentrated and strategically distributed in three organizations – G7, BRICS, OPEC. Twenty-five countries. Their decisions, plans, strategies, agreements, and conflicts were followed by the other 170.

It was clear – power lay with the one who dealt the cards. But how could we change the course of a game in which no new players were allowed?

Twenty-five was the number of people that physically represented in public the three organizations and their positions. For us, that number became more important than to anyone else – these were the casualties that needed to be suffered in exchange for the chance to demolish the system.

Twenty-five members of our organization were about to voluntarily alter the lives they knew to supplant the faces around the round table and take hold of the levers of power.

This was our chance for success; the moment had come. We could now gradually change the course in the right, constructive direction.

Only two decades ago, our intentions would have sounded like science fiction, born in the mind of an ultra-futuristic wacko. But things were different in our time. The possibilities of medicine and plastic surgery allowed two individuals to become 99% identical.

Not to speak of the fact that for a long time now, it had been known that heads of state often prefer to use doubles for events with a high security threat.

Despite sounding exotic, this approach needed little more than time, lots of money, a similarity in basic physical characteristics, and behavior coaching.

We realized that all these elements were at our disposal. To start with, the funds our organization had accumulated over the years were enough to finance any absurd idea, as long as it brought us closer to our goal. With our resources, we needed little more than terrifically good surgeons, the faked deaths of our doubles, and the dedicated study of the originals – their families, history, beliefs, politics, and public behavior. And of course, we had to prepare the new government program that we were to gradually implement. All that, from the point of view of the doubles.

From the standpoint of the actual replacement, we had at least as many factors to consider, and the questions were unending. *How far into their term was each leader? What were their chances of reelection? What would be the most opportune moment to replace a particular individual?*

These were the reasons that imposed the more gradual replacement over a period of four years. Strict organization and being able to predict several moves forward were going to be our only chance.

The stakes were high; taking control of these countries meant taking control of the whole world. The most valuable resources on earth would be in the palms of our hands – money, technology, manufacturing, military power.

It was true that the individuals we were replacing were pretty disapproved of for their wrong decisions during their overly long terms of service and their ulterior motives driven by self-interest. But their image was going to get a makeover – after all, we believed that the purpose of the new policies we meant to put on the table was more important. The advantages of it were going to be more tangible. The future that it allowed for would be appreciated.

Luckily, the decision to replace as opposed to taking down was made more or less on time. In that same year of 2019, we started preparing our doubles. The construction of twenty-five secret bases on the territory of each country where we meant to replace the leader was no easy task, but it was possible, given enough funding. Each of them cost a significant sum, but one meager when compared to the totality of what we had at our disposal.

Considering that the bases were underground, their use was restricted to the missions of our replacements. We couldn't afford to risk one of them being spotted, and we couldn't build them above ground so they could be used after their intended purpose. But we did believe that finding use for them was only a question of time, which was definitely not now, right before the *Conference.*

The day when we were going to present a new perspective for the world.

But a lot of work had to be done before that. We needed to psychologically and physically prepare our doubles, and gradually replace all twenty-five presidents and prime ministers.

And all of that – in the period between 2020 and 2026. We had calculated that our chances decreased exponentially with each following year.

Considering the scale of our capabilities, we decided that we could now act. What was more, we already had at our disposal a serious presence in the circles of those leaders, which was a surplus of the previous plan, since it required embedding agents among their party cadres, their security details, and their confidantes. Actually, we were already halfway to our goal – both the old and new plan called for similar tools. When it came to executing the actual cloning, at this stage of the organization's development we had eight top-notch plastic surgeons at our disposal, and with their help, we recruited five more. Each of them could take on the transformation and observation of three doubles. That worked, even though each leader had a replacement for their replacement, who wouldn't be undergoing surgery unless necessary. Besides, the agendas of the different doubles were to start at different times and move at a different pace; the replacements were to happen gradually, depending on the situation and length of their terms.

Despite its complexity, the selection of the replacements was unencumbered. We chose from people who were part of our network. Each one of them would execute their tasks flawlessly. The fact that they were among us spoke volumes about their ideology and it wasn't necessary to convince them, even though the change we were seeking required sacrifices. There was no projected scenario without sacrifice, and we all knew that one day, ours would come.

Some of our doubles had families. Their choice was the hardest. On one hand, they were aware of the pain that their "death" would cause their loved ones. On the other, the stake was even more valuable than all the shared moments – it gave them, their children, and their grandchildren a real chance for a better future.

That reminded me of Yon Chey, our double in China. In about thirteen months he was to take on the role of President Hau Lin, who was to start his third mandate at the helm of the empire. We could claim with nearly absolute certainty that he would have a fourth one. Communist or not, he was one of our most established leaders for years to come.

In a few weeks I was to travel to Guangzhou to check on Yon's recovery. He was in the last phase of the transformation.

Staged death – Psychological conditioning – Behavioral conditioning –

Surgery – Recovery – Fully taking on the role

This was the procedure that all our doubles followed. It took about two years, and since the initial stages didn't involve isolation, in early 2020, our first doubles were already preparing. By mid 2022, all five of them were successfully embedded. I still remembered the commotion that surrounded our first replacement, the prime minister of Canada Gerard Bardot. He was around the middle of his term when our Gassien replaced him. The switch happened during a fishing competition which the country's elite organized annually. Bardot liked fishing and he got lucky – where he ended up, he could do that all day long. Until his last.

In the next few months, the presidents of Brazil, Ecuador, Venezuela, and Italy's prime minister followed suit. Although they came from different places around the globe, fate ironically put them together for their last trip.

Not that we kill them!

We could just say that they went on vacation with a one-way ticket.

By the end of the year, they were joined by the prime ministers of Japan and India, and by mid-2023 – the presidents of Algeria and Angola.

But the largest-scale replacement operation was yet to come – next fall. We were going to have the chance to insert eight more doubles within the span of three days – during an OPEC meeting regarding the increased global demand for oil and the measures needed to balance the crisis. Regardless of how much they shook international relations and the economy, Russia's actions in Ukraine considerably aided our mission. The regular meetings and conferences at the "top level" once

133

again gave us the chance to act en masse.

By replacing the leaders of Congo, UAE, Gabon, Iraq, Iran, Kuwait, Nigeria, and Saudi Arabia, by the end of 2023, we had control over twelve of the thirteen members of the largest among the three international organizations. Only Libya was left. We took care of it a few months later, at the beginning of this year. And by August, we were done with replacing the presidents of South Africa and France.

Last month our team in the UK completed the last replacement for this year – that of prime minister Jones.

Although it sounded like mission impossible, our organization worked on every continent, and our network expanded with each passing day. Thanks to that, we could act on several fronts, even simultaneously, if the need **arose**. Besides, as I mentioned, a significant part of the entourages of the leaders were our infiltrated instruments, so the successful completion of each operation was a question of teamwork and a tight schedule.

"Tight" was an understatement, by the way.

And so, we made it to this point – the end of 2024. On the eve of the last four operations – the most crucial.

Germany – Russia – the US – China.

2.

"We're moving on to the next hunt" was one of those phrases that I loved to hear Fiona say. At the base today, we had three "interns" who had successfully passed through the sieve of our international bases. As the mission advanced, we increasingly felt the need to have a larger team here at HQ.

Two of the young men we reassigned were from the US, and one from Valencia. I looked them over carefully as I walked to the large screen where they were gathered to familiarize themselves with our next target. The rest of us, of course, had long known who we were about to deal with.

Their excitement showed despite the thorough preparation they had undergone in the last few years.

They greeted me with a somewhat rigid nod.

"We've reached the two main players in Russia," Fiona said as she introduced the two faces on the screen. "This one here" – she pointed to the face on the left, the more likable one. "That's our guy, Andrey Romanov."

In his late fifties and good shape, with silver hair and a clear, piercing look in his eyes. I knew him well, even though we had yet to meet face to face. The other man was about the same age. A very unpleasant mug. Flabby cheeks and eyelids, drooping on the outside corners. With dyed hair, on top of everything! Like he was going to fool anybody!

"He had a lot of fun in his day," continued Fiona. "Drugs, arms trafficking, the usual. He still has fun, actually," she added. "Only now it's out in the open."

To clarify the latter, she clicked on one of the links in his file, which led to a video. Romanov, clearly the guest of a TV talk show, was smugly discussing his role as a patron of the arts.

"Not the usual platform for a gangster, right?" Fiona smiled at the newbies and moved a few wisps of hair that had escaped her ponytail. "The man has spun his net very nicely. Right now, he's perceived as an influential benefactor. The biggest in Russia. He owns one of the most extensive collections of antiques on the planet."

"It's the first time we've dealt with such highly-cultured individuals," Ryan, one of the youngsters, quipped sarcastically. It was clear that he was cooler than his colleagues.

"No need to be shy, he isn't all that elevated," she said with a tap on Ryan's shoulder. "He's been cleaning up his image for years."

"Clubs, hotels, you know how it goes," summarized Matt. "But the snake has put his hands on the most valuable asset in Russia."

He made a short pause and looked around at the three young men. He was challenging them to guess. Fiona and I watched them voicelessly giving way to each other.

"Illegal alcohol?" Ryan shot first.

"Anyone else?" Fiona looked around theatrically.

Silence. It seemed that Ryan had summed up the group's guesses.

"Slim?" Fiona shouted. Sometimes we forgot that Austin was around.

"Not now!" Austin wildly flailed his hand about. "I nearly broke into the chancellor's networks."

For some time now he had been trying to hack the personal computer of one of our next targets. Austin was Fiona's main instrument – her research began with his breakthroughs.

"Saint Petersburg," she continued. "The Hermitage, one of the largest art museums in the world. Pieces that are worth six-figure sums and beyond. Romanov is one of the collectors known around the world. Lately, he's been the Prince Charming that donates his prized artifacts to the museum. Something of an official donor."

"And in reality?" asked Mitch, another one of the interns.

"Let's just say that the four million tourists that visit the museum each year are unlikely to have seen a single original," I chimed in. "The originals, or what's left of them, are kept in underground chambers. And the trash that Romanov takes to the museum are just convincing fakes. The things he takes out, on the other hand..."

We paused for a moment. We let the newbies sort out who exactly we were dealing with.

"You mean to say that the man still traffics?" concluded Ryan.

Fiona nodded.

"But on a much higher level. We're talking solid positions in the Russian elite. The global elite, too."

Everything sounded so clear and easy... The way Romanov had spun his net was almost impressive.

"And the authorities? No one's breathing down his neck?" the Spaniard asked.

"The opposite, actually," Fiona replied. "Luckily, he's

very close to President Mirov. That's what makes him so valuable to us."

Another silence ensued, surprisingly interrupted by Austin.

"Should we move on to the plan? How would we go about it?" he challenged Fiona. "You can't just meet that guy."

"Officially," she answered firmly. "We'll go to his turf."

I could already guess what she was talking about. Two years ago we recruited someone similar in South America. The difference was that, unlike Romanov, he truly did buy antiques for a higher purpose – he wanted to return to his country everything that had been looted over the centuries.

"Ramirez?" I voiced my guess.

"Ramirez," she confirmed. "He'll give us something we can use to bait Romanov and get a meeting."

"A private collector that wants to sell an artifact?" I followed, giving a hint to the newbies.

"Precisely." She cut in and headed to the computer by the entrance. That's where our archive was – the contacts and files of all our recruits.

I thought about the upcoming St. Petersburg meeting. I hoped Romanov's English was good. My Russian never took off.

While I was trying to figure out how long this particular hunt would take, I remembered the one in Sicily a few years ago that was the longest one. I was stuck there for over two months. And even longer on the continent. I could've had a better time of it, but my stay coincided with one of the last waves of the covid pandemic. Lockdowns, masks, curfews... I hated that circus. And all the people that got rich off it. At least while they were playing immunologists, they were careless enough to overlook some important aspects. We managed to embed our people in four of the largest pharma companies. We couldn't miss the chance. After all, pharma was one of our main targets.

We stole money, reports, research, formulas and patents – all the things that should be in the service of the people, yet never reached them. Every year billions were invested in scientific research. But as it turned out, with a focus on increasing the number of patients, instead of the opposite.

"Ramirez agreed!" Fiona interrupted the rage that always took over me at the thought of the twisted pharma industry. "He'll help. He said he has something appropriate for the occasion."

"What'll he give?" Matt's curious eyes lifted his thick eyebrows.

"Golden vessels from the Mayan Golden Age. He said they're from the sixth century."

"Would they arouse Romanov's interest?" wondered Ryan.

"I asked him the same thing, he said that we can trust him. Let's go over the script."

My role. Playing it out always made me anxious. Even though I trusted Fiona unconditionally, I subconsciously lived through all the unfavorable, yet entirely possible outcomes. It showed in the wrinkles that multiplied in the corners of my eyes. I could avoid at least some of them with more autonomy between thoughts and mimicry. But in any case, my lifestyle didn't require a well-rested visage and a California tan.

"The workday in Russia is over," she started. "Tomorrow I'll get in touch with Romanov's assistant and make an appointment for Ron Price.

Ron Price was one of my fake identities. One of five, to be precise. Born in Chicago to a wealthy family, second generation immigrants from the Balkans. His father was a jeweler and his mother an art critic. Ron Price claimed to be a professional historian and an antiques collector. He wasn't one of the prominent collectors, but he certainly had items that could tickle the interest of someone like Romanov. We started building his cover story in 2013. We had foreseen the need – history and art are favorites among people with money.

"Let's go!" She spurred us on in an almost soldierly manner. "The schedule's on my computer."

A few meters in and we were at the far end of the base, by the last computer. She opened one of ten folders on the screen. It was labeled 2024. Inside of it there were ten more named after each month of the year. November held the plan for our upcoming hunt.

"You leave next week, on Friday the 12th. The flight is at 6:30 a.m.; you have two transfers," she recited sternly without letting me out of her sight. "First stop – New York, JFK, a few hours of layover. Then Moscow. You'll have a few hours there before continuing to St. Petersburg."

"Wasn't there a direct flight?" I whined, although I knew the answer.

"I want you to be as invisible and hard to track as possible."

"And if Romanov doesn't agree to meet during my stay?"

Fiona smiled knowingly. "Did you really think you have a two-way ticket?" Beyond the appearance of sympathy, her colorful eyes were secretly mocking me. "You'll stay until you get a meeting. I'll do my best to present the bait appealingly."

"Speaking of the bait, how will these things travel?" asked Matt. "Will the boss carry them?"

"Are you serious?" Fiona snapped. "You don't carry such items around just like that! Ramirez helped me come up with something that's better. You'll like it!" she said mischievously, before she changed the subject. "More on that later. As far as the safe house..."

The safe house. I couldn't just go and check into a hotel. Invisibility was our goal. For this reason, every time I hunted, I stayed with different people. Some of them were interesting; others, annoying. Sometimes I never exchanged a single word with them. Like that old sailor in Valencia. Not a single word in two months. That hunt that took me all over Europe – I needed to recruit in Italy, the Czech Republic, Spain, Austria... Finally, we did it, even with an added bonus – organizations from Germany and the UK joined us later. But that wasn't entirely my doing. They joined as a sign of trust in their neighbors.

Fiona had already started to organize this hunt in 2016. Only that the pandemic caught her by surprise. And not so much the pandemic itself – by 2017 we already had information about it. We didn't, however, anticipate such massive changes.

We expected everything to quiet down by 2020; we knew that it was the plan. But we couldn't have any influence over that process. It was too early for our organization to be a factor. We continued to adhere to our own plans very strictly, even though we had just undergone a major change relative to our initial intentions.

Fiona returned me to the conversation and the roof under which I was to dwell in St. Petersburg.

"Lorenzo Mozzi, 58. An informer for the Italians. He's been living there for ten years."

"Did Alberto recommend him?"

My question was basically rhetorical.

"As you know, Alberto Razzini is the boss of one of the three largest organizations in history," she clarified for the new guys.

We worked with all of them. I didn't want to qualify them as criminal, because they weren't entirely. Most of the people who pulled the strings there did so as heirs with the task of enforcing the rules, maintaining the hierarchy and the clearly defined boundaries that must never be crossed. Nothing had changed in the Italian mafia. Tradition and respect were still values, and ordering hits, a method.

"But he isn't the friendliest, as you recall," Fiona said apologetically.

Like I give a fuck!

"I'm not a tourist."

"Alberto said that the apartment was close to the Hermitage."

"Romanov's second home, huh?" Matt suggested, this time hitting the nail on the head.

"Sounds good. Will he pick me up from the airport or wait for me at the apartment?"

"You'll meet at the safe house. You may not even see each other for the first few days. You'll have a card key to get in."

The fewer contacts, the better.

One of my most complicated tasks was still ahead of me. I had to recruit Romanov into our network, and his participation in our operation was of crucial importance to our plan.

Fiona continued with the schedule.

"We're hoping you can meet Romanov on the 16th or 17th. Our cover story is that you have valuable antiques that you need to offload. He'll agree, because that's his game – buy a treasure, make a fake, and donate it to the museum, while the original vanishes forever. So don't worry about it, you won't wait long. Just focus on how the meeting will go."

Although I didn't show it, this target unnerved me more than any other. His power didn't just extend to the underworld, and his influence went beyond Russia. The need to recruit Romanov was great. In a strategic aspect, rather than financial. Especially now, when we had already executed half of our plan. Romanov had a special role that he needed to perform very soon. A refusal on his part would create serious difficulties for us.

"It will go like any other." I tried to sound as convincing as possible. I couldn't afford to let anyone from the team – let alone the newbies – sense my nervousness. "Romanov will be ours."

"I'm sure of it," Fiona assured me. "But as important as he is to the mission, his refusal won't mean failure. We'll find another way to get to the president."

"We've already replaced twenty-one leaders – we're in the final stretch!" Austin emphasized his agreement.

Recruiting Romanov brought benefits to both sides. For us, his agreement would mean that other figures of his rank could join. Not just figures – factors with influence. And means. Very considerable means. But there was another, more important thing.

What did he gain? What did any of our investors gain?

The same as us – freedom.

People like Romanov paid dearly for it. And he happened to be paying someone in particular – someone we wanted to get to. As soon as possible. That was why he was so important to us – he was our easiest path to Pavel Mirov, the president of Russia.

The story behind Romanov's partnership with the Russian government was the usual. As often happened, the political enticement started as a promise by the courts to overlook this or that. Then it was the turn of favors – bribes, support for the party, hits. And so, the noose got tighter and tighter, and our hero soon realized that his money didn't belong to him, and neither did his independence or name. The moment that his services were no longer useful to his corrupt "partner," he would himself become the target of a hit.

"So we're going according to schedule?" I wanted to make sure.

"You could say that," Matt said with a nod. "If everything goes according to plan, by this time next year we'll have changed everything."

It was strange to inhabit reality while also knowing what we were doing and what was about to happen in a few years. The world was going to take on a new way of progress. At first, we ourselves doubted that we would manage to open a path to a new system. We knew what we wanted to achieve, but the means and way to our goal could change at any moment.

3.

I never managed to get used to long flights, especially the early ones. At least the first one of the three would be short. Besides, I liked JFK.

Winter in Seattle wasn't in the habit of arriving early.

We usually started feeling it at the end of November. Still, the damp, dark streets are not the most inspiring at 4:55 a.m. even in Belltown, one of the upscale neighborhoods that I barely ever left. Our eleven-story shield called Tech Progress, our base, my apartment – everything was here.

"Tacoma airport?" the cabbie asked with surprising cheerfulness. At the end of his night shift, he was probably on at least five cups of coffee.

"Main terminal," I nodded and sat in the passenger seat.

Luckily, he wasn't talkative. I generally avoid pointless conversations.

Twenty minutes later I stepped onto the terminal's granite floor. It can only be seen in the small hours of the day. It's surprisingly resilient, considering the serious foot traffic that it supports for most of the day.

At this time of day, us travel enthusiasts were few, and the luggage and passport check went without a hitch. As I expected.

"Have a nice flight, Mr. Price"

The three times I heard this phrase today helped me get into character, although I had been tuning in to Ron for two days. I thought about how long it had been since I had heard my own name – Ian Dunne – the orphan son of the famous lawyer Jeffrey Dunne. Officially, the poor boy's tracks vanished sometime after the sale of Dunne's Central. People said he was still in Africa.

Ron Price, Alex Smith, Miles Bush, Leonard Doe, and Rick Evans. The gentleman at the end was my most frequent landlord. For the last twelve years, I had toiled under his identity. I was known as Rick even to my own team.

The plane took off exactly on schedule. I still hadn't had my coffee so I impatiently waited for the flight attendants to finish their safety presentation. I spent the entire flight staring down at the maps on my tablet, going over the routes we planned. I knew Moscow well but knew barely anything about St. Petersburg. I didn't know how long I would be staying, so I needed to be able to find my way around. I had to be prepared for anything – unforeseen circumstances, secret locations, shortcuts to my main locations, Romanov's estate, the warehouse where he kept the originals before taking them out to sea, the port...

After about five hours in the air and three absorbed by the time difference, I landed at my favorite airport. JFK was like a home to me. I had come back here so many times, but now I was just passing through. I had a little over an hour to get on the flight to Moscow. I was hoping that the Boeing would be at the furthest possible gate. These were going to be the only steps to stimulate my circulation in the next ten hours.

Inactivity always drives me nuts.

As for the really bad news, I wasn't going to sleep a wink for the entire flight. Maybe the lucky ones flying to New York could. But for my biological clock, the landing in Moscow would happen at 10 p.m. Well, at least I could finally have time for a movie... But who was I fooling? Certainly not the millions of exterminated brain cells. I've heard that some people can switch off, even for days. Not me. In the last two decades, even before I started the organization, I could only think of one thing – the new order that we needed to establish. For better or worse – always awake.

This agony of a flight finally reached its destination, even if slightly late. I doubt it was as torturous for the large man in front, whose seat was brazenly reclined all the way into my lap from the thirtieth minute to the tenth hour. It definitely didn't deserve a more detailed mention, and neither did the flight to St. Petersburg.

A ten-hour time difference. That's what I call jet lag!

For me, it was 5 a.m. after a sleepless night. For the Russians, the afternoon would soon be poured into glasses.

The St. Petersburg airport was relatively big, but easy to get around. It was on a par with the one in Moscow and the ones back home. Modern, well-lit, full of tourists. I have traveled a lot, especially in the last few years. But still, I found the alphabet to be quite different from anything I was accustomed to.

I stepped beyond the sliding doors that separated the arrivals from their impatient families. To be honest, that always made me feel a bit awkward. I usually sped through without looking around. Besides, there was usually no one waiting for me. Except – to my great surprise – this time.

At the end of the line of parents, spouses, aunts and uncles, stood a tall man with a shaved head, sunglasses, and a stony expression. If I hadn't seen *Price* on his sign, I would have never thought of looking for my other name.

Damn it!

It *was* my name on that sign!

I started to slow down, hoping it wasn't obvious. Ron Price – I wasn't wrong. The tall man clearly noticed me because he suddenly straightened up, and the focus with which he observed me seemed to gather his whole face in one spot. I pretended not to notice him. I was still wondering how to proceed.

"Mr. Price?" he said with a thick Russian accent and icy intonation.

Well, I had no choice now, but I still acted distracted at first.

"Mr. Price!" he repeated, this time with an imperative instead of a question.

I was half a meter from him, there was no escape. There was probably no point, either.

"Can I help you? I'm not expecting anyone..? I said mechanically.

"I know, Sir. You are being expected." His tone was firm, but didn't sound threatening. "Mr. Romanov wanted you to receive a personal welcome."

I had about fifteen meters at my disposal to restructure my attitude. The last time I spoke to Fiona was at the New York airport. The plan was the same – I land, I go to the safe house, I wait for an appointment. We expected it to take a few days. I had switched my cellphone on as soon as I landed, but there were no messages or missed calls. Whatever was going on, she didn't organize it.

"This way, please." The tall man pulled me toward the exit.

We turned right, probably to the black Chrysler that stood out between all the cabs. In the meantime, I established that the Russian November was nothing like ours.

I could see my reflection in the car's tinted windows – disheveled and surly because of the harsh combination of cold and wind. The latter considerably worsened the feeling. I picked up my suitcase and headed for the car's trunk.

"I'll take care of that, Mr. Price." He took it from my hands and opened the door for me. Then encouraged me with a hint of annoyance. "Please, take a seat."

As comfortable as the Chrysler's back seat was, I couldn't enjoy it.

I don't know what the fuck's going on!

The trunk clicked shut. My companion walked around and sat in the driver's seat. I guessed he was Romanov's personal driver.

We slowly drove off, and the realization that I was getting into a scenario that could develop very unfavorably sunk in ever deeper. I knocked twice on the black window that separated the back seat from the driver. Instead of rolling it down as I expected, he only deigned to use the intercom.

"Yes, Mr. Price?"

Even without seeing him, I could swear he said it through clenched teeth. "Could you please tell me where I'm meeting Mr. Romanov? Honestly, I hadn't planned for this, and I have an engagement later..."

I hated to make excuses, but my role required it. This was exactly the kind of behavior to be expected from Ron Price. The man was simply an antiques lover and collector who'd come across a good find. Yet suddenly he found himself in the limo of one of the godfathers of the Russian mafia. Of course, presently with a very rebranded image, but still...

"Mr. Romanov will welcome you to his estate. It isn't far."

We drove for about fifteen minutes in the opposite direction of town. There were fewer and fewer buildings, until finally there were scattered shrubs on either side of the newly patched asphalt road.

I took the tablet out of my pocket. I needed to figure out where I was and send my location to the base. Fiona would no doubt notice my detour from the plan, but probably not for the next two or three hours. Considering that I was heading straight for the lair of the beast, that could be too late.

Alas, not one of my devices had coverage. I couldn't say I was surprised. The opposite would have been more surprising.

We turned off the asphalt and continued down a narrow dirt road toward a much more forested area. I kept shuffling different scenarios in my head, until I realized that the realistic options were very few. We had never underestimated our targets, especially ones with Romanov's rank. But still, it seems we'd made a mistake that could cost us everything.

Soon the car stopped between two men. Both were armed and in uniform. The window on my left rolled down. One of them walked up to the car and leaned down to look me over. The driver stuck his hand out and waved him in. We drove past them slowly as the guard on my side relayed some sort of information through his radio. We were clearly getting close to the estate, even though there were still only trees around. It was to be expected with such properties.

We went for another kilometer and a half before reaching the next checkpoint. Access here was controlled by four guards. Again, the driver rolled the window down so they could look at me. More or less, we repeated the scene from a few minutes ago.

After another five minutes and some ten kilometers, we found ourselves at the highest point of an elevation that wound down to a solid, cold, limestone house in minimalist style. The building was at least a thousand square meters, three stories, and the still-green gardens surrounding it were no less than two acres.

The car stopped in front of a tall metal fence with an automatic sliding door. We slowly went through and drove around a classic fountain, also made of limestone, before we stopped by the fortress's entrance. I got off and looked around. In addition to the two guards by the gate, three more patrolled the yard. They wore suits but were heavily armed. Just like all the others in a fifteen-kilometer radius.

Escaping won't be an option for me.

"Follow me, Mr. Price." The driver led me forward and opened the door with a key card. I was conscious of the fact that there may be no way back through it.

We found ourselves in a giant lobby with left and right extensions to what probably were other huge rooms. I did my best to not stare too much. Yet another two-meter giant rushed over to thoroughly pat me down. After his approval, we crossed the lobby and climbed the marble stairs to the house's second floor. Then we turned right along a lengthy corridor. I noticed that the space lacked any paintings, statues, or any works of art whatsoever.

Just doors, all on the left side. Five in total, spaced at four meters from one other. We stopped in front of the fourth. The driver went around my right side to open the door.

"Mr. Romanov is expecting you," he said coldly.

After a few steps on the massive wooden floor, I heard the door close behind me. It sounded like a dead sentence. The space looked more like a funeral home than a room. The floor, furniture, and walls merged into one. Wood, probably walnut, was the predominant material.

On one wall there was the trophy head of a reindeer. On the floor, underneath my feet, there was a similar trophy – a glossy white pelt, probably from a polar bear. I knew that the polar bear was nearly extinct in Russia as a result of hunting by similar *aficionados*. It appeared that Romanov enjoyed gazing at his victims.

I wonder what's in the other rooms...

"Welcome, Mr. Price!" my host greeted me.

Except for a few wrinkles around the eyes, the pictures I had seen in the bunker seemed current. His gray eyes flickered predatorily as he slowly walked toward me.

"Mr. Romanov, I'm pleased to meet you. Quite the surprising welcome," I hinted. "You probably got in touch with my assistant? She failed to inform me."

He headed to the long table on my left. He pulled out a chair and encouraged me to do the same.

"I hear that you're offering something quite valuable. I'm assuming you don't have it on you?" he asked rhetorically, without replying to my last question.

"I don't, of course. This is one of my most valuable possessions. I wouldn't take the risk."

"I don't doubt it. It truly is very, very valuable," he said and stroked his thick, short beard with apparent nonchalance. "Few people would voluntarily part with such an object."

He put emphasis on voluntarily. I could sense that the direction the conversation was taking wouldn't lead to a good outcome. In any case, I meant to continue with my story until I was absolutely certain he was not bluffing.

"To be honest, these types of artifacts aren't of particular interest to me. But I knew they were a find, so I bought them."

"And I know people that would die for such a find."

He made long pauses between sentences. He was slow roasting me, and I needed to prepare for the potential results of this conversation. For now, I stayed in character. "Is it as valuable to you?"

Romanov abruptly changed his intonation. He started to sound a bit overexcited. "Do you know what's important to me, Ron?" he said.

I shook my head, showing I was ready to listen.

"To me, it's very important to have cleanliness. Rats... disgust me." He stared at me icily, without blinking.

There was no room for doubt. From this point on, every word was life or death. I had to fight for the chance to make it to the essence of the conversation in one piece.

"That is so for everyone who has been inside Cheboksary," I replied, pulling my first trump card. "I hear the prison there has become unrecognizable. They say everything in it is brand new. Except the occupants, of course."

His expression sharpened. "You seem well informed about Russian prisons."

"I figured that it would be nice to find another conversation subject. We may even have friends in common." I knew perfectly well that the mere thought of his past having survived bothered him. After all the blood, money, and power he had expended to erase it. I had definitely challenged him.

"We certainly have friends in common... Juan Ramirez, for instance," he remarked with a malicious smile and pulled a heavy silver knife from the right pocket of his pants. Beautiful craftsmanship, almost like lace. He then added, "You should have been more careful when sniffing around someone like me, Ron!"

There was no way that Ramirez betrayed me and set me up. True, he and I didn't start out well, we had plenty of conflicts before our mission united us completely. But that was years ago. Maybe he tried to recruit Romanov...

"Do you know what your mistake was?" He asked as he walked around to stand behind me. It seemed that the questions in my head were predictable.

"I'd like to hear it."

"I admit that you made a great effort to get here. A comfortable cover, a credible past... I know how hard it is," he added smugly. He walked around me patiently, steadily, like a hyena circling a wounded antelope. Apparently, that's how he perceived me. What a mistake! "Very clever! To use antiques to get to me. And not just any antique."

While I was too busy trying to figure out what he knew and from whom, I had evidently missed the threat that was coming behind me. People had tried to kill me many times. But in Romanov I recognized a particular passion for such things. He would have done it with singular relish. Somewhere between the sound of his last step and the ongoing second, the elaborate knife was loudly and deeply plunged into the massive wooden table in front of me. Right between my middle and ring fingers. Romanov was literally breathing down my neck.

"Only you underestimated me!" He hissed in my left

ear.

Romanov pulled the chair next to me and sat very close to me. He pulled the knife out of the table and started playing with it again, without letting me out of his sight.

"I've been after these artifacts for a long time, my friend. Juan Ramirez won't just refuse to sell them. He'll be ready to kill to safeguard them. Like any other item in his collection. It seems you were really keen to get to me..."

Romanov stood up and walked to the center of the room. Then, he turned around and theatrically spread his hands.

"Well, you made it! Now let me hear why this was so important to you. And then you can personally tell Ramirez if it was worth losing his life over this meeting."

"Are you done yet?" I asked with the most arrogant expression I could muster. That surprised him, even though he tried to hide it.

"Ramirez isn't dead. He provided the items so I could reach you. We're preparing something you will want to know about.

"Ah, so *you* are," he retorted condescendingly. "And what exactly are *you* doing?" he underscored again.

"I'm here because I believe it should be *us*. Your place is among us.

"I don't form alliances."

"Your friend in parliament may be disappointed to hear that," I provoked him.

"That's about interests," he interrupted dismissively. "I act alone, it's always been like that. You should know it, having investigated me in such detail."

"You're lying again! The symbol on your back says otherwise. Ten isn't a lot, but it isn't like you're alone, either."

These last words caught him unprepared. In a couple of seconds, he went through surprise, anger, and bewilderment, which spilled over his face like scenes on a reel. Then, he took hold of himself and restored his usual icy expression.

"Ten?" he asked. He seemed to understand exactly what I

was telling him.

It was no coincidence that the conversation with Romanov had been postponed until this point. The plan for our secret operation had reached the moment when he was necessary to us. Aside from needing more individuals of his rank by our side, his recruitment required a few years to win the support of eight other people. They were key to Romanov's decision to join.

The griffin is a controversial mythical beast. It isn't entirely good, but not entirely evil, either. Much like the leaders of most criminal organizations that we had already recruited and others that we were about to. Much like Romanov himself. Much like his eight brethren. And each one of them had inked the enigmatic beast on his back – in an attacking pose, with wings spread and a word written between them. One word out of ten, arranged as an oath between them.

I kept repeating it to myself as I unbuttoned my shirt. Although the tattoo that concerned Romanov covered the left side of my back, he probably wouldn't miss the samurai on the right. It was one of the signatures of Japan's oldest criminal syndicate. It was also a much more bearable way to mark members. The second was infinitely less pleasant.

"Duty..." Romanov pronounced the four sounds that meant so much to him. Not so much for their own significance, but because of their importance in combination with the rest of the words that adorned the backs of the other eight members.

Rule over the beasts

Gaze beyond the wings

Ten equals – lifelong duty

Duty was the last word of the oath. The one tattooed on the tenth and latest member of the union between them. These were people with power and positions in both the underworld and out there, in the open. They created their alliance twenty-five years ago with an oath of loyalty, regardless of circumstances and interests. All eight of them embraced our mission and its significance. They agreed to use their power in the service of a new beginning, without backroom deals and dirty tricks.

The agreement I had with each of the other eight was that I would only be fully accepted after the approval of Romanov. If he allowed it and inked a full stop after the word tattooed on my back, I would become the last member among ten equals, and the new order became a considerably more achievable goal.

"When?" Romanov hissed and I discerned something else in him. He was offended.

"The last one was Diego. Last year. The rest, one by one, starting in 2017."

"Why didn't I know about it?" He paced the room from one end to the other like a mad dog.

"Because our cause is even bigger than your oath! Each of you has power that will be needed to achieve different goals. And every goal has its turn."

"And what? What's the last goal?" he put his hands up, as if praying for enlightenment. "What's my power?"

He was still angry; he couldn't accept that for years his brethren had known something which he only found out now.

"In addition to all the others, one of your biggest vices, actually. It seems that in the last few years you've been working for interests beyond your own. State interests, to be precise," I said sarcastically.

He sat by the table again, one chair over from mine, and let out a long, heavy sigh.

"Speak directly!" he ordered commandingly.

"You made a deal some time ago." I put my hand to my temple in a mock military salute. I knew that Romanov understood exactly what I meant. "To clear the way for the father of all the people in your circles that obstruct him. Then in return, your fatherland closes its eyes to most of your activities."

Romanov loudly swallowed his ego. The reminder that he had sold out to the state stung.

"Look around you, Mr. Moral! The war is not over! 'Most of my activities' are Russia's least problem right now! Let alone the trash I clean up!" – he downplayed it. "I told you, it's a question of interests. The price is low, considering what's left for me. Besides, we had the same thorn in our sides."

"The war is a whole lot of different play – I'm talking about you! You yourself know that it's always a question of time." I was voicing what we both knew. "First they put their hands on your money, then come the conditions, favors, purges.... Until the moment when your power, honor, and name are crippled, and you just become the next victim of their new partner."

"So what, you've organized a rescue mission?" he sneered sarcastically.

"Something like that. But not for you. Since 2011, I've been leading an organization dedicated to breaking this vicious cycle. For you, and for everyone else. You're aware of how the system works. In its essence, it treats us all the same. You can feel it on your back," I continued convincing him, without taking my eyes off him "So we devised a way to uproot it. To reform it. And you, people like you, are needed for their money, power, and contacts."

"Reform the system? You're absolutely nuts!" he said with a laugh that wasn't an expression of amusement. "We could have all the power in the world, but a coup requires instruments. Physical instruments."

"We don't call it a coup anymore. We call it a replacement. As for the instruments, we have them, too. Almost three hundred organizations. Including these." I lifted my left hand and wiggled the stub of my amputated little finger.

Romanov knew perfectly well who branded their members like that. And exactly how astounding their scale was.-

"We divide our members into investors and instruments," I continued with my disclosure. "And you have the luck to be in both groups."

I had never had a case when my words were so quickly accepted by the target. The idea didn't surprise him as much as I expected.

Although he was yet to hear the culmination.

In my meetings with the other griffins, I had realized the greatness of their alliance. But only now did it dawn on me that the ninth member took it to heart the most. As soon as he established that his brethren had accepted me as one of their own, his mind isolated the thousands of possible arguments and reasons to turn me down before even hearing me out. Instead, Romanov went straight for the instruments that we were going to need. In addition to being an investor, he happened to be – as he was soon to find out – one of our principal instruments.

He kept observing me with that piercing look, never removing his gaze. He was still listening. I doubted I would get a second chance with him. Regardless of the approval of his brethren, his refusal would shut the doors to them as well as other people that we were going to need very soon.

"If your mission is so noble, why are people like me in it? Do you know all the cruelties we're guilty of? Every single one of us!" He was provoking me with a valid question.

"I believe that crime is a relative concept. It entirely depends on the motive. You stole to give away... You killed to punish an unforgivable trespass," I enumerated. "You maimed in the name of discipline when someone didn't keep their word."

"So what? I'm a good man to you?" He raised his brows mischievously.

"Do you remember the neighborhood where you grew up? You and your sister?" I started as I walked over to his desk. "Very different from what surrounds you today. There was barely a house with windows, let alone heating. Yours wasn't an exception. It was probably hard on you." I gradually penetrated his deeply buried past.

I put my palms on the desk, facing Romanov. I wanted to observe his reaction. For now, he was edgy and definitely restrained. I knew that childhood memories were painful for him. Especially if they involved his sister Lina.

"You spent your days wandering the dusty streets, waiting for your mother to finish her twelve-hour shift at the textile factory. You needed to be far from home when your father woke from yet another one of his alcoholic blackouts and be back only after he'd left to begin the next one. The only truly happy moment of your day was seeing your mother come out of the gray hall where you spent hours waiting for her, so all three of you could go home together..."

I watched his face. He was confused... Vulnerable. It was understandable, given that he was hearing his most private memories retold by a complete stranger.

"The way home took you by the only colorful shop window in the area – Glaze. You've set foot in that pastry shop just once, right?"

Romanov had crossed his arms on his chest. Obviously, it was a response to the emotional threat he was feeling. But he remained silent, so I continued.

"The scene of your first crime. It suited your age, of course. You weren't even ten yet. In that far away year of 1975, you did something without comprehending that it would determine your path forward. You knew you'd probably get in trouble, but it was worth it. What was the name of that cake?"

I imitated an effort to remember the story, even though I knew its name very well, just like every detail of his past. He had stolen a whole cake to surprise his sister for her birthday.

"What are you getting to, boy?" he finally interrupted me.

"Don't rush. You'll understand why I'm telling you all this."

Romanov clenched his teeth and leaned back.

"*Medovik*?" I added after a moment. "Just a cake... something so regular for those on the other side of the window. And so beyond reach for Lina."

His eyes moistened when her name was mentioned.

"You judged that stealing it would be an act of justice, even if it gave only a moment of hope and joy to someone you loved," I stated, as he looked at me accusingly for having dared encroach on his painful memories.

"Let's jump another ten years ahead," I suggested. "Your first murder. A triple homicide, if I'm not mistaken. They deserved it for what they did to her, right?"

"Every cut on their rotten flesh!" Romanov hissed. "I'd do it a thousand times over!"

"It was worth every day spent with the rats in Cheboksary!" I nodded. "I'll skip your other crimes... the thirty murders, along with all the hits you've ordered."

I was holding his attention.

156

"And we get to your last war – Nikita Orlov. The piece of shit you share the Russian underground with. Your beliefs and approaches were quite different, but you put up with him as long as he stuck to the basic rules."

I paced slowly and looked at him from time to time to gauge his reaction. He seemed to have come to terms with the fact that I knew a lot about him. Likely, more than anyone else. Instead, he probably expected me to clarify the point of this retrospection.

"After he crossed the line and reached for your territory, he received severe retribution."

"That's what happens when you turn your back on rules established for years," he cut in coldly.

"Probably... As you can imagine, I haven't heard his side of the story. He hasn't given many signs of life after your... reeducation."

"You've investigated me well," he remarked and stood up. "I doubt that anyone besides me could know how difficult it must've been to dig as deep. You know that I'll do likewise. But I've yet to hear what connects us..."

"You've never been a good man. But you had your motives," I said. "Justifiable, even. Until the moment when riches and power became your motive. And then a bargaining chip for your independence."

Once again, a brief expression of surprise ran through Romanov's face. It seemed like my honesty was having a refreshing effect on him. I doubt anyone had spoken to him like that lately.

"So what kind of person are you?"

"It depends on whether you judge me for my crimes or my motives. You could say that my victims exceed yours a hundred times over."

Romanov, who had been sitting motionlessly with his arms crossed on his chest and his palms under his armpits, unsuccessfully attempted to hide the fact that this "advantage" bothered him. Only his slight forward weight shift and the furrowing of his gray brows betrayed the change in his poise.

"The difference being that my motives always remained honest."

"Really?" he asked before remarking sarcastically. "What a gentleman!"

He walked behind my back again. I looked over my right shoulder. He stepped up to a fountain pen stand and took one.

"You can't have change without casualties," I concluded. "The bigger it is, the more they are."

I didn't want to turn again so as to not betray the fact that his movements behind my back unnerved me. But in any case, I was here alone and in his hands. A second later I heard the sound of breaking plastic.

"Well," he let out a heavy sigh and started pacing. "You're certainly right about one thing. I prefer to do the work myself," he said, now in front of me.

He took an inkwell and nodded toward the chair behind the desk. Then I saw the broken plastic. He took one half of the splintered pen and squeezed some ink out in the well.

I sat on the chair, trying to appear unfazed. The tension hadn't left me for a single second ever since the bold driver had abducted me from the airport.

Romanov opened a drawer and gave me a sign to take off my shirt. He took a gold lighter with one of those antiquated flint mechanisms. Then he took out a thin needle from the inside pocket of his jacket.

"I remember what it's like to have... how did you say it... a justifiable motive?" he said as he heated the tip of the needle. "Let's hear what yours are. Clearly, they're justifiable enough," he added with a quick glance at the stub of my missing finger.

"Everyone who joined us before you was, in one way or another, pressured by the weight of our power. Each one of your brethren was given proof before he inked his word on my back. I'm not going to give you any theatrics. I'm the face of a network the scale of which will become apparent to you soon enough."

"You've come here with at least eight arguments that are weighty enough for me to give you a chance," Romanov said as he dipped the tip of the needle in the ink and leaned over me. "If you fuck me over, the scale of your network will mean nothing," he added, piercing my skin with the needle.

The act only continued for a few seconds. The full stop symbol he was inking on my back allowed us to continue toward our goal on schedule. Toward the new order and laws, toward the new world. It was only now that I felt the veins on the back of my neck relax, together with my jaws. Romanov's decision – or rather, his refusal – could have seriously complicated our agenda. And everything that we still needed to accomplish.

My new brother headed back to the long conference table. I could see for myself that it could be sacrificial. I wondered how many offerings it had seen...

This time, he didn't sit by it but walked around to a tall glass cabinet with six different bottles of vodka, and as far as I could see – three sets of glasses. He was about to be disappointed – I hadn't had a drop in years.

He opened the cabinet and reached down. He skipped the four visible racks and headed for a fifth one, hidden below the line of the window. He pulled out a solid-gold knife engraved on both sides and a half-full bottle of vodka. I'm not a connoisseur, but it looked quite different from the others. The glass was visibly thicker, and it had a metal "label" that looked like a wedding ring made of old silver. There was a word engraved on it that I couldn't see.

He sat in one of the chairs that was already pulled out. The same one I had sat in when the possibility of becoming yet another one of Romanov's victims was very real.

"I don't suppose you've heard the expression 'ink brothers'?" he asked rhetorically, hinting that we weren't done with the marking.

He opened the bottle, rubbed some of the liquid between his palms, and put it back on the table. He didn't need to urge me. I knew what he had in mind.

I did the same but remained standing. I put my left palm forward. He stood up and opened his. A dark, protruding scar ran from his middle finger down to his wrist. Evidently, this was going to be the ninth and last time he was going to open it.

"Power over the beasts, gaze beyond the wings," he recited with unshakeable foreboding, as he slid the knife down the long line of the twenty-five-year-old oath.

He handed me the knife and I saw the engraving. It was the same line he had just spoken. Before he handed it to me, he turned it around to reveal the other side. The second part of the oath was engraved on it.

"Ten equals lifelong duty," I read and opened the way for the blood under my skin.

This ritual seemed unnecessarily exaggerated to me. I've always been a man of my word. That was the legacy my father left me – the weight of one's word. I found everything beyond that to be melodramatic.

Not anymore. This was an oath that I truly had to defend with my life. An oath that ensured my ability to continue fighting for the new order the world deserved.

He gripped my palm and pulled me toward him.

"*Lifelong duty*," he repeated. "There's forgiveness for those that err, but not for those who betray. Don't forget it, *brother*."

"I don't need forgiveness. As you can see, I guarantee my intentions with my life."

Barely breaking eye contact, we cleaned the cuts with the alcohol. I looked at the bottle. I didn't understand what the letters said.

"*Klyatva*," he said. "It means oath."

I walked over to the other end of the room again. I went around the desk and sat on his chair. Romanov watched me expectantly. I was unpredictable to him, and that made him anxious.

I reached for one of the drawers on the right-hand side. I had known for a long time that he basically never used it.

"As for the meaning of my word, you're about to receive more assurances."

The drawer wasn't exactly the ideal height, but enough to fit something special.

I put the heavy box on the desk and lifted the lid. The gold in it reflected a bright light on my face. Strangely enough, this was also my first time seeing the artifacts. A flat and broad golden necklace and a mask, probably ritual.

The expression, details, and ornaments on it stunned me. As much as we knew about these civilizations, their skills and abilities never failed to impress me.

Romanov, who still stood where we had taken the oath, slowly stepped toward me. He was shocked by the supposition of what I could be looking at. It was as if he were trying to contain the fantasy that these were the items from Ramirez's collection. He knew perfectly well that there was no way they could be. He stopped a couple of meters from the desk.

"With this oath, it isn't just me that's entering a new relationship. You're also joining a new alliance. A lot of people are expecting you there," I said before turning the box toward him.

He gazed at it, almost in horror. He probably was truly terrified by the thought that I or one of his new allies had entered his home – had gotten past the dozens of goons, somehow – and had delivered one of the most valuable antiques Romanov had ever seen to his own desk, where he sat every day. Every single day!

"This isn't possible..." he barely managed to mutter.

"You're right. It isn't!" I admitted with a certain degree of smugness. "Just like a new order isn't possible."

A second later, after he had shaken off the initial stupor, my host put his palms on the desk so firmly that they almost created a vacuum with the surface.

"How long have you been watching me?" he asked. It was obvious that he wasn't thrilled.

"Let's see... As I said, I started recruiting your brothers in 2017. This means that..." I started counting on my fingers. "That I know you very, very well," I concluded after the seventh finger.

Romanov bowed his head and exhaled. Slowly, with his eyes closed. It wasn't hard to guess that he was swallowing substantial irritation. Maybe even rage.

"Okay," he finally snapped after a second and pushed away from the desk. "You're testing my patience very bravely, especially considering the fact that you've obviously known me for a long time. What's next?"

I stood up from the chair and walked toward him, despite my unwillingness to trample the polar bear with the soles of my boots.

"Mirov. You'll have to help us get to him. That's all you need to know for the time being," I declared. "I'm going back to the US to organize the next trip. I'll let you know the time and the place when it comes time to plan the operation."

"Now you listen to me carefully, boy!" he said before crossing his arms on his chest again.

"Rick," I interrupted him. He surely knew that my name wasn't Ron Price, but I certainly didn't like to be called "boy."

"I doubt that," he answered quickly. He seemed like he couldn't care less about my "real" name. "All your talk about change, a coup, a replacement, or whatever it is you call it... I don't know who else is in that alliance."

"Aside from your eight brothers?" I reminded him, only to be ignored. "I told you that you'll know when the time is right."

"Oh, I'll be waiting with baited breath," he muttered before he looked toward the missing finger on my hand. "You clearly have strong backing for this operation, but that doesn't mean that you'll be leading me by the nose – neither you, nor them. What you're asking of me is serious. I could be accused of many things, but I've never been a traitor."

"Is that so?" I countered. "Interesting that you mention that. I've heard that a lot from people like you. Someone *always* gets betrayed," I emphasized. "You just took the wrong side, Andrey. Instruments in the wrong hands."

I decided that I wouldn't accomplish much more in this first meeting. I didn't need to remind him that, already, he was indeed on call, but for those that ran the state.

"Today you're on top of the pyramid. You've long forgotten the people whom you're actually betraying... You don't see them around you. But they're still out there somewhere, beyond your stone palace." I pointed outside. "There, in the poor neighborhoods where you yourself came from. I didn't come here to overpower you, but to win you to our cause. What we're fighting for is way beyond any personal rivalry or struggle for power. Your strength, the power you've conquered at the expense of your life, will be redirected to something of global significance."

"I still haven't heard what's in it for me," he said, and I could read the irritation on his face. He definitely seemed to have doubts, or even to regret having rushed to agree.

"An exit," I reminded him. "I'll take you out of this game before your replacement takes you out. You know how it goes."

Romanov looked me in the eyes, and every once in a while, winced in agreement with the rebellion that showed through my words.

"We'll put an end to that!" I declared.

"And then what? You think things will be better with us?"

"In the world we're preparing, yes, I think so." I headed toward the exit and left without saying anything else. It wasn't necessary at this stage.

I took to the right, toward the staircase. I'd walked barely five steps before one of the lackeys rushed toward me. It seemed like he'd been standing guard somewhere on the left side of the door, because I hadn't noticed him on my way out.

"I'll escort you, sir," I heard him say. Romanov had probably barked a command through his earpiece, to keep me on a short leash until I left the property.

We went down the stairs to the spacious and currently empty lobby. Halfway through, it was teeming with robot-like guards wearing suits, some of whose faces I already knew.

Luckily, I'm good with faces.

I even noticed that one of them was missing. His long, crooked nose had left an impression.

There was a robocop guard at each of the three doors that led to other rooms, while the two goons that searched me on arrival were waiting for me on either side of the exit. When I

163

reached them, the one on the left opened the door.

I did walk through it twice, after all!

The same Chrysler that had brought me was waiting outside. The driver was the same, too. He stood by the car's open back door.

I hadn't considered the risks that could possibly accompany my way out of Romanov's estate, but I realized I was getting off too easily and freely. Not that I was worried about something in particular. My new brother, regardless of how much he wanted to, wasn't going to attack me, at least for now. After all, he wasn't quite sure who he was dealing with.

"I've missed you," I teased my bald companion as I entered the car. This time he wasn't wearing sunglasses, revealing the empty gaze in his glass-blue eyes.

He closed the door after me and walked around the car to his workstation behind the wheel.

"Where should I take you?"

I had written down the address of the safe house in which I was supposed to have settled long ago. I remembered that it was close to the Hermitage and opted to keep the precise location to myself, if at all possible. I assumed that it wouldn't be a secret to Romanov, but I had to do what was up to me.

"Alexander Nevsky boulevard," I replied.

Close enough, but also far enough.

4.

I checked my gadgets. As I expected, there was still no reception. It had been six hours since I landed in St. Petersburg, and HQ were certain to have noticed my deviation from the schedule. The Italian in whose house I was to stay had probably also noticed my worrying absence. Such things usually set off bright red lights in the minds of our team.

In any case, there was nothing I could do at the moment. Especially not from the backseat of Romanov's car, where I didn't even get a signal. In about an hour I was to reconnect with the team so we could coordinate our actions in light of the new circumstances.

The recruitment of Andrey Romanov was significant, even though I remained unsure of whether he was with us or not. I knew that it would be so until the end of the mission. He seemed to be the type. It was true that his devotion to his brothers and the oath they had taken was obvious. But as we spoke, I felt like something changed the second he found out they had acted behind his back. They made an extremely important decision without consulting him, although the final decision remained his. Suddenly, all the weight of his own devotion had turned against him, against his ego. I could only hope that he would grasp the significance of our alliance before returning to his true nature as a lone wolf.

There could be a lot of changes to our plan depending on the outcome of my meeting with Romanov. For this reason, we had a question mark on the next stage.

Immersed in thoughts about things to come, I was surprised when we came upon the city. I never noticed the deserted road during our return.

St. Petersburg by night was completely different. I didn't have a daytime impression, as I'd only seen the airport and the outskirts, which didn't seem very appealing against the gray and gloomy backdrop. Besides, the city's charm was about the last thing on my mind.

I rarely allowed myself to get sentimental, but the night ride gifted to me by the bald man with icy unwillingness brought back long-forgotten emotions. For some time now, I considered myself incapable of feelings like nostalgia, sadness... But this evening, this city, these lights, took me back to warm memories buried very, very deep. St. Petersburg's sights reminded me of one of our family trips. Vienna, before Christmas, maybe in 2003.

The broad boulevards, the opulent architecture, even the freezing cold outside took me back to where I didn't want to go. I didn't need the distraction of something that made me vulnerable... even a dear memory could be dangerous.

Still, the city is beautiful.

"Nevsky Boulevard," the driver loudly interrupted my thoughts.

I looked ahead. This boulevard was a lot longer than I had expected.

"I'll get out here."

"Mr. Romanov's orders were to leave you at your doorstep."

"There's no need, I'll walk."

He was certainly going to follow me, but at least I would make it difficult for him.

The satisfaction from knowing that I was complicating his job exceeded even his irritation. He could barely maintain his stony expression as he walked around the car to get the suitcase from the trunk.

"Goodbye," he snapped without even looking at me and sat back in the driver's seat.

He slowly drove forward. He was probably going to pull over in an alley. As for me, I had no idea where I needed to walk. It was more important to get in touch with HQ and coordinate our actions. I needed to move my muscles. Naturally, I had no intention of walking all the way to the Hermitage and the safe house, but the last few hours had been a bit more static than I would have liked and was used to.

I started walking among the crowds of people. It wasn't too crowded, but it was still rather busy. Everyone looked the same to me. Red cheeks and noses, wrapped in all kinds of scarves and hats, eyes moist from the wind. I probably looked like them myself; only the absence of wool around my head and neck betrayed the fact that I was a tourist.

I took the phone out of my pocket. Normally, Fiona was the first person I called after such meetings. Not this time.

"You said that I must get you a meeting..." said the voice on the other line.

"Damn it, Ramirez, you could have warned me!" I was still mad at him.

"It always hangs in the balance. The goal is worth the risk." He sounded amused by my anger. "If you hadn't impressed him by making him think you killed me to get to him, he would have wiped you out in a second. And that's if you got a meeting at all."

"You have a history with those items?"

"Not a long one, but very eventful."

I thought I felt a hint of nostalgia in his laughter.

"Andrey is a passionate researcher of ancient civilizations. But his collection barely has anything of the sort. In other words, he heard about my artifacts, he came, asked to buy them, and I flat-out refused..."

"To be honest, he didn't seem happy you're dead," I confided. In the meantime, I felt that the cold was starting to seriously affect my articulation.

"He knows me well enough to figure that the person who managed to kill me is not to be underestimated."

"Just one more thing," I asked. "Who was in charge of the 'drawer bomb' operation? Whoever it was, they did an excellent job. I could see for myself that it must've been exceptionally difficult."

"I told you! I don't train criminals. I make ghosts," he said smugly.

"Everything went according to plan. Good job!"

"I knew that those two artifacts would spin such a story in Andrey's head, and if I just laid low for a day or two, he'd decide I'd been removed by a serious new player. I strengthened your position, no need to thank me!" Ramirez kept showing off.

"Well, it worked. I survived by a hair's breadth, but... I suppose it couldn't have worked any other way. In any case, he already knows you aren't dead. You can stop hiding."

"Got it! The thought that he'd lost me forever probably made him more amenable," he concluded wittily.

During our entire conversion, I could hear the beep from another call. Fiona was about to *melt* the receiver. I interrupted the call with Ramirez to take on the wave of outrage that I could feel coming. Ever since Austin had ensured the confidentiality of our calls, I could no longer save myself with the excuse that we were being listened to.

"Have you lost your fucking mind?!" rang in my ears before I said a word.

"At least I'm alive, thank you for asking! When did you realize I wasn't on schedule?"

"Too fucking long ago! Where were you? You've been unreachable for hours!" She fired her questions so quickly that I wondered how she breathed. "New York was the last time I heard from you! We concocted all kinds of scenarios!"

"Maybe you got close to the truth with one of them. But it's unlikely…"

"I watched you through the security cameras until you left the airport with some goon, and then you vanished completely! I managed to find you just now!"

"Well, they greeted me with a pleasant outing to Mr. Romanov's estate. I realized my phone had no signal, but I figured you could follow through the security cameras. Didn't you hack them?"

As a matter of fact, before I left they assured me they had access to the estate's security cameras.

"We couldn't connect to the network. At all. We must've underestimated Romanov. He was prepared, he deactivated the cameras," she reasoned. "Besides, I didn't really anticipate having to hack into them today. His assistant never gave me a time and date."

My adrenaline surged again. Maybe because I wasn't used to hearing Fiona surprised, unprepared…

Although I was no longer in danger, all the mystery surrounding this meeting made me realize even more clearly how deep in the mud I'd found myself earlier.

"So what happened, Rick?" she asked after a pause, which I used to look around. I couldn't see the stony face anywhere. I'd been walking for a while, naturally using the side streets west of the boulevard. I meant to take a cab to the safe house as soon as I finished my conversation with Fiona.

"It seems that our buddy Ramirez tossed us some pretty

special antiques."

"That was the idea, right? Something that would definitely attract Romanov's attention."

"He executed his task more than perfectly. Only he put *me* on the line."

"What do you mean? Tell me straight!" Fiona insisted.

"The two artifacts really drew his attention. He obviously knew them from before and had tried to buy them from Juan. Of course, he'd refused in his outspoken way."

"So what?" she asked, still baffled. "Why wouldn't he sell them to Ron Price?"

"Obviously Ramirez has never turned you down," I replied sarcastically. "When he sells, he sells. Without demands. If he isn't selling, though, your chance of getting it is only over his dead body..."

"Romanov thought you killed Ramirez?"

"Precisely! Enough for him to have heard that Ramirez hadn't been seen for a while to end up believing in the illusion that I killed him."

"Which would make you a pretty dangerous individual... The sneaky bastard!" she exclaimed with a hint of admiration for Ramirez's audacity.

Even though he nearly got me killed, I agreed with her approval. That fox Ramirez managed to get me a meeting in the shortest time possible and saved me from being initially underestimated by the target to boot.

"I'll organize your return trip. Why are you there, by the way? The safe house is quite far."

"I'm trying to get rid of Romanov's driver. I'm heading over."

"I'll warn Mozzi, he was wondering what's going on."

Only after I returned my hand to my pocket for a second to drop the phone did I realize how frozen it was. I could barely move my fingers. There was a digital clock that showed the temperature on one of the buildings. Minus 8 C, but it felt much colder; the wind was blowing even harder.

I noticed that traffic had increased considerably. One of

the main St. Petersburg boulevards at a peak hour. I stood there with a raised hand for a while before the waves of cars brought what was likely the only available cab around. I'd hoped to find him before Romanov's empty-headed goon saw me.

"*Kuda napravlyayetyes'*?" the driver asked as he sniffed.

"Hermitage," I said stiffly. It was clear what he'd asked.

We joined the thick columns of cars. Many of them spewed dense clouds of carbon smoke. Electric cars weren't exactly winning the race to replace fossil fuels. Luckily, the language barrier spared me from a conversation with the driver.

After we crawled through traffic for 20 minutes, we reached two bronze statues, symmetrically placed on both sides of a bridge. As far as I could see, there was a figure of a fallen man under each of them. Knocked down from a horse, probably. But I couldn't understand why they were naked... Who rides a horse naked?

"*Anichkin most*," the driver explained. Then he clarified, this time in English. "Anichkov Bridge."

I'd never heard of it. As we drove over it, I noticed two identical statues at the other end. Soon, something colorful attracted my attention. I wasn't used to seeing such colors on tall buildings.

A church?

Looked a lot like another one I've seen in Moscow.

"The Savior in Blood," the blondish driver chimed in again. "*Spas na kroki*."

I'd just decided that exhaustion left me indifferent to the city's charms, when we stopped on a giant square. I recognized the Hermitage.

"*Spasibo*." At least I knew how to say thank you.

I paid and took the suitcase out of the trunk. At this point, I couldn't help but be impressed. Even dry and arrogant me.

It was no wonder I'd never seen pictures of the entire square. It was *immense*. There was a tall column in the middle of it, but I quickly ignored it against the backdrop of the Hermitage behind. It was a lot more stunning than I'd imagined. Actually, I'd never really tried to imagine it. During the last 20 years I'd ignored historic, cultural, and all kinds of landmarks.

I copied the safe house's address into my phone's navigation. I knew it was close by and that put me at ease, because I really needed to lay down. According to the directions, no more than ten minutes separated me from my bed.

I was just getting used to the unpleasant wind that pierced my neck when I made it to the apartment building. I took the two key cards which I had moved to my pocket from the suitcase before I loaded it into the cab. I put one of them to the reader, unsuccessfully. It was probably for the apartment door; it had C15 written on the back. The other one did the trick. The signs on the right informed me that C15 was on the 3rd floor.

The seven-story building was old but well-maintained. Once I crossed the apartment's threshold, I established the same thing. It was rather spacious for a safe house. Judging by its size and location, it seemed that this Mozzi character wasn't hiding at all.

I quickly identified the bathroom and my bed. They were all that I needed right now.

Seven hours later, I awoke, prompted by my impatience to get back to HQ and plan my visit to the base of our replacement in Guangzhou, Yon Chey. Although the distances covered and the flights were far from inconsiderable, I was ready to head back. After all, at the cost of generous helpings of stress and adrenaline, the previous day had given me the chance to immediately complete a task that otherwise was of unpredictable duration. Considering that I could have been stuck here for days, I really wouldn't change anything.

I needed strong coffee. Last night I had noticed plenty of coffee shops, so it wasn't going to take long.

Once outside I dialed Fiona, while I looked over the shop windows on both sides of the street. The weather was still gloomy, but at least the wind wasn't howling like last night.

"You can leave tonight. But you'll have a longer layover in

Moscow," Fiona explained.

"How long?"

"Seven hours."

No way!

"Other options?" I asked as I stepped inside a small coffee shop. From the outside, I noticed they had a high-end coffee grinder.

"In four days."

Even more ridiculous!

"Espresso, please," I said to the girl behind the counter and looked around for a place to sit. "What time should I be at the airport?"

"At 8:30 p.m., your plane leaves at 10. I'll send you the boarding cards for all the flights in a bit."

"Thank you. I'll see you tomorrow, hopefully."

"More like the day after. We'll pick you up from Tacoma."

The growl of my stomach reminded me I hadn't eaten anything since yesterday morning. That was normal for me during a mission, but it really made me feel unwell. Unfortunately, I lost weight very easily. After a hunt, I regularly dropped to 84 kg, and the 10 kg difference made me look scrawny. Luckily, this hunt was over in less than a day.

"Would you like anything else?" the girl asked in proper English with the characteristic Russian accent. She must've noticed I was eyeing the baked goods.

"I'd like three of these," I said, pointing to one of the trays of small round cookies.

"*Pryaniki,*" she explained as she arranged them in a porcelain saucer. "250 rubles, please."

"And one order of these," I added pointing to the pelmeni dumplings in the hot food stand. At least I knew what to expect from those.

I sat on one of the barstools by the wooden counter at the window. It wasn't often that I had free time to manage. I had the whole day ahead of me. If I was the tourist type, I would have been more than happy to have ten hours at my disposal in St. Petersburg. For me though, these were 600 minutes stolen from the mission. There was no landmark or sight in the world capable of removing it from my mind.

5.

The only thing that made me forget my murderous headache for a moment was the sunny weather in Seattle. It was at least 15º C warmer than in St. Petersburg. The time difference, the distance covered, and the meeting with Romanov may have been a bit too much for me, even with my level of tolerance.

My phone had been off since I boarded the plane in St. Petersburg. As expected, the first message was from Fiona.

We'll wait for you at HQ, something came up.

I had asked myself why they felt the need to pick me up from the airport. The meeting with Romanov truly was a turning point in our mission. Its success had clearly excited everyone.

As I walked to the exit, I couldn't stop thinking about the *newly emerged* problem. That phrase seldom came without consequence. If it was, Fiona wouldn't have mentioned it at all. On the other hand, she was unlikely to have mentioned a serious problem in a message instead of discussing it at HQ.

"The Tech Progress building, please," I instructed the driver. As usual, I avoided eye contact so as to not look like I was interested in conversation.

"Belltown?" he asked without even looking, which put me at ease.

After all these years of hunting, replacements, and the pursuit of our final goal, I barely registered the fact that we had done quite well as entrepreneurs. We may have built Tech as a cover for what we were doing underneath, but with time it had become one of Seattle's most emblematic buildings. We were yet to establish whether its location in one of the city's most affluent neighborhoods benefited our mission or put it at risk, but it was certainly a gold mine from an investment point of view.

Twenty minutes later the cab dropped me off by the main gate. Naturally, it wasn't meant for me. But we didn't use invisible sliding doors like in a cartoon either. Our entrance was at the lowest level of the underground garage. A door at the bottom of the security room. It wasn't super innovative, but it did an excellent job. All three security guard shifts were staffed by our members. Just like every Tuesday and Thursday, Johnny Penn was at his post today. He was one of the youngsters who had been working with us for three years. A self-taught hacker, he was also Slim's protege.

"Hi Johnny," I greeted him without hiding my intention to quickly open the door behind him.

"Congratulations on Romanov, boss!"

I looked toward HQ and noticed that everyone was gathered around Matt's computer. It seemed like there were more people than usual. They still hadn't heard me.

As I walked over, I counted four more people with Fiona, Matt, and Slim. When I got closer, I recognized them – three boys and a girl. They were some of our other computer specialists. They wouldn't be here otherwise; only ITs came to HQ.

"Glad to see you, boss!" As usual, Fiona was the first to notice me.

"I hope I'll have at least a few days at my disposal before you send me out again. Is everything organized for China?" I asked as I pulled up a chair.

"There's a small change of plan," Fiona began. Evidently, she was to have the honor of dropping the bomb. "Does the name Layla Pierce mean anything to you?"

"I'm not sure." I vaguely remembered hearing it, but that was all. "Should that name mean something to me?"

Fiona opened one of the folders on screen and picked one of about twenty files. Three pictures filled the screen. A beautiful woman, probably about my age. I didn't know her. At this stage, I could establish nothing else.

"Layla Pierce," Fiona repeated. "An investigative journalist, one of the best in the country. Corruption and fraud at the highest levels of government are her specialty. Actually..."

The short pause added to the tension which was already starting to irritate me.

"Actually what?" I spurred her on.

"The senator Preston and Thomas Mason saga in 2005 was one of her first serious cases."

I finally understood their unease but didn't find it to be justified. After all, I'd long accepted this as part of my life.

"Alright," I said flatly. "It seems that the lady swam in the gutter that took my father's life. At least she preserved hers..."

"Yes, you could say she only lost her job. At the time, she'd just started to work for one of the most prestigious political publications," Fiona explained. "After a few articles that were highly critical of the senator, she left. She worked at two other newspapers over the next few years. As far as I could find out, her name is associated with more trouble than it's worth for media owners. It seems that for her, freedom of speech remains an ideal, despite all the censorship they tried to impose on her."

"Admirable! But I still haven't heard anything that would call for a change in *our* plan," I remarked hastily.

Matt turned his chair toward me and took on the task of enlightening me on what was clearly evading me.

"For some time now, we've noticed increased searches for your name. Key terms like Ian Dunne, Jeffrey Dunne's son, Africa, etc., and all of them from the same IP address. The red flags started flying."

"We've seen similar searches before, but never as systematic," Fiona added.

"Let her search for whatever she wants," I instinctively reacted. "I've yet to hear why that should bother us, let alone make us change our schedule. I have no intention of wasting time with reporters."

"Right, but after we checked her articles, we found one about Miles Bush," Slim chimed in.

He spoke so rarely that in such cases we immediately stopped talking to hear him out.

"In a series of pieces she did on the 2016 Athens power plant explosion... She tried to connect it to Miles."

Now *that* explained their concern. Miles Bush was one of my all-time favorite identities. It was a pity that we only went on one hunt together – the recruitment of the Greek magnate Alexis Khoros.

Not all our investors came from the criminal world. Many of them were entrepreneurs and businessmen whose past and development made them suitable to have a place among us. Money was an important, but far from the only, requirement for admission.

Khoros was one of those enterprising individuals who carried the passion for victory in their blood. Although his origins didn't in any way indicate the status he had achieved over the years, he started to build it in his youth. Slowly and methodically. While his peers played, he studied. While they went through their first romantic thrills, he worked to support his widowed mother. From a sausage workshop, through a photo studio, a framing store, to a real estate agency. These seven years quickly filled out his leadership qualities with the necessary experience and contacts to support his way up. And so on, until he became one of the richest businessmen in Greece. Nonetheless, he never forgot where he came from, his city, the people in need, his country. He continuously donated to schools, foster homes and nursing homes, and organized charitable and educational initiatives.

Since people like him were a rarity, we couldn't judge him for having his doubts regarding me and our organization as a whole. This required a demonstration of our capabilities. On one hand, it needed to provide spectacular and irrefutable proof of our organization's reach, and on the other, it had to avoid victims, just as we always did.

Well, that mission really made us sweat!

"So what did she find out about Miles?" I wondered. "At the end of the day, they declared the blast was an accident due to negligence, right? Miles's name was never mentioned in the media."

"Except in her blog," Fiona countered. "Luckily, her publications didn't get much circulation. Just as we hoped, mainstream media opted to sweep it under the rug and didn't give her articles any publicity. No one wants to dwell on such incidents at a state-run facility."

We looked at each other with disappointment. It was the moment we realized we'd overlooked information that damaged us.

"Honestly, we're still trying to figure out how she managed to dig Bush up. He was a fabrication meant to exist in official registers just long enough for you to move from point A to point B. Athens, in this case," Matt mused.

"I think you're starting to understand why we want you to talk to her," Fiona stated. "She's digging too deep for us to ignore. The fact that the same person managed to get any information on the existence of Miles Bush, and then searched for Ian Dunne, means that there's a real danger of them putting two and two together at some point."

Her tone betrayed a concern that I very rarely observed. And it was warranted.

"What about the articles?" I only now thought to ask. "What do they say exactly?"

"Fortunately, very little," Matt said with a barely noticeable smile. "She looked at the flight manifests around the days of the incident. She came across Miles's name, and she thought the lack of any information about him suspicious. She wrote that it was as if he were born to go to Greece and disappear after his short stay there."

"It seems her readers found all of that too conspiracy-minded and didn't pay much attention to these articles," Fiona interjected.

"In the meantime, the official version of a tragic incident has settled comfortably enough between the lines," I concluded.

This woman was obviously a bloodhound. We needed

to be especially careful with her kind. I looked at her pictures again. I was disturbed to realize that the things that I had just learned about her somehow made her stand out in my mind. Layla Pierce was a danger. A beautiful one.

Fiona's voice brought me out of my thoughts.

"You need to speak to her, boss. This woman isn't just digging for a sensation or out of curiosity. We read dozens of her articles. She's a *fighter*. Truth and justice are the motives that drive her, and she's sacrificed plenty for that."

"Do you think we should recruit her?"

Fiona nodded with an expression that confirmed the answer was obvious.

"Why is she more inappropriate than other targets?" Slim asked. "She could be just as useful. Besides, it'd be nice to have someone else on the team from whom a stab in the back wouldn't be an actual possibility."

I laughed. He was right! Even though we had many members with proven values and morals, it was also true that we were yet to find out if a wolf can truly change its skin. Or rather, put back on its original, considerably more honest one. The fact that they were among us was a manifestation of our belief that our environment and context are the main factors that place us in the category of good or bad. For now, every member had convinced us in one way or another of their capacity to go along with the change that was to occur on a global level. Because each one of them believed that transitory power in a world of deceit and compromised values is an extremely low bar when compared to what we offered – to mark the beginning of a radical reform with a sustainable perspective, unlike the current system, which would forever remain attached to one-night stands.

We'd all seen enough of this world. No half measures were going to shake the establishment.

The house always wins.

The game seemed to give and give – freedom of choice, entertainment, profit, and social mobility. But actually, it managed to limit our ambition to little more than the above. And convinced us of how dear it was, how vitally important.

And it was going to continue. The direction needed to change, and it was now or never.

"I've prepared Pierce's addresses, both home and office," Fiona said, pulling me back out of my thoughts. "There's an early flight to New York tomorrow morning, if you feel like you're up to it."

"We have no time to waste," I answered. "We all agree I need to speak to her, so let's do it!"

After we discussed my St. Petersburg adventures, my meeting with Romanov, and, finally, Ramirez's ingenuity, I headed over to my apartment. Finally. For some years now, I resided comfortably on the ninth floor of the Tech building. We had designed it for a multifunctional role, both office and residential.

Riding the elevator always amused me. All these people that had no idea of what was going on literally under their noses.

After a few minutes, I finally reached my apartment's door. I needed at least one quiet night. I missed the night view of Seattle.

I opened the boarding card that Fiona had sent me. The flight was early in the morning, I needed to be at the airport by 6 a.m. I looked up Pierce's addresses. Both her place and her office were in Chelsea. She lived on 22nd and 8th Avenue, and her office was right next door to her, much like mine.

6.

I left JFK and took yet another cab to get to Chelsea. At this time of day, the trip was likely to take at least 40 minutes, and I had to hope that Ms. Pierce worked regular office hours, so I could avoid having to go to her apartment.

I felt a sense of excitement, this time of a slightly different character. It was as if I were about to reunite with an old friend.

What was behind this feeling? On one hand, she

seemed to know the story that branded my life forever. On the other, she was getting increasingly close to my life now.

In New York, I felt like I was on my turf. Some of my carefree years were spent here. College, friends, dreams... I didn't remember what it was like to live like that anymore. Chelsea, however, was one of the neighborhoods I didn't know well. Of course, technology made that irrelevant.

I watched the madness outside as the cab crawled along. Empty eyes, autopilot... what was started by social media saw its completion during the pandemic. This pattern made the end of interaction inevitable. Online communication still successfully masked the absence of actual contact, real and face to face. The virus had made people afraid of closeness. The new era gave them the virtual world, and COVID locked them inside. Sometimes I wondered if that process was at all reversible, even with the actions we had planned.

The cab pulled over in front of Pierce's gray apartment building. It had two entrances; the left one was hers. The office was a few hundred meters away. I meant to walk there. I had just stepped onto 8th Avenue when, to my surprise, I saw her walk out of a bakery across the street. The pictures I'd seen at HQ helped me recognize her. She was smaller than I'd imagined. Somehow more fragile than my preconceived image of an investigative reporter.

Her long, fiery red hair flowed casually down to her waist. Her pace was rhythmic and nimble despite the high heels on her boots. She had a large paper cup in one hand and a brown bag with telltale grease spots in the other.

I impatiently waited for the light to turn green so I could cross over and follow her. I looked around, wondering how many more pieces of junk needed to drive by before allowing me to go after her. To calm the vein insistently pulsating on my forehead, I reminded myself that I knew where she was going.

As expected, by the time I finally got across, she was long out of my sight. After two blocks I turned left and walked for a bit before checking my location on the phone. I was heading the right way and was very close to her office. Fifty meters later, the app let me know I'd reached my destination.

The building had three entrances, and her office was in the middle. I needed to find a way to introduce myself and convince her to let me in. I'd underestimated that detail. Luckily, the door opened and the lady who came out spared me the inconvenience. Or at least delayed it another two minutes, when I was to fully experience it at Pierce's doorstep. I walked past the lady and reached out to catch the door before it closed.

"Are you here to see someone?" she shouted after me.

"Layla Pierce."

"Oh, alright then. Second floor, I think," the lady added cordially.

As in many other apartment buildings in New York, this one had no elevator.

I looked at the second-floor hallway in front of me. There were ten doors evenly spread on both sides. I walked forward, trying to find B8 as Fiona had instructed me. I saw it at the end of the corridor and once again remembered that I needed a way to introduce myself. Then I stopped fooling myself. I was going to improvise as usual.

In the meantime, a man walked out of Pierce's office. I examined him thoroughly. He was probably a bit older than me, with a suit, a leather bag, and slicked-back hair. I bet he wasn't a colleague. Maybe a lawyer.

Once in front of B8, I wondered if a few prepared lines might not be a bad strategy after all. My arm's robotic motion outpaced the answer that I never gave. I knocked twice as per protocol and went inside.

"My answer is still *no!*" Layla said calmly, but very firmly, without looking up from the notebook in which she was writing something. After receiving no reply, she looked up and gaped at me from behind the glasses on her nose.

"I'm sorry, I thought you're someone else," she said and

181

put the glasses on the desk.

She had twisted her hair up in a small bun. It should have looked more conservative, but in fact had the exact opposite effect. Her white face blended with the soft afternoon light that flowed from the window behind the chair.

"Can I help you?" she asked, seemingly nearly convinced that I was some sort of halfwit. I remained quiet for at least three minutes.

"Maybe I should help *you*," I answered pointedly.

"Oh yeah?" she laughed, probably dismayed by the dumb reply.

I had no idea where this smart-ass attitude was coming from – I couldn't remember behaving like this since high school.

"And how would you help me, Mr....?" she asked with sincere curiosity.

"... Dunne."

Her face froze immediately. She didn't find things as funny anymore.

"Dunne as in..."

"As in Ian Dunne. As in Jeffrey Dunne," I said slowly as I walked to her desk.

It took seven steps to reach it. I felt a lot better now that I had wrested control of the situation and Layla Pierce was studying me like a quantum physicist would study a chunk of dark matter. I pulled over the chair set against the wall and sat across from her.

"I figured that you may need assistance. It seems like you're trying to find information about me."

It could have just been my imagination, but she seemed disturbed by the fact that I'd caught her in the act, so to speak. It took her about five seconds to recover her businesslike attitude.

"And why do you think so?" she asked coolly.

"I don't know... Ian Dunne, Jeffrey Dunne's son, Dunne's Central, Africa," I enumerated slightly theatrically. "You have been very tenaciously performing keyword searches, Miss Pierce. So I guessed that I could be of assistance."

"Interesting." She folded her arms on her chest and leaned back. "And did you know that cyber espionage is a serious crime in the United States, Mr. Dunne?"

"Indeed, and also extremely difficult to prove. But you know that full well, I believe..."

Although she was playing her hand skillfully, it was obvious that she knew nothing of our activities.

"So you've come to warn me to not stick my nose where it doesn't belong?" she asked and winced. She pushed her chair forward to the desk and rested her folded arms on top. "It looks like my curiosity made you nervous. If I were to trust my professional instincts, I'd bet you're hiding something."

"Maybe... But maybe I've come to do the exact opposite," I suggested. "Now you have the chance to drink straight from the source. What would you like to know, Ms. Pierce? How did I come to your attention?" I asked as I evaluated the environment. I was trying to learn as much as possible about her. I noticed that the rest of her office was very neat.

She stood up and very slowly walked around the desk. She stopped and leaned on it not very far from my knees.

Without being much of a psychologist, I could sense that my snooping around irritated her. She preferred that I focus on her. She was certainly focused on me.

I could see her trying to measure me up, torn between what she knew about the poor orphan whose dramatic story she had followed from the front row, and the jerk she was now playing cat and mouse with.

"I'm not sure how well acquainted you are with my work, Mr. Dune. My resolution is relentless. I cannot stand injustices, and I never let off once I've smelled one. In this case, I mean senator Preston." She paused for a moment, expecting some reaction from me. She didn't get one. "Since I first came across his treachery in your father's case 20 years ago, I've never stopped trying to uncover compromising materials about him."

She paused again. Once more, I didn't react. I just motioned for her to continue.

"Back then, he got away with it. He's been getting away with it ever since. At his point, though, I believe I have enough evidence against him. When I was covering the 2005 case, I obviously found out that Jeffrey Dunne had a son. I found out that you'd gone to Africa and given most of the proceeds you received from the sale of your father's building to charity."

I listened to her carefully, searching for an indication that she'd connected my real identity to that of Miles Bush. I still didn't register one.

"I'm glad you found me first. Either way, my intention was to get in touch with you soon for two reasons," she continued. "First, I assumed there's a possibility that after all these years, you'd found information that would help me expose Preston. But even if you haven't, I believe that you deserve to be part of this in the name of your parents. I think it's only right that we fight this battle together."

I couldn't hide from myself the fact that her attitude moved me. My intuition was telling me to ignore my initial concern and reveal our mission to her and try and recruit her.

I could now claim with certainty that she hadn't made the connections that would threaten us. This gave me the chance to just tell her that I don't know anything else about Preston, and I thank her for her sympathy, but would rather stand aside from it all and return to my own tasks. Only in the course of our conversation, it became clear that she was an honest and capable individual with a genuine sense of justice. These three reasons were enough for me to act.

As I conducted this internal dialog, Pierce went back behind the desk.

"So, what do you think? Are we going to fight together?"

I stood up. I always felt more comfortable moving during such conversations. It helped me focus.

"First of all, I'm impressed by your willingness to devote your life and career to pursuing the truth. Many of your colleagues sacrificed it to gain promotions or acclaim, which in our day comes with more censorship than facts."

I slowly paced back and forth and tried to look in her direction as little as possible. Her reactions affected me more than my concentration could allow.

"Yes, Ms. Pierce. I do believe that we should fight together."

I was about to continue, but she interrupted.

"I'm glad to hear that, Ian. It won't be easy, but we *have* to do it," she answered with emotion, which I found flattering.

"Oh, you have no idea of how hard it will be. The battle is of a much larger magnitude than you imagine."

"So I'm assuming that you have more facts at your disposal. That's fantastic."

"I have a lot more, Layla." I accepted her invitation to use our first names. "What I'm fighting for is global change. Radical change."

I looked at her. She was clearly not understanding, and I decided it made sense to lead her directly into the deep end. There was no need to beat around the bush, put on an act and such. Layla was someone with an outlook like ours. I thought it over for a second and reached the conclusion that even if the idea of such a fight frightened her, she wouldn't misuse the information.

She didn't look away, expecting me to continue.

"You probably noticed that Ian Dunne evaporated after he left for Africa," I started.

"I heard you did some great things there," she remarked. I ignored her, I didn't like recognition.

"I'll try to introduce you to the second half of my life as briefly as possible. One of the projects that I worked on in Africa gave me the chance to meet a brilliant IT engineer. To our mutual surprise, our points of view coincided to a degree where his and my abilities became the prerequisite for realization."

185

"Realization of what... ?" Layla raised her brow.

"Let's begin with the essentials," I suggested. "My father's case and the things I discovered about the system, power and injustice, left me truly disgusted with the world. Up to the moment I met my first ally, I'd spent years thinking about where the world was headed and what could cause a radical change in politics, the legislative system, media, education, the environment... When we established how aligned our viewpoints were, we also realized that if we could find capable and skilled allies and enough resources, we could initiate the beginning of change."

Layla seemed completely surprised by the turn of our conversation. If I was reading her expression correctly, I could even discern pity. All of this probably sounded to her like a naive and absurd utopia.

"Right... Yes," she muttered. "It sounds good, but..."

"There's no way it could work," I interrupted. "Not peacefully and quietly. It quickly became apparent to us that the moral degradation of those in power would require a complete uprooting of their influence and a shift in the direction in which they lead humanity. Laws, heads of state, governments... Brainwashing with superficial values and detrimental models of behavior," I added.

"I'm having thoughts that I don't like, Ian," she admitted. "I think that our paths are beginning to diverge."

"It isn't our path, Layla. Our methods differ. You believe that by revealing the truth, you'll bring about change. It doesn't work. At most, you may get retribution for one person. Or two, or three..."

I kept pacing, doing my best to keep my emotions from overwhelming my voice.

"I've devoted years to make this change possible. And I'm succeeding. I run a global network with members in more than 50 countries. I don't want to lie to you; our path is neither peaceful, nor fair."

"What are you telling me, Ian? That you mean to organize a massive coup, because you're disappointed by all the injustice around us?" she quipped sarcastically. "And what, you'll change the world with 10,000 people?"

"More like 30 times that number," I quickly calculated. I didn't really know precisely, but counting our instruments, it was a lot more.

The pink hue on Layla's face quickly went pale.

"Yes, quite a few of us," I remarked calmly. "Radical measures require radical means. And those who are currently giving and distributing global capital now are, as you can imagine, not part of our plan. Our money comes from elsewhere."

"Just say it. And I hope it isn't what I'm thinking," Layla interrupted me sharply.

"And why not? As if all these presidents and prime ministers, with their loyal entourages of corrupt judges, prosecutors, and all the other protectors of 'law and order' – as if they're any better? All their greed and arrogance, all their schemes and theater, is that something we should just settle for? Put up with it and hope that the next one won't be too corrupt?" I could feel myself getting angry. "Believe me, I've found a lot more honor and justice in the underworld than in in the US Congress!"

"God!" Layla blurted and then sighed inside her palms, which she'd raised to her face. "Do you really believe that the mafia has a place in government?"

"We aren't the mafia, Layla," I corrected her. "We're not exactly diplomats. As far as the people we work with, we don't ally with just anyone. I can assure you that money, although extremely important to the organization, is far from being the sole or even the leading selection criteria." After a few seconds of hesitation, I continued, "Our members can be either investors or instruments. To date, we've attracted more than 300 organizations. They're our investors. You have a good idea of what such structures are like, so you can estimate the human and financial capital."

Layla stared at me, increasingly horrified by the scale of my "deception."

"And your instruments?" she asked dryly. "Who are they?"

"Specialists from all fields relevant to the overhaul of the system – technology, medicine, architecture, green engineering, construction, and pretty much every scientific field you can think of... The ones that will help us build solid foundations for the future."

She didn't hear her own profession in the list, but it was far from complete, anyway.

"Alright, but what would happen to international relations?" she insisted. "How would government policies be discussed? The participants will shoot at each other over a round table and whoever survives, decides? Is that your solution, Ian?" she concluded angrily.

It was in the cards... that she could disagree. Maybe it was too soon to tell her about our organization? Maybe I was too direct? I hadn't even told her what we *really* did, the essence of our mission. I could only imagine how she would take the part about supplanting all world leaders...

I sat back on the chair across from her to shorten the distance and cool the situation down. "Look, I can understand your suspicion. I can't say that I didn't expect it. Maybe I should even apologize for involving you without asking for your consent. After what you've just learned, nothing will be the same anymore."

I paused for a few seconds. I gave her time to prepare. I had recognized that the moment for her to decide was close. She took a breath and sat back again, while I continued. "The way I see it, you have two options. One," I lifted the index finger on my right hand, "I walk away, and you try to live like before. Only you can't, because now you know something that threatens the lives of many, many people. You could betray me, but you won't. Because you'll realize that you'd be depriving the world of a chance for a better future. You'd be condemning it to the past and present that you've been fighting your entire life. So, you'll just wait. Day after day, you'll wait to find out if what I shared with you is true."

I spoke slowly and calmly, without removing my eyes from hers. They seemed to show that she was living through every single one of the cards I was putting on the table. Still, she didn't move.

I lifted the index and middle fingers of my left hand to indicate the second option. "Or you could do otherwise." I turned my wrist to show her the display of my watch. "We could be at my HQ in Seattle shortly after midnight. Come with me and see with your own eyes before you pick a side."

Layla's expression told me that she knew how to make immediate decisions. Even one like that! In a fraction of a second, she cycled through about five facial expressions. I interpreted them in the following order:

What?

Are you crazy?!

Maybe I should go.

Do I need luggage?

Fuck it!

"Give me half an hour," she finished out loud, once again back to her comfortable, businesslike demeanor. With lightning speed, she scooped up her phone and notebook in one hand. "Let's go!" She motioned with her free hand. "I need to get a few things from my place."

Before I knew it, Layla was waiting for me by the door. I didn't even see her get the purse and coat that hung on her hand. I walked past her, wondering if I'd made a mistake. I felt more nervous than usual, especially when I recognized the length of the flight we were to share. Six and a half hours made for a pretty long first date.

"Could you please hold this?" She shoved everything she was holding, minus the coat, into my hands and locked the door.

Maybe I don't need to be nervous; it seemed like the ice was breaking quickly between us.

Layla darted ahead of me and her heels rhythmically clacked on the floor.

"Ready. Thank you," she said and stretched her hand out as she pulled the gray coat on.

I handed her the notebook, the phone, and the purse. Until a very short time ago, I considered this a pathetic scene – a man with a purse walking three steps behind his wife.

7.

It was dusk. At this time of year, less than an hour separated 5 p.m. from darkness.

Aside from a couple of logistical questions from Layla, we walked briskly to her place mostly in silence.

"Give me seven minutes," she shouted before climbing up the stairs to the front door.

I secretly hoped she would be late. I wanted her to irritate me with at least something, so I could start perceiving her like just another associate, and nothing more. While I waited for her, I watched with restlessness as the traffic swelled. Against the backdrop of the incoming darkness, the red stoplights of the cars multiplied and became denser and denser, like dozens of alarms going off in my head reminding me we were chasing a flight.

I consciously restricted any other thoughts. I counted on my tunnel vision to return me to my customary autopilot working state. Any type of emotion was about the last thing I needed.

Right before the seventh minute, with relief and a measure of satisfaction, I verified that Layla still wasn't here. But the squeaking door behind my back a moment later disturbed my peace. The telltale rhythm of the steps confirmed it was her, although it wasn't the sound of heels.

My hopes were completely dashed. First, she was right on the dot, and second, she had foresight. Only now did I realize how absurd the high heels would have looked at HQ. Somehow, she'd accounted for that too. I turned around and with irritation noticed the third thing – she wasn't dragging a huge suitcase like I'd expect from someone with her appearance.

I had to reconcile myself with it. Obviously, to *not* be charmed by Layla Pierce was going to cost me considerable effort.

The bag she had, if you could even call it that, was twice

the size of her purse. No wonder she'd packed in four minutes.

"We're leaving from JFK, right?" she asked as she walked toward me.

"At eight," I confirmed. "We have time, as long as we manage to get a cab in the next five minutes."

"It'll be here in three," she said right next to me. "I called one while I was packing."

We stood next to each other on the sidewalk like schoolchildren at a bus stop. At least that's how I felt.

"The last time I went to Seattle was last year." The breath she exhaled floated forward like a thin fog and vanished, carried away by the cold wind. The red lights of the cars reflected off her cheekbones making her even more beautiful. "The flight was pretty long. We'll land around 2:30 a.m., right?"

"11:30 p.m. local time," I replied.

In the meantime, the cab pulled over.

"JFK?" the driver asked as soon as I opened the back door for Layla.

"That's us," she said as she slid over to the driver's side to make room for me and spare me the walk around the cab.

She sat against the opposite door and put her purse and bag between us. She took her phone out, and I inadvertently looked at the display, its brightness nailing my attention in the dark. I saw a list of hotels she must've checked earlier. This woman was multifunctional in the full sense of the word... I guess it was normal, given her occupation. And I needed to stop blowing her qualities out of proportion.

"What side of town is your HQ on? Or are we heading to your place? Just so I know where to get a hotel room."

"HQ is in the basement. When it comes to comfort, I've outdone even you. They're in the same building."

"You're living my dream!" she joked.

"I have a neighbor that rents his apartment to visitors, if you'd like. He's on the floor below. As far as comfort, it's a pretty adequate option."

"Sounds good," she agreed looked out the window. Then she leaned toward me again.

"So how come your HQ is in the basement?" she quietly asked with genuine curiosity.

"Well…"

"So either your base is pretty small," she interrupted. "Or the building is huge."

It was my turn to lean toward her.

"My HQ is definitely not small," I said conspiratorially.

Demonstratively, and in the spirit of our little act, Layla returned to her spot. "We'll see about that," she replied with mock severity.

Somehow, I could feel that we both felt comfortable in each other's company. We spent the rest of the trip in silence. Immersed in our own thoughts, and Layla – occasionally in her phone.

We made it to the airport a bit before 6:30 p.m. Right on time.

As soon as I stepped into the terminal, I headed for the security line out of habit.

"I need to get my boarding card from the check-in," Layla stopped me. She had booked her flight from the cab.

"You don't have it on your phone?" I said, surprised.

"I couldn't check in so soon before the flight," she explained quickly, already a few meters away.

There were so many flights in my life that it seemed absurd for me to not know this detail. Thanks to Fiona, I never had to think of such things.

"Get in line, I'll be there in a minute," she turned back and shouted. She was at least six or seven meters away, and I realized that my eyes were still fixed on her, even though my thoughts had wandered.

I did what she said, but it annoyed me.

I would have thought of that, thank you!

Even my favorite JFK was an unpleasant place at this time. Crammed with locals and tourists to the point where you needed to shout just to hear your own voice. Not to speak of the exotic compilation of languages that confused my thoughts. And still, I preferred that to the alien feeling that came over me in

Layla's presence.

Some 15 minutes later, I saw her trotting over. I raised my hand so she could see me in the crowd. Luckily for her, I had moved quite ahead, but she had to withstand the disapproving looks as she made her way to me. She swiftly squeezed under the black rope that kept the line in an S-shape.

When she finally went through, her embarrassment was betrayed by the redness of her cheeks, regardless of how hard she tried to hide it. I don't know if it was in contrast to that, or because of the white light in the terminal, but I only now noticed her eyes. I had so far ignored them, too busy with her general demeanor.

Green, deep, unending, just like the Amazon jungle. I once had to spend some time in such a place. In Peru, seven years ago. Now I was experiencing the same feeling – excitement and adrenaline from the unpredictable danger ahead of me.

The approaching echo of her voice brought me back to the jungle in the terminal.

"Where's your seat?" she repeated. Shouted, actually. This time I heard her very clearly.

"37B, toward the back."

"You got away!" she joked. "I'm in front, 4A."

We went through security relatively quickly, considering the long lines. In my experience, this was one of the few airports where nearly all lines were open. I rarely saw one that wasn't.

We were doing well on time, and thanks to that, the tedious wait at the gate was cut down to a minimum, only 20 minutes.

"Boarding card, please!" the airline clerk asked politely at the gate.

I handed my phone over. Layla, who was right next to me, started to feverishly fumble through her purse. It seemed she had put her card away while we waited.

Finally, something annoying!

"Please go ahead, Mr. Evans." The clerk handed me the phone back, and Layla raised her wide open eyes to me, surprised by what she'd heard. She didn't move them away as she handed her card over.

We walked inside the jetway.

"Mr. Evans?" Layla retorted shortly after and looked away as if I'd betrayed her.

"Rick Evans," I introduced myself. "Today I spoke and heard my real name for the first time in a very, very long while."

"Why?" she asked with a degree of compassion.

We were standing increasingly closer to each other. On one hand, we were whispering, and on the other, it was getting crowded.

"No one needs Ian Dunne at the moment. No one has in a long time. I'm known as Rick even to my own team, although they do know my real name."

"Don't you miss it?" she asked. She didn't seem to believe this was easier for me.

"I'm Rick Evans. I live inside his mind and with his mission."

I looked around to make sure no one was listening. I realized I could hardly see anyone but her... "Ian's life ended with the death of his parents," I added.

Meanwhile, as the jetway took a turn, Layla stumbled, lost her balance, and fell right into my arms. What a cliché!

I've lived too many clichés in the last few hours.

Layla got back on her own feet and we both straightened ourselves up. Our conversation's natural conclusion coincided with the incident, and since our seats were at opposite ends, I headed to the back.

"See you later," I smiled. We were supposed to land sometime before midnight.

I headed to my seat with a great degree of relief. I worried that just one more hour spent with her would awaken things in me that I consciously kept dormant. During my missions, I often came across attractive women. And even though I couldn't complain of a lack of attention, I always perceived them as a beautiful accessory that my targets used to showcase their wealth and power. Nothing more.

With Layla, it was different. I couldn't get her out of my mind for the entire flight. Finally, after three hours of consideration, I reached the conclusion that my best strategy would be to just stop thinking about all the reasons that made this woman so interesting to me. It was futile to resist it. Something could happen at some point, at some stage of our acquaintance, or it would just fizzle out with time... The important thing was that none of it mattered now. My focus needed to be fully committed to the mission. Anything surrounding it could happen or not happen, without affecting the goal I'd been pursuing since I was 25.

Three hours, two tiny packets of pretzels, and a liter of mineral water later, I seriously needed to use the restroom. Despite that, I sacrificed a few minutes trying to decide whether to go to the one behind me or the one in front and ahead of Layla. It wasn't the best excuse, but it would do.

I abruptly shook these thoughts off. Maybe it was the pressing biological need that sobered me up; I really felt like slapping my own face. Every second I let my mind wander beyond my conscious control, it raced toward her! And I hadn't even known her for half a day!

During the second half of the flight, I made sure to clear my head up by watching the dumbest movie possible. It was absurd, considering all the important things I had to reflect on. I knew myself well. Rick Evans, Ian Dunne, and the other four. This state of mind wasn't characteristic of any of us. So I opted for a cheap action flick to numb my thoughts instead of letting menial thoughts disturb my strategy.

Right on schedule, our plane landed at Tacoma, two minutes before 11:30 p.m. I felt fully energetic. After all, I had woken up in the same time zone this morning.

I joined Layla and we headed out. In her time zone, these were the early hours of the new day. Regardless, she didn't seem tired.

"So, how do you feel?" I asked her.

"Alright. Lately, my schedule's been pretty similar. I go

to bed early, I wake up around 2 a.m., I write until four and then go back to sleep."

"So you managed to sleep during the flight?"

"The first phase is complete," she nodded. "If I can get to a pillow in the next two or three hours, you'll barely take me out of my comfort zone."

If she only knew how far from the truth that was! Soon, she wouldn't be able to remember what a comfort zone was.

We left the terminal quickly, as usual. When we stepped out, we headed for the first cab in sight.

"Belltown, please," I said to the driver.

"Belltown?" Layla seemed surprised as she whispered: "You aren't even trying to hide."

I imagined the 11 floors under which I was actually hiding and smirked.

We drove toward Tech Progress. Layla was exploring the city through the cab's window, while I tried to figure out what to do with her phone. I really wasn't worried about her, but I couldn't afford to be negligent. After all, I knew full well what could be achieved with such a device. Considering her work, I didn't exclude the possibility that someone was keeping an eye on her.

About 15 minutes later I could see the giant letters lit up in bright green that made our building stand out from its surroundings.

"You can pull over here." I pointed to the sidewalk on the right.

We were two blocks from Tech. Layla started to look around, probably searching for a building high enough to house an HQ in its basement.

"Are you still feeling alright?" I asked.

"Depends. What do you mean?"

I took a step back and pointed to the bar behind me. One of the ten we ran in key points of the city. They were all under 24-hour surveillance. Naturally, they were all staffed with our people, and there was no need to hide.

196

"Let's go in for a bit," I suggested. "I'd like you to know a few things before we continue forward."

"Okay," she agreed, without much enthusiasm.

I opened the heavy door for her. The bar was called Chester's. The name was one of the few things from my past that I allowed. I did think of my old friend once in a while.

"The coziest HQ I've ever visited," she said quietly as she walked past me to get inside.

I didn't answer. I pointed to the bottom of the empty saloon. She chose one of the last booths.

I looked over the bar and rang the bell to announce my presence. I tried to remember whose shift it was. Andrew beat me to it by coming out of the storage room. Good kid. I'd known him for six years. We let him and his brother, Jim, manage Chester's. Orphans from a very young age, Andrew raised his little brother on his own. He raised him to be hard working, honest, and brave. We didn't let such people slip.

"Hello," he greeted me with some reservation. He wasn't sure if I was under cover.

"Good to see you, Andrew." I indicated that I wasn't hiding. "Could you please get me a mint tea, and..." I turned to Layla.

"The same," she said as she sat on the cherry-red bench.

"Coming up!" Andrew answered.

While he walked away across the chessboard tiles on the floor, I noticed the whimsical expression on Layla's face.

"Mint tea, a pub... hard rock..." she added after pausing to listen. "I'm really beginning to wonder how you managed to drag me all the way here, *Rick*!"

I remained serious.

"Listen, this isn't a game," I assured her. "You're yet to find out why you're here. To begin with, I must ask you to remove the SIM card from your phone and leave it here."

"Seriously? After all the things you told me in New York, you're worried about a phone?"

"Believe me, I know perfectly well what technology can do. I know what we're capable of achieving, and I don't believe we're the only ones taking advantage of that. The nature of your job makes it possible."

In the meantime, Andrew brought the tea. After he left, Layla took the phone out of her purse and followed my request. Seconds later, she turned it off and left it on the table with the card.

"What now?" she asked nervously.

"Soon I'll take you to a place that only my team associates me with. Have you heard of Tech Progress?"

"Yes, some sort of tech company. I saw the building from the cab."

"It's *our* tech company," I confirmed. "As well as the entire perimeter. We rented different floors to a number of IT companies that we also own. These people are our legitimate facade for the public. They're all our people, from the assistant to the CEO. And they all report to us underground, even though we aren't on any register."

"Underground?" Layla repeated. She was expressionless; she didn't seem to believe me. "You're still trying to convince me that your HQ is in a basement?"

"I'm not trying to convince you of anything," I retorted coldly. "From this moment on, while you're here in Seattle, I won't hide anything from you. You'll see and hear everything we're doing. Then, you'll choose whether to join us, or we'll shake hands and continue our separate ways."

"What if I talk?" she raised her eyebrows. "How do you expect me to believe this, if you're revealing it all to someone you met ten hours ago?"

"I know you indirectly, I know your work. I don't expect you to harm ours, at least not for now. After you verify what we're doing and what you're getting mixed up in, I believe that you yourself wouldn't consider such an idea."

"How can you be so sure? I'm a reporter. If you know my work, you're aware of the type of mess I usually investigate," Layla provoked me.

"It's pointless to discuss that now. You'll make your choice tomorrow," I interrupted her argument. "But you need to know, Layla, that I won't let anything stand in our way."

I wanted her to understand me properly, even though my words sounded threatening. They were, however, true. "I believe that you'll soon be persuaded," I added. That was true as well.

Layla slowly took a sip of tea, without looking away from me or saying anything. I stood up and did likewise as I took my wallet out. "I think it's time to go, or we risk disrupting the second cycle of your sleep."

I took the phone and the card from the table, and I headed for the bar. I left ten dollars on the mahogany counter, and I handed him the phone and the card.

"Keep them here for now. Put them in the back and return them to the lady when she comes to get them."

The sharp difference between the temperature in the bar and on the dark street outside refreshed us enough to quickly walk the 500 meters to Tech. Layla's pace was more than brisk, likely not only because she wanted to get someplace warm at 1 a.m. on a December night, the temperature near freezing.

"Are you cold?" I asked from several steps behind her.

"It's fine, we're nearly there," she answered. She was so focused she didn't even look at me, just turned her head to one side. She stopped to wait for me only when she reached the goal.

What an honor... I thought.

"Good morning," said the security guard.

We crossed the spacious white lobby and headed straight for the elevator. The white Italian marble on the floor was so polished that it reflected the lights from the ceiling, even though they were 12 meters away. Against the setting of a fine glass facade and open spaces, the stone gave a sense of solidity.

As soon as we entered the stainless steel elevator cabin, Layla glued herself to the panoramic window. It covered three-quarters of the cabin, providing the ride up with a view that could easily match the one from the London Eye.

We stopped on the eighth floor. There were ten apartments in the building, all on the upper three floors. The key card in my pocket opened all of them.

"Is this me?" Layla asked. At this point she was walking behind me.

"A4," I pointed to the door at the end of the hallway. "Does anyone beside you live here?

I was starting to fully grasp the nature of her job.

"You'll find out yourself, I suppose..." I replied pointedly and put the card on the receptor.

Layla walked in and headed to the living room. I turned the lights on, although the glow that came through the panoramic windows from the other buildings was enough. It wasn't that the rest of the apartment was unimpressive, but the view certainly thrilled her, as I expected.

I stood by the living room door.

"See you in the morning, then," I said.

"What time are we meeting?" Layla shouted from somewhere in the kitchen.

"Wait for me here. I'll pick you up at eight."

I walked out and headed for my apartment on the upper floor, confused by the ease with which I let Layla get close to me and the organization, but also somehow certain of her place in it.

8.

The mug with the coffee I drank before leaving in the morning was still on the counter. There were footprints on the floor from when I returned to pick up an extra key card for Layla. I had foreseen the possibility of her staying in one of our apartments.

I habitually finished the day with an analysis of my activities and meetings. I could analyze today in thorough detail if I wasn't so tired. The attitude with which I'd flown to New York only a few hours earlier now seemed very distant. At this stage, my initial goal to recruit a talented reporter or neutralize them as a risk factor had turned into something personal. I couldn't ignore the fact that I was convinced Layla's place was among us. As far as her role in our mission was concerned, I believed that defining it was just a question of a few meetings with the team.

Six hours later, the alarm brought me out of a deep slumber. I jumped out of bed, although I could have slept for at least another hour.

Aside from having to deal with the general turmoil in the base for bringing an outsider to HQ – and on top of that, without a warning – I was also supposed to hear some news from Fiona about something that had come up while I was gone.

At 8 a.m., I knocked twice on Layla's door. She opened a second before my fist delivered the third knock. The right side of her body was still in front of the mirror. Judging by the comb between her teeth, she was fixing her ponytail.

Her laser focus on this action was incomprehensible to me. I didn't see anything that required improvement.

"Just a sec," she smiled nervously.

"I'll wait for you by the elevator," I answered and walked away.

I thought about waiting for her downstairs, but I opted against it once I imagined her going around the other floors to investigate our mysterious "tenants." She wouldn't have missed the opportunity. I was still a few steps away from the elevator when I heard the door slam and the clear sound of her steps as she ran over. She caught up to me before the elevator door opened.

"So, what's the plan?" she asked eagerly.

"We're going to HQ, as promised."

The day was sunny and clear. The rays that entered the white lobby through the glass panels nearly blinded us.

"I thought HQ was downstairs, isn't that what you said?" Layla continued with the questions.

"Did you think it has direct access from the elevator?" I cut her off. "Try to listen more and ask less... at least for today," I added with a wink, concealing my mild irritation.

Surprisingly, she didn't reply. And my initial impression indicated that she rarely let someone else have the last word.

We took the long way around the building. I usually snuck out at night, and I didn't need to be as paranoid, especially given that we controlled the surveillance within the wider perimeter. We walked to the parking's entrance on the back side and went inside toward the security booth at the bottom.

Porter Finch was manning it today, a 30-year-old retired military man. He wasn't particularly intelligent, but he was honest and loyal. He was taken aback as soon as he saw me approach with a stranger, although he tried to hide it. I had never brought an outsider here before.

Just like Andrew, when Porter saw an alien element, he first pretended to not know me.

"How can I help you?" he asked convincingly.

"Everything's fine." I patted his shoulder.

Layla greeted him with a silent nod and came to stand quite close behind me. She was certainly starting to worry. Before I opened the door, I turned to her.

"Keep in mind that they aren't expecting you. Everything will be fine, just please don't speak before I explain."

"Understood," she replied and took a deep breath. She wasn't as confident anymore.

I went inside first, pulled Layla behind me and closed the door.

"Careful," I warned her. I took her hand as we went down the stairs. Not as a result of any romantic intent – I just knew that, prompted by her curiosity to look around, she'd probably forget to look down. The last step was treacherous.

Unlike Layla, I could already make out Fiona, Slim, and Matt, who, after hearing us, turned around one by one, and subsequently froze in the same order as soon as they spotted the intruder. As I expected, Fiona was the first to speak. She approached Layla slowly, sizing her up from head to toe. It wasn't a warm welcome.

"Miss Pierce..." she stretched her hand out and coldly introduced herself. "Fiona Rider."

Her otherwise warm brown eyes now examined the unexpected visitor with deadly seriousness.

"Your boss forbade me to speak before he explained my presence here. But maybe he needs to hurry up," replied Layla and gave me a sideway glance. "Silence isn't my strongest suit."

The boys didn't appear to be as disturbed, despite the unprecedented situation. It seemed that the sparks between Fiona and the newbie interested them more.

Fiona turned to me, but not before she kept her warning stare on Layla for another second or two. "*Boss*?" she stressed, pointing the scanner to me. We were clearly equals, regardless of the "title." "To what do we owe this *surprise*?"

I cleared my throat.

"Are you done?" I said to both of them. "Layla has, in one way or another, long been close to us, as you, Fiona, discovered out yourself."

Layla gave me a confused look.

"Greece is pretty far from here, Rick," Fiona hissed.

"I'm sorry, am I missing something?" Layla interjected, still not suspecting that the fate of the Dunne family was not the only time she investigated me over the years.

"You didn't get to know each other that well, huh?" Fiona said with a palpably condescending tone.

"Look, I don't know what you're thinking, but I didn't come here on my own initiative! My first big investigation was the Preston and Mason scandal. The murder of Jeffrey Dunne and his wife," Layla started with an ascending tone. "I got to the bottom of the story. They tried to shut me up. They couldn't. But I couldn't break through Preston's alibi, either. He's still up to the same schemes. The Henderson foundation, Future Life, Second Chance… they all duplicate Mason's operation. I'm just as ready now to scream until they hear me. I decided that Ian must be part of that. For his family, for his loss, for the future of those he helped in Africa. Suddenly, one day, as in yesterday, he came to my door and announced he's set up a secret network of Nobel prize winners and criminal organizations that will eliminate corrupt governments and found a new society… And all of this is run from a secret HQ in the basement of a building in downtown Seattle!" She spread her hands theatrically.

"Does that sound funny to you?" Fiona bit back.

"It seemed a lot funnier before I realized it could be true," Layla replied with complete seriousness. Then she turned to me. "You told me to come so I could see for myself and decide whether I want to take part. I want to know exactly where I am and what I'm doing here!"

I tried to speak but Fiona beat me to it.

"You're here because we registered periodic searches for keywords that trigger an alarm in our system. We follow the source of every such search. With these two," she pointed to Matt and Austin, "We can get access to any smart device that we deem worthwhile. And that's how we got to you," Fiona explained, now considerably calmer. "We found out who you are, we looked at your investigations. We decided that you're digging too deep and we need to intervene. Our intervention can come in two forms – we recruit you, or we remove you. Given the efforts you've made, we'd prefer the former."

"My efforts to chase down the truth? Unfortunately, it rarely leads to any result," Layla said with a shrug.

"You know that words don't change anything," I added. "We need action, global action, synchronized and irrevocable."

"So how is someone like me useful to you?"

"You already are," Matt chimed in. "Reporters that chase the truth aren't so few. But the ones that actually find it are. And this could be a hiccup for us."

Fiona went over to her desk and came back with something in her hand. In the context of this conversation, I knew what it was.

"We aren't recruiting you because you found Ian Dunne," Fiona began. "We need you because you're the only one that sniffed out one of our phantoms, created to carry out only one mission."

A puzzled expression took over Layla's face again. Instinctively, she first turned to me for an explanation. After all, she'd known me the longest – a whole day.

"Do you remember the 2016 Athens blast?" I asked as Fiona put an ID card in my hand.

"Greece..." Layla said, going back to the blank spot from the beginning of our conversation.

"Nice to meet you," I said and handed her Miles Bush's ID.

"That's why we need you," Fiona explained. "Although it was nearly impossible to get to us, the fact you knew that name turned you into a threat. Or an essential instrument."

Layla was speechless. She recovered quickly. "What else?" she raised her eyebrows inquisitively.

"The Norma file leaks. The Federal Reserve explosion, the hack into the FBI, the system disruption at the Paris airport," Fiona enumerated.

"The end of John Rich, Pablo Ria, Yurii Malich," Matt added.

"Wasn't your strategy to recruit people like them?" Layla interrupted.

"Not like *them*!" I frowned. "We didn't set out to pursue every criminal with money. We work with *people* and their values, beliefs, reach... Not just their money."

"In any case, we're involved in 80% of crime headlines," Fiona summarized. "I'm guessing you already know our network is large. Our members continue their work regarding the scale of our organization, while we here carry out the execution of the main plan, the essence of our mission."

"Which is at a very advanced stage, actually," Matt chipped in, but stopped himself there. He wasn't sure how far he could go.

Maybe that would have been for the best, if only fate hadn't presented us with one of its tricks now, of all times. Matt's computer started beeping hysterically and insistently.

That could only mean one thing.

"Do I need to put my seatbelt on?" Layla smirked.

Only a second later though, she started to suspect that her witty comment could turn out to be prophetic. She could feel the explosive charge within Matt as he rushed toward her – or rather toward his station, which was right behind her. He nearly shoved her aside in his attempt to prevent revealing the culmination, which was seconds away from materializing on the screen and blowing up her mind like a nuclear blast that swept away the limits of the possible and realistic.

"What's with you?" Layla jumped out of his way with indignation, when her eyes became fixed on the word Hermes that was blinking in her face in tune with the alarm.

Matt was too late. And the collective unease that took over HQ didn't escape Layla, only increasing her anxiety.

"What's Hermes?" She looked at me with trepidation.

Hermes was our little corner of paradise in the waters of the Indian Ocean, separated from any other land by 300 kilometers. We named the island after the god of thieves partly because of the mythological vibe, but mostly due to a love of irony.

After every replacement we transported the real individuals to transit points located in deserted and difficult to locate coastal areas, strategically placed around the final destination. Once they arrived at the transit points, every one of them had a microchip implanted in their palm. Although we had thousands of cameras around the island, we needed to know the location of all our special guests at absolutely all times. The first ones arrived in 2022.

"You know, maybe that's enough for today..." Fiona tried to postpone the explosion.

"Matt..." I interrupted her, and motioned to him to move aside. Then I pointed the monitor to Layla. "Go ahead, open it."

She drew a deep breath, closed her eyes for a moment – her last one of blissful ignorance – and clicked on the blinking icon. I observed her bewilderment as the click revealed a satellite image of the island, a piece of land in the middle of a large expanse of water. With 21 red dots scattered around the shore. Two of them, right next to each other, were blinking in tune with the alarm, while the others were static. Layla instinctively put the cursor on one of them and clicked.

"What the fuck!" she yelled, almost panicking.

"Prime minister J—" Matt politely tried to clarify.

"I can recognize the fucking British prime minister, thank you very much!"

The rest of us remained silent to give her a chance to recover.

"What is the meaning of this?" she kept thinking out loud. "The other day he was on Downing street, I watched his statement!"

"He was right here, I can assure you," Slim said calmly and somewhat mischievously.

"No! No!" Layla waved her finger around patronizingly, as if she believed that she could prevent us from doing something terrible... which we had already done, apparently. "This can't be true!"

"Alright, alright. Come here, just sit for a sec."

Layla ignored Fiona's attempt to calm her down and went back to the mouse to click on the other blinking dot.

"Ooh, God..." she seemed to be getting dizzy. "The president of Brazil? What the fuck have you done?"

This time, Fiona abruptly, and without asking, pulled Layla to the side and made her sit.

"Listen, Pierce, you wanted proof and you got it! You asked to come here. This is not a joke, you hear me?"

"Oh, forgive me! I was having so much fun!" Layla answered hysterically.

"Enough!" I intervened. "Layla, it wasn't my intention to show you everything today, but what's done is done."

Remarkably, I didn't hear a reply or comment from her, so I continued.

"You must have already realized that the other 19 dots on the island aren't there by coincidence."

Once again, silence.

I zoomed in on the image so she could get a better idea about the location and its inhabitants.

"I'll get straight to it," I announced. As you can see, the real Jones is quite far from Downing Street. He and 20 other world leaders are sharing 200 square kilometers in the middle of the Indian Ocean."

"Hermes?" she asked.

"That's what we call it," I confirmed. "In 2020, we started preparing doubles for the leaders of BRICS, OPEC, and G-7 countries. Up to now, we've replaced 21 of them."

"Up to now?"

"You are aware there's 25 of them. This year we'll replace the last four."

"So you need to replace the last four... okey dokey..." Layla kept repeating my words. She was clearly having a lot of difficulty finding her own position. Shock, judgment, awe, rage... I could see them all on her face.

"Matt, can you please get me Yon's file," I asked.

While he looked for it among the thousands of files, I kept disclosing.

"All of the doubles are members of our organization. Each one of them was given two years to undergo several stages of preparation. We faked their deaths, isolated them in a secret base, they went through surgical transformation, familiarized themselves with the target, and took on their traits."

I followed Layla's eyes to the screen, where Matt had already pulled up two photos. One was of Yon and the other of the Chinese president.

"Yon is the double for President Hau Lin. He's undergoing the last of his surgeries. Until the moment we replace the president with him..."

"This coming December," added Fiona.

"... he'll continue preparing in our secret base near Guangzhou."

Layla was in a stupor. It seemed that the adrenaline from the first shock was wearing off.

"Why? Why are you doing this?" she asked, exhausted. "You could have helped so many people with all these resources..."

"Do you really believe that?" Matt snarled.

"We must penetrate the system itself, where everything originates..."I added. "This is our only chance. Leading the countries and alliances that run the world will allow us to breach the matrix and integrate a new type of government."

"Even so, you're working with the m-a-f-i-a" snapped Layla. "How benevolent can that be?"

"The ends justify the means, you've heard that. The elements necessary to complete our mission can only be found there, in their world."

"All the organizations we work with, all the investors, we didn't select them randomly," Slim chimed in again as he rolled his chair over. "We pick them the same way we chose our members. They're all people that the system uses the same way it uses us. They all want their freedom. And they're all capable of changing in order to gain it."

"The world isn't just black or white, Layla..." Fiona put a hand on Layla's shoulder. Matt opened the camera feed for Yon's base, specifically the training center. Then he showed her the base in Russia, where the president's double was practicing a speech.

"President Mirov?" Layla recognized him.

I nodded.

"In a few months' time, Alexey will take his place. Before that, we still have to replace chancellor Mulitz, then president Mayden, and finally, Hau Lin."

"So soon?" she frowned skeptically.

"If we don't do it now, we'll never get another chance. Terms end, and preparations take time. We won't get another opportunity to act so completely."

"Now or never, huh?" she remarked, and I felt like I was starting to see understanding in her eyes. "And then what?"

"The conference," Fiona announced. "January 12th, 2027. By then, they will have all spent between one and five years in office. Each of them will know the system well enough to understand how to fully influence it. And a little over a year later, the president of China..."

"Yon?" Layla guessed.

"... will make a public announcement and an invitation to the leaders of all three organizations to join a debate regarding the new policies he intends to implement."

"And the general direction of the world," added Matt.

Layla exhaled and thought something over for a second, before turning to me again. "And the victims? How many innocent people have suffered?"

"We've always strived to avoid damage, as much as possible," I answered. "If you go through the reports of all the operations, you can verify it yourself. As far as the kidnapped, you can see they're having a great time on the island."

Layla remained silent and sat on the chair by the other computer. But she was only given a few seconds to collect her thoughts before the forceful yank with which Austin stood up from his chair returned her to the disturbing new reality that we had just plunged her in.

Slim's expression betrayed the tension of something that was kept quiet for too long. He exchanged looks with Matt and Fiona, only confirming my hunch.

"What's going on, just say it!" I spurred them on.

"Actually, boss, funny we mentioned Oliver Preston earlier... your mutual... friend." Matt started and stood up to get closer.

"He was here yesterday," Fiona continued. "Upstairs, to be precise. He wanted to meet with Tech's investor."

"Who did he talk to?"

"Dean Horton," Matt answered.

Dean Horton was the CEO and chief representative of the owner of Nova, the company that owned Tech Progress. The company and its accounts were offshore, and no one could find the actual owner. Even if it seemed like they did, it would be just another shell company.

"Get him on the phone, I want him to tell me everything."

"There's no need," Matt countered. "The conversation

210

was very brief. Preston wanted Nova to make a donation to one of the foundations he's been working with a lot lately. He insisted on speaking with the owner personally."

"And what did Dean say?"

"Whatever he's supposed to," Fiona replied. "That his boss doesn't appear in public and he's fully authorized to make any decisions regarding the company."

Matt continued. "He told Preston that he'd submit the request at the next board meeting, when they'll be discussing donations for next year."

"I bet Preston didn't like that!" Layla jeered.

"He really did not!" Fiona confirmed. "He made a direct threat and said that if they turn him down, he'll initiate investigations into the company. That he knew very well what kind of people work with this approach and that the owner needed to make an exception and get in touch with him, to avoid, and I quote, 'serious problems.'"

Maybe it wasn't a coincidence that Preston's path was crossing mine again. That crook was clearly not ashamed of playing the same old game, all these years later.

"Did he mention anything about other foundations that he works for?" I asked Fiona.

"He usually works with several at the same time. He always aims to direct the largest sums possible toward them, and then appropriates nearly all of it..."

"Like Mason's foundation?" Matt asked.

"His classic scheme," Fiona confirmed.

I wondered how many lives that bastard had ruined. How many people he had destroyed, how much he had taken from people in need.

I sat on the empty chair next to Layla and tried to ignore the fact that everyone was staring at me. They expected a reaction or decision. I gave myself a few long seconds to weigh out the consequences of my decision. I had already made it.

"Fiona, can you call Dean, please," I asked and stood up.

After a few rings, his voice echoed from the far side of the bunker.

"What did you decide?" he asked directly.

"You did great, Dean. Now I want you to call Preston and tell him that Nova's owner will be delighted to invite him to his estate on December 30th, to attend his exclusive annual New Year's cocktail party..." I paused and took a few steps, to give myself time to embellish the story.

Briefly, I met Fiona's glance. She was stunned and annoyed. She hated last-minute plans. But on the other hand, she had to do it all the time.

"Got it, boss!"

"Wait, I haven't said the most important part!" I shouted. The four pairs of eyes that were staring at the floor, trying to assimilate my words, suddenly shot up at me in expectation of the climax.

"Yes?" Apparently, the same was true of Dean.

"The limo of the CEO, what was his name?"

"Bill Tyson," Fiona answered.

"Right!" I remembered. Please ask Preston to inform you once he chooses a hotel for his stay, since Mr. Tyson insists on sending his personal driver to pick him up."

"Got it," Dean repeated. He was as confused as everyone else.

I endured several seconds of silent, along with universal – and probably deserved – reproach, before Fiona finally exploded.

"What the hell are you doing?" she asked in all seriousness.

"When have I ever let you down?" I hurried to reassure her.

"You mean to say that you thought it over in the two minutes since you learned of Preston's visit?" she shot back.

The eyes of Layla and the boys darted between me and Fiona like they were watching a Wimbledon match.

"Trust me, I did think it over. Sometimes it only takes a few seconds."

With a deep sigh, Fiona shifted her weight to her right leg and crossed her arms on her chest. It was her way of showing me she was listening.

"What do you have in mind, boss?" Austin relieved some of the tension.

"We'll give the bastard what he wants." My reply startled them. "This year, our company will actually celebrate the new year with an exclusive cocktail party at Mr. Tyson's winter residence."

I made short, dramatic pauses as I opened the curtain around my plan, like I was giving a performance. I was convinced that they would eventually appreciate my idea. And its execution – even more.

"Yes, yes, I know, we don't have a residence," I continued, trying to ignore the pessimism on their faces. "Fiona will find something appropriate... A cozy spot out in the country," I winked at her conspiratorially. "We'll gather to officially present the esteemed Mr. Preston with a 20-million dollar check for his foundation."

***

We devoted the next few hours to Layla. We told her about the doubles, the plan they were going to follow, about some of the cases – mostly ones she had heard of or even investigated. But still, there was no way to introduce her to everything in just a few hours. We did make an effort to give her enough details to allow her to make an informed decision on whether to join us in our mission.

As we spoke, I could see that she seemed lost. Not because she disagreed with our vision for the future. She believed it was sound. The doubts she had regarding the execution – especially that of the conference that was to take place two years later – evaporated as we revealed every stage, replacement and hunt. She was more worried about the risks this represented for ordinary people. Maybe if she could measure those risks against the consequences of letting the world continue on its old, rusty tracks, she would realize they were acceptable.

In the late afternoon, I led her out of the building, and we headed for Tacoma. Earlier, Fiona had booked Layla a flight for 8 p.m., but before that we needed to drop by Chester's to get her phone.

"You don't need to decide right now," Fiona reassured as she emailed Layla the boarding card. The ice between them had thawed. "But don't underestimate the role you could play among us."

"We're fighting for something big" Matt added and stretched his hand out.

"I've always relied on research and analysis, including my own boundaries," Layla said, cooling their enthusiasm. "I'll need some time."

"Sometimes the perceptions of others are more objective than self-evaluation." Surprisingly, even Austin had spoken.

"Well, we still made it this far without you, somehow..." I tried to lighten up the conversation. "Let's get going, so we can get you home in time for the next phase."

"What phase?" Fiona said, puzzled, while Layla smiled and waved her hand nonchalantly.

After we took her things from the apartment and left Tech, we headed for the bar. It was right after 5 p.m. and the offices were beginning to empty out, while the streets were starting to fill with cars and people. That didn't bother me. No one knew me, and even if someone did, they wouldn't have recognized me under the hat and scarf.

I called a cab shortly before we reached Chester's. I asked Layla to wait outside while I exchanged a few words with Jim. From the inside, I saw the car arrive at exactly 5:23, right on schedule. I had put off the decision on whether to accompany Layla to the airport till the last moment. Part of me wanted to, but I could also feel that I was starting to see her more like a future member of our team. As if my desire to work with her had displaced emotions, at least for now.

Finally, I decided to leave it. I left the bar and walked up to her. She was waiting by the passenger door. She seemed to be under the impression that we'd be traveling together.

"Wait," I said and motioned for her to stop. "It's better if I stay here, I have a few things to deal with. I won't ask if you'll manage. You're the fearless Layla Pierce, after all!"

"We'll see about that," she smiled uncomfortably, confirming I was right. She definitely expected me to go with her.

I was silent for a moment, then I put the phone in her hand.

"Thank you for trusting me. Most reporters wouldn't have given it up."

"Most rebels won't take a reporter to their HQ," she countered and extended her hand. "I'm glad you found me, Ian."

"Rick," I corrected her. "I think we can make a great team."

"Who knows..." she opened the car door.

"Is that a yes?"

She stopped and looked down. I could swear she smirked, even though she had her back to me.

"Let's just say it isn't a no." She climbed in without turning around.

"We'll await your decision," I said and closed the door.
    * * *

I went back to HQ to coordinate the plan for the cocktail party, the star of which I was very impatient to meet.

"That, we didn't expect!" Fiona bit onto me as soon as I stepped in.

"We unanimously thought she's a good reporter, but bringing her here..." Matt added.

Austin also joined the feast of the other vultures.

"If you always picked them as pretty, we could have enjoyed more visitors for much longer!" he said underhand-

215

edly.

"Alright, alright, that's enough!" I put both hands up. "That's how I judged the situation, and I acted. And I didn't bring an investor, but an instrument. You'll agree that there's a huge difference, even if the risk's about the same."

Fiona clapped her hands a few times, as if gathering a junior football team around her. "Alright boys, we have work to do, enough nonsense!" Next, she turned to me. "'A cozy spot in the country,' right?" she asked, demonstratively quoting the words I had said earlier.

"You know what I mean. We need an isolated enough place, a few dressed-up colleagues, expensive champagne, and a limo that will bring our special guest."

"But mostly to carry him out," Matt quipped sarcastically.

"Which brings us to the most important part," Fiona continued. "If I understand you correctly, I'll need to ask Fitz to prepare an Elektra capsule for next week?"

David Fitz had started synthesizing Elektra a year and a half after we had him infiltrate the research team of one of the largest pharmaceutical companies in the US. We had tested it enough times to know it had a guaranteed effect – dependable and final. Over the last five years, this substance served us very efficiently.

How would Zenith Pharma react to the fact that one of their employees created the perfect biological weapon? I wondered whether they'd murder him or cover him in gold.

Gradually, over a period of a couple of hours, Elektra interrupted all systems that made a body function – digestive, nervous, motor, respiratory, articulatory... Until the victim was left in a state very similar to sleep paralysis, with an unresponsive body, but also fully aware. In real time, the subject experienced horrific visions and feelings, without being able to move or speak, despite all efforts.

Elektra gave us enough time to disappear from the crime scene way before the victim's actual death. No witnesses, no traces.

"Let's make it two capsules," I suggested. "Anything could happen, we don't want to take chances."

Fiona nodded and made a note in her pad.

"What are we going to do with the corpse?" Slim asked.

"That's my favorite part!" I replied.

I had never been a fan of shady games and predetermined scenarios, but that was before. Now, our mission demanded that every step I took in the real world and all my identities be staged. As an active participant in this creative process, I was certain that I could give that man the best of shows.

9.

December 30th. I felt like this was going to be one of the most important days of my life. Until very recently, I'd thought there were no loose ends left behind me. This newly presented chance to finish with Preston, however, made me realize that this was one page I had never turned. Maybe I would have never done so without this opportunity. I was always racing to the future and my role in it. I had no time for personal vendettas.

And now, the bastard had appeared on his own accord to receive his retribution.

The thick forests around the Snoqualmie river made, in my opinion, the Three Forks region one of the most picturesque not just around Seattle, but in the entire country. Seclusion, silence, nature – only 30 minutes from town. Everything that a major businessman would want for his winter residence.

I arrived at the estate around noon. I wanted to check the place and its atmosphere – I *was* going to have guests. We didn't expect more than 35 people – it was exclusive, after all. Mr. Tyson didn't like big crowds.

The house, if one could call it that, was as large as a mid-sized hotel. Only that it was a Swiss Alpine chalet from the architectural standpoint. Three floors of wood, glass, and stone.

The snow crunched under the tire of the heavy Dodge

Ram as I drove down the private road that connected the estate's gate to the large parking lot in front of the mansion. It could fit about 15 cars.

I thought that I needed to ask Fiona who she rented it from. He could easily turn out to be a potential investor. But I also knew that if it were an option, she would probably introduce the person in question shortly after the event.

The building's windows, or rather glass walls, extended almost to the ceiling. If it weren't for the thick pine forest around, I would have doubted Fiona's understanding of secluded. But now I could see how the area was completely detached from anything that one could possibly stumble upon.

I parked on the left side of the lot and headed in the same direction to walk around the mansion. A backyard, entrances, basements, garages, workshops... I wanted to be familiar with every corner of it.

My route took me back to my departure point. I didn't notice any unusual or troublesome features. It was just a regular backyard covered in snow, and a separate building that acted as a garden shed. Naturally, it was in tune with the luxurious look and didn't disrupt it with its menial purpose.

It was difficult to open the front door with one hand. I had to lean on it with some of my body weight to push the robust solid-wood door.

The place was fabulous. I liked it at first sight. The first floor was 150 square meters of almost entirely open space. The huge pieces of furniture were distributed in four different corners – one with soft furniture centered around a home theater, another one around the fireplace in the central part, as well as a giant dining table with 15 seats on each side and a long stone counter on one side.

The hanging fireplace came down from the wood beams on the ceiling. The floor of the upper level had an opening in the center, which left about eight meters of open space in this part of the room.

It was more important to me to explore the two upper floors, and in particular, to find an office where I could speak to my special guest.

At about 6 p.m., three hours before the event's official start, the other guests started to arrive. They consisted of our *instrument* associates. It was particularly amusing to watch them unload boxes of expensive alcohol and arrange catering trays while dressed in their Hugo Boss and Vera Wang outfits. At the end of the day, nothing less than Dom Perignon and black caviar was expected at an event like this one.

Fiona and the boys arrived even earlier, somewhere around 4 p.m. We placed cameras and microphones everywhere for surveillance and arranged the special platform for the senator's speech.

Around 8:10 p.m., my personal driver Pete informed me that our guest was in the backseat of the limo and on his way to Three Forks. Preston decided to stay at the Four Seasons in Seattle, which meant that we had about an hour until they arrived. Pete had a lot of experience behind the wheel but traffic the night before New Year's Eve was congested.

We awaited the senator fully prepared. Our people were transforming into their roles of top-level players, the bar and the hors d'oeuvres table were arranged, even the 20-million dollar check patiently waited for its moment of stardom. We had planned that to happen an hour, an hour and a half after Preston's arrival, or around 11 p.m.

According to my calculations, the most important part of the night, and one of the most important moments in my life, or rather Ian's life, was going to take place around midnight. How dramatic!

I chose a room on the third floor for my office. The owner had obviously intended it as an independent and isolated whisky and cigar lounge, which suited me ideally. It just needed a few touches to look completely believable. We took a few generic paintings off the walls, of the sort normally seen in rental properties. We arranged bottles of MaCallan, Dalmore, and other outstanding malts in the liquor cabinet. We tossed around some "personal" items like books, souvenirs, and other things that indicated a more permanent presence.

Impatient to go into action, Elektra was spread at the bottom of a glass.

I only needed to follow my associates and immerse myself in my role for the first part of the evening – that of billionaire investor Bill Tyson. Slightly unnerved by the pressure the guest had exerted to achieve his goal, yet full of the cold politeness appropriate for people like him.

The holiday light jazz and the guests made the party look amazingly realistic. Everything was ready for the night, but I still decided that this was a good time to go over the plan. I gathered everyone to once again practice all the stages. We couldn't afford to forget why we were here for even one second.

The three main stages of the plan were handing over the check, getting Elektra into Preston's digestive tract, and the finale at the hotel. Allison and Sharon were already in place a few blocks from the Four Seasons, waiting to climb inside the limo with the inebriated lowlife. We needed to deal with the two stages that were to take place here. We had to make sure they would follow one another without a glitch. One advantage we held was that like basically never before, the time factor only became critical once Preston ingested Elektra. From that point on, we had about half an hour to load him into the car that would take him to the hotel.

We went over our individual roles – who was who according to their business card, what subjects they could discuss with Preston, the kind of bait they could throw at him to entice his appetite for money at the expense of caution.

In the meantime, the vibration in the pocket of my pants made them even more uncomfortable. The tuxedo was definitely not my thing. The code name that came up on the display, however, alleviated the feeling. *Mist* was what I called Layla after she decided to join our team. Technically, it was meant to be about her function of creating a mist around us. In reality, though, she still did that to my mind. At least in the moments when I allowed her to enter it...

I went inside the office before taking the call. The plan called for me to retire for a bit, and it also gave me a chance to speak to her.

"It's perfect," I said as soon as I answered. I meant the article she had sent me the day before. The one that was going to take over the media like a virus in the morning.

"It's waiting for me to hit the *Submit* button. By 8 a.m. everyone will be talking about it. Are you ready?"

"I certainly am. We're expecting the guest of honor any time now. Everything's going according to plan."

"Are you *really* okay?" she asked with concern. She understood how difficult the first part of the plan was going to be for me – the polite phrases, the false niceties, speaking of our "mutual interests..."

The goal is worth it, damn it!

"Everything comes with a price. We'll manage."

"Just checking." I could feel her winking from the other end of the line. Her intonation was that expressive.

"Make sure to be by the Four Seasons at 1:30 a.m. Your presence there must be verified. After all, you'll be the first one to get the story."

"Don't worry about that, everything's in place," she assured me.

Just then, the Lincoln's headlights lit up the road. The office's window had excellent visibility.

"I have to go, they're here."

I moved away from the window. It was 9:23 and the plan called for giving him an hour to get used to the environment, engage with a few prospective contacts, and have some fun... They were going to hand him over to me tipsy and merry, just the way I wanted him.

While I patiently waited for him to warm up to the required temperature, I used the opportunity to prepare myself for the show. I ran all possible scenarios through my mind. Several times. I was *ready*.

***

At exactly 10:39, I closed the office door behind me

and headed downstairs. By the time I was on the last step, I had already surveyed the situation. I was satisfied; everything looked as planned. The music was just loud enough to allow the pleasant buzz of the ongoing conversations to be heard. The guests were spread evenly in groups of a few people.

I registered Preston at the other end of the hall in the company of one of our men. Judging by his gesticulation, he was probably bragging about his fabulous charity deeds with the hope of hooking yet another wealthy businessman. He had no way of knowing that Jeremy Cobbs wasn't the heir of a rich family with mining concessions on two continents that he was pretending to be.

I got a drink from one of the mobile bars and walked in Preston's direction. I stopped at a distance that was neither too far nor too close. I joined Kaleeb Lin and Maya Smith, who according to their covers were a development investor and the daughter of the owner of a large Austrian pharmaceutical company. Not long after, my peripheral vision caught Jeremy motioning toward me. With a polite toast I ended the "conversation" and headed over. I was the host, after all.

"Mr. Preston! The special guest of our modest party!" I greeted him and shook his hand.

The lively and calculating look in his eyes that I remembered from his days as a California senator had by now become overtly arrogant under his swollen eyelids. Probably swollen because of the sleepless nights filled with thoughts of more "charity."

"I need another drink, I'll catch you later," Jeremy said and tactfully stepped away.

"Do you know, I've never received such an obliging offer before," I continued. "It's quite refreshing in someone from my social circle."

Preston tapped my shoulder with a condescending smile and directed me toward the more isolated corner between the bar and the window to the backyard.

"You're still young, Mr. Tyson. Someday you'll realize that power gets cold quickly and it needs to be consumed while still hot," he started in with his self-satisfied, patronizing tone. "Diplomacy is just a waste of time, even for people like yourself."

"You seem to know them quite well. And... What was it..." I tried to quote his own words when he threatened Dean: 'the approach they work with.'"

"Oh please, Bill." He waved his hand. "We're more alike than you realize. Offshore companies, straw men, hidden owners. Should we bet on whether you're squeaky clean?" He laughed disdainfully. "I may turn out to be cleaner than you!?"

"I don't doubt it! But as you know, if the dish is too hot, your receptors could mislead you. Sometimes you only realize how spicy it is after you start sweating."

Preston gave his own reflection in the window a sardonic smile. "My receptors are fully functional, my friend. I know exactly what I'm doing. And I take care that everyone around me is satisfied." He looked at me to make sure that I understood him.

"So I've heard. Some people I know were left very satisfied with their investment in your funds."

"As I said, I make sure everyone's happy, that's all," he said with faux humility. "And, as I also said, power isn't a given. I worked hard for my privileges, and I have many, I assure you."

"That part I understood, Mr. Preston. And you're right that we aren't very different. Our privileges, as you called them, mean that sooner or later, we're destined to work together."

"Why, too late, if you ask me," he smirked again, relieved by the similarity in our way of thinking, of which I had just managed to convince him.

"To the common good!" The amber bourbon swirled on the bottom of my glass as it clinked against Preston's. "Now let's reward all your efforts!" I put my arm on his shoulder and guided him toward the podium where I was supposed to hand him the check. It was especially arranged to represent his moment of triumph. "And then I propose that we step into my office to coordinate our actions in private. That's where I keep the best stuff," I assured him as I took the last sip.

This was another one of the many exceptions that I had to make. The shot of whisky with which I decided to celebrate my guest's grand finale also played a role in my upcoming speech. This type of activity was far from my favorite.

After he answered my toast, Preston left his glass on the bar to free up his hands and straighten up his white jacket before he joined me.

"Ladies and gentlemen, may I please have your attention!" I shouted, using one of the silver knives from the table to clink on the champagne glass I brought on stage with me. I had seen other people do that. I nodded to Peter Mills to lower the volume of the music, and I continued. "I believe most of you already met our special guest this year. Mr. Oliver Preston, former California senator and an exemplary citizen devoted to charity for the last 20 years!" I pointed to him "excitedly" as he took the applause in with his well-practiced fake humility. "Please step up and join me, my friend! It's truly an honor for me to announce my support for one of the many causes with which you help the needy!" I put my arm over his shoulder, while Rich Mayer handed me the check.

Preston clasped the check from one side and took the floor.

"Thank you, Mr. Tyson! Your generosity is worthy of respect! Applause, please!" This time, he was pointing at me. Then he went on with emphatic emotion. "I see a room full of young, capable, successful people! And a world full of need..." He made a dramatic pause. "And do you know, dear friends, there's no feeling more satisfying than that of helping others. It's our duty as people of certain means to be socially engaged and to employ our resources to make the world a better place."

As he spoke, I carefully observed the behavior of the "guests." They were acting magnificently, much like "noble" Preston himself. They reacted to his inspirational speech realistically and genuinely enough to feed his bottomless ego.

"Just like our esteemed host has already chosen to do!" He added. "I'm happy to be surrounded by people who, like me,

224

Mr. Tyson, and our other benefactors, believe in the need to do good and to reach out to those who are disadvantaged!"

I joined in the applause that followed to solidify the impression I wanted to imprint on Preston's mind.

"I know my guests well, Mr. Preston. Everyone gathered here shares the same beliefs. I believe that tonight will change the fates of many people," I declared with irony, at least one truth amid the dozens of lies. "Please contribute, dear friends! What is money for, if we don't use it to help, right?"

The thunderous applause made Preston purr with delight. Frank Sinatra, whose crooning came louder after the speeches ended, sounded rather mediocre compared to the music that my words represented to the ears of the greedy son of a bitch. I was sure that to his eyes, every face in the room looked like a green dollar bill.

With an oily smile, he bowed left and right with his hand on his heart.

The moment we were all expecting was approaching as scheduled. I met Fiona's eyes among all the "dollar bills." I was used to seeing her in her t-shirt and camouflage pants, but her dark blue dress changed her dramatically. The same could be said of Matt, who had chosen a graphite-blue suit that was in stark contrast with his usual jeans and baggy sweatshirt. Good thing Slim wasn't here – seeing him in a tuxedo would have caused a culture shock to many who knew him.

Fiona winked at me. It was time to go upstairs.

I walked toward Preston, who was giving a passionate speech to a smaller group of potential investors. When he saw me approach, he somewhat unwillingly came over to pay some attention to the host. The potential investors were probably more interesting to him at this point, although he was unlikely to underestimate the portion of the 20 million that he was going to gulp down.

"Wonderful speech, Bill!" He acknowledged admiringly. "It's as if we've worked together for years!"

"The more investors, the more investments!" I tapped him on the shoulder. "And the bigger the investment, the bigger our interest. Isn't that right?"

"I think it will be a pleasure to work together, my friend," he agreed.

"I see that your glass is empty," I remarked. "Our new partnership deserves a special toast."

As we climbed up the stairs like we agreed before the ceremony, I could feel the stares of everyone behind. They needed to act quickly.

We went into the office. Curiously, it now seemed changed, maybe a bit smaller. I was probably getting used to it...

"Please make yourself comfortable." I pointed to the armchair by the desk as I opened the liquor cabinet.

He looked around, but he was probably not seeing anything. He was likely making mental calculations.

I took two glasses out, put them on the wooden table, and poured three fingers of the limited-edition Dalmore in each. Elektra needed about 10 seconds to dissolve completely.

"Would you share this pleasure?" I asked as I offered him the cigar box. I knew that the selection wasn't random.

"Red Dragon? Good choice," Preston remarked. "You don't see them every day."

"Well, I'm not your everyday guy!" I assured him as I handed him the glass. "And neither are you!" I added and raised my glass with a wink. "To profitable power!"

"While it's hot!" Preston concluded wittily.

That bastard likes to play with words as much as I do.

He took a generous gulp. He closed his eyes and put the glass under his nose to inhale the aroma. Then he drank again. It was more than enough.

A feeling overtook me that I didn't remember having felt since my adolescence. *Peace of mind.* I had forgotten the meaning of that.

I sat behind the desk, thanking fate for bringing the bastard to his end. And his own greed, of course. The only thing I wanted now was for the poison to hold him conscious long enough for me to tell him about all the things he had missed.

"So, what kind of percentage will I be getting back?" I

asked. "Or maybe you'll offer something else?"

"Straight to the point, huh?" He answered with amusement. "You know that there's no better way to save on taxes than charity. And for getting rid of dirty money, we all have it... My network is tightly knit, and you can be confident that no one is going to come sniffing around you," he boasted and lit his cigar. "People like us rarely get chances like these. You free yourself of your dirty laundry, you put on the crown of a benefactor, you get some cash back. Clean money, nobody knows, nobody asks."

"A tightly knit network, huh?" I said pensively. "Tighter than in 2006?"

"Of course it's tighter!" Preston gaped at me. "A lot of things change in 20 years."

"Indeed! You were under a lot of pressure back then, weren't you?" I reminded him with delight.

"Pressure?" He repeated dismissively. "I make things happen without pressure, Bill. A few inconsequential victims, nothing more," he "reassured" me and blew a thick puff of Peruvian smoke in my face before adding, "What do you know about these times, you were too young!"

"Not young enough, unfortunately," I answered. His expression was starting to change with every sentence I spoke. "If I'd been younger, it would have spared me from having certain memories."

"Memories of what?"

Elektra had entered Preston's body only about three minutes ago, but I could already see the first signs of it taking effect. He scratched his left arm and I knew that he was already feeling bugs crawling under his skin. A second later he tried to take a deeper breath and looked around a bit nervously, like he was checking his coordination, but he still didn't suspect any of what was actually happening to him.

I smiled back at his question as if he had taken me back to a cherished but forgotten memory.

"I remember your years as a California senator..." I answered, and then remarked casually: "Is everything alright,

Oliver? You seem tense."

"Please continue, I..." He waved his hand and looked around again. "You know, it's a bit stuffy in here, can you open the window?" he asked and added with annoyance: "I may have overdone it with the toasts."

"Just sit still, senator," I answered and headed for the window. "You'll feel better soon enough."

I went back to the desk, but this time I sat on top of it, right in front of Preston. I could see he was starting to lose focus, so I hurried to continue.

"So, as I was saying, your career – especially in that year – changed my life..."

"Bill, I think... I think... I need to get going..." He said with a drawl as he wiped the tiny drops of sweat from his forehead. "Something's not right."

"*Ian*," I emphasized.

He grimaced at me questioningly, and the immense difficulty that each word now cost him was evident.

"Does the name Ian Dunne mean anything to you?" I repeated. "It's better if you don't answer, you'll need all your strength."

I knew that he would hear the story until the end. He was going to understand everything I said, but I needed to resign myself to the fact that it would be a monologue. As much as I wanted to hear the verbal expression of his bewilderment, I had to content myself with his tortured facial expressions, which was the only thing he would be able to do from now until his demise. Which, according to my calculations, would take place in less than an hour.

"One of your inconsequential victims and his wife were blown up on Connecticut Avenue. Attorney Jeffrey Dunne, do you remember?"

The horror in Preston's eyes said more than all the words he could possibly say. He realized that somewhere along the way, he had stepped on a landmine. I enjoyed watching panic take over him. And I had so many other things to tell him!

"Listen, there's no point in resisting. You just ingested a

large dose of something very special. Just about every system in your body will shut down almost completely about an hour from now. You can't speak, and you can't move. Your oxygen saturation will keep decreasing. But you won't die of asphyxiation, your end will be more traditional..."

I winked and turned the TV on. It was hooked to two of the cameras on the first floor.

"You were definitely the life of the party," I remarked sarcastically and turned his head to the screen. Only the twenty-million-dollar check was left on our impromptu podium. The empty hall perfectly illustrated the charade that our event had been. "Our special guest," I tapped his shoulder. "That's how easy you are, Senator! A man with your sins should have been a lot more careful!"

Preston slouched in the chair with half-closed eyes and droopy lips, just like a heroin junky that had taken a little too much. The two states were very similar, the main difference being that Preston still had a clear mind – his harshest punishment.

"Let me tell you how you'll be spending the rest of the night... I mean, of your life." I changed the feed on the TV. The Four Seasons lobby appeared on screen. "Very soon, you'll walk through the front door propped up by two tipsy girls. Only minutes later, the poison you swallowed will cause a cardiac arrest. The postmortem will determine you died from a heart attack induced by consumption of alcohol, cocaine, and Viagra... At your age, it's dangerous to act like a playboy, you should have thought of that!"

I gripped him firmly by the shoulders to prop him up and I whispered in his ear, "Tomorrow morning, the whole world will be laughing at the sorry way you died. But don't worry, you'll be neither the first, nor the last. A lot of deadbeats will follow you," I added. And you know, you should thank me! Your companions could have been underage!"

***

We ended the evening just the way we had planned, and the last day of the year was marked by the sad news of the passing of former California senator Oliver Preston.

As expected, the media carefully limited the official version to an unexpected heart attack. Layla, however, made sure to make some suggestions about his last lecherous escapade with the corresponding visual and factual materials. We didn't go into too many details, since they would cause indignation and uproar, and that wasn't our goal. First, it wasn't necessary, and most of all – we wanted to avoid unnecessary attention being directed at the girls who shared his last moments. Our reward and my personal revenge were the horror in the bastard's eyes at the thought of the humiliating way in which he lost the game.

Still, the article that was reposted in a number of internet media outlets made sure to pay respect to some of the most brazen scams of his long political and "philanthropic" service to society.

10.

December 31st. The last morning of this year. I headed for HQ; I still had enough time to get ready for my trip to Guangzhou and Yon's preparation. I remembered how he had found his way to us.

Before he joined us, he felt like he could achieve anything he wanted. He was a young man from a good family, with a prestigious degree and a happy family of his own – a wife and two children. The future promised him many opportunities for realization in the sphere of politics, which had been his major.

The problems for Yon began when the internal rationalizations with which he explained actions of the upper echelon of power to himself the began to bring him first disappointment, then rage. Apparently, the Ivy League schools didn't teach students to be dickheads – you were either a natural talent, or else you kept silent and just took it. It seemed that Yon didn't belong in either category.

He spent some anxious moments worrying about his future and that of his family. On the one hand, his education ensured that he had contacts in the existing and newly forming upper classes, a position in one of the most influential media conglomerates in Silicon Valley, as well as a six-figure starting salary. He was given the chance to provide his family with everything – financial stability, comfort, good education, travel.

On the other hand were the dirty games, shady dealings, and corruption that reigned in those same circles.

Life brought him to us at the right time. In the end, Yon was able to provide to his family with more than he had ever dreamed of, without betraying his principles and values. And yes, the price for it was insurmountable to many – he had to watch his loved ones bury the urn with his "ashes," together with the shared future that had, until recently, belonged to them. He had to live with the knowledge that he would never again see the eyes that gave purpose to his whole world. Yon overcame all that with the unshakeable belief that his sacrifice would open the way to a better future for everyone.

He was one of the last replacements that we approved. And his task was the hardest – he was to be the voice behind everything we were fighting for.

The main reasons for choosing him, however, were more prosaic. Physical characteristics were of paramount importance. We needed to find members with similar features for every one of the 25 leaders we were replacing. We wanted to make the work of the surgeons as easy as possible, and it also minimized the risks of complications for the double.

Aside from Yon, we had two other candidates to replace President Hau Lin. They didn't have families, which could only be of help to us. One of them was even left-handed, just like Hau Lin. All three were equally suitable to undergo the changes. Ultimately, the scales were tipped by the distance between Yon's eyes, the height of his forehead, and the pitch of his voice – they were closest to the original. Some may have found this insignificant, but for us and our team of surgeons – and for Yon himself – they were particularly valuable.

Today, on the eve of 2025, approximately one year separated Yon from the replacement and another two years from the day of the conference, when his new face would be recorded in history. The credit was going to go to the real Hau Lin, but to us, this detail was of no consequence. Until then, Yon's days would consist of diction and gesticulation exercises, as well as the study of the president's political credo, his personality, ideas, governing style, and even his posture, facial expression, and vocabulary. Naturally, the double spent considerable amounts of time studying the development of China over the last 50 years. Even as a political scientist, he didn't have knowledge of the things that our experts revealed to him.

Additionally, we paid a lot of attention to the president's family. Lin was a widower, a convenient turn of events that happened about a year after we began preparing. He had a son and daughter that we knew well, and Yon knew as well as his own children.

Just like with all our doubles, we had found a way for him to have almost complete access to the lives of his family. Aside from making sure that the families lacked nothing and enjoyed a string of impossible-to-explain strokes of good luck and favorable circumstances, we also did our best to provide our doubles with regular footage of the lives of their loved ones.

Yon was the only double who chose to completely sever any links to his family, however one sided. He planned to allow himself to observe them only a few years after the replacement and the conference.

The Seattle city sign brought me back to the present and the preparation for my upcoming trip that awaited at HQ.

* * *

I made it back first, a little after 9 p.m. Fiona and the others were still on their way.

It was rare for me to be alone among the 30 computers and the archives, the thousands of files that detailed every operation since 2011. Moments of privacy like this one stimulated my mind in a different way. Solitude seemed to make me somewhat more rational.

I sat in Fiona's station. The sheer number of files that inhabited her workspace would have brought on a fit of claustrophobia for anyone but our people. Luckily, I was very familiar with this view. I quickly figured out where to find the information I needed. I opened the folder labeled 2025, the year that was about to begin.

Yon was my first task. More of a verification, really.

At the end of January, when I was to meet him, he would be 99% Hau Lin and 1% Yon Chei. That 1% existed only in his head and ours. But it was a lot more significant than the other 99%. It was the living memory. The memory of the reason, function, and meaning of the replacements.

I was to depart on Sunday, January 28th. My schedule once again reminded me of all the hours of my life that were wasted because of the damned time difference that accompanied all my missions. This was the case in this situation. My plane left at 5:30 p.m., and then I had a six-hour overnight layover in Vancouver. The flight to Guangzhou was to leave one hour after midnight and land 16 hours later. And this was the funny part. According to my biological clock, the date would be January 29th, around 5:30 p,m., and I would have spent 24 hours on the road. In this part of China though, it would be the morning of the 30th. So, 16 hours lost, just like that.

As usual, I consoled myself with the thought of my return flight. I only needed to board it alive to make up for the lost time.

233

"Are you already feeling sick?" Fiona teased me as she opened the door.

"Why are you bluffing?" I parried. "I know you can't see me from there.

"She doesn't really need to, after all this time," Matt added from somewhere behind her.

I could now make out their approaching figures. Luckily, they were back to their usual selves. The puffed-up individuals from last night – myself included – needed to exist only there and then.

"So what's the feedback on the last operation?" I asked. They knew that I didn't listen to the radio in the car. I always took advantage of that time and devoted it to thoughts that required silence.

"Layla's article did its job," Matt announced.

"About 70% of outlets we checked on the way over quoted her article when announcing the news," Fiona clarified.

"The rest opted for a postmortem polish of Preston's reputation," Austin interjected, already sitting by his station by the last computer.

"The usual..." I concluded. "And now, back to Yon," I said, changing the subject.

Before we examined the data regarding his metamorphosis, we went over his file.

Considering time and our goals, plus the fact that they were many and multiplied every day, there was no way for us to know everything in detail. For this, we counted on our dispatchers.

Over the years, we built key recruitment centers around the globe to optimize the selection of candidates on a more localized level.

The people who managed them were called dispatchers. They were closest to us in management. Their task was to seek out and recruit suitable instruments for our organization. After we reached a number that made strict control difficult, the dispatchers opened subcenters and appointed managers who reported back to them.

We received the files of all new recruits on a weekly basis. Among them, there were usually several key individuals. They were either people that played a central role in a recent mission, or they had contributed to the overall development, optimization or facilitation of our plan. Of course, Yon was one of the key members. All doubles were, and in particular – under the latter criteria.

Basically, we were about to let them rule the world!

"Let's see... Yon..." Fiona started to look for his file. "Two months after his final surgery..." She linked her screen to the multi-monitor. "A little different from the last time you saw him, right?" She said smugly.

Although we had spoken two months earlier, it was still before he underwent the final operations that Fiona mentioned. During our video call, he showed me the results of the previous corrections – an elevation of his hairline, thickening of his brows, ceramic caps on his teeth. Even back then it was obvious that the end result would be outstanding. Just like it had been for everyone before him. So, the answer was – not really, Yon's transformation was not a surprise to me. I couldn't detect even one inconsistent detail in his expression. The job was flawless.

I often felt like a magician who has nearly come to believe his own trick.

We went back to the file. The first 10 pages contained all the information about Yon, everything he had been before turning his back to his old life and becoming a double. Everything that happened after, and everything that was to come. I went straight to the last section. I knew the first two pretty well, especially when it came to Yon.

11.

The thousands of kilometers that I traveled to get to Guangzhou had turned the clock around just like my opportunity to sleep. Here, it was a little after 9 a.m. on January 30th. I struggled to make my way through the colorful crowds at the

Baiyun airport.

In similar situations I usually applied an approach of my own invention, which I called selective seeing. I visualized just one or more targets in my mind. It could be a gate number, an exit sign, a rent-a-car office. I imagined the target in question and tuned everything else out of focus, walking like a ghost between the other passengers until I saw my destination. I was secretly proud of the military efficiency with which I got around such places. That's why, this time – just like every other – I tried to fully ignore the robotic stares around me, which made me believe that everyone on the terminal was using my method.

Soon I spotted a suitable target ahead – the sign for the metro. I needed to get to the Tianhe stadium downtown, where I was to meet Adam Royce, the psychologist who had worked with Yon throughout his entire transformation – ever since he received the news he would be a double, through overcoming his "death," to his first look in the mirror.

The two of them, just like the rest of the Hau Lin team, had been based in Guangzhou for about a year. Overall, this was the central stage of Yon's program – the preparation, surgery, and recovery. Everything else happened in Xiamen, where he was born and "buried." As the specialists from the team drafted the plan, they advised us not to interrupt the lives of doubles outright. They needed to be aware that at least the ground they had been stepping on was still the same. For this reason, we made sure the first five or six months – when doubles had to overcome the grief of separation from their past, become familiar with their new roles, and take the step across the two characters until the real transformation occurred – were spent in familiar territory, even if in complete isolation. Despite their modest names, the bases where we moved them were provided with all comforts, especially since our doubles spent 90% of their time there. With all the physical changes, we didn't want anyone to recognize them.

Each base was around 250 square meters. The electric grid was autonomous, charged by lithium batteries housed in a special room. In addition to that, there were six other rooms

– one for surveillance, a medical station, a conference room, a dining room, a bedroom, and a gym. We delivered food and other necessities twice a week. The double and the psychologist lived there permanently, while the other specialists visited the base on a schedule to conduct instruction in political science and international relations, verbal and non-verbal communication, the biography of the original. When we prepared a double that was to take on his first mandate, we paid particular attention to the differences in policies when compared to the acting ones at the moment.

I decided on the go that a cab would be a better way of getting around. I would have made it twice as fast underground, but the metro had cameras everywhere. I had no reason to worry now, but I had no intention of taking risks, either.

Less than 15 minutes later I was speeding down the six-lane freeway on my way downtown, as I stared at the map of the area on my screen. Adam was supposed to meet me at 10:30 a.m. on a street corner across the stadium. Although on the roads on the map looked perfectly rational, I knew from experience how difficult it could be to make your way in some large Asian cities. For one thing, new buildings and entire districts popped up from one day to the next, which made navigation unreliable. On top of that, these were the most densely populated cities on the planet.

Still, the crowd didn't worry me. To the contrary – it allowed me to become invisible, which put me at ease. In any case, Alan and I weren't going to be looking for each other long. Our dots on the satellite map continued approaching one other. We called the app *Crosspoint*, and we had been developing it for five years. Red dots located each of our members on the map in real time. The ones nearest pulsated in bright red. This way, we all knew who was closest at every moment.

We needed another hour to get to Conghua. The location we picked for the base was in a much quieter region, about 75 kilometers north of the city. The picturesque landscape wasn't just a mere bonus, but a condition. Our doubles were undergoing training; they weren't in exile. We had enough surveillance scattered around to have the comfort of observing the perimeter strictly and being able to allow people to see the sun and breathe clean air.

Even the laser focus I applied to my preparation for the meeting with Yon couldn't close my eyes to the impressive megapolis. As we entered the downtown, the city's skyline encroached on my peripheral vision. The skyscrapers rose imposingly one after the other.

Personally, I felt at ease in Asia. Especially in China. The contrast between the population's density and the at least superficial lack of emotion in people made me feel at home and invisible enough.

Tianhe stood about a kilometer ahead and looked gloomy on the foggy January day. The spacious park around it made me conclude that it was one of the city's attractions. I had never seen so much open space in a Chinese city. Not that I could be counted on. After all, my travels around the world were pretty much limited to landing, action, and departure. My impression of a particular place came down to what I could see on the road between each of the three stages.

Tiny cold droplets covered my face when I climbed out of the car and looked around. I tried to reconcile my surroundings with the map. I headed in the right direction with the assumption that I would intersect with Adam in a few minutes.

I put my earpiece in and continued with the voice assistant. I didn't like having the look of a tourist crisscrossing the streets while grasping their phone.

The mechanical voice in my ear was encouraging me to continue forward when the sound of an incoming call silenced it.

"In 200 meters you'll get to the entrance of an underpass," Adam said. "I'll meet you there, in a gray combi."

I pulled the jacket's hood over my head and accelerated my pace. I walked on the edge of the sidewalk, then I saw his car slightly behind, on the other side of the road.

I turned Crosspoint off and put the phone and earpiece back in my pocket.

"Welcome, boss," Adam greeted me when I climbed in.

His deep, calm voice contrasted with his disheveled hair and the yellow frames of his glasses, as well as his driving style. I had realized that in Xiamen, when we were setting up Yon's first base. Adam had been living in China since 2012. He was 36 when he first went to a conference in Shanghai. He never returned to his native Chicago. He was rather impulsive in a professional way. He liked to joke that he had been attracted by the concentration of crazy people per square meter. We never actually found out his real reason for staying in China. Or how far he had managed to understand the locals. But from personal experience, I knew that his behavior on the road was a result of the Chinese culture he had undoubtedly assimilated over the years.

"Good to see you, doc." I patted him on the shoulder. "How do you feel with all this civilization around?"

"I already miss the isolation," he admitted with a melancholic smile. "Presently, my place is there. And the base is great, you'll like it."

I knew Adam well. Regardless of his words, I knew that staying at the base was as challenging for him as it was for Yon. But he was the sort of person for whom work was life itself. He knew perfectly how to adapt to the goal and the means it required. He did it organically, with his entire being.

"Any intruders?" I changed the subject a bit.

"Rarely. Barely anyone's come closer than eight kilometers."

"Barely?"

"We had a few cases. All innocent..." he said dismissively.

He clearly understood my insistence on finding out exactly how innocent, because he continued despite my silence.

"Last year..." he started slowly as he brazenly cut in toward the last lane on the right. "There were two, actually..."

The sharp turn with which we merged into a different boulevard forced me to grip the handle so tightly that even my clipped fingernails left a mark on my palm.

"This young couple... students maybe. They liked the old tree on the hill."

"They could have found us because of some tree?" I tried to swallow my indignation at the absurdly naive encroachment on our mission.

It probably showed, because Adam cheered up and hurried to explain, "It's beautiful." He shrugged his shoulders. "It's a camphor tree. Very old. I can show it to you when we get near."

"No need. And how did that nonsense end?"

"The same as for the other two!" He smirked. "Wild boars!" he announced proudly, as if exposing some long researched conclusion that his professional path had led him to. "We scared them for good!"

I didn't even know how to reply.

"The problem was that these people found exactly what they were looking for," Adam continued. "Silence, isolation, far from anything. We needed to show them that nature is not so welcoming."

"Any accidents?" I asked after a few seconds, during which I wondered if I even cared where they found the wild beasts.

"Nothing serious." He winked and pointed to my right. "This is one of the last ones."

He meant one of the giant skyscrapers outside. Its top was hiding up in the clouds.

"It's a little taller than our Tech," he teased.

"By at least 20 floors. How's Yon doing?" I got to the point.

"We stopped calling him that a year and a half ago," Adam corrected me. "He is Hau Lin. To the bone. The way it should be."

"And is it really like that?"

"It is now. But still, considering I'm with him 24/7, I think that after your meeting we'll know more about his state of mind than I could assess on my own."

"More than he could, too," I agreed.

As precise as our preparation was, they were isolated at the base, mostly in a theoretical environment. Both Adam and I assumed that any outcome was possible after my visit. The encounter with someone from the outside world, even if I had put him in that position, could derail Yon from everything they had been trying to erase. It could cause psychological issues that we would have to deal with. It was precisely because of it that we decided this phase was the right time for a personal visit.

In the short distance to Conghua, we mostly discussed Yon's state of mind. This was in addition to the full report on the surgery and training results we received in Seattle. For me, it was important to hear Adam's honest opinion of his mental state.

Adam categorized it as synchronized. Yon felt comfortable and confident in his role. He believed he had achieved a complete acceptance and readiness to live as Hau Lin in a personal and political sense, without risking his own mental health. He had overcome the absence of his previous life. He looked on the future of his family as an incentive to achieve his mission in the best possible way.

In short, Adam believed Yon was ready.

As much as I was glad to hear that, I needed to confirm it in person.

Conghua was not an independent region, but a province of Guangzhou. Adam claimed there were lots of tourists because of the mineral springs scattered around the beautiful area. The Pearl River I managed to see in Guangzhou despite Adam's manic driving watered the base of the snowy mountains. Its name was a poetic attempt to beautify reality.

Shortly after 11:30, we left the more populated areas as we were close to the base.

"This is the shortest way possible," Adam explained when he saw me look around the hills on the other side of the river.

"Wasn't there a road on the other side?" I pointed to the woods beyond the water boundary.

"There was! Until they discovered yet another spring."

Until this moment I had only seen a satellite image

of this area, but I understood Adam's disappointment. This "shortest possible way" we were on was six kilometers longer. Considering it was mountainous and winding, this seemingly small difference was about to delay us by at least 20 minutes.

"How did the students actually approach?" As we barely crawled up the primitive road, I found it difficult to imagine how two lovebirds decided to climb the stony slopes.

"Through the closed road. Some ecologist told them about the new spring, and they went to look for it."

"The camphor tree," I ventured, "was probably not enough for them."

Adam turned right and we found ourselves going down a shaded incline.

"Do you see the stump?" He pointed to the remains of a tree that must've been magnificent. It was in the narrow gully between the opposite hill and the one we were descending. We had left the river behind.

"The one on top of Yon's bedroom?" I joked, but I also knew I wasn't far from the truth. As far as I could tell, our base was right around there.

"You nearly guessed it," Adam replied and shut off the engine.

He led me to the place I had pointed to, and we veered slightly to the right. According to the blueprints I had seen, the entrance to the base was probably about 50 meters ahead.

"What are we stopping on top of right now?" I asked Adam, who had gone ahead as I explored a bit.

"The dining room!" he announced excitedly, as if he were showing me a penthouse on 5th Avenue.

This clarified the picture somewhat. The base's floor plan was reminiscent of a 50-meter rectangular submarine. All the halls and rooms were on the right side. They were connected to the other facilities by a long corridor. Which meant that if I was now on top of the dining room, we would reach the entrance in about 20 paces.

Adam lifted the hatch, which was covered by a thin layer of dirt and snow. He unlocked it by scanning his thumb. A long staircase descended into the hiding place of the "Chinese president."

I entered before him, and if the pale daylight hadn't seeped through from above my head, the tunnel would have been pitch dark.

I descended carefully, putting my palms and soles on the cold metal. From time to time I looked down, trying to see where the bottom was.

"You'll get used to it by the second time," Adam remarked smugly from above.

I didn't look at him to avoid getting blinded by the light; I had just become used to the blackness down here.

My right foot was the first to touch the concrete. The entire base was made of it. I couldn't see much, but what I knew beforehand helped me shape an image of the immediate surroundings after Adam closed the hatch.

"Keep going forward, a few more steps," Adam instructed.

I made it to a digital panel, the only source of light.

"Six-three-eight-five," Adam instructed.

Then I scanned my right-hand thumb. My prints were on file in every base, allowing access. The groan of the heavy door echoed around the silent bunker. I let my host go ahead, even though I knew the layout well.

A few meters separated the entrance from the first camera. The internal doors were automated and opened with iris recognition.

"We'll need to scan you later," Adam remarked.

"Let's hope this is my last visit! Besides, who would open the lid for me?"

"Just in case."

We went across the battery room and walked into the next.

"The surveillance hub," I noted as I looked around.

It was about 15 square meters, with 10 monitors linked

to a number of surveillance networks placed around a wide perimeter. We had several on the Guangzhou Road, others covered all the approaching roads, and the rest formed a ring around the base. The feed was received both by the base and the dispatchers in our China HQ.

We continued down the long corridor to the next room. Adam pointed to the door on my right. It was large, gray and chrome plated, just like every other one.

"I'll go in alone."

"That might be better," he agreed. "I'll be in the operating room if you need me. You know, down at the bottom."

"You forget who you're talking to."

All our bases followed the same blueprint. And all the blueprints had passed through my mind and hands. I knew exactly where the operating room was.

"Go!" I urged him and put my hand on the handle.

The central panel at the bottom of the room ahead of me displayed an official meeting between Hau Lin and the Russian president in Beijing, 2021.

"We cannot fall prey to the provocations of the West!" said the man in front of the screen slowly and clearly.

I had heard this speech, and I recognized its ending.

Several seconds later, the man *on* the screen repeated the same words. With the same tone and intonation.

The double heard my steps behind him. He didn't turn around, but I knew that when he did, I would not be looking into Yon's eyes. Hau Lin was speaking. In front of me and on the screen.

"It is so good to see you, Mr. Evans," he said decorously as he walked over.

While he crossed the few meters between us to shake hands, I struggled to subdue the paradox confronting my mind. There was what I saw, and what I knew. I saw President Hau Lin. I also knew it was not him.

"May I address you by Hau?" I asked and extended my hand. "Or do you prefer Mr. President?"

"Did Adam confuse you?" he asked with amusement

as he executed his handshake according to protocol.

"It does stand to reason," I replied.

"I prefer to go back to Yon for this meeting," he said and invited me to one of the three tables in front of the screen. His expression, diction, and nonverbals, however, remained those of Lin.

We sat at the table and spent a few seconds observing the original and the Russian president on screen. Yon interrupted the silence.

"As far as I can follow, my colleagues are doing pretty well," he began. "We can kind of see the end of it, right?"

"More like the beginning," I winked. "Everything's going according to plan. Only three left before you."

Yon remained silent for a moment. He smiled and looked down pensively. I realized that the number had reminded him of the three most important people in his life. The ones the cause had taken away from him.

"I'm here for you, if you need to talk about it." I put my hand on his shoulder.

I looked at him, ready to answer his questions. I hoped he would ask me how his girl and the boys were doing, so I could assure him everything was fine, and they were alright. Dzhou and Min went to the best schools and were straight-A students. They played sports, traveled, and explored the world exactly the way Yon would want them to. They were young when their father "perished." One day their mother received a call from a lady who claimed to represent a private organization that recruited talented youth and sponsored their education without further obligations. They had noticed Min's mathematical mind and Dzhou's sporting prowess and wanted to transfer them to one of the most prestigious schools in Shanghai. In reality, neither of the boys had any special talents, but at this tender age and with the proper education, they could make it up to fulfill the realization of this white lie. As for their mother, she received a generous stipend from the same organization for being willing to relocate in the name of the country's bright future. In addition to the initial sum equivalent to 350,000 dollars, she received a monthly wire transfer the size of a diplomatic salary, plus various bonuses for the kids to travel and explore the world. Anything that could widen their perspective. Su Chey herself used the opportunity to pursue her calling – she was a talented seamstress and was in the process of opening her own boutique in the center of the megapolis, very near the famous Shanghai tower.

Such were the happy coincidences with which we rearranged the lives of the families of all our doubles. Yon knew about some of these events, enough to be able to guess the rest. It probably helped him stay true to his strategy, because he never asked.

"I'll make up for what I've missed," he said resolutely, as if to himself. "But not before I make sure I fully control the outcome of our mission.

He was right. I didn't need to convince him that his family was safe and happy, because that could distract his focus.

"You said everything is going according to plan," he said, changing the subject. "How are the others doing? Chris should be next, right?"

"It looks like it'll be Alexey. A good opportunity presented itself and we must act."

In the following 11 months we were to substitute the remaining four leaders. Yon had the most time at his disposal. By the end of 2025, when he was going to take on his role, the leaders of Russia, Germany, and the US were to be replaced.

Mirov, Mulitz, Mayden.

"And Prime Minister Jones?" he added.

"He's already on site. Since November," I refreshed his memory.

"Two more years until the conference," Yon remarked. "In the last few weeks I find the excitement about that day is taking over me."

His training was meant to remain focused on Lin's character, even though the political scientist Nancy Forks was already instructing him on the new program. Three months from now, the emphasis was going to be on her agenda.

"Shouldn't you be more excited about the replacement?" I teased him with a nudge, although he was not to be underestimated. "Are you ready? It's only a few months away." I looked into his eyes.

"I couldn't be readier." After a moment of retrospection, he added, "I've spent all these months learning how to think, look, and breathe like this man. I've studied the movements of every centimeter of his body. I know his home as well as my own. I'm ready to hug his children the way I would hug mine. And most of all," he emphasized, "I'm ready to be what *he* should have been."

The unshakeable resolve in his eyes was convincing enough for me. That's what I had come for! And this was only the beginning. I could only imagine Yon after he spent one year governing China and had that experience on the day of the conference.

"The main focus from now on should be on the position of BRICS regarding the changes," I announced. "Even though China will officially be the first one to initiate the new policies and put them on the table, the alliance must build a credible symbiosis. The choreography of your statements, if you will..." I added metaphorically.

BRICS was a significant player with great economic, energy, and manufacturing capabilities. As a country with thousands of years of history, as well as one of the two major economic powers and an enormous territory, China had the weight to make the world listen. There was no voice more appropriate to announce the changes we wanted to implement.

The doubles that represented the G7 and OPEC were going to act in opposition, at least at the beginning of the debate. That was the logical, realistic scenario. In spite of the perspective for a future of united international relations, we had to expect a backlash against the measures that Lin was to propose.

"Where would we show the strongest resistance?" Yon

asked.

"Oil exporters would be the last to accept alternative sources of energy," I said. "Just like the US will be the last to want to hear about the problems in the monetary system."

"The world's currency printing press... the conductor of the financial markets..." Yon listed with uninhibited disapproval. "All your might rests on financial dependency!"

I couldn't just close my eyes to this. Although we were tightly bound by our mutual goal and a consensus of ideas, subconsciously Yon still saw himself as China and me as the US.

The primal instinct to accuse, to defend one's ego – this is what a human is.

"Not our might," I corrected him. "We're all sides of the same coin. The whole world hangs on an illusion! Is China any different? Or Russia, or Europe?"

Yon anxiously stood up and paced over to the screen on the wall.

"You know what, you're right! It's unforgivable!" he hissed despite his effort to contain his anger. "So *much* effort! So much work and sacrifices to be like him!" He pointed to the president on the screen, whose speech on climate change from last May was running on mute. It seems like I've done *too* well," he said, the disappointment written all over his face.

Although we were about the same age, I could relate to Yon's insecurity. I generally didn't believe in hierarchies, especially within our organization, but at that moment my position required me to act as a mentor. In part, because he was doing something he had never done. Partly, because he was yet to do something else he had never done. And last but not least, because the stakes were immeasurable.

I remained seated as I spoke, wanted to avoid shaking him up additionally. "No one can do what you're about to do better than you. The words you spoke are just a reminder of what the system has done to us, of what we're up against. I myself am a product of that system, Yon," I assured him. "To change people is not our mission. People are a reflection of their environment. *That's* what needs to change. Your children could reflect a more meaningful world."

I rarely allowed myself such inspirational speeches, even though I completely believed every word. I just didn't like the role they put me into.

"It's time you stopped studying Lin's personality," I said so suddenly that I heard myself articulate it before it even registered in my mind. "I think you've gone deep enough inside his skin. The three months you have left for this phase... You don't need more." I could see he was ready. "Let's shift the focus to the political program. It will be up to you to open the door to all the changes. To explain to everyone who will watch, hear, or cover the conference why politics cannot remain as they are. We can stage the dialogue between BRICS, OPEC, and G7, but not the questions of people, the media, or even your own 'family'... You'll be alone out there," I concluded. "You need to be ready. Completely resolute. Nancy is preparing you with the basics, right?" I asked rhetorically at the end.

Nancy was a passionate political expert and one of our most valuable associates. A key member, just like Yon. She followed, analyzed, and commented on every major or minor development in international relations. She was also a historian, which made her assessments even more relevant. It was precisely because of her perspective on the past that she was deeply convinced of the non-productivity of the interactions between the great powers and the internal policies of states. She was an example of exactly the kind of people we needed to draft a functional political program for the world and implement it. In this discipline we had 10 senior experts, and Nancy was one of them. They, on the other hand, trained another 40 young experts to actively work on the development of strategies. We also had 25 political scientists working with our doubles. Yon had the honor of working with Nancy personally. Until the last phase of the program, the visits to the base were weekly, which allowed some flexibility for Nancy and her colleagues. With the onset of the final phase, however, instruction was almost daily.

"She is," he confirmed. "Every Tuesday."

"In that case we'll move to four times a week, as planned. We'll just start earlier," I reasoned.

Yon stared at me in full concentration and expressionless. He was still considering the schedule change. After a few long seconds he lowered his arms from his chest and walked back.

"You're right," he said and sat in the chair next to me. "I've given enough time to the old Hau Lin. Time to build the new one."

12.

I stayed at the base for several hours more. The decision to move to the next phase earlier than planned wasn't radical, but we needed to coordinate it with Adam. After our conversation, we called him to hear his opinion. At first, he didn't seem to approve, which I expected. Not because he believed that Yon wasn't ready, but because he was convinced that every step played an important role. He had, after all, devised a lot of it himself. Finally, we reached a consensus.

By 5:40 p.m., we were once again driving down the six-lane freeway on our way to the airport. Thanks to Adam and his driving style, I could try to get on the 7:45 flight that night. Otherwise, I would have to spend a lot longer in Guangzhou. I preferred not to.

I took my passport out of the bag and put it in my pocket, getting ready for a serious sprint through the terminal.

"Every meeting with you ends up changing my plans!" Adam teased me after he pulled over at departures. And he was right – just off the top of my head, I could remember at least three cases.

"Do you have any concerns?" I asked, although I had already opened the door in readiness to get a flying start.

"I'm a psychiatrist, boss. If you ask me, there's no better preparation than a thorough one."

I stepped out of the car, swung the bag over my shoulder, and leaned down to the window. "It still won't ease your doubts, right doc?" I winked.

I wasn't closing my eyes to the possibility of complications. There was always something. But Yon had undergone a sufficiently thorough preparation. At this stage, the magnitude of a potential error was far beyond the critical levels. We could gain a lot more by using the time for this final, most important phase.

Adam raised his hands from the wheel, admitting his guilt.

"We'll hold the line and make it happen," he said humbly. "Have a nice flight, boss!"

By 6:10, I was already standing in the long border control line. The many missions and flights had not spared me from experiencing nervousness. Even though I had mastered all my identities excellently.

To top that off, my helpful mind found a breach and retrieved the memory of Layla. Yet another flight I had to chase, but the first one with her...

I thought of her often, although I kept my emotions under control. I was supposed to be good at it, but... They say that there's no good or bad time for such things. I could definitely argue with this careless statement. A growing number of links connected me to Layla, which increased parallel to her involvement in the organization. We spoke regularly, but seeing her was rare.

Luckily, my phone vibrated just on time to tear through the cloud of thoughts that didn't need to be inside me, especially right now.

"How did you know I needed a wakeup call?" I answered Fiona's call.

"I wish it was telepathy!" She sounded like an amateur who'd just run a 5k fun run. "But since it isn't, you need to send me the access codes for Mira on Crosspoint immediately! It's urgent."

Mira was an encrypted database to which I had sole access, precisely because Fiona insisted. This cloud contained our entire archive and detailed every past and future action of our organization.

It was impossible to even reach Mira. Although it wasn't for a lack of trying.

It had been a while since we dealt with any secret services, especially the FBI. Surprisingly, despite their supposed jurisdiction, MI-6 was sniffing closer to us. Unlike their US colleagues, where we managed to infiltrate about 30 people, the UK agency was more difficult to influence. We had recruited seven people from their ranks and introduced three more, but that service remained a serious threat to us.

I always thought that between me and Fiona, I was the wrong person as far as protecting data was concerned. The probability of getting caught, questioned, or terminated were a lot larger than with her or the others. Fiona, who was a core component of our team, suffered from one obsessive fear – to somehow be the source of an information leak that compromised our entire mission. We all knew that wasn't going to happen if she was conscious. What really terrified her were the new methods of interrogating the unconscious.

Finally, the codes for Mira were held only by me. That was probably the reason why for a split second, I felt the blood drain from my head and leave only dry icy shivers behind. It sounded like someone was on the verge of breaking into our organization.

I opened Crosspoint and sent her the code.

B..EB.CE

"Just like we discussed, letters for numbers and periods for zeros," I reminded her.

20052035. 20 May 2035. I vividly dreamed that on this day I would be able to hang my hat and go far away from it all. I didn't know if that moment would ever come, but it was a comforting thought in which I could find refuge every once in a while.

"Who's sniffing?" I asked.

"Same place. I think it's Emerson," hissed Fiona. "That

hound won't give up!"

She was rarely this enraged. Actually, it had happened only twice. Ironically enough, the other case also involved Emerson. A nasty man and an outstanding agent. One of the old dogs in MI-6. If James Bond were real, he would have been the only one to survive his brutal training.

"What did he get?" I couldn't help asking, even though I knew she wasn't going to tell me over the phone.

The line had advanced considerably since the last time I looked around.

"Just make sure to catch your flight. We'll manage," she snapped and hung up.

Whatever Fiona was fighting, I knew that she was going to make a copy of Mira. I wasn't worried about the loss of data, even if from now on everything was scattered between different servers. The question was to act before Emerson and his bloodthirsty dogs.

An agile operator! If he wasn't so brainwashed by the system, we could have worked together very well.

Despite the turmoil that was clearly ongoing at HQ, Fiona had managed to find me a good flight. Four hours later, a little before midnight, I would land in Tokyo. I had a 20-hour layover there. I couldn't think of a more comfortable option. Sometimes I wondered if I had been endowed with more energy than the average person, or my high cortisol levels had become a comfortable constant for my body. Endowed or not, however, over the last few days I had accumulated a desperate need for sleep and exactly zero requirements about where to satisfy that need.

Tokyo it was.

On the following day, or rather the same one, after I spent most of it sleeping, was my nine-hour flight to Seattle.

*＊＊

I wished I was one of the lucky people who could make use of night flights as intended. The ones who could announce they didn't even feel the plane land. I often heard this at different airports.

Well, I wasn't that lucky. I clocked every minute from the long flight to Seattle. The lack of information regarding the reason for moving Mira made it even longer. While still in Tokyo, I tried to get more details from Fiona – to no avail. She only confirmed they were still working on it. She sounded calm, but I could easily imagine the atmosphere at HQ, especially Slim's frown and the colorful curses he hurled at his monitor.

By the time I set foot in Seattle, it was late afternoon. I jumped into the first available cab and headed to Tech, while trying to go through all the different versions of what could have happened and the possible consequences.

I trusted my team. We had taken care to have contingency plans for nearly every realistic or absurd scenario that could develop over the course of our mission. Besides, we were more than used to dealing with risky situations. In our struggle, barely a day passed without one.

Nonetheless, I was still worried. From inside the organization that we had all been inhabiting for years, it was sometimes possible to lose perspective of the monstrous magnitude of our operation. Interferences like this one that made us regain it were sobering – they reminded us of how enormous the elephant that we needed to hide was.

I spent the 20-minute ride to Belltown deeply immersed in a projection of probabilities and developments of the near future, with *if* and *would* being the major landmarks. Then I burst into the garage and flew past the guard on duty entirely on autopilot. I didn't even see who it was.

"Are you sure? 100%?" I heard Fiona's voice from the other end of the hall.

Ten steps later, they saw me. Matt did, to be precise. As soon as our eyes met, he lifted his index finger, telling me to be quiet. He sat across from Fiona, who was leaning against his desk with her back to me and speaking on the phone.

I darted in between them and tried to hear more of her conversation. She noticed me and winked at me comfortingly with a barely noticeable nod. A small gesture that finally managed to restore the flow of blood to my head.

"Keep an eye on things and call me later!" she ordered the person on the other end of the line. Visibly relieved, Matt stood up and tapped my shoulder.

"Everything's under control!" He said, and then added loudly and clearly, "Welcome back!"

Fiona left the phone on the desk with a sigh heavier than the stormy wind that blew outside. `

"We were super close this time! Am I exaggerating, or are you always gone when things get hot?" She teased, "Don't you think so, Matt?"

"I think we deserve a raise," he said, conspiratorially joining the provocation.

"What happened? What did they find?" I asked anxiously.

"Emerson followed one of Ramirez's transactions to the account from which we rerouted it... you know." She cut the explanation short with an eye roll. "The important thing is that he doesn't know where it went."

"But he still caught a trace of South," Matt remarked.

South was our HQ in Texas. It was called that because our people there were responsible for processing data and funds to South America. It was relatively small compared to the North American one.

"I spoke to Emily," Fiona added.

Emily was one of our agents at MI-6. She was exceptionally valuable due to her close proximity to Emerson and his team.

"She said that Emerson believes he could find more clues in our region. He intends to investigate personally."

"Where did he travel from? How long do we have?"

"Canada. And he's still there." Fiona grabbed my shoulders. "The danger's passed. We baited him with something else."

"Em confirmed we're fine," Austin assured me. "He canceled his flight to the US, he's going back to London."

"Back to the royal court," Matt added.

"And Mira?"

"Taken down, moved, hidden even deeper," he answered.

"So what are we doing about South?" I returned to the neutralized threat.

"We already did it." Fiona glanced at me smugly. "We relocated the boys to Arizona. They have temporary places to stay until we organize a new HQ."

I myself couldn't remember what it was to live without the constant feeling of a storm cloud hanging over. Danger and risk had become our shadows. Still, I couldn't shake the feeling of guilt when I didn't manage to be with my team in a time of crisis. An unfounded worry, considering their capabilities. They exceeded anything that I could hope for. Sometimes I even wondered if my absence actually helped them.

"How's Yon?" Matt asked.

"Ready. Almost *too* ready," I emphasized. "His nationalism is more authentic than that of Lin himself, I think."

Austin was carefully looking at me from his chair, while Matt's expression showed absolute bewilderment.

"I'm exaggerating," I assured them. "But we decided it was time to move on to the main phases of the political program. It will be more beneficial if he skips the last phase of becoming Hau Lin. He seems to have assimilated it well. Instead, we'll increase the period of preparation concerning the new way of governing."

"Did you tell Nancy?" Matt asked.

They were close and he knew how much she loved impulsive decisions.

"I gave her a week to arrange her move to the base in Conghua," I confirmed. "She and Alan will manage."

"I won't ask about the surgery," Austin said as he arranged the pages in Yon's file.

"Don't! It's unbelievable, even his glare is the same! When's my trip to Germany?" I asked after I remembered all

256

the thoughts that went through my mind during the interrupted sleep on the plane.

Our next replacement was that of the German chancellor. Robert Mulitz had been in power for about a year and half, but he'd been present in senior political circles for about three. After the first one, it had become very clear that he would inherit the chancellorship. We had inside information, but the prognosis was part of the public discourse as well, so we started preparing his double in time. Not that we had much of a choice, but in general it was easier to prepare doubles for the leaders with more time at the post; they could be assimilated and studied in more detail. This wasn't the case with Mulitz, but he compensated for it by having straightforward views and behavior. He was a typical German through and through. Married, and lucky for us – with no children. Public support for Mulitz was halfhearted at best. It was the same with the EU, the influence of which was expected to subside.

Christopher Miech was born and raised in Berlin. He was 35 when he joined the program, and he was recruited two years earlier. An architect by profession, he was earnest, rational, and principled.

"According to the schedule, in June," Fiona informed me.

"We're doing it earlier! The meeting with Yon gave me a new perspective. We'll accelerate all the other visits, too."

"Maybe you have a point," Matt said.

"I'll revise the schedule," Fiona agreed.

"Let's see if we can speed up the last phases of their programs," I added. "Did Romanov confirm his meeting with Mirov?"

"Not definitively, but he's almost certain," Matt informed me. "The other day we talked to Alexey's supervisor."

"Yes, me too," I replied. "He believes he's ready."

Which meant that I needed to get ready for a new trip to Russia and the base where Alexey was being trained to replace Mirov. If Romanov confirmed the meeting, the swap was going to happen at the end of March, and not in mid-July as we had planned.

Regardless of the team's assurances regarding Alexey's readiness, I insisted on approving it personally.

"In that case, I'll look for a flight to Omsk."

13.

For Jay Markins, April 16th started with 20 push-ups and 50 crunches. US president Mayden was in excellent shape, especially for his age. Besides, the weather in Alaska where our base was located called for a morning shake-up for warmth and circulation. Then, he played the president's speech from last year's Independence Day, and he turned on the coffee machine on his way to the shower. That had been his morning routine for the last six months.

In the context of how he spent the rest of his time, the calm, even prosaic mornings seemed like a paradox. They were the only *nearly* free hours before the beginning of yet another day devoted to his mission – to become the president of the United States.

Jay went to the bathroom around 7:10. We knew that because his alarm woke him at 7 a.m., one hour before his nonverbal communication training.

He was ready. He said it himself, and his supervisors confirmed the evaluation. He was five months away from the swap.

At 8:10, the psychologist Rich Sagan, who worked with Jay, knocked on his door. After knocking two more times without receiving an answer, he went inside. Being late was unlike Jay, and that gave Rich reason to worry. He was relieved to hear the water in the shower, but something made him go and check if everything was alright. He shouted a few times before opening the door.

Sometimes fate can be cruel. Jay often joked that he had drawn the short straw when selected to replace the US president. He claimed that an attempt on his life or terrorist attack were most likely.

At the end, the dangers that lurked outside with their jaws greedily opened in expectation were left hanging in the realm of possibility. We were convinced we had taken every precaution possible. From the credible erasure of his identity to the tough preparation and internal security of the base. The absurd incident that took Jay's life mercilessly laughed in our organization's face.

That morning, Rich found Jay naked on his bathroom's white-tiled floor. The water was still flowing at a high pressure. It seemed that he had stumbled while trying to grab the soap which was still on the sink. His death wasn't caused by head trauma, but by the tragic blow against the toilet bowl, which snapped his neck.

The news of the incident found me in Hamburg. I was here to clear up some details regarding Mulitz's replacement with Chris. For a moment, I imagined what would have become of us if we had been negligent about the unpredictable twists of fate, if we didn't have a plan B, if we had decided to skip the effort of training reserves. On the verge of the final phases, a similarly absurd turn of events threatened to derail it all.

What if we didn't have a backup for Jay? Were we about to impose global changes without the US? Every single one of the other 25 leaders was important, but the president of the US? The country's fist still hung heavily despite the shakier influence of the last few years. The potential refusal of the real US president could freeze all the new policies proposed at the conference.

I would never forget the terrifying feeling that cut through my chest when I found out about Jay's death. The nightmarish combination of helplessness, panic, and guilt. Sometimes I wondered if it would be the same if one of the scenarios, he liked to joke about had come to pass. Would have I felt more guilty, or less? Would have I felt like I contributed as much?

It took me a while to realize that in reality, I had no reason to feel either. And I really didn't have time for that.

I was forced to go back to the memory of my parents in the hope that I would be able to give it meaning. Just like Jay's. I had realized long ago that that meaning was the most sustainable motor of our mission. We couldn't afford to lose it, not with everything that was at stake. For this reason, we did everything possible to predict the unpredictable. The things that could storm over us at any moment and devastate everything in an instant.

Simon Henderson had started preparing about a month after Jay. Just like the other back-ups, he trained at a similar tempo, but under a different schedule and more relaxed conditions. One of them was that their deaths were never confirmed publicly. The back-ups were listed as missing in circumstances and places that no one wanted to investigate. Although it wouldn't be easy, this meant they could, if necessary, return to their lives if it didn't become necessary to use them. For this reason, more invasive surgery was also postponed until the moment it became absolutely certain it was needed. For Simon, all these challenges were still ahead, just like his complete isolation.

He was to be moved to the Alaska base a few days later. Rich and the other experts were going to adapt the program to his progress. By the time of my visit in August they were expected to have advanced considerably, to have undergone the most difficult surgery and be ready for replacement by the end of October, after Chris and before Yon. We had already put Alexey in place thanks to the opportunity that Romanov gave us at the end of last month.

By the end of 2025, we were supposed to have replaced all the leaders.

In the meantime, Romanov and his brethren, Ramirez, the Japanese, the Italians, and all other investors were to continue multiplying their networks and recruit like-minded individuals from the underground who were ready to change. Their parallel struggle to change the system wasn't any easier than ours. Aside from financing the mission, their main task was to clear the criminal world for change. An assignment that was going to continue long after the replacements.

Layla and the team she had trained in a relatively short time after she joined us were covering our backs in the media. Each one of them was deeply involved with different internet news outlets, which had become a serious tool for spreading influence. They were on the lookout for leaked information 24/7, ready to counteract it at once. Sometimes they needed to publish obfuscating articles that aimed to distract, while other times they ignored or refuted legitimate suspicions.

During the last few months, their assignment was to be different. They were to credibly and delicately begin building a positive image for the leaders already replaced and the ones that were about to be. Considering the quality of the originals, this was a tough responsibility. We forced ourselves to keep our critical voice quiet, and we shed more light on positive developments, which Layla and her team often concocted. This was supposed to make it considerably easier for us to win public trust after the conference. It would have been difficult to convince people to believe in a new system proposed by the old greedy and corrupt leadership.

Layla also had another, personal mission. We knew that we would invariably need to inform the public of our activities. That's what Layla had taken on – the acknowledgement. We intended to be honest and believed it was only fair for people to one day learn of what we had done and why. It could happen – five, six, or even ten years later. We meant to assess that depending on how the situation developed.

But the facts needed to be known, as well as the reasons.

Besides, true change wasn't going to happen overnight; it was going to take time.

Terms for leaders in democratic countries ended, and we were already in the process of preparing new candidates. Naturally, we hoped that societies would organically accumulate worthy successors, but we also had to do everything possible to prevent the reentry of elements from the old system. And speaking of it, who knew, maybe in the foreseeable future there could be a live program from Hermes. After 10 years spent in isolation and retrospection, maybe its inhabitants would want to share something with society.

We had started outfitting the island with surveillance technology six months before the first "guests" arrived. At this point there were 22 of them, and by the end of the year we planned to deliver the other three. With time, their number was going to grow. They were going to be joined by players from other spheres. The system was rotten way beyond politics.

Now Hermes was far from me, in the capable hands of the team that was exclusively dedicated to it and its residents.

Here, we were prioritizing the conference. January 12th, 2027 was going to be an unforgettable day. One of the few in modern history that had true significance for civilization. This first official meeting of the great powers represented by the three coalitions was going to take place in Beijing and be broadcasted worldwide. The Chinese president was going to stand up and voice all the sick and festering aspects of world politics. All the ones we railed against but accepted as a necessary evil. Hau Lin was going to become part of history as the first head of state who proposed real steps toward a completely new – and until then unthinkable – global political, economic, and social order. He was to conduct a debate – even if staged – of the relative positives and negatives of such a change. At the end of the day, nobody expected all members to agree on day one.

The goal of the event was to present these different methods of global government to the public and provoke their initial questions even before they were raised as a counterpoint by the "opposition" during the publicized debate.

After the official summit and the declarations of intent of the three alliances to join forces in the preparation to implement the new system, the time would come for the first of many press conferences. Like never before, the media would really give voice to society. They would ask, wonder, assume, and analyze.

We believed that after this first appeal for the reorganization of the world, change would come gradually and naturally.

14.

The long alleyway in front of Tech was deserted. I rarely had the chance to sit on one of the benches here and observe the surroundings at this time of day. On a regular weekday, the place would have been full of people from our and the surrounding buildings headed for their favorite lunch spot. But today, the first Saturday of November, there was no one around.

The lack of wind made the sunny autumn day even more pleasant. The aroma of freshly brewed coffee steamed from under the lid of the paper cup. The comfort that the scent provided, however, could not push away the anxiety rising in me. In our entire team, in fact. We had very recently successfully completed the replacement of German chancellor Mulitz. Which brought us to our penultimate swap – that of the US president.

I tried to keep my phone stationary and unaffected by the nervous tapping of my right foot. The noon sun fell on my screen and made visibility irritatingly difficult. I had to sit crouching with my elbows on my knees and my hand sheltering the display to see anything on the map at all.

For more than an hour now I had been watching the area around the Capitol in DC on Crosspoints. According to the app, Adrian was in position. His red dot flickered in the immediate vicinity of the Library of Congress.

What worried me was that I still didn't have Fiona's confirmation that the presidential car had reached the perimeter of Brioche, the old bakery. There, Mayden was supposed to meet his sister, and this was only known to us, them, his closest associates, and the select staff at the bakery. Although Simon had been ready weeks ago, we assessed this to be the most opportune moment. The bakery opened for just the two of them, and the visibility while they were on their preferred second floor remained extremely limited. Usually, they stayed for about two and a half hours. Just as we did. We had been observing them since the inception of their little tradition. These atypical and unknown quirks and habits all of us – including the leaders – had were key reference points in our planning.

Adrian's car was parked a few meters from Brioche's backdoor. Lucky for us, it was only used to take the garbage out.

Ironic, considering what else was about to be taken out of there.

The area was under intense surveillance. That wasn't really a challenge for us, but it raised the pressure levels. Especially now, when we were about to execute one of the last two replacements. I did my best to avoid focusing on the importance of the event and see it just like any other operation, at least until it was done.

We chose this particular moment for a number of other reasons. The principal one was that even though the area was heavily guarded, this was one of the very few occasions when the president moved around relatively incognito and without his motorcade, which left him with only four Secret Service agents. Despite Mayden's prickly personality, the Secret Service team in charge of his security kept him tightly confined. His outbursts against that quickly subsided completely after the prevented attempt that would have ended his life one year into his term. Some psychologically unstable young man had tried to assassinate him during the Super Bowl. The sociopath clearly craved an audience – few events reached such proportions.

We had observed Mayden's every move since he took office, and we knew that there were only two other such instances – when he visited the family residence in the Hamptons over Christmas, and his son's birthday. These were our three windows of opportunity. The rest of the time he was surrounded by bigger details and his team, by other politicians and their security, or reporters.

For objective reasons, the family gathering wasn't our best chance, especially for Simon. Regardless of how prepared he was to inhabit Mayden's skin, the close family circle was too risky to be his first role. The president's sister, however, was a much more adequate option. They weren't very close, and they saw each other once or twice a year. Their conversations revolved around Emma Mayden's business interests and the perks the family name brought. The president himself was willing to sacrifice a little effort and goodwill, as long as their meetings didn't become more frequent.

The self-absorbed Ms. Mayden was certainly not going to notice any changes in her brother's behavior, even if Simon's first performance was clumsy, unless it was because of a blunt misstep.

The meeting was scheduled for 12 p.m. The staff selected was to appear at 10 a.m. Of course, most of the preparation was done in advance the previous day. Brioche's status and reputation didn't allow for anything to be left to chance. They had two hours left to put on the final touches, and four for a deep clean in honor of their special guests.

Mia Pope was an art student in her last year of college when her brother Aaron recruited her. He was eight years older than her and a member for three. He knew about wires and electrical panels, but he still had a lot to learn. He was valuable mostly because of the five languages he spoke fluently, his potential for growth, and the views we shared about the future direction of the world. When we suggested using his sister in the operation to replace the US president, Aaron was working on Hermes's surveillance system.

One month after she joined us, Mia started work at Brioche as just another young girl who was trying to get extra income to pay her student loans. She was hired as a janitor, which is what we needed for the operation. No other job position offered us better opportunities for action. It was always the cleaning staff who arrived to work early, and they were often alone.

That morning though, she went in there with company. Shortly after she started her work for the day around 8:15, Simon entered through the backdoor and went up to the second-floor bathroom. He was to remain there for a few hours, until nature called the president or the hygienic requirement to wash his hands before the meal brought him to the arms of his double. Simon could then replace him and take over the conversation first, and his new life later.

When Simon sneaked through the back, the surveillance cameras were going to transmit footage from a previous time that showed no trace of our presence. This meant that Fiona and her team were going to spend the time until Mayden's arrival in readiness to deactivate the cameras in the area around Brioche. There was nothing especially innovative about the method and it didn't require great hacking skills, but it worked because we acted quickly and only needed to apply it for short periods of time. If everything went according to plan, we were going to carry the unconscious Mayden out through the back-door once Mia gave the signal.

Right on schedule, the bakery's manager and one of the servers arrived at 10 a.m. After they pedantically inspected Mia's work, they moved on to the details – tablecloths, napkins, silverware, dishes. Naturally, the master baker had arrived earlier. Brioche bore the name of his famous specialty.

I spoke to Adrian at 12:15, five minutes after Ms. Mayden had taken her seat at the table reserved for the occasion. The president's car, however, was running late. Fiona confirmed that he had left his residence on time and taken the established route. He passed through three of our observation posts, but something had delayed him and his three goons in the last section before his destination. Ironically, it was precisely the two kilometers that we had decided not to watch.

I couldn't remain unfazed by the change in schedule, but I knew from experience that when one, two, and three were in place, there was rarely a problem with four. What irritated me was that I had no choice but to sit on this damn bench thousands of kilometers away and just watch. But my job required gigantic amounts of resignation. I just couldn't allow myself to appear there. Right from the beginning of our mission we had decided that it would be wiser if I was nowhere near the locations of the replacements. In case of any complication, this would give me a chance to react and vanish.

As if on demand, thick clouds crept over the sun just as my Crosspoint chat with Fiona popped up.

He's three blocks away.

Four minutes later Mason's car stopped out front. My phone received a direct feed from the entrance, the back-door, the receiver under the president's table, and the one in Simon's ear. He was in position, Mia was ready to report on the president's every move, and Adrian was ready to take his body after her signal. Fiona and the others were in our den in DC, and we had equipped a small studio in Brentwood after Mulitz's replacement.

"Sorry about the delay, Em," I faintly heard the president say. He was probably some distance from the table and the mic under it. "Some clowns blocked the intersection right next to us!" He continued with annoyance. "It took them 10 minutes to drag themselves to the other side!"

The sound of a chair moving on the floor – she probably stood up to hug him – prevented me from hearing her first words. What she said next was a lot clearer.

"You didn't even look, did you?" Mayden's sister asked an obviously rhetorical question, clearly not expecting him to deny it. "It wasn't a protest, it was a breast cancer early awareness march!"

"I don't know, I saw pink and decided it was a gay-pride parade," the president admitted, unperturbed. "If I paid attention to everyone complaining, I would have run away from the White House a long time ago!"

"Or they would have kicked you out," his sister teased again.

Maybe we should have included her in the operation. Listening to her, I would bet that she would readily give her brother over.

During the next hour they discussed a lot of subjects that had nothing to do with politics or Mayden's presidential deeds. Rather, he passionately told her about his family and bragged about the academic and financial success of his sons, until the moment came to talk about his support for Emma's enterprises. Soon, my concentration began to fade from the conversation. Time went by and I could only imagine what Simon felt, sitting in the restroom waiting for his twin. I didn't need to imagine, actually. I spoke to him several times trying to gauge his mood, and I could feel he was getting anxious, despite his attempts to hide it.

Very soon, the president was going to get his brioche, which – as we know – even he ate with his hands.

As I reminded myself that our star moment was near, a new, unexpected call from Simon made my stomach turn.

"Boss, I need to..." He couldn't finish.

His stomach obviously felt much worse than mine. The sound of the liquids he shot out of his mouth helped me very clearly picture what was happening behind the last door in the row of five, where he was hiding. We had only left one camera running and it pointed to the sinks, so at the moment I was unable to see Simon's face, but...

For fuck's sake, what exactly is protecting the fucking president?!

Yet more absurdity swirled around us with Mayden's replacement, this time drawing us into a much riskier situation. The boiling point, as I found out from Adrian's call, was yet to come. The baker had just placed the two special brioches on the first-floor kitchen line.

"Mia just confirmed that they'll be served in a second," he added.

"Simon will need help," I said. "Tell her to go to the men's toilet at once." Meanwhile, I went back to the conversation on the table.

"I'll go after you do," we heard Emma Mayden say.

Simon had heard it as well. So ready or not, he needed to be ready to go into action at any moment.

"Simon, listen to me," I said intensely in his ear. "You are ready for this. Get yourself together and act! You have 15 seconds."

I heard him take a deep breath.

Mayden went into the bathroom and headed to one of the sinks. After the careful inspection in front of the mirror while he washed the soap off his hands, he used the remaining moisture to smooth down the lock of gray hair that had dared to deviate from the rest.

Simon exhaled in my ear. From this point on, I could only hope that it gave him courage, and it didn't indicate that he was about to abort the mission.

The president was already by the drier right next to the fifth door, where his fate hid. He turned to the mirror on his left again.

"What the f..." he choked.

His horrified expression confirmed Simon's appearance behind him, fractions of a second before I saw him. He was gripping the rag soaked in chloroform, and with a few leaps he made his way to the president. Mayden initiated a furious self-defense. His survival instinct very quickly overrode the shock. In the meantime, Mia also burst into the restroom and rushed to activate the drier, the noise of which muffled the noises of the two men wrestling. Then she helped Adrian subdue the still struggling, but by now half-sedated president. Simon's mic transmitted grunts interrupted by the fight. Finally, Mayden stumbled to the ground. Mia hastily took his jacket off and started to unfasten his tie, while Simon pulled on his pants. One minute and thirty seconds later, the double left the restroom to complete the rest of the operation.

The new president headed for the table.

Mia signaled Adrian to approach the backdoor, where he was to pick up the former president's body.

I knew that Simon had been prepared as rigorously as all the other doubles. But the physical manifestation of tension that had overtaken him at the key moment worried me deeply. Something that at first glance appeared innocent could be the cause of many, many complications.

"I thought that only women dolled up in the restroom," I heard Emma tease. It had been six minutes since Mayden left the table.

"Yeah, you should give it a try sometime!" was Simon's biting retort – entirely in her brother's style. Then the conversation continued from where it had stopped, and I switched to Adrian.

"I'm in the back; the boys went in to take him," he reported.

According to the plan, Mia was to drag the blissfully unconscious Mayden down the middle of the corridor to the back door. The practicality that Brioche's designer had applied so long ago was so valuable to us now that he deserved a post-mortem membership! The bathrooms were located in a hallway that led straight to the backdoor. On top of that, instead of stairs, there was a ramp to facilitate disposal. He couldn't have made it any easier for us if he'd tried.

Four minutes later, Adrian's dot in Crosspoint was in motion. Only then did I allow myself to relax a bit. It had been a nervous five hours. I could feel the tension that had gripped my body from my heels to the last hair on my head gradually release its powerful hold.

"Number 24 has successfully departed for Neverland!"[2] Fiona always became charmingly poetic in such moments. She assured me that Adrian and another one of the "Lost Boys" were on the planned route to transit point Argentina.

It was tucked away in a deserted coastal area a few hundred kilometers south of Buenos Aires. Before Mayden, the prime minister of Canada and the president of Brazil had also stayed there. It was the most convenient and direct location from where to sail away.

Just like the others, in two days he was going to wake up on an empty (maybe) beach in the middle of nowhere. He would have no idea of all the old "friends" he would encounter on Hermes. But first he had to seek them out somewhere among the golden dunes. Like the rest of his peers, he would probably notice the cameras spread all over the island. Who

[2] *A reference to the island of Neverland, where the hero of J. M. Barrie's eponymous novel lives with his band of Lost Boys and other fantastic creatures.*

knows, maybe someday they would count them and discover there were exactly 3000 surveillance points. Or maybe they'd find out from me, during our first official conversation after the conference. The special moment when they would finally be told where they were and why. Mayden was one of the lucky ones; all the others before him had spent from a few months to four years without that privilege.

I could still not allow my mind to travel to Hermes too often. Here, on the mainland, we still had work to do. One last swap before we replaced the leaders of all 25 countries in the three alliances.

Next month, Yon was to take power in place of President Hau Lin. It was contrary to logic for him to be the last one. But we had learned that logic can't always be applied, especially to our mission. *Opportunity* was the driving force that we took into consideration. In the case of Hau Lin, the most opportune moment would be December 2nd, 2025, the day of daughter's wedding. We had been planning the swap since 2023, and it was going to be executed following a well-practiced scenario that we had accepted as final eight months earlier. For this reason, as strange as it seemed, the most important replacement was going to happen last. That was the opportunity. Many people, friends, strong emotions…

Euphoria is a powerful ally.

All these factors would make the operation go a lot smoother. Which meant that a few months on high alert for Yon was worth it. Either way, he was excellently prepared and would have an entire year in office before the conference.

By that time, each of our doubles would have acquired deeper firsthand knowledge of the system. Some of them had been in office for years. This gave them the chance to gradually prepare the ground for an optimization of government and international relations. That was our focus at this stage of the mission, and the big day was drawing near.

The countdown had started. 13 months…

III.

2027

1.

Six weeks before January 12, 2027, and the upcoming summit between the members of OPEC, BRICS and G-7, the media started to circulate reports about it. The president of the People's Republic of China personally invited his allies and the other organizations to an open debate.

Everyone accepted.

What a shock!

They also agreed, despite the initial turmoil, to forego protocol and announce beforehand the topics and tasks that were to be discussed.

In a televised speech from the presidential palace, Lin appealed for the meeting and described it as "pressing in the context of current global development and critical in terms of its potential consequences." After he announced the time and date of the conference, Lin emphasized that regardless of the decisions made, "the world will be different the morning after."

Thirteen hours before the video was posted on the official presidential site, the sensational piece of news was alluded to by a reporter from *Global World*. It was one of the many news outlets that existed on the internet. It didn't have the scale of the *Washington Post* or the *New York Times*, but it enjoyed a solid following and a high level of trust. Especially for those readers who knew how "trustworthy" the media giants were.

Zachary Fisch had started *Global World* and eight other socio-cultural websites in 2025. That was four months after he joined Layla's team.

Hours after the publication of the dramatic news, the article wasn't shared a single time. It was being completely ignored. It was probable that other reporters, as well as the audience, considered it too improbable to be true. Either way, we didn't aim for that. We didn't need a commotion. The only thing we wanted was to be first. Nothing else.

The fact that *Global World* had obtained the information before anyone else was going to increase trust in our media. From then on, we could participate in shaping public opinion on the new program and social order that Hau Lin, or rather Yon, was going to propose several weeks later. The mission of this outlet was to give the audience the necessary tools to analyze the different points of view before it rejected the idea. People were going to need that – a place that allowed for constructive dialogue outside of the other publications with the keywords "shock" and "unprecedented." They needed someone to ask *What if? Could it?*

We were going to widely discuss potential pros and cons to be taken into consideration before ignorance and fear of the unknown hurled society back to the destructive – but familiar – comfort zone.

The days passed imperceptibly, and, in spite of the rigorous preparations, we felt like we'd been directly teleported to the conference. On January 6, Beijing welcomed its first guest, Mirov, the Russian president. One month after his term had begun, we had started preparing Alexey Kraev, who took over two years later. We had to act quickly once again, but Romanov had created the perfect opportunity and we had to take advantage of it.

Until then, Mirov hadn't exactly displayed a very remarkable personality, which may have been a good move, considering his predecessor, the controversial figure that ruled the country for two decades. Some worshiped him; others hated him. Especially after the Ukraine conflict.

Still, some people did realize that it was not just between the two countries. There was, as always, a backstage provoker – third party interests, backroom dealings, and billions of dollars laundered at the cost of hundreds of thousands of lives.

But whatever the reason, international relations had deteriorated to critical levels, there were armed conflicts in many other countries, and the financial crisis that started with the covid pandemic had shaken the global economy to the core.

In any case, it was clear that Mirov was to continue the policy of his predecessor to preserve cooperation with China and the other members of BRICS. After 2022, his country had suffered a blow to its prestige, but still wielded influence thanks to its nuclear arsenal, and no one was under the illusion that they would cease to be a factor. .

For this reason, Alexey's political training was geared toward preserving that line. Luckily, he was similar to Mirov physically, and the surgical intervention didn't have to be as extreme as with some other doubles.

Following the remaining six days to the conference, the other 23 leaders arrived one by one. Our leaders.

The big day started for me at 5:58 a.m. Not that I had made use of the night as intended – I didn't really sleep a wink. I started watching the empty square in front of the National People's Congress, where the summit was to take place, long before the sun came up. The first rays tried to break through the thick clouds about an hour later. The emblematic political center of Beijing could rarely be seen so deserted. I had been observing it for a week now, and I knew that soon the early-rising administrative officials would begin crisscrossing it. And only four hours later, the 25 instruments with which we were going to fix the social and political machine would walk across as well.

Did even one of them get any sleep?

The morning promised another gloomy day, even though the winter here seemed bearable. Not that it affected me directly – I was going to spend the next few hours in my hotel room, staring at the Congress building as the conference went on behind its columns.

Layla and Alex Stevens were here to cover the event for one of our channels, the one that managed to secure a pass. They arrived a day after me and were going to leave immediately after the end of the meeting. Our stay here was going to be strictly autonomous; we were not to meet or call. We needed to maintain strict security. Even the smallest hint that we might be connected could inflict damage.

Minutes grew into hours, and each hour dragged by. I had the nagging feeling that the air in my room was stuffy enough to cause any normal person claustrophobia.

I had no way of communicating with any of our 25 associates. That they would be followed and surveilled was more of a guarantee than a possibility. By contrast, I called Fiona four times. The time difference meant nothing on this day.

At 9:42, I looked out to the square again. Only after I let out a deep breath did I realize that I had been holding it as I watched our people walk across the square surrounded by the human shield of the bodyguards. These in turn were surrounded by journalists, but none of them was given access. With minor exceptions, our channel included, very few outlets were allowed to attend outside of the official national broadcaster of each country. This was a provocative condition that had been arranged by Layla long ago. The US was represented by FOX.

Fiona made sure we had access to the camera feed from the official hall. I could follow the conference in its entirety, but I was more interested in the reactions of the reporters. I planned to watch FOX on my laptop. They sent Tiffany Walls, who had just interviewed chancellor Mulitz. Or more accurately, Chris.

"Germany is always open to unifying our positions, as long as there is constructive dialogue and rational decisions," he responded when she asked him about Germany's predisposition before the conference.

I also kept an eye on the TV. Thanks to the Chinese media's courtesy for foreigners wanting to follow the event, there were subtitles, and I didn't need to freely interpret the faces, mimicry, and gestures. The Chinese national channel was showing an interview with Indian prime minister Amir Vind:

"President Lin invited the three largest organizations to discuss the possibilities for *global* development," Vind resumed. "I believe that global interest should and *must* be a unifying force. India hopes that the discussions will give rise to policies that are detailed and sustainable, with measurable benefits to society, especially when it comes to social responsibility."

"You mean to say that the economy is not the first priority?" the reporter sharply reproached him. That angered even me, and I wondered how Khalid managed to keep president Vind's kind facial expression.

"It is not my intention to provide a deep analysis before I have heard the announcement of our honored host," Khalid countered calmly. "The economic profile should be the result of social policies, not an excuse for its unavailability to society. And as to your question: I believe that if a certain perspective is beneficial to people, even if it's in the long term, it could, to an extent, justify temporary economic difficulties. Thank you. If you'll excuse me..." He ended the conversation politely when he saw the selected reporters and the leaders head for the hall.

I followed them on both channels. Before they went inside, all 25 leaders posed for a picture.

A picture that in my mind marked the beginning of a new phase in our mission.

The beginning of the new order!

2.

At exactly 10 a.m., Hau Lin welcomed his guests. They sat around an enormous round table set to the left of the hall's entrance. The hall was around 150 square meters and seemed somewhat sterile, in a Scandinavian way. It was probably because of the light oakwood that covered the floor, the paneling, and the table.

The representatives of the media were arranged alongside the inside wall. The thick glass cabins from where the interpreters worked were right above their heads. The light that entered the hall through the panoramic windows certainly didn't help the camera operators, but the interior didn't offer any alternatives.

The central spot from their point of view was occupied by President Lin. On his left side were his allies from BRICS: Russia, India, Brazil, South Africa. Then came the oil exporters – the OPEC members. The G7 leaders were on the right side of the host.

The cameras jumped among all the leaders:

Lin, Murad, Mulitz, Suhama, Albriani, Mayden... That is, China, Saudi Arabia, Germany, Japan, Italy, the United States...

The whole world understood the unprecedented magnitude of the event. It had provoked historic levels of engagement – for weeks political analysts and social scientists commented on the public reaction to the upcoming summit. Such a reaction had not been recorded since the outbreak of the covid pandemic.

Once again, the world felt it was facing something unknown. We heard all sorts of interpretations, speculations, and hypotheses on the purpose of the meeting. Some thought that gathering the leaders of all these countries, some of which were involved in years-long active or latent conflicts, heralded a threat of a very different and catastrophic nature.

The more optimistic ones believed that China had made a scientific or technological discovery which was so sensational that it required an official international presentation because of the changes it was going to bring to the world. There were suppositions that the conference's aim was for China to publicly flex its military muscle and deliver some kind of ultimatum, leading in turn to the official Third World War, which had been barely avoided in the last years.

The noise in the hall quieted down, and the insufficient amount of air in my lungs forced me to regulate my breathing. This was the moment I had been waiting for my entire *truly* conscious life.

"Esteemed gentlemen," Hau Lin stood up and began. "I would like to present my sincere apologies for not following established protocol and announcing the precise reason for this summit in advance, as diplomacy requires. I convey my personal gratitude and appreciation, as well as that of the People's Republic of China, for your acceptance of the invitation, the inconvenience notwithstanding." He spoke slowly and clearly. "We have many different political outlooks on this table today," he remarked as he pointed to both sides of the table, without pointing at anyone in particular. "We will be hearing different opinions in the course of our conversation. Since we are not following a political scenario, I would like to open our conference with an appeal for a reasonable, unprejudiced, and constructive dialogue.

Everyone was all ears, trying to hear the purpose of the meeting. The cameras skillfully captured everyone present, both around the table and their colleagues along the wall. I carefully examined each of them in the hall through the "eyes" of Chinese state security, who were guarding the president and observing the conference with four cameras. Fiona made sure we were connected to all four.

Given that there were several theories on the reason for the meeting, the leaders of the countries hosted by Hau Lin had facial expressions that betrayed tension. Or at least that was the look for the broader public. But I could read something different in the eyes of every one of *our* associates. *Our* members, whose hands I had shaken years ago, who had accepted the sacrifice of their former lives for everything that was beginning with this conference. The members whose families we had sworn to protect after the deep grief we caused them. The associates whose souls I had seen behind the changed faces that had become unrecognizable.

There, I now read the thoughts in my own head. I was certain that such were the thoughts of every member of our organization. We were here – the moment of truth. The culmination of our operations and the starting point of change.

"As you know, China takes pride in its thousands of years of history and deeply appreciates the moral legacy of its ancestors," Lin said decorously. "For us, the inheritors of this memory, the meaning of life has always been a value beyond our daily existence. We live with the thought of our own function within the whole – our society and its future development and wellbeing. Before, it was within the empire, then the people's republic, and now – the world."

Yon, from inside Hau Lin's skin, continued to carefully examine the reactions of everyone after each word. Especially after the last one, which caused a quick exchange of excited, but somewhat disturbed glances between reporters. I could see it through the cameras in the hall, and I could see it through the "eyes" of the FOX cameraman.

I knew how many times Yon had prepared for this moment – the moment when he needed to mobilize all his self-control and present our organization's mission to the world. Our further actions now depended on his facial expression, speech, and intonation. Even the most remote hint of doubt in his words could turn what was said into parody. Into something that the media and the public could ruthlessly mock.

But his performance was flawless.

"Regretfully, in the last few decades we have watched humanity tear itself apart in spite of the level of global interconnectedness brought on by new technologies. We have gathered here in our capacity as leaders of the most powerful countries on earth. The three organizations that hold the planet's most precious resources."

With each word Lin said and every camera shot that showed the other leaders around the table, I became more convinced of how exceptionally well we had prepared for this. Although they were still hearing out Lin's welcome address and their roles were passive, their expressions intentionally showed surprise, skepticism, even mockery.

"We are here today," he emphasized again, "because in spite of its natural and economic resources, in spite of its technologic and intellectual progress, humanity has not been moving forward or upward." He paused and looked over his guests on both sides. "We are sinking ever faster, and we are doing so in disunity. We surely do not want to live in a world like that. We believe that the world does not want such a future for itself."

He paused again, before getting to the heart of the matter. "We invited you here with the hope of laying the foundations of a new path to our collective future. For that to occur, we must speak some truths."

A wave of unease went over the attendees; they shifted uncomfortably and looked to the side.

"I will begin," Lin continued. "You are welcome to object, refute, or agree with the proposals of the People's Republic of China.

All eyes were on him. The interpreters in the cabins on the second level seemed the most stunned. After all, they were to be the first ones to repeat the uncomfortable truths they could feel were coming.

I stared at my laptop's screen. A close, frontal shot of Lin's face once again reminded me of how far we had traveled in seven years. Then it returned me to the speech.

"We humans are superior to other living beings in having the privilege of being able to make use of reason and feeling. A privilege that should lead us to progress." His face betrayed that the next words would rub salt in some wounds. "The memory of time, unfortunately, clearly shows that for us, these opportunities have led to self-destruction. We have allowed ourselves to be lost in the age of technological super-progress – we are educating a generation relying entirely on artificial intelligence and robbing it of the conditions in which to develop the ability to survive with the help of their own hands and knowledge if it ever became necessary. We have lost ourselves in the modern understanding of freedom and democracy. Our education system prepares personnel in all sorts of fields and spheres of the modern world and culture. Spheres which would have no value and function in a human lifestyle where man develops naturally, as part of nature, without the need to sell, manipulate, or judge.

The eye contact Lin made with each one of the leaders added meaning to his speech and converted it to an appeal.

"Additionally... It was precisely the modern world and its new opportunities that taught us consumerism as a way of life, with transitory values and brutal stress levels provoked and maintained by the surrounding "comfortable" environment. And that, it seems, brings on more disease than pollution and poverty. Millions of people and households are forced to think about surviving instead of thriving. Worrying about how they will feed their families, whether they will lose their jobs, or how to pay off their home, how to provide a good education for their children and their chance for a better life... What about the air we breathe? The food and medicine we are poisoned with? Who hasn't lost at least someone in their family after a battle with cancer?"

I could wager that the bitter lump stuck in Yon's throat could be felt by everyone in the hall. It took him a few long seconds to swallow it and continue his speech.

"Ladies and gentlemen, we have become victims of our own "progress"! And in the name of the people of the People's Republic of China, I declare that henceforth, we shall devote our efforts entirely to creating the conditions for a better life. Not in that discredited modern sense of a better life. We will strive to return to the ideal meaning of an advanced civilization. As the leader of our country, it is my personal duty to declare this to you and the entire world. And to do everything in my power to persuade you to take up this direction together." Now it was time to move smoothly on to the next point. "China's global influence is well known. We remember the consequences of the pandemic that has been gradually bringing us down for years. Our own inability to produce what the world was used to getting from us, and at the price it had taken for granted, had a disastrous effect on the world economy and led to the manufacturing collapse of some of the largest companies in the world. Let us remember the Russian invasion of Ukraine at that time. It was as if the focus of the public was on the expected gas crisis rather than on the hundreds of thousands of victims of that invasion. Although it was criticized, we all felt the painful withdrawal of Russia as the largest exporter of this resource from international exchanges. At that time, we were also convinced once again that, although NATO was seen as an interstate alliance, the US dictated the rules. The country with the most expansionist military."

At this stage the president personally turned to each one of the leaders he was addressing.

"Global control over oil, agricultural, and financial resources of the countries we represent..." Lin paused once again and looked over the hall, while the tension on his face dissipated. "I point out these aspects to emphasize man's tendency to use his advantages as a means of power. It seems to be in our nature to strive for domination, monopoly, subordination; to choose our allies by the destructive force of the weapon in their hands, even if it is at the expense of tolerating certain differences in values." He shook his head. "We are ready to do anything to increase our share of the whole, and we are deeply convinced it belongs to us."

Lin stopped and looked away for a moment. It seemed like a way for him to find a solution for an internal hesitation.

"Before you interpose, I'll be the first to say that I, as head of state, I have also been part of the vicious circle I am exposing. But in due course I recognized that things could be different... How much longer are we going to scare people with scarcity? How much longer are we going to hide the fact that it is just an illusion we use to prop up the system? That the resources we have could allow us to live comfortably and in an environmentally friendly way? A comfort for which today we pay the state, corporations, and cartels, institutions whose material interest turns out to be more important not only than the future of people, but of our planet itself! And who knows – maybe someday we will realize that the centralized monetary system is no longer needed! We may reach a stage in our development where the economy will exceed the dimension of buying and selling resources. Perhaps we will share them?"

The hall fell into a nearly dead silence, interrupted only by Hau Lin's voice and the camera clicks of the journalists.

"It is also true that the gold standard in the monetary system has not worked for a long time, that has been apparent for decades. We believe that control of the money supply is considerably more important than its value, and we mean to explore more appropriate alternatives to government control of money. We won't remain blind to the fact that there are more and more opportunities for decentralized currencies, and we believe it is a matter of time and constructive collaboration to build a new one that would benefit society," he announced encouragingly, before adding, "We are inclined to believe that there is a path to move toward a sustainable economy, based on natural resources. If the planet has enough sunlight, water sources, and wind, which it does, then the idea of scarcity imprinted for so many years is illusory. What's more, we should not have to pay for the comfort that these resources afford us. But we ought to start thinking about their present state!" Hau Lin appealed. "We need clean air, water, and food, and we need sustainable, environmentally friendly energy. This will be the focus of our country in the coming years."

It seemed that everyone present was more and more stunned with each additional sentence spoken by the host. It was as if they were getting shocked by the new statement even before they had time to assimilate the previous one. It was obvious that no one had expected to hear similar words here. Maybe from an eco-activist, even from a conspiratorially-minded individual, but not from a government representative. Even less from a president.

"Today the People's Republic of China formally declares its disagreement with the system imposed in the civilized world. We find it unsuitable for development. We believe that it plunders and enslaves." Hau Lin spoke the last sentence with a calm but firm tone.

"Dear guests and compatriots, I would like to announce to all of you the first steps we are taking in this direction. To begin with, from now on, none of our countrymen will pay for the right to have electricity, water, heating, or transportation. It is common knowledge that as the largest manufacturer of solar panels in the world, it is entirely feasible for us to produce eighty percent of our electricity from sunlight. You are also aware that the technologies for converting water into electricity that we have been developing for years are achieving promising results. Provided there is strict control and consideration of the impact on water sources, we could achieve good results without affecting their sustainability. I can assure you that the decision to provide these free services is neither shortsighted nor temporary. We have made a concerted effort to look for opportunities to realize this policy. And while we have found ways to start, we believe that with the help of your experts, and all the other countries around the world, we will perpetually continue to improve all that we mentioned here, until we can finally create a single, comprehensive, truly working model!"

From time to time, I switched over to the cameras in the hall, and I could once again appreciate the preparedness of our doubles. Although at this stage of the meeting their roles were entirely nonverbal, their reactions to Hau Lin's words seemed genuine. Exactly as would be expected from heads of state who are being informed publicly and in front of the entire world that a new order is coming to the People's Republic of China. The anxiety they tried to hide behind their calm expressions seeped through their body language.

"For this model to work sustainably, we plan to work hard toward phasing out the monetary system and dependence on banking institutions in the next ten years. I am not saying that it will be easy, nor that it will happen quickly. However, we certainly know that this is the direction we will take. The best economists, mathematicians, sociologists and analysts of our country have invested years in research, calculations, and projections to create the agenda that is in the folder in front of each of you, and that we are about to distribute to our people. By the end of our meeting, it will be delivered to you digitally. Attached is the complete research report on the implications and prospects for this program, as well as a projected plan for the next 50 years. It details the most favorable, as well as the negative, scenarios of global adaptation to this new system."

One by one, and still in a general state of disbelief, the guests opened the thick folders that had been placed in front of them minutes earlier. Most directed their attention to the Table of Contents.

It contained six main points, with four or five sub-points, which all present, as well as their governments, would be thoroughly acquainted with in the coming months.

Lin used these moments to put his thoughts in order.

"We also had the obligation to present the probable outcomes for international relations in the event of a possible refusal of the proposed changes by the other countries," he said regretfully, as if he actually imagined such a development.

Everyone put their folders aside and focused. It seemed like this aspect interested them more than any other. The hall fell silent.

"You all understand that the relationship of the People's Republic of China with other countries will not continue to develop in the established way," the host went on to reveal. "To put it bluntly, your disagreement with our new government model could put an end to them altogether. Although this is not the outcome we hope that today's meeting will have, I assure you our country is capable of adapting to a self-sufficient model of functioning. But I remind you" – he held up his hand – "that it does not wish such an outcome. The changes we are introducing into our system aim to isolate the preconditions for extreme dependence on an international exchange of any kind. Of course, we will not destroy our military equipment and leave our country defenseless. Although in our new system, the sense of military conflict and action is minimized, we should not forget that the human ego remains prone to that as a way of overcoming differences. Military conflicts will remain a serious threat to us should the world refuse to join, or at least accept, the different path China is taking."

If until now the other leaders looked stunned, after

Lin's last words, their expressions started to betray great tension. Every once in a while, the cameras caught their eyes, with which they seemed to decipher the attitude toward the message. Naturally, these were just reflections of the reactions that the world expected them to have.

"But the purpose of today's meeting and your honorable presence here is not simply to inform you of our actions. It is to convince you that we should walk this path together," Lin assured them. "My sincere wish and mission is that we build together; that we put together the beginnings and the rules of a new world, better and more promising for the sake of our children. That is why we will soon make education accessible to all of them. Not just accessible, but also mandatory! Because they are our future and the safest investment."

The host spread his arms and continued to his closing words: "Thank you for the respect with which you listened to the message of the Republic of China. With the same respect, I am ready to listen to your attitude or considerations on the points raised."

A silence as absorbing as dark matter spread over the hall in the ten seconds that separated his last words from the interjection of the President of India.

"President Lin," Vind started. "I have the honor of ruling a country where spirit and personal development are indeed held in high esteem, despite the economic situation which we have consistently, though not always successfully, sought to optimize." He spoke slowly and coolly, but the honesty of his words was genuine and palpable. "A moment ago you mentioned intellectual resources. For India, education is also a supreme value. Extraordinary efforts on the part of the government to incentivize teachers have resulted in considerable progress over the last decade. You understand that we are talking about a financial incentive, provided at the expense of budgets for industrial, manufacturing, and infrastructure development. Based on my experience with an aspect similar to the complex reforms you proposed,

I am willing to hold in-depth discussions with our experts about the prospects for a new global socio-economic system. It would be a sign of poor diplomatic culture to oppose or object before I have examined the detailed report," declared Vind. "Today I will only ask you to consider the answer to a single question."

The cameras darted back to President Lin, eager to capture the reaction to the request, which they must have seen as a political provocation.

"Please!" The host replied with a welcoming gesture.

Vind placed the palm of his right hand on his heart and bowed back, but with what seemed like appreciation. "You are aware that, just like the People's Republic of China, India is a country with a multi-million population. What will happen to education in a country where the problem of a lack of teachers and teaching staff can only be solved by financial benefits? In a world without the worry of material deprivation, what would inspire a young and educated person to dedicate his life to the cause of passing on his knowledge to others?"

"Your question is reasonable, President Vind. In modern times, to be an educator is much more than a calling. In many ways, it is a sacrifice that few are capable of," he admitted before concluding: "Your government has adopted a financial incentive strategy. What are its parameters, if I may ask?"

"We aim to offer monthly salaries that are significantly higher than average monthly salaries. A key focus of our policy is also the provision of sufficiently satisfactory social benefits – medical care, property insurance, tax breaks, retirement benefits..."

"What is at the heart of this proposal, Mr. President?" Lin asked with a confidence that hinted at his readiness to answer. "What is its true meaning?"

"Peace of mind, of course," Vind replied. 'We need to convince these people that by dedicating themselves to the cause of educating their countrymen, they are not ruining their chances of the better life that their intellect and knowledge merit and that they could potentially achieve."

"It seems like you found a way. In their essence, the measures that you have taken and those we are proposing are in unison. Scientists, teachers, doctors – that is the foundation of a healthy society! Financial or not, the benefits they deserve for their service should allow them to live with dignity and without material concerns. What is more, they should be at the peak of the social pyramid!"

The majority of those present showed neither opposition to Lin's words nor agreement with them. This lack of reaction allowed him to finish his statement.

"And please do not misunderstand me – I'm not ignoring entrepreneurs and businessmen who are presently standing at the top. To amass a fortune, through perseverance, visionary thinking, and market savvy is worthy of respect in the highly competitive environment of the 21st century." He paused for a second to formulate his next thought.

In his responses to politicians and the media, Yon did not stick to a literal script, but to the facts and values of our program, which he had to present in the most convincing way.

"The problem is that powerful corporations, property tycoons, stockbrokers... their activities are based on exactly that consumerist behavior that we want to confront. Although it sounds extreme, it does not lead to the development of society," Lin explained. "At its core, it is based on taking, not on sharing."

"'I would like to interrupt, if I may," said Mayden. "You seem to be striking a blow at certain democratic values, which, after many years and effort, we have fought to impose as the birthright of the individual!" he remarked defensively. "At the heart of the modern understanding of civil liberty is precisely the chance to develop according to one's own abilities. The American Dream..." Mayden reminded them. "The assurance that with the inner fervor of a dream, the power of character and will, you can achieve anything

288

you wish!" he said theatrically.

"Of course, President Mayden," Lin conceded. "The United States of America has succeeded in convincing the world that anything is possible if you are driven and confident enough in your abilities. The problem is in what we have taught people to pursue. Precisely," he turned to the others. "We all did it. And what did it lead to? Corporations worth billions, a corrupt judiciary, the disappearance of the middle class. Educated individuals living on the verge of poverty?" After his last rhetorical question, he kept his eyes on the table before turning to his opponent. "Who are your wealthiest citizens?"

"If you're trying to insinuate something, President Lin, let's consider a three-dimensional view of the circumstances," Mayden retorted with an arrogance that bordered on the impermissible. "Things cannot be black or white. The elite is the elite everywhere. The most educated or the hardest working do not always make it to the top of the pyramid. Power also requires a set of distinctive qualities and characteristics, sometimes even more important than a diploma and hard work. Sometimes these are inherited," he added. "Fair or not, it has been so for centuries. It's the way the world carries on." He confidently concluded his thesis.

"Exactly. It's the way the world carries on," Lin repeated. "Let us take a three-dimensional view. What propels it to carry on like that?"

"Please, Mr. Lin!" Mayden replied with amusement. "I understand the hint that we humans have set it up this way. But I cannot agree, at least not entirely. Mother Nature functions according to a principle called natural selection! It is not about the survival of the biggest, the bravest, or even the strongest! Sometimes the fastest survive. Sometimes – the most cunning. And at other times – the most inconspicuous. What I mean to say is that, in the end, life doesn't follow a script, and it's definitely not always fair!"

There was some movement in the hall. The various cameramen were filming the other leaders. Some of them had to demonstrate agreement with Mayden, and others showed irritation with his way of thinking.

Hau Lin took the floor again to parry.

"And this is the time, President Mayden, to go back to the beginning and my opening remarks. Unlike nearly all other animal species, man is endowed with the ability to reason, to evolve. To evolve," he emphasized. "Mother Nature did not create politics, correct? Neither did she invent medicine, technology, art, education, artificial intelligence... If you think about it, she did not even create time, which subdues us as if it were a law of nature!" Lin rightly pointed out. "We created them."

"Much like we created war..." The German chancellor interjected. "At least the kind fought over money."

"Chancellor Mulitz, with all due respect," Albriani spoke out, "we must remind ourselves that wars are not fought for money alone. Some nations fight because of a fanatical drive for superiority."

The reference of the Italian president did not appeal to many of those present, especially Mulitz, but had to be present in one form or another. Similar moderately sardonic remarks made the debate more credible.

"Let us please refrain from going in that direction!" Havi cut in. He was our replacement for Saudi monarch, Salim Murad. The ironic part was that they were relatives, even if distant. "As I understand it, the future you are designing does not involve mining or the use of oil," he remarked reservedly after closing the folder in front of him. "Would you care to explain how you plan to replace it? What will cars run on? Or are you suggesting we all ride bicycles?"

"President Lin, this meeting is beginning to take on somewhat utopian dimensions, don't you think?" provoked Mayden in his turn. "Does this folder really contain the absurd proposal to discontinue the use of oil? You are about to make me refuse to even take it with me!" Then he added more diplomatically. "In principle, I accept the idea of a greener future, but you are focusing on a plan for the next ten years! We will not be ready to phase out fossil fuels on such short notice!"

"You will be persuaded once you familiarize yourself with the program. As you know," he added, "scientists have been working on alternatives for years. I am happy to reassure you that in recent years we have discovered the missing elements of Yull Brown's oxyhydrogen gas technology,[3] as well as its successful application."

"Oh Lord!" Mayden rolled his eyes wearily.

"This, and many other good discoveries, have been suppressed in an attempt to protect certain interests." Lin raised an eyebrow and looked around at the others, apparently to confirm to himself intuitively that they all knew what he meant.

"No one has proven that works!" Mirov interjected and snorted dismissively. "Water for fuel!"

The last president of France was among those who held views closest to ours. At least that is how he sounded in his media appearances. Unfortunately, he succumbed to material seduction as easily as the rest. At least he was among those who posed the lowest risk of an abrupt change in behavior.

"President Lin's team has attempted to create a comprehensive program to initiate a number of measures aimed at an entirely new, more humane and socially responsible system," he began. "It would be appropriate for the skepticism expected in assemblies like this to be in moderation. As state leaders, we have no right to react with hasty opinions and positions, especially regarding a subject of such global importance," he announced, and then turned to Hau Lin. "I am assuming that you allocated a reasonable time frame during which we could review the plan with our relevant ministries?"

Lin nodded in confirmation and proceeded toward

---

[3] The inventor (with a Bulgarian origin), known for his belief that water could be used as a fuel, developed into the corresponding Brownian gas.

closing the session. "I propose that the meeting for the second consideration of the measures be held in six months. In the meantime, a team from the People's Republic of China will remain available for extraordinary discussions and consultations on the sections on the plan at both governmental and scientific levels."

At this point, no further sarcastic or skeptical expressions could be noticed. The faces of the leaders showed a rather neutral stance, as we believed they should.

"Esteemed colleagues," Lin continued. "Thank you for your presence and participation in the official announcement of the proposal to restructure the global economic and social system. I would like to reiterate that this is a proposal for collaborative change, but our country has already decided to take real steps in this direction and hopes that they will be mutual. I call for tolerance and willingness to consider the measures thoroughly, and I declare the conference to be finalized."

3.

During the following press conference with the media in attendance, many of the issues were renegotiated, while others were still being raised. Some journalists showed hope and inspiration, others skepticism and even hostility. Naturally, Yon was expected to be the main source of information and clarification, although the attitude of the other leaders toward the new world order was just as relevant to the media.

As for me, I was more than happy with the outcome of the summit. Everyone played their roles brilliantly and realistically; I had no doubts about that. Regardless of how well we were prepared, I couldn't get the human variable out of my head. At our core, we always remain human. Vulnerable to our greatest virtue – the ability to feel. To oppose that purely human inclination was a heavy burden that everyone at that table shouldered.

Yon could have suffered a collapse at the thought of the entire world staring at him... or at the thought that the mission to which hundreds of thousands of members had dedicated their lives could have failed with just one wrong message. Or by the provocative questions of the media that none of us could have foreseen.

Simon was only a step away from going too far in his attempts to provoke president Lin. Instead of demonstrating the credible, characteristic skepticism and mild arrogance so typical of Mayden, he could have provoked mass disapproval among his countrymen over the new proposals.

In turn, Alexey may have been tempted to follow his desire to take a more prominent role in the dialogue. He sincerely believed that Russia should be more involved and be a more relevant voice at the meeting. We had discussed his conviction more than once with political scientists and sociologists in our organization. The consensus was that such a request would be interpreted as a Sino-Russian threat to the rest of the world.

In the minutes after the end of the conference, I considered whether the absence of any mistakes on this day was a reason to be satisfied or to be disappointed. This was probably the biggest sacrifice we had made. The price we all paid.

If to err is human, does that mean that there's very little human left in us?

Ultimately, the day went exactly as we wanted, and that was the only thing that mattered. The most critical points of the program had been laid on the table. There were arguments and counterarguments. Many questions were yet to receive answers, regarding many aspects that were yet to be decided. But the direction had been taken.

The first ring of my phone returned me to reality, and the second, to my task.

"I still can't believe it worked!" Fiona admitted with a tone that I had never heard from her before. Balanced, thoughtful, even somewhat sentimental.

"Why?" I pretended to downplay it. "It went as expected. No surprises."

"Come on, even you aren't such a robot!" She had intuitively felt the vein of my thinking a moment ago. "I'm ready to

293

connect you."

"So am I."

"You're going live in five minutes."

I paced around the room a few times and took a couple of deep breaths before I went back to my spot by the laptop. It was my turn now – time for my solo performance.

Unfortunately for its inhabitants, the weather on Hermes didn't appear the most congenial. Despite the pouring rain, I could see the 25 faces I had just watched in Beijing, assembled sort of "below" me, or rather, below the screen that was showing my face. Only now, there was no trace of the intimidating concentration of power that they radiated when together. They had no confidence, decisiveness, or diplomacy. There was no formal clothing, either. Or maybe some – a few of them still wore the suits they came in. But at this stage, their appearance was far from the intended imposing effect.

I was glad to see them together. It had taken a while to gather them all together, and some more time for them to get acquainted.

It seemed that over there on the island, Mayden still played an important role. Although he had been one of the last to arrive on Hermes, he had quickly oriented himself in the new environment. Lucky for him, he had stumbled across Lucas Meyro and Mirov, who were trying to resolve a disagreement on one of the beaches. The Russian's English had the characteristic hard accent of Russian, while the Brazilian spoke melodically, but was difficult to understand. Three presidents on the same beach was a coincidence that could not have arisen through pure coincidence, so Mayden started to deduce what was happening. And though he could have never guessed that he would be in such a situation, he quickly steeled himself and tried his best to take leadership of the island – we were often the spectators of his statements and speeches.

"Gentlemen," I began. "If you still had any doubts as to your presence here, I believe that witnessing the event has clarified some of the unknown parts of the equation."

"What kind of fucking charade is this?" Mayden exploded. His irritable nature had not left him.

"We will now solve the puzzle, Mr. President," I answered patiently. "The day is January 12th. Today, you inscribed your names in history. Or rather, we did for you. No need to thank us!" I added sarcastically, examining their lowered heads and confused looks. "I suppose that each one of you remembers their kidnapping, but you were unsure of the reason. I'll begin by telling you that your families are doing great and are in excellent health. They haven't really missed you, to be honest. As you yourselves saw, your doubles are quite convincing."

"You won't get away with this! It's only a question of time before the Secret Service and the feds realize what's happening!" Albriani fumed. "You think they won't know?"

"I can assure you that we won't stain your reputation in front of your corrupt friends in the intelligence services. We have made sure to maintain your webs as you spun them. And you'll keep spinning them, until we eliminate your team members one by one. And yes," I clarified somewhat threateningly, "this island will become increasingly populated."

"The intelligence services will be the least of your problems, you clowns!" Mayden vowed. "Do you really believe that we're the only ones standing between you and your idiotic utopia? That your little circus will uproot the system?"

"Let me tell you something about me and my little circus. My name is Ian Dunne. I also have four other identities that all your services slept through. I spent the first half of my life in that wonderful, centuries-old system that you took such care to maintain. It didn't end well. So, I had to devote the second half to democracy's favorite credo: 'Be the change you wish to see in this world.' Don't you see, President Mayden? I bought into the American dream! I started with a small team, like most young entrepreneurs. Once we proved to ourselves that our capabilities allowed it, we set out to develop prototypes of a social system. If you followed the summit that was just broadcast live for your special island, its main objectives are clear to you. Your doubles did an excellent job with presenting them. And for these goals to be fulfilled, we only had to pull the weeds." I pointed to them so they would understand me correctly. "All the way to the root."

My audience, so active until now, was mute. They were probably wondering if 'all the way to the root' meant that their exile was a preamble to their death.

"You'd be surprised to know how many people actually hate you. You understand that what happened to you required a considerable investment... I'd even argue that you made some of it yourself. But, as it turned out, your dirty games no longer apply even in the underworld you thought was in your hands."

"And you imagine that they'll remain loyal to you? That you'll live in your fantasy world, and the murderers will turn into fairies and unicorns?" Mirov hissed.

"Every system has a life cycle, gentlemen," I began again. "The breaking point when the cup overflows. In our next live calls, some of the 'fairies' will personally tell you what this point was for them, and why they chose our tale. Anyway," I changed the subject, "time to talk about your world. You're on a 200-square-kilometer island. Very remote from anything that can be called civilization. I'd advise against trying to swim out! You may have already noticed that there are cameras all around the perimeter. Believe it or not, it's important for us to know that you're safe and not killing each other." I surrendered to the irony that bubbled up in me with increasing pressure. "Although I remember you prefer others to do that for you. However, as a gesture of goodwill, we have unanimously decided to keep you updated on how things are going out there. Every third and sixth day of the week, at 6 p.m. sharp, you will be kept up to speed on the latest developments. Just like we're doing right now. It's up to you to find a way to keep track of time. Note that today is Wednesday."

Even though the conversation was a pleasure for me, I couldn't ignore the rage I saw smoldering in their eyes. And I had to be honest with myself – this made the pleasure even greater.

"As far as food goes, I can see you're doing fine. There's plenty of fish in the sea, as they say. Don't complain. After all, entire civilizations have survived under similar conditions."

At this point, I heard two or three comments uncharacteristic of heads of state, which amused me more than it irritated me.

"To end today's meeting on a positive note, I can assure you that you will not be bored. I repeat – new and interesting people will constantly arrive on your island. You will meet old friends and make new, promising acquaintances." I consoled them with a solid dose of sarcasm and satisfaction. "That was all for today, dear guests! Welcome to the rest of your lives!"

I had imagined their expressions after that first polite conversation many times. They managed to surprise me – they were humbler than I'd expected. Maybe I had secretly hoped for a more challenging dialogue, but I didn't rush to any judgments. I attributed it to the shock of realizing the circumstances.

After all, however much evidence of their exile they collected on the island, I assumed that due to the lack of information, they still had a glimmer of hope that there was another explanation. The kind that wouldn't be a guarantee of spending the rest of their lives on these 200 square meters, or finding certain death in the depths of the Indian ocean.

EPILOGUE

In the following weeks, all the media repeated, interpreted, and analyzed the different policies of the new program. Hours after its announcement, it fundamentally shook the global notion of order and prospects for society.

Over time, the limits of perception and tolerance of the changes broadened. People were gradually becoming convinced that the proposed new order was not as unrealistic as it had seemed at first.

The optimistic attitude of the most outstanding businessmen, visionaries, and tech giants also contributed its fair share. Much as we expected, there were considerable exceptions, with a serious public platform and dubious backroom connections. Only that now, we stood in the backroom, and the path for the people of their kind was well trodden.

In June of that year, at the summit for the second discussion, the 25 countries reached a consensus on the individual points and ultimately approved the program unanimously. After the agreement was announced, each of them was given a period of time to submit their own plan and timetable for enforcing the new measures. Then, the timetables were to be coordinated to ensure that reforms were conducted in a suitable way, at an appropriate pace, and were tailored to the local specifics.

Many other leaders around the world also expressed a position. We played a role in some of these countries, where we helped tip the scales. But the factor with the most influential relevance was that the rules were dictated by the great powers.

How about us?

This was a good ending to the first phase of our plan. But the mission was far from over. We had populated the first island with puppet masters, but we also knew that somewhere behind the scenes, someone was pulling their strings, too. And the ones pulling them also had their own strings. For centuries, dozens of grotesque, greedy generations were given power over people, governments, and media. Dynasties that were already fast on our heels...

* * *

The first rays of sunlight glowed on the asphalt of the twentieth mile of Route 66. Despite the sparse vegetation, the aroma of the blooming summer hung in the air. It could almost make Layla and me forget that we were on our way to a mission. We were heading to London. We meant to personally investigate our first target from the Clan.

The flight to the center of the monarchy left from Chicago. But that was six days from now.

"Sugar?" Layla asked as she stirred the contents of one of the two packets she was holding in her coffee.

"Just Michael."[4] I winked and turned the volume up.

No more lies
No more lies in the morning
No more lies
No more lies in the day

Long ago, I used to love this song. Long ago, before I forgot about music.

The wind insistently tried to scatter the ponytail that Layla gathered her hair into when she asked me to put the hatch down. The calm in her eyes looked like a promise for tomorrow.

I could get used to this.

I had long ago realized that the fight we started was not going to end in my lifetime, let alone by that May 20, 2035. Which meant that I needed to find a way to live a fast life in every intermission, and work with what I had.

And right now, I had a 1959 Cadillac El Dorado and 4000 kilometers ahead of me.

---

[4] *"One More Night" by Michael Kiwanuka.*

SYSTEM: THE LIMIT

ZARDI CROSS

English
First edition

Made in the USA
Middletown, DE
05 December 2024

66208186R00179